THE HIGHLANDER'S ENCHANTMENT

ELIZA KNIGHT

ABOUT THE BOOK

Lady Blair Sutherland has always followed the rules. As the youngest of five, she's spent years observing her older siblings misbehaving—but even more importantly, she's learned a lot about smoothing over disputes. Dared by her cousins, Blair writes a note, and puts it in a bottle, but at the last minute, refuses to follow along with the dare and send it out to sea. As the months pass, she forgets about what she's written until a warrior lays siege to her clan's castle—in her name—claiming her brother is a murderer. For a lass who's never been in trouble, her world is about to turn itself inside out.

Since the murder of his older brother, Laird Edan Rose has looked for a way to prove himself to his clan. When he was a lad, his father sent him to foster with Robert the Bruce, but never asked him to return home. Gone all these years serving his king, he has to make his mark and show his clan he has what it takes to lead by finding his brother's killer. When the possible answer to his deliberations comes in the form of a message in a bottle, he wastes no time in taking action. Though he hopes the man responsible for his clan's pain will surrender, Edan is not afraid to wage war. If he has to, he'll lay siege to the castle, rescue the lass, and take out his enemies, gaining the respect he seeks.

When a Highlander rides on her brother's castle, Blair is aware the blame lies at her feet. In order to clear her family's name, she chooses to give herself up to a stranger and help him find the true assassin—for she's certain it is not her brother. But once she's in Edan's arms, the only thing that comes to mind is wondering if his kiss is as powerful as his embrace. Having desired to show his worth to his clan, Edan is now determined to show he is worthy of Blair's heart. However, their passion is halted when the one who wanted his brother dead, decides the two of them are a loftier prize.

Cover Design by Kim Killion @ The Killion Group, Inc.

Edited by Heidi Shoham & Erica Monroe

Published by:

MORE BOOKS BY ELIZA KNIGHT

THE SUTHERLAND LEGACY

The Highlander's Gift
The Highlander's Quest
The Highlander's Stolen Bride
The Highlander's Hellion
The Highlander's Secret Vow
The Highlander's Enchantment

PIRATES OF BRITANNIA: DEVILS OF THE DEEP

Savage of the Sea
The Sea Devil
A Pirate's Bounty

THE THISTLES AND ROSES SERIES

Promise of a Knight
Eternally Bound
Breath from the Sea

THE HIGHLAND BOUND SERIES (EROTIC TIME-TRAVEL)

Behind the Plaid
Bared to the Laird
Dark Side of the Laird
Highlander's Touch
Highlander Undone
Highlander Unraveled

WICKED WOMEN

Her Desperate Gamble
Seducing the Sheriff
Kiss Me, Cowboy

UNDER THE NAME E. KNIGHT

TALES FROM THE TUDOR COURT

My Lady Viper
Prisoner of the Queen

ANCIENT HISTORICAL FICTION

A Day of Fire: a novel of Pompeii
A Year of Ravens: a novel of Boudica's Rebellion

FRENCH REVOLUTION

Ribbons of Scarlet: a novel of the French Revolution

PROLOGUE

Somewhere in the Scottish Highlands
1325

He was not her first kill.

She suspected he wouldn't be her last. *The plotting, the careful implementing of each detail, and the watching. Oh, how it still sent a shiver racing up her spine when she thought over each incredible detail.*

But the very best part by far had been the death.

She'd sat back, well away from the crowd, and observed her handiwork as it unfolded. Watched the life slowly, painfully slip from his body. Felt that same life punch to her chest, renewing her in some odd sense. She'd gasped, sucking in the last of his breath and feeling her body tingle with what could only be known as rapture.

People had thought she'd gasped from the shock of his surprising demise, and she'd let them think so.

She knew she would get away with it. Hell, it was hard to keep in her laugh. Those bloody fools were going to take the fall for her; she knew they would. Because she'd made sure of it.

Deciding to take his life had been easy—he deserved it for what he'd done. He'd needed to suffer, and so did everyone else he loved.

Who was she going to kill next?

A bubble of excitement expanded in her throat, and she turned to flee the great hall before anyone could see it burst.

CHAPTER 1

Castle Ross
Scottish Highlands
Late March, 1325

Lady Blair Sutherland always did what she was told.

And yet, she was far from perfect.

She followed rules as though they were carved into her very limbs, and to break one would be to sever a very important part of herself—or bring war upon her family. That was an event she did not care to encounter...again.

Blair didn't have archery or storytelling skills like her eldest sister, Bella. Nor did she hold any talent with sailing or swimming, as was the case with her older sister, Greer. Though she'd tried both, it had ended in disaster. She'd nearly taken her father's eye out with an arrow, and Greer did not yet know that it was in fact Blair who'd caused the horrid series of events that led to Greer's husband being speared in the leg.

She was not good at playing music or singing. Nor was she any good at embroidery, though she tried her darndest to see the task done, because that was what a proper lady was supposed to do. In the end, she often hurt more ears than she pleased and left whatever fabric she was working on covered in droplets of red.

She was not a warrior like her brothers, though she could probably defend herself if necessary, as was the way for most younger siblings who were forced to defend themselves from one rivalry or another. Her defense, however, was scrappier than it was coordinated, as attested when she had to scurry out of the way of an older brother's desire to wrestle.

But Blair was really good at keeping secrets.

So here she was, sitting in the great hall of her brother's newly refurbished castle at Ross, where her brother, Liam, was the new laird. This seemed strange, considering the Ross clan had been her family's mortal enemy since before she was born. Yet, here they were, dining as they'd done the past several nights as though nothing were out of ordinary. And all around her, it seemed love was blossoming with the first buds of spring.

Blair was at a complete loss as to what she could do about procuring a husband.

Liam's lovely English bride stared at him with such love that it was enough to make Blair yearn for that same feeling. She glanced around the crowded hall where everyone was eating, drinking and being overly boisterous, but she found no man in the vicinity that made her feel even the slightest inkling of joy. And even if there had been, she had no way to entice him. Yet, that did not detract from her desire to gain a husband.

Aye, marriage... It had been on her mind a great deal as of late. Her parents had yet to broach the topic with her, though she'd waited patiently for that day to come. She was not like her sisters who had resisted marriage. In fact, Blair wished very much to take up the mantle of wife. To find purpose in running a household and bearing children. After all, if she couldn't excel at any one thing in particular, she knew for a fact she would be gifted at fulfilling her duties as a wife. Well...most duties. She knew nothing of the marital bed, and she didn't think she needed to, as it was a husband's duty to see it done. But she could take the skills she'd learned from her mother about running a kitchen to see her husband and children well fed. She would organize the house to keep it clean, and she aid her husband in dispensing judgments and rewards on his people.

Above all, she knew she could help bring peace to any clan. After all, since she was a wee lass, she'd made it her goal to do just that. It was, without a doubt, the only other thing she was good at besides keeping secrets. And only because of one very large, unforgettable mistake. Funny how the various mistakes she'd made had not led to her developing multiple talents.

Alas, life was as life was, and one had to foster what they were given.

Once the vows were exchanged, her life would be different. More exciting. More purposeful. She was certain that a husband was exactly what she needed to fulfill her purpose in life.

Now, how to go about getting one?

At her age of nearly twenty, it was a wonder her parents hadn't been entertaining offers at all. Unless they weren't telling her about it, which seemed impossible given how involved they'd allowed her sisters to be with their own marriage planning. Well, if they were planning something, she sincerely hoped it wasn't with any of the fools here today.

With a great sigh, she stood to excuse herself, hoping to catch at least some semblance of a walk and fresh air before the sun set completely. She loved to be outside, to feel the sun on her face no matter how cold or warm the air was.

Blair managed to slip from her place at the table and through the great hall unheeded until she reached the wide oak doors. Suddenly, she found herself flanked by two of her cousins. Aislinn and Aurora were the youngest twin daughters of her mother's twin sister, Aliah.

They were the spitting image of their mother. Blair had always found that to be rather eerie. She also felt a slight twinge of jealousy, given she looked so very different from the rest of her family. They were all golden-haired, pink-cheeked and had sunny smiles, while she was dark-haired, sun-kissed and rather reserved.

The twins were also forever getting into trouble, more so even than her sister Greer, which meant Blair did her best to avoid them at all costs. She couldn't allow her cousins to ruin the reputation she'd so carefully been building.

The twins slipped their arms around hers, on either side, and fairly carried her from the great hall in their exuberance and haste.

"We're so glad ye got up to leave," Aurora gushed with a roll of her big blue eyes.

"We were so bored," Aislinn continued in a drawn-out groan, obviously an exaggeration, as they both seemed to be having plenty of fun flirting and fawning over her brother's men.

Before Blair could say she was looking for some time alone, her cousins cut in with their own back-and-forth banter.

"So stuffy in there."

"And not enough music."

"Aye, they could have done a better job of that."

"I didna like the chicken."

"Was it chicken? I thought it was goose."

"Gross. Goose?"

Peals of laughter from her cousins left Blair both confused and slightly irritated. She furrowed her brow, trying to figure out a way to disengage herself from them post haste. Aislinn started in on a story of a stuffed goose, and Aurora shouted about how they'd thought it was alive. Blair frowned, glad she'd not been a part of whatever it was they were discussing and wishing very much not to be a part of anything else.

When they finally ceased their chatter, she cut in with a tight smile. "Rather tedious, aye. If ye'll excuse me, I'm going to take a short walk before I retire."

"We'll come with ye." Aurora peered around Blair at her sister, a mischievous grin on her face.

"Aye, 'twill be fun."

Blair gritted her teeth and forced a smile; certain their idea of fun was going to be far different than her own.

They exited the castle with the twins talking so fast, and without catching their breath, all the while finishing one another's sentences. They talked over top of one another so much that Blair could barely keep up, and so, she quit trying. The courtyard was mostly empty as the clansmen and women were either in the great hall dining, or home with their families doing much the same. Soon, the only ones awake would be those guards on watch, and perhaps her own brother, who never seemed to sleep in his quest to be the perfect laird.

Guards lined the castle ramparts, staring out over the lands beyond, always prepared for an attack. It made Blair nervous the way they stood like that. Always had. Especially after what had happened a few years before with her brother, Strath... Blair had almost single-handedly been the downfall of their entire clan. She shuddered at the memory. She was glad that what could have happened had never came to pass. But, oh Lord...if she had only *thought* before speaking...

Every day when she woke, she thanked the heavens for being as safe as she was. Thanked her lucky stars to never have been a part of an attack, like her sister-by-marriage, Cora, or Bella, when she'd come so very close.

As the bairn of five, she'd been well-protected—unless the attack came from an older sibling trying to steal her scone or her favorite pair of hose. As a lass just coming into her own, she'd nearly destroyed thousands of lives when she had caught her brother's betrothed with a lover. Shocked at what she'd found, Blair had immediately gone to her brother and told him everything. Insulted and in a rage, Strath had taken his bride back to her father, humiliated. A war had started soon after. And it had been all Blair's fault. Well, not all her fault exactly; it wasn't like she'd insisted Jean Guinn bed another, but if she'd kept quiet, or maybe told her father instead of her brother, war could have been avoided.

A husband would protect her. Maybe even keep her safe from her own blunders that inevitably put other people in danger, for even though she tried hard to follow all the rules, unexpected and some-times unpleasant things still happened.

One of the guards called out a greeting to Aurora, who ducked her head in feigned shyness. That lass had not one shy bone in her body.

Blair narrowed her eyes, wondering if this contrived coyness was something that she should adopt to gain the attention of a man. Was that what they wanted?

Blair swiveled her gaze back to the guard, who was nodding with appreciation at her cousin. She recognized him as one of her brother's men from their lands up north. Though the guards at Ross Castle were a mix of both Ross and Sutherlands, at night, only Sutherlands stood watch. Watching him ogle her cousin left her with a sour feeling in her belly. She would do her best not to act coy, as she did not want this kind of attention. He looked to be fairly drooling, like a dog over a bone.

Blair cleared her throat and gave him a hard stare. He seemed to come back to himself and returned to his duties.

Undermining her father, and the safety of his people.

"Och, Blair, ye're no fun," Aurora murmured.

"He is not here to ogle, but to keep the castle guarded."

"Life is not all about work. We have to have some fun," Aurora said.

"There is a place and time for fun," Blair retorted.

"And where would that be for ye, Cousin? Do ye ever have fun?"

Blair frowned, pursing her lips. She had fun. Certainly, she did...

Liam had not come by this castle by birth or inheritance, rather by siege. He needed his men to be on guard at all times, not distracted by baser desires. And if she could help with that, she would.

Though Liam had laid siege to Ross in the name of the king—and been rewarded with it by Robert the Bruce—to some people, he was not the rightful laird. And since her brother had taken his position, there had been a few instances of Ross men rebelling.

They were wrong, of course, to go against her brother, and anyone with half a brain would know that. They should see him as a savior.

No longer were Ross lands, and Scotland, to be tormented by Ina Ross and her *Sassenach* husband, Ughtred. Not that Blair had anything against English people in general. Her mother was English, as was her grandfather, her aunt and uncle, and even Cora. But she had much against the English who wished to oppress the Scots. And with good reason. They'd been oppressing her people, murdering them in cold blood for generations. Infiltrating Scottish ranks in order to undermine the kingdom and Robert the Bruce's rule.

"I wish we could go down to the loch. It's such a beautiful evening," Aislinn whined in a way that Blair was certain was meant to be cute.

"Let's go. For certain, the three of us can convince one of the ninnies on guard to open the gate or accompany us," Aurora answered. "That is if *Blair* doesna try to spoil our fun."

Blair let out an exaggerated yawn. *Nay! Not on my life!* "Not today. I'm tired. Perhaps on the morrow?"

"See, I told ye," Aurora said to her sister.

"We're going to hold ye to it, Blair. On the morrow."

Blair nodded but said nothing, so that her words could not be held against her, for she would not agree, and it was just dark enough that she could tell them they'd confused her nod for a shake of her head.

As they walked back to the castle, Aislinn and Aurora murmured on about their various beaus, and how they expected to soon gain proposals of marriage. They couldn't wait to be married. A surge of what could only be jealousy stirred in Blair's belly. If one of them were to get married before her, when she'd spent her whole life thus far following rules in order to be the perfect wife and mother...

"How about ye, Blair?"

How was she supposed to answer? Blair was not ever one to confess her deepest desires to anyone. She placated everyone, went with what they wished, knowing that one day, all her good deeds would be rewarded. She didn't want to say that her parents had yet to broach the topic of marriage with her, as it was clear nuptials were a large matter in the twins' household—and they a year younger! She frowned, perhaps just a moment too long, because it was this very frown that drew her cousins' attention.

They both stopped dead in their tracks, halting Blair with them, mouths agape. "What is it? Have Aunt and Uncle found ye a man to wed? One ye dinna like? Oh, do tell, Cousin. Ye can trust us to keep your secrets."

Blair shook her head, fierce enough that a few locks fell from the tightly bound knot at the nape of her neck, causing them to brush against her cheeks. The hairs tickled her skin, and she itched to tuck them back in place.

What was this burning heat she felt in her chest? It was unsettling, and spread like fiery fingers outward, up her throat, and out her arms. Her feet stilled and couldn't move. Not another inch. And her voice, it disappeared with her breath. She was...angry. Was that the right word? How could this be?

Blair was *never* angry. Aye, a little irritated sometimes, like right now, and for the past quarter of an hour. Mayhap a little longer. But for some reason, that irritation was quickly escalating. She swallowed, working to shove down these unpleasant feelings. Working to keep herself under control. She drew in a deep, ragged breath and let it out slowly.

Blair was always everything she was supposed to be—docile and happy and chipper.

She did not allow herself to be angry. Anger was for her siblings, for warriors and those who mattered. Not for the bairn of the family, who had to remain neutral in all things in order to keep the peace.

Aye, that was what she was, the peacemaker. A title she wholly embraced, else she make another blunder that tossed their clan into a war.

And peacemakers shouldn't feel like raising hell, which was exactly what she felt like doing at the moment.

This burning feeling in her chest had to go away. Right this instant. She stomped her foot, dragged in a gasp of air at both her feelings and the unnatural stomp. Goodness... She needed to go to her chamber. To quiet down. Calm herself, so she'd not do something even more unladylike.

"I'm verra tired," she said in a near growl and tried to rip away from her cousins' grips that seemed to have grown tighter on her arms.

They wouldn't let go, and she felt them crowding closer, looks of concern on their beautiful faces.

"Och, dearest Blair, ye must tell us what has ye so cross," Aurora breathed out.

Aislinn made a clucking noise of concurrence. "I've never seen ye so."

"I am not cross," Blair said. "And I am not betrothed." *Nor do I have any beau. Or anyone even remotely interested.* Biting the tip of her tongue, she held back any more words from spilling out. A lady did not share the secrets of her heart. Especially not with her busybody cousins, who couldn't wait to tell the world all of her problems, because they were so much more interesting than their own.

"Then what is wrong?"

When she said nothing, her cousins dragged her to the side of the keep, well out of earshot of anyone else. They stood in the shadows now, and Blair pressed her back to the cool stone wall, grateful for its solidness to hold her up.

"We willna tell anyone. Ye can trust us."

Blair studied her cousins' features, so similar to her mother. Golden locks and eyes the color of bluebells. They were beautiful. Flawless. Her sisters were much the same. Beauties. Bella took after their mother, and Greer's hair was more ginger like their father's. But Blair... Her tendrils were unnaturally dark, black as a raven, which set her apart from everyone in her immediate family. Perhaps so much so it was the reason no one had yet to offer marriage. She simply wasn't that pretty. And her body... That was another thing altogether. She was a bit too rounded in her hips with a bottom that bounced too much when she walked, lacking completely in the lithe beauty of her siblings and mother.

Even her skin was different, prone to darkening with the slightest touch of the sun. The only thing that was the same were her eyes, an identical blue as her mother's. At least by seeing her eyes reflected in the loch, she knew she belonged, that she wasn't some changeling brought in by the fairies.

Her entire life had been about belonging. About doing the right thing in order to be accepted and valued, for she had no talent, no beauty, and no penchant for anything that might set her apart from anyone else. And her lack of standing out only made her stand out all the more.

Every once in a while, she'd try to step outside of her shell and join one of her siblings on an adventure, telling herself that to do so was to protect them. If she were there, she could make peace should they get into trouble.

But she couldn't help knowing deep down that doing things she shouldn't sometimes sparked a bit of joy inside her, even if she quashed it.

And then something would happen, to remind her of why she should remain as she'd set out—a rule follower.

"Blair..." Aurora called her back to the present, and she stared into her cousins' eager expressions.

Blair felt that desire to cause mischief, for a moment of excitement, if only for a second, before the practical side of her shoved it aside.

"Ye can tell us anything, Blair," Aislinn murmured, soothing and calm. A manner she must use quite a bit in order to get her way, for she seemed very good at it.

"Aye, anything. I'll even tell ye a secret so ye know ye can trust us," Aurora added.

Blair's eyes widened. Did she want to know a secret? *Nay, definitely not!* Look what had happened the last time she knew a secret...

Aislinn's grin widened, for she must already know what secret Aurora kept, and now Blair was certain she didn't want to know.

"I kissed one of the stable hands today," Aurora confessed. "The one with the long ginger hair."

Blair's mouth fell open.

"Didna even ask him. Just did it. And it was a lot of fun." Aurora winked at her sister.

"That wasna even her first kiss," Aislinn said with a roll of her eyes.

Not her first kiss?

Blair touched her own lips without thinking. What would it be like to kiss a man? She'd not even got that far in her fantasies. Nay, she thought mostly of sitting beside a fire, drinking a glass of warm spiced almond milk, and having a handsome man completely mesmerized by some fascinating thing she said. Although she had no idea what it would be because she never felt clever, but in her fantasy, she was incredibly witty. Her man would hang on her every word. Admire her. Tell her she was beautiful.

Blair sighed.

"Have ye kissed a man?" Aurora asked.

Blair shook her head.

"Do ye want to practice on the stable hand? I assure ye he was more than willing. I could bring ye to him right now."

Blair's stomach did a flop. She shook her head vigorously. "Nay, nay, I dinna want to do that."

Aurora frowned with disappointment. "All right, well, then tell us what has ye so cross. Ye promised."

Blair had given no such promise, but she supposed by listening to her cousin's confession about the kiss, she had perhaps in some unspoken way given her word to share. Even if the confession had been thrust on her. She had no one else to talk to though, and from what she was guessing, Aurora wouldn't want it spread around that she'd been kissing the stable hand. Perhaps there was a measure of trust Blair could find in that.

"I canna describe it," Blair started, biting her lip and frowning. "But when ye started to talk about your beau, I was reminded that I dinna have one."

"And ye want one." It was a statement, not a question.

"Aye, I do."

The twins glanced at each other, and Blair could practically hear their minds turning. "We can help with that," they said at the same time.

A little niggling feeling inside her gut told her that perhaps now would be a good time to say "nay, thank ye," and to be on her way. To say, "never mind, I'll handle this on my own."

But she didn't.

In fact, she opened her mouth and started to share with her cousins one of her longest-held fantasies, the one about the hearth and husband. How her husband would come riding upon the castle, confess his undying love, and rescue her from the doldrums of a sheltered life.

Their eyes widened until they were so large, Blair feared they would pop out of their heads.

"I never would have thought ye had it in ye, Blair," Aislinn said.

"Aye, I thought ye were destined for the church," Aurora added.

"Aye, I think everyone did," Aislinn agreed.

Aurora pressed her hands to Blair's shoulders. "We must do this."

"We must make this happen."

"Nay," Blair protested, removing her cousin's hands from her shoulders. "'Tis silly. We canna. And there is no way about it."

"I know a way." Aurora grinned. "A message in a bottle."

"Nay!" Blair shook her head. "I canna."

"Oh, but ye can. Tomorrow. Be ready at dawn."

Blair swallowed hard and considered telling her parents they must leave before dawn the following morning in order to avoid this blunder. Or if she might be able to run away and escape the fate her cousins had planned for her.

"My parents would be terribly upset if I did something so reckless." Blair shook her head. "I canna."

Aurora shrugged. "They will never know. Trust us."

There was that word again—*trust*. Blair was fairly certain her cousins had no earthly idea how much they were asking of her, nor that they were likely the last people she would ever trust so deeply with her future.

"Let's go inside before anyone worries about us. Best not cause a riot tonight when we've plans to make Blair's dreams come true tomorrow." Aislinn giggled and rubbed her elbow into Blair's ribs.

While the twins chortled over their ridiculous plan, Blair felt very much like losing the contents of her dinner. She allowed herself to be dragged back into the castle, up the steep, winding stairs to her chamber, where her cousins rummaged through her writing desk until they produced ink, quill and parchment.

They tapped the parchment, their eyes gleaming with delight. "Write. Write something glorious."

"I'm no writer," Blair said feebly, wishing she'd spent more time paying attention to her sister Bella, who was well-known for her story-telling capabilities.

Blair could barely string two words together, and if she did, they rarely made sense. She knew the basics of giving direction. Of writing a missive that got across the important parts—*all is well, weather is good, I still hate mutton, and cheese is my favorite dish.*

All very mundane and boring.

Just like her life up to this point. Again, that little spark of want, of desire to do something beyond the rules lit in her belly. *Nay!* She pushed it aside. *Dinna be stupid.*

She nodded to her cousins, already knowing that on the morrow, she was going to disappoint them when she burned whatever letter she'd pen right now to get them out of her room.

Och, what a mess she'd gotten herself into. Blair took the quill and scribbled hastily on the parchment. Aurora squealed with delight as Aislinn sprinkled sand over the ink to dry it.

As soon as they were gone, she tossed the parchment into the fire, watching it crinkle and seize in the heat, the edges turning black before shifting into ash. A moment later, her maid arrived to undress her for the night. She sat quietly as her hair was brushed out and replaited, and then she was tucked safely into bed like the bairn everyone considered her to be.

Within seconds, her mother slipped into the room, as though she'd been waiting on the other side of the door. Did she know that Blair's cousins had been there? Did she know their plans? Without a word about it, her mother gave her a kiss on the forehead and wished her a good night's sleep.

Blair stared after her mother's retreating figure, wondering if she'd ever done a wrong thing in her life. Lady Arbella Sutherland was kind, beautiful, smart and cared for everyone. She always had a smile, a soft word, but she could be strong and take anyone who went against her to task.

Lady Arbella was perfect.

Even her sister Greer, with her penchant for troublemaking, was perfect. Bella was of course untouchable, a goddess among women. And Blair...she was just...not.

That burning sensation came into Blair's chest again. Was she *jealous?*

She rolled toward the window covered in thick fur to keep out the night's chill. As much as the fur tried to do its job, her chamber was still quite cold, and a subtle draft blew over her skin.

"I'm like the fur," she murmured to no one. Trying so hard all the time to do what was expected, and for all intents and purposes, succeeding enough that everyone kept on using her. But when it came down to it, she just wasn't perfect or really that great at what she was supposed to be doing, evidenced plainly by the blunders she'd managed to keep secret for so long.

The letter she'd penned and burned came to mind. A blunder averted. Thank the heavens.

But what had it hurt to play at making her fantasy, her dream husband, come to life? It wasn't like it would have actually worked if she went through with it—which she wouldn't. She would never toss the message into the loch, unless it was simply the ash from the hearth. Oh, this was all silly nonsense that her cousins and she would laugh about until they were old ladies.

However, for a few moments, it had made Blair smile.

A true, genuine smile, because she had been doing something just for her, and for the pure goal of enjoyment. When did she ever let go just to have a little fun?

The sad truth of not knowing the answer to that sank in quite deeply.

CHAPTER 2

Kilravock Castle
Scottish Highlands

E dan Rose had not been home in a long time.

And the last thing he'd expected to come home for was to help solve his brother's murder.

Well over a year had passed since last he'd traversed this road, and then, his brother had been full of life and soon to be married.

Now, Edan was laird and hadn't even had the chance to say goodbye to Connor before his brother's life was swiftly stolen. Gone were any imagined days of them as older men, telling war stories before a hearth to younger generations. Gone was the idea of ever getting to know the brother he'd missed.

Guilt ate at Edan's gut. If he'd been there... If he'd come home... He might have been able to put a stop to whatever plan had been put in place to end his brother's death. Tell the murdered to take him instead, at least, the one trained to fight in battles, who regularly put his life on the line. Let his brother, the one who was wed, and duty bound to produce the next heir to the Rose Clan, live.

Fate had dealt them both a cruel hand.

Why had he not made family a priority? Why had he given himself wholly to the crown? Questions he was certain to ask himself for the rest of his days. Questions his people might be asking as well. The very least he could do was give them the answers they sought and lay the head of the traitor at their feet.

In the past, Edan's visits had always been brief. He'd deemed his duty to the king more important than duty to family. Enough so that many faces within the clan were not well known to him. Edan had been fostered out to the king's army captain when he was just a wee lad, his father's gift to the realm since he had one heir already, Edan's half-brother, Connor, born of their father's first wife. Though his father never told him exactly why he sent him away, Edan wondered if it was because he looked so much like his mother, that when his father looked upon him, he was only reminded of his own broken heart.

In fact, the last time he'd been home was to pay his respects to his brother as the new laird when their father died. A keen sense of dread threatened as he approached the castle gates. The men up on the thick stone wall shouted down to him, recognizing the Rose banner even from this distance. The pulleys of the portcullis grinded, and the gates were swung wide, yawning as though they'd swallow him up as he went inside.

The keep rose two stories higher than the wall itself, solid and familiar, yet never feeling quite like home.

And now, possibly home to an assassin, too.

Rose lands were not as vast as some of the more powerful clans in the Highlands. In fact, he could ride from one end to the other in less than a day, sometimes twice depending on the weather. Despite their small size, the clan did occupy several miles of shore along the Moray Firth between the Campbell and Hay clans, which gave them further abilities to trade and fish. In essence, what they lacked for in land, they more than made up for in sea.

Across the firth, such clans as the Mackenzie, Urquhart, Munro and Ross battled for space. To their left were the Frasers and Mackin-tosh clans. It was a source of pride for Clan Rose that they were able to keep their hold on the water despite battling with some of the most powerful clans in Scotland.

Most of them got along well, other than the occasional raid—all except Clan Ross, who'd been the bane of nearly everyone's existence since time itself stood still. Whether by land or sea, whenever there was trouble, it was the Ross clan to blame, for certain.

In fact, the reason he was here at all, the reason he felt a gaping hole in his chest from the loss of a brother he wished he'd known better, was probably due to those bastards.

Edan rode through the gate into the bailey, surrendering the reins of his horse to a waiting stable hand before dismounting to plant his feet on the ground. *His* ground.

"Welcome home, my laird," his guard Raibert said, sweeping an arm out to indicate the slowly gathering crowd and the imposing keep.

All of this was his, as was the responsibility of seeing that the people were safe, cared for and thriving. All things his brother and father before him had done perfectly. All of which Edan felt completely unprepared for.

He could lead an army. Take down his enemies. Make sure they were safe—aye, he had that down. But lead a clan? Comfort a wife who'd lost her husband? Solve disputes between neighboring crofters?

Covered in dust, not yet washed from his hasty journey north from Stirling, Edan climbed the worn stone steps of the keep facing his people. Some folks were familiar, having changed over time, but some were not recognizable at all. There he stood watching as the bailey slowly filled with weary clansmen and women; children even appeared subdued as they stared up at him. Edan imagined that each one wished his brother was still alive. He longed to be back out on the battlefield or traversing the land with his men.

He was not a laird. He was a warrior. A brutal man of his word who'd helped protect the King of Scotland for the past decade.

Why did Connor have to go and die on him?

Upon the death of his brother, an urgent missive had been sent to

Edan, carried by Raibert. On the long journey back to the Highlands from Stirling, Raibert had filled him in on all the goings-on at Rose, and that the elders had voted unanimously for Edan to take his natural place as heir to his brother and leader of their clan.

If they'd voted against it, honor and duty would have made it impossible for Edan not to challenge the successor.

Being laird had never been on his list of things to do in life. In fact, since his brother had wed a pretty Highland lass, he'd assumed he'd never need to worry over it. Now it would appear that the very same lass had never had a child, leaving Edan as the first in line as blood heir, even if they were only half-related. They shared the same father, both of them born into a strong line of Rose leaders.

Even though he'd been voted in as laird, that could change.

There would be a waiting period to see if Connor's wife was early on in a pregnancy, though it did not seem likely. Her maid had explained to the housekeeper, who had relayed the message to the steward, who had relayed it to Raibert, who then blundered through it to Edan, to make clear at this moment, due to some things known privately to women, that it was likely she was not carrying a child at this time.

But if they were all mistaken, Edan would take his place as their laird until the time came that the child could rule instead—which was essentially a lifetime from now.

Edan let out a long sigh.

He'd yet to have a moment to deal with his own grief. How was he supposed to face these people and try to offer them comfort? With his men, comfort was a rousing slap on the back, thumping of chests and hearty jests, a round of whisky, and perhaps a challenge to cheat death once more.

Doing so with the clan would likely be frowned upon.

They stared up at him now, waiting patiently for him to speak.

The death of his brother was under investigation, as Connor had died rather suddenly when in such good health. Connor had been dining in the great hall with several guests when he'd suddenly clutched at his chest and fallen face-first into his supper, never to wake. When they'd examined him, his tongue had been purple, and the whites of his eyes red.

Poison, Edan was certain, having seen the effects of it before. Lady Rose had been cleared of any wrong doing, but the guests had been retained in the dungeon, each under suspicion.

Edan wondered if the suspicion should go beyond their guests and to any of the people who faced him now. He drew in a long breath, feeling the pulse of his jaw muscle flex at the side of his cheek. What did a laird say when his people did not expect him to be laird? When they knew so little about him? He might have been brother to Connor, a Rose through and through, but he'd spent most of his life away.

He cleared his throat and hoped to hell they didn't toss him out on his ear. He racked his brain for wise words he'd heard from his father or his king, or hell, his sword master. But it was all a jumble, and nothing specific came to mind.

Well, there was no way about this other than to simply dive right in. "People of Rose, my family, my friends, ye were loyal to my brother, my father, and my grandfather before him, all strong and able-bodied men in service to the clan. Great leaders, brave warriors." Edan's gut twisted in an unexpected knot as the people stared back at him blank-faced.

Add failure to move a crowd to the list of his deficiencies.

It was utterly ridiculous that he should feel unworthy. He was a battle-hardened warrior. He'd certainly roused his men to fight, to risk their lives when he spoke. He was well-respected by his king, and the first to mount his horse and ride into battle. He'd single-handedly taken on a dozen men at a time and saved countless lives.

Edan Rose was worthy, dammit.

And yet, the more they stared, the smaller he felt.

Wasn't that ballocks...

He straightened his shoulders, puffed his chest a little. He was Edan bloody Rose, slayer of *Sassenachs* and lassies' inhibitions. And now he was a blasted laird, ruler of men and protector of his clan. Add that to his list of undertakings. "My predecessors left large boots to fill, and I can promise ye that I'll work day and night to make them fit."

Several of the older clansmen nodded approvingly. A few of the younger lassies whispered, and even more still simply stared at him. He'd take that as a partial win—at least they were not all blank-faced.

"Though I may have been away serving the king, I assure ye, I have always been and always will be a Rose."

Edan's gaze went toward the kirk, the steeple climbing high enough for him to see it above the wall. Just there behind that holy house was his brother's body. They'd left him out in state long enough for his people to pay their respects, but not for Edan to do the same.

He still remembered being a lad of perhaps seven or so when his mother had passed. Seeing her body laid out, so still, so pale, a linen cloth wrapped around her. Her lips had been blue, and he remembered thinking she must be so cold. And the linen blanket, so thin. He'd run up to his room, tugged off the fur blanket on his bed and brought it to the kirk where he'd placed it over her body. But it hadn't helped. Within days they'd covered her face with the linen before placing her in the ground, and the fur blanket had been put back on his bed.

But Edan had never used it again. If it couldn't warm his mother, how was it going to warm him?

Foolish thoughts, he knew, but what was a lad of that age to think when no one told him anything? Less than a sennight later, his father had packed him off to Stirling.

Lady Mary Rose, née Guinn, who Edan had yet to meet as he'd not been able to attend their wedding celebration, took that moment to open the great doors. All eyes left him, going to her. Edan studied her, and she gaped at him, her mouth falling open in horror.

He knew what she was staring at—the scar on his face that cut a path from the right side of his forehead, through his brow and to the center of his cheek. He was lucky he still had vision in his eye, though it was weaker than before. Women either found his scars enticing or horrifying. It didn't take much to realize what she thought of them.

Before Mary had the chance to faint, or run back into the castle screaming, thinking him some monster come to attack, Edan bowed.

"My lady, I am Edan."

Seeming to get control of her fright, and concentrating her gaze on his nose, she held out her hand. "I am...pleased to meet ye." He could hear the opposite in her tone. "Connor spoke verra highly of ye," she offered, though it didn't sound sincere. Dark circles were smudged beneath her brown eyes, lack of sleep and tears, he'd guess. There was a haughty lift to her chin, and no doubt, she wondered why he should be here, and not her own husband.

Edan said softly, "I'm sorry for your loss, my lady, and that this should be the reason we finally meet."

She pursed her lips. "And I am sorry for yours." Her gaze once more centered on his scar. "I trust your journey was...uneventful."

"Aye." The lass chose an odd word to describe his journey, and he surmised it must have something to do with his battle scar, as she continued to concentrate on it.

She smoothed shaking hands down her unwrinkled blue gown and glanced at the assembled clan. "I shall let ye get back to it. I came out to see why everyone had gathered."

"Ye're welcome to stay, my lady. We are still your people."

She shook her head abruptly, her lips a firm line, shoulders rigid. "I am packing."

Edan was taken aback by that, but he forced himself to remain neutral, a hard thing considering what Connor would likely think if his wife were to leave so shortly after his death. He had to attribute her behavior to grief and not guilt. "Packing? Ye dinna have to leave so soon. Ye've only just..." He let his words trail off as tears gathered in her eyes. There was no need to remind her of what she'd just lost. To do so would only be cruel. And he had no idea how to comfort her. A woman in tears was more terrifying than any enemy on the battlefield.

"I've no reason to stay," she said tersely. "Despite what others might think will happen." She touched her belly, relaying to him in her own way that she was not with child. Mary had wed his brother nearly a year before. She should have, by all accounts, been well-rounded with Connor's child, but her belly appeared as flat as the stone wall. "My father will be coming to collect me before nightfall."

"Laird Guinn." Edan didn't know much about the Highland laird, other than there had been a scandal involving his eldest daughter a year or so before his youngest daughter married Connor, and Connor had been worried the scandal would carry down to him.

"Aye." She pressed her lips together and gave a curt nod, dismissing him as she turned her back and re-entered the castle.

Edan frowned at the closed door, uncertain how he felt about the exchange. It had been awkward and strained. When he'd been riding for the castle, he'd thought up many ways in which he could try to offer comfort to Connor's wife, knowing if he'd been in this position, his brother would do the same. But the lass wanted none of that. She simply wanted to get the hell off Rose property.

Unsettled, he returned his gaze to the crowd, trying to assess how they felt about the situation. They weren't much help. A few gave judgment negatively toward the door, but the rest looked just as impassive as they had before. That told him a lot, even when words were not expressed. His sister-by-marriage had not made an impression on the Rose people. Whether she stayed or went, it meant little to them.

The fact that her father was coming so quickly to retrieve her after the death of her husband didn't sit well with Edan, almost as if he'd been coming anyway. The Guinns were more northward, which meant a messenger would take at least a week to get there, and a week back. That was two weeks. It had taken Raibert four days to ride to Stirling, and four days for them to ride back together. That meant for her father to be arriving now, his trip had to be pre-planned, didn't it?

Edan supposed the man could have been coming for a visit. Or a messenger could have ridden faster. But to know that he'd be there that day?

He shook his head, his thoughts turning dark. The lass wasn't responsible for his brother's death. Their marriage had been arranged, a useful alliance. She was not happy here. It had to be as simple as that. And she must not want to be a part of their clan. Perhaps their marriage had not been a happy one. Indeed, if it had, wouldn't she want to stay among the people where she had found happiness? Was that not a wife's place? Edan ran his hand through his long, untamed hair. What did he know of women? Or of their thoughts? Naught.

His frown deepened even more as he tried to recall everything his brother had relayed about his bride in his missives. Not much other to say how bonny she was, and that he was honored to have her as a bride. Her father's land did not border theirs, so he wasn't sure the significance of an alliance, save for it could help with any issues arising from the Brodies or Stuarts, of which they had none. But there had to be something, as they had not wed for love.

Edan cleared his throat once more and directed his attention back to the people. He had to focus on them right now, and not the awkwardness of meeting his sister-by-marriage for the first time.

"As I was saying, I'm proud to be a Rose, and proud to be your laird. Within the king's army, I trained my own unit. My brother commended the Rose warriors, and I'm honored to lead ye. I will begin each day by training the men here, along with Raibert." He nodded to his guard. "I'll hold attendance to hear disputes each week as my brother did. And every day, I will work to discover what happened to Connor. I will not rest until we have uncovered the truth behind his death." That was quite enough. His shoulders were tense, and he felt as though he held the weight of the keep on his back. "Does anyone have any questions?"

More blank faces, enough that he wanted to sigh with frustration.

Then Raibert raised a hand and called out, "What if the king should need ye?"

Edan was glad he'd brought up the topic, as he was certain the others were wondering the same thing. "Every warrior in Scotland's duty is first to king and country."

Raibert nodded. "And the men here?"

Several of the women stiffened, shifting closer to their husbands as though Edan had come all this way from Stirling Castle to deprive them. He hadn't, but if the king called, he was duty bound to obey. "We *all* owe our loyalty to Robert the Bruce, do we nay?"

"Aye," Raibert said, glancing at the men.

"Aye!" they shouted in unison, their faces reflecting pride back at Edan.

The Rose men, small in number, were not oft called up by the king.

Maybe a few here and there to bolster numbers, but nothing like some of the larger clans who sent men by the hundreds.

"What of the Campbells? They've taken to reiving since the laird's passing."

"Are ye certain 'tis the Campbells?" Edan asked.

"Aye, Murtagh captured one of the bastards. Beat his arse bloody, too."

Edan frowned. "Did anyone reive after?"

"Nay."

"And do ye suspect them of having anything to do with my brother's death?"

"Canna say."

"I will send a missive to Chief Campbell. With the return of his bloodied warrior, he'll be expecting it, I'm certain."

"What happened to your eye?" This unwelcome, yet not entirely unexpected, inquiry came from a lad no more than six or eight summers who'd crept in front of his da and was staring up at Edan with a mixture of horror and awe.

Edan wondered if he'd ever get used to the looks of disgust tossed his way by women and children—it was a noted difference than what he was used to. The men always looked on him with appreciation and reverence, for he'd survived.

"A battle wound, lad."

"Aye, but what happened?" the lad insisted.

"I saved my king's life."

The lad let out an exasperated sound, shoulders rising and falling with the huff of his breath. "Aye, but, laird, what *happened?*"

Edan flattened his lips, considering whether to say it was a story for another time. He decided he'd best not for two reasons. One, he didn't want the lad to ask again, or cause someone else to ask in his place. And two, perhaps his story would lend just a drop of clout to his position. If they knew he could protect the king, was willing to take blows that should have led to death, then perhaps they would see him as a strong leader capable of keeping them safe.

"A *Sassenach* aimed to thrust his sword into King Robert's chest. I leapt from my horse, taking the blow myself."

"And ye dinna wear a patch?" the lad asked, before his father shoved him behind his back and made profuse apologies.

Edan chuckled. "There's nay need to apologize. The lad is only curious. Though I will caution that being curious can put one in danger." He met the gaze of the lad from where he peered from behind his father. "I dinna wear a patch, because I'm not ashamed of my scars, and because a patch would leave me half-blind, whereas now I still have us of my eye. I earned my scars in battle serving my king." He broke eye contact with the lad and turned to the rest of the crowd. "Are there any other questions afore I seek out my brother's final resting place?"

As he suspected, with that particular line, none raised their hand or dared shout out.

"Then I shall ask ye all to join me in the great hall for supper tonight."

"Wait," Raibert called out before the people could disperse. "We must pledge our allegiance to ye, our new laird."

Edan swallowed, wanting to say it could wait and knowing it could not. He nodded, not sure he could find his voice if he wanted to, as one by one the men, women and children of his clan knelt before him, hands over their hearts, just as they had before his brother, da and grandfather, loudly professing their loyalty, their allegiance. His chest swelled with bridled emotion that yearned to be unleashed, but he kept himself contained, lest he break one of the rules he'd given himself—never show emotion, whether they be friend or foe.

"I accept your pledges and am honored to be your laird. Rise," he said, his voice stronger, perhaps more guttural than he intended.

The clansmen rose and slowly dispersed, all but Raibert, whose gaze fanned over the people and the kirk before finding Edan's.

"I'll take ye to the kirk," Raibert said.

"I know where it is." Edan's throat was tight.

"Aye." Raibert shifted, and Edan could tell that he wanted to go with him, but this was something Edan needed to do on his own.

He needed to be alone right now, lest he break.

Edan cleared his throat, forcing himself to speak steadily. "I appreciate it, Raibert. But 'tis not necessary."

At last, Raibert relented. He turned to attend his own duties as Edan made his way out of the postern gate toward the kirk and the graves beyond. His parents were buried there, along with two little bairns, his brothers who'd never made it past their third and fifth summers respectively.

Oh, how his mother had grieved for them. The death of a child was not uncommon; it was to be expected even. But that didn't make it any less painful. Edan was certain that losing her bairns had eventually led to his mother's own demise. Her health had grown worse as the years went on, and then one evening just a few days before their annual Yule and Hogmanay celebration, her heart had given out. Though the healers had been hopeful, she'd never recovered. She'd slipped peacefully into the night.

Edan's father had married two years later, and his new wife had borne a daughter. However, both mother and child passed not two weeks later. After that, his father had devoted his time to growing his clan's ability to travel by sea, building *birlinns* and making attempts to sail them to France to trade. Journeys he completed twice, but on the third, he never returned. There was no word from him in France from the inquiries Connor made, and so he had been pronounced dead two years ago.

The gate to the graveyard creaked as Edan pushed it open. His father's grave was empty, but said a prayer over it anyway, before finding Connor's freshly dug final resting place.

Edan knelt before the grave, his knees sinking into the sun-warmed earth. He crossed himself, pressed a hand to the freshly turned mound and whispered, his voice choked with emotion, "Och, brother, if ye'd wanted me home, all ye needed to do was ask."

Why did ye have to die?

As long as he'd been away, Edan had always known he had people at home. His brother, his da. And now they were both gone.

He was well and truly alone in the world.

CHAPTER 3

Blair jolted out of sleep to find her two cousins bouncing on her bed, their eyes gleaming from the glow of a candle they must have brought into her room and now sat on her bedside table.

"Has something happened?" She rubbed the sleep from her eyes, thinking someone would only wake her so cruelly in the middle of the night if there were an emergency. Goodness, were they under attack?

"Not yet. But finally, ye're awake," Aurora said with a giggle. "We've been calling your name forever."

Aislinn wiggled her brows and rubbed her hands together. "Are ye ready for all your dreams to come true?"

Blair looked from one of them to the other, not fully comprehending what they were doing in her chamber. "We're not under attack?"

The twins looked at one another with identical expressions of bewilderment and then turned back to face her.

"Do ye nae remember, silly? Your letter." Aislinn rolled her eyes.

Blair resisted the urge to roll her own eyes. Were they still serious about going through with this mad plan? Aye, she'd attempted to make a fun game out of their idea last night, but that didn't mean she was going to go through with it. Not on her life. Thank goodness she'd already burned the letter. Now it was time to let her cousins know that while it had been fun yesterday, she wasn't going through with it today —or tonight, whatever time it was.

She scooted herself up by the elbows and attempted to reflect the smile on her cousins' faces.

"I do remember," she said softly. "But I'm afraid I had to toss the letter into the fire."

"Och, nay! Did your mother see it? Was she cross?"

Blair decided to go with the solution so easily given to her. "She almost did. I burned it before she had a chance to read it." And that was theoretically not a lie. They didn't need to know she'd burned it before her mother even came into the room.

Aislinn bounced off the bed and went toward the writing table. "Ye'll have to write another, and this time, we'll be sure she doesna see it."

Blair cringed, pulling her knees up to her chest. "I'm nae so sure 'tis a good idea anymore."

"What? Come on," Aurora said, taking Blair's hand and tugging her up a little more, forcing her knees to drop back down. Then, as if to soothe her into agreeing, she said softly while nodding, "Dinna ye want to get married?"

Blair tried not to laugh. If only her cousins knew how many times Greer had tried to trick her into doing things with the same subliminal cues. "I do, but this is probably not the best way to go about it," Blair said, quite logically, she was certain.

Aurora laughed. "How about we do it just for fun? Pretend then." She glanced at her twin sister, and Blair felt a warning bell go off inside her mind.

"Pretend?"

"Aye. Write the letter. We'll sneak down to the firth, but we won't toss it in. If anything, we can just dip our toes in the water to say we did it. I'll even help ye burn it when we're done."

"I'm nae certain I want to do that." Blair was finding it hard to fight her cousins on this. Pretending wouldn't cause harm to come to her family, but it was most definitely still the middle of the night and going out to the firth required sneaking out of the castle and beyond the walls. "Is it nae dangerous?"

"Have ye never snuck out of your castle at Dunrobin?" They both looked shocked.

Snuck out? Nay, with a capital "N." Of course she hadn't snuck out. "I would prefer to sleep."

"Blair," Aurora said, her voice dragging in a note of authority. "Ye promised."

Had she? "'Tis just a silly game. And one not worth getting hurt over." Blair returned her cousin's words with her own note of authority.

"Who is going to get hurt? We do it all the time."

Blair let out a long, ragged sigh. She was going to be at Castle Ross for several more weeks, and at this rate, her cousins were not going to relent until she did what they wanted. All she wanted to do was go back to sleep, back to her strict adherence to the rules. Even if the idea of sneaking out to the firth held a bit of excitement to it.

Perhaps, just this once, she could do something truly risky. Och, but the repercussions should they be caught... Was it worth it? Nay! Definitely not.

And yet, she found her voice betraying her. "All right."

"I can write the letter for ye." Aislinn's grin turned downright treacherous, which had Blair tossing back the covers just so she could take control of the situation.

"Nay, nay," she called as she bounded across the cold stone floor and practically ripped the quill from Aislinn's fingers. It might be quite possible that her twin cousins were even more mischievous than Greer. "I want to do it. 'Tis my fantasy husband, is it nay?"

"Aye, 'tis." The twins rubbed their hands in unison. "And make it better than the one ye penned last night."

Relief flooded her as the quill touched her fingers. If she was going to go through with it, then at least she was going to be in charge.

Oh, this was such a bad idea. Her fingers trembled, causing the feather of the quill to tremble, which she tried to hide. With her back to her cousins, feeling their breath on the nape of her neck, she leaned over the table and pressed the top of the quill into the ink, leaving a droplet of black on the parchment.

Just pretend.

Blair had to take a deep, steadying breath to calm herself, for she was only a heartbeat away from calling the whole thing off and allowing them to torment her for the foreseeable future. She was willing to bet her sisters never found themselves in a situation like this.

They should call me Blundering Blair. Though she would keep this small act of idiocy a secret, too.

"Well, hurry then," Aurora encouraged. "Everyone will be up soon."

"Aye, and we can only distract the guards for so long."

Blair curled her toes on the wooden floor, feeling a chill rise through the soles of her feet up through her legs and centering around her heart. How did they plan to distract the guards? Because she was fairly certain it would be a lot like what Aurora did with the stable hand.

Biting her lip, she pressed the quill to the parchment, the black blot growing larger. What would Bella do? She wrote about knights saving ladies, and ladies saving knights. Blair closed her eyes, imagining a warrior riding over the moors to save her. That seemed a good fantasy, did it not? A secret fantasy. She scribbled hastily before she lost her nerve. This was all pretend; besides, what did it matter?

"There, all done," she breathed out, her heart leaping up to somewhere in her neck.

"*Blair the Not So Fair*," Aislinn teased, pointing to where the words were scratched in ink. "A winning touch."

Aislinn and Aurora grinned like little she-devils and nodded, pride in their eyes. "There just may be hope for you after all, Cousin Blair."

Blair didn't like the sound of that at all. Hope for being a hellion... Nay, she'd never survive. Her heart couldn't take it. She couldn't be filled with any more doubts or regrets.

Do the right thing. Be the right thing. Calm. Reserved. Follow the rules.

"Get dressed," Aurora ordered as she tucked the rolled parchment into a bottle and shoved a cork deep into it. She slipped the bottle beneath her cloak and out of sight.

Blair noted then that her cousins were fully clothed—even had their boots laced and cloaks on. And she had the sudden realization they had been planning to sneak out to the firth, whether Blair agreed or not.

Goodness. How many nights had they done this before now? Perhaps at their own castle they were used to doing such, knew the way, were safer. But here? This was a new place. New even to Liam. How could they be so certain they would be safe? If Blair didn't go and they got hurt, she would never forgive herself.

Perhaps it was best to join them, only because she would be the only levelheaded one among them. This had often been the stance she took with Greer. If there was one sensible person among them, then disaster could be averted. And she preferred to be the one making certain that any catastrophe was dashed.

"If anything should appear amiss, we will come back," Blair said, attempting to use her own no-nonsense tone.

"Aye, of course." They rushed to agree, nodding emphatically, which only did the opposite of alleviating her worry.

"And I want to hold the bottle."

With a pout, Aurora produced the bottle and pressed it into Blair's hand, the glass cool to the touch on her palm.

Her stomach did a not-so-tiny flip as she allowed her cousins to toss a gown over her head and tie it in place. She slipped into her boots, and then she was in her cloak, and they were rushing her from the room.

The corridor was dimly lit, illuminated only by a single torch at the end. No one was about, not even those in charge of stoking the morning fires. What time was it? Surely it couldn't be close to dawn if no one was moving around yet.

Her cousins led her down the servant's stairs, away from the front entrance and back toward the kitchen, startling awake a wee lad who slept curled before the hearth.

"Shh..." Aurora said, holding a finger to her lips.

Aislinn produced a sweet from within her cloak and handed it to the spit-boy for his assurance that he'd not seen them and would allow them back in when they knocked. The next thing Blair knew, they were out in the gardens and racing through the chilly, dewy grasses toward the postern gate.

Her heart was pounding so hard she could hardly make out the sounds of her steps, or the whisper of grass against her boots. The leather covering the tips of her toes grew damp, and a chill nipped through her limbs.

When they reached the gate, the guard on top frowned down at them, causing Blair to breathe a deep sigh of relief. Good, he would tell them to go back to bed, and she could finally slip back between her sheets and warm blankets, this nonsense over with.

But with a gentle bat of her lashes and the promise of a kiss, Aurora had the guard practically vaulting over the wall in his haste to open the gate to meet her. Blair gaped in horror.

"Sir," she started to hiss, but Aislinn pinched her hard on the arm, redirecting her attention, and before she could gain her senses, Blair was being tugged away from the couple enfolding themselves in a heated kiss.

"Come on. We dinna want to watch that," Aislinn admonished, as if Blair had been intent on doing just that.

They raced toward the Moray Firth, which gurgled not too far in the distance.

"Will she be all right with the guard?" Blair called in a pitch slightly higher than a whisper. Goodness, this was going from bad to worse.

Aislinn snorted. "The proper question is: will *he* be all right with her?"

Blair wasn't certain what that meant, and it had her feeling more and more naïve. How sheltered a life she'd led up until now. Blair assumed a lass didn't receive her first kiss until it was with the man she was to wed, unless one was a lightskirt—but ladies were never harlots, and yet her cousin...

How very straight and narrow Blair was. Aislinn and Aurora acted as though kissing were the most natural thing in the world. Perhaps it was. Possibly Blair was even more shielded than even she realized. What a silly notion that she'd thought by going with her cousins she could protect them. More the fool her. By the time they reached the water's edge, Blair had to bend over to catch her breath, while standing beside her, Aislinn looked as though she could have made the run a hundred more times and still not been tired.

"I dinna feel good about this, about leaving her. What if she is to lose her virtue? I could never forgive myself."

"Ye're not responsible for her."

"I am older."

Aislinn shrugged. "So am I, but thirty seconds." She giggled. "But Aurora has always done what she wants."

"What does Aunt Aliah think of it?"

"She doesna know, of course, ye ninny. And ye're not going to tell her. Besides, Aurora would never lose her virtue afore she was wed. She's not an idiot."

"What if she doesna have a choice in the matter?" Blair wrinkled her nose, realizing that perhaps she was in fact the wisest of the three.

"What do ye mean?"

"The guard may decide what she's offered is more than what she was in fact willing to give."

"Are ye talking about...*rape?*" Aislinn whispered the last word.

"Aye." There was no use in hedging around the topic, and perhaps a dose of something scary might help her cousin see the seriousness of it.

"Och, Blair, not every man is out to pillage a woman's virtue." She laughed, and Blair felt bad for her cousin.

"Ye're right. Not every man is. But without a dose of caution, how is a woman to know?"

Aislinn grunted and then pointed toward the bottle in Blair's hand. "Toss your message into the water. Wish it a good journey. And pray the man who answers doesna have the same notions of a simple kiss as ye do."

"I told ye I wasna tossing it in."

"Scaredy cat," Aislinn scoffed.

"I am not."

"Then toss it in. I dare ye to live beyond the extreme tightness of your plait. And the fortifications of your virtue."

Blair frowned at the downright rude accusations. Was her cousin trying to get back at her for what she'd suggested could happen to Aurora? The two of them needed a healthy measure of reality.

Blair stared down at the bottle in her hand that seemed to signify in that moment the difference between an uptight and prudish miss, and a jovial, teasing enchantress.

Aislinn was ignoring her now. Apparently having made up her mind that Blair would not go through with it, she was sitting down to unlace her boots. Blair was certain she was doing it to delay their time here in order to torment her all the more. Because while she'd relented in leaving Aurora in the arms of a guard, Aislinn had to know that Blair would never leave her cousin alone and unprotected outside the walls and quite alone.

Frustration and the same burning heat of anger she'd felt earlier in the day burned through her. How had she allowed herself to get into this situation where she felt so out of control? So at a loss for words and actions?

This was ridiculous. Blair was not this person. She wanted to have fun, aye, but not at the cost of what sending out a plea for rescue would bring to her family. Bringing war to her clan, to the people she cared, about was an experience she didn't care to visit again. With Aislinn's eyes averted, Blair uncorked the bottle and pulled out the rolled parchment. She tucked it up her sleeve, then recorked the bottle, her cousin none the wiser.

Her cousins didn't need to know who she was. They only wanted to know she was willing to take as many reckless risks as they were. So be it. Besides, it was Aurora herself who'd said *pretend*.

"All right," Blair said, a little too loudly, to gain her cousin's attention.

As predicted, Aislinn's head jerked up, her fingers still on her laces, mouth forming a little "O," her eyes reflecting the moonlight.

Blair closed her eyes, wrenched back her arm and threw the bottle as far as she possibly could—which didn't end up being very far. The plunk of the jar hitting the water, and a small spray after, reached her from what could only be a couple dozen feet away. Perhaps that was fate's way of letting her know that even if she had left the missive inside, the jar would just wash up on this shore, and she'd never have to worry about it again.

But then, a swift wind picked up, causing the water in the firth to swirl in the moonlight, and the bottle drifted ever speedily away until she could see it no longer. Thank goodness she'd had the foresight to send it empty.

"Saints preserve me," Blair whispered, touching her hand to her chest. She let out a long breath of relief.

Beside her, Aislinn giggled, relaced her books and leapt to her feet. She grabbed for Blair's hand, her warm fingers clashing against the cold of Blair's.

"Ye did it. Now we wait and see." Aislinn's voice was filled with mirth and a bit of surprise.

Despite the bottle being empty, it was oddly freeing that Blair had tossed it into the firth's depths. Almost as if she were releasing herself from the grasp of her cousin's overbearing attempts to influence her. Perhaps now, Aurora and Aislinn would no longer feel the need to treat her as their lost cause. At least she could hope.

They ran back to the castle. Aislinn grabbed her sister's arm and tugged her out of the embrace of the knight, because if their fathers or brothers saw what was going on, they would take him to the stocks.

The guard called out after them, begging Aurora for her name, but they only laughed and kept on running. Blair wasn't sure if she was rushing away from the impression she'd just given her cousins of who she was, or the fear of the danger she'd come so close to causing if her missive had ever seen the light of day. What she was certain of, was that she was hurrying toward her chamber and away from being caught having snuck out of the castle in the middle of the night.

This was the most reckless thing she'd ever done by far, and if her father found out, he'd have her hide.

Ha! Her family wouldn't believe it even if presented with the truth.

A rush of something hot and cold at the same time stormed inside her.

Back safely inside the keep, her cousins gone off to their own rooms, Blair tugged the rolled parchment from her sleeve and tossed it into the fire. She kicked off her boots, tucked them safely into the wardrobe with her cloak and then snuggled deep within her blankets, trying to warm up her limbs.

But no matter how much she rubbed at her chilled arms and legs, the rush of all that had happened continued to tunnel through her body, causing her to shiver and lie awake for the better part of the night.

EDAN SWIPED a hand over his face in frustration.

The dungeon was lit by several flaming torches, but still the darkness left shadows along the cell housing the men suspected of murdering his brother.

The four accused were ragged and bruised, having put up quite a fight when they were seized by the Rose men as they dined at Connor's table, nearly a fortnight before. Their *leine* shirts were stained with their dried blood. Their plaids, the colors muted beyond recognition with filth, lay in heaps on the floor where they'd made themselves makeshift beds, the pins removed to keep from using them as weapons.

From what Edan had been told, these four prisoners had been invited to dine after a feat of heroism on the road outside the castle. Her ladyship had been out for a ride with a guard and her maid when they were intercepted on the road by a trio of outlaws, their faces painted blue.

Her guard had tried to fight them off but was losing badly until these four had shown up. No one knew where they'd come from.

Connor had seen them as heroes and awarded them a warm dinner and beds for the night—until he'd fallen dead in his own stew. Now, it was suspected they'd been part of a trap set for the lady, in order to gain entry to the castle and the laird.

Edan had been questioning the men in the dungeon for what felt like hours and barely gotten anywhere with them. Bloody stubborn fools. He could not entice them to widen their traps, even with the promise of a warm meal. The most he'd gleaned from their tight lips was their claim to hailing from Ross lands—knowledge that did not surprise Edan in the least.

The Ross men had plagued the country for years and didn't seem in any hurry to quit.

Edan had been at Stirling several months prior when Liam Sutherland, son of the infamous Magnus Sutherland, had brought a captured Ughtred Ross to their king. The idiot and his wife, Ina, were still imprisoned in the castle's dungeon awaiting execution.

With them still alive, the Ross clansmen who had not aligned themselves with Sutherland were doing just about anything they could to regain power, and possibly break their leaders out of Stirling's dungeon. One reckless attempt had already been made by Ughtred's brother—a plan that had been thwarted rather quickly by Liam's own wife, Lady Cora.

That was about the extent of what Edan knew about the Ross clan and their wayward plans to allow *Sassenachs* to take over the country.

But why had his brother been a target?

Had Connor gotten in the way of some plan of attack? Had he thwarted them somehow, and so they'd felt the need to take his life with the elaborate ruse of saving his lady? None of it was making sense.

What a massive load of horse manure that was. Edan clenched his fists at his sides and resisted the urge to beat the lot of them bloody. Then his anger shifted toward Liam Sutherland—why hadn't he dealt with these unruly traitors before they'd been able to kill his brother?

Aye, Liam held some of the blame for this. After all, the king had tasked him with taking care of the bastards. Even now, he was residing at their castle, acting as laird to their people.

A bitter taste soured Edan's tongue. To hell with the lot of them. What use were they to him? What use were they to anyone, save misery? This was the Highlands of Scotland, and he too was a laird. He was judge, jury and executioner. Perhaps it was time he laid down his decision and be done with it.

"'Haps ye'll all face execution the same day as your treacherous leaders." Edan scowled, already imagining the weight of his sword in hand as he brought it down upon their necks, exacting vengeance for his brother on behalf of the whole clan.

Then his people would know they could trust him because he would have put to rest the men who'd betrayed them, killed their leader, put them all in the situation they now found themselves.

Edan would be recognized as a worthy adversary. No longer would they have to rely on word alone, stories told around campfires from men who may have fought beside him in the king's army. They would know him as a powerful leader, one that would give no mercy to anyone who'd wronged them.

And yet, he scowled, because putting these devils to death would still leave the unanswered question—who'd put them up to it?

"Or what," one of them scoffed, "rot here in your dungeon? If ye wouldna mind, I'll take my execution now."

They were goading him, seeing how far they could push, and if he'd break. Edan worked hard to keep himself calm when all he wanted to do was lash out.

"I'll not give ye the pleasure of an easy death." Edan pinned the man with a mighty glower, his fingers itching to be around the traitor's throat. "Tell me who put ye up to poisoning my brother, and I'll see your death done swiftly."

"Och, nay, ye fool." The whoreson spit on the ground only a few inches from Edan's boot. "We'll tell ye nothing. If ye want the truth, ye must agree to letting us go free first."

Edan ground his teeth, fighting the need to cut these men down, and his desire to know the truth of who was behind their design. Was it worth setting these bastards free so he could go after the man, or woman, truly responsible? The mastermind behind their murderous plot?

The muscle over his eye twitched, causing an ache to spread

through his skull, pulsing in a line over his scar. He gritted his teeth, keeping his hands flexed at his sides and refusing the impulse to rub the painful mark.

In a voice so tight it came out a growl, he said, "Tell me, and I will consider it."

The men eyed each other, realizing this was the best offer they would get if they wanted a chance to live at all. They seemed to have a private, silent conversation, proof they'd schemed together for a long time.

Then boldly, the man who'd taken up speaking jutted his jaw forward and said, "'Twas Liam Sutherland. Now that he has Ross lands in his power, he plans to conquer every inch of land along the firth, whether by marriage or by war. Greedy bastard." He spit again for emphasis, only this time, rather than landing a few inches from Edan's boot—it hit him square in the center of his bare knee.

Without hesitation, Edan swung his fist and connected it with the man's jaw. Pure rage, at having been spit on and with the lie this man was willing to utter in order to save himself and his disgusting friends, erupted through him.

"Ye lie," Edan bellowed. "And for that lie, ye'll die tomorrow."

He turned his back on them and marched toward the lowered ladder deep in the dungeon where two of his men waited on either side.

The men all protested at once.

"I swear to ye, my laird, we tell the truth, 'twas Liam Sutherland."

"We heard him ourselves. He issued us the orders, and we but complied to keep our heads."

"He has our families held hostage, our wives and daughters. We had no choice if we wanted to save them."

Their words bounced hollowly off Liam's back. "And look what good that did ye," he tossed over his shoulder.

The largest of the four men kneeling on the dungeon floor started to cry like a bairn, big fat angry tears streaking down his cheeks. He scooted forward on his grubby knees, the hem of his shirt getting caught beneath. He blubbered and held out his hands in resignation.

"Please, I have a family. A wife about to birth our firstborn any day now, and I've been so worried. I swear to ye, we dinna lie."

The pain in Edan's head only grew until his lucky eye started to blur, as it did in times of stress. How could they possibly be telling the truth? Liam Sutherland was the most loyal warrior he'd ever met. And, aye, Edan was furious that Liam could have allowed these pustules to roam the land, but that did not make him a killer. Liam was deemed one of the greatest warriors in all of Scotland. How could a man like that decide that power and greed were more important than order and alliances? Edan just couldn't fathom it.

Taking the lands along the firth by force would be frowned upon by the king. Indeed, his newfound Ross lands and lairdship could be stripped from him. Why would Liam risk that? Or had the king agreed to the plan?

Edan's brows knitted even tighter together, and he was in danger of lashing out again. To think that his own king might be behind his brother's attack sent a shiver of revulsion running through him. *Nay. Nay. Bloody nay.*

"Lies," he said through clenched teeth. He turned his back on the men again and shouted orders to the guard, "No food or water until they are ready to tell the truth."

He'd stay their execution and hope that a hungry belly and a tongue dying of thirst would get their mouths moving in a more truthful direction.

Out of the dungeon, head pounding, he exited the castle with determined strides. Edan wanted nothing more than to call his men into the bailey for an impromptu training session in order to work out the fury in his blood. Alas, he was stopped by the housekeeper. She wrung her hands and her brows screwed up in worry.

"The lady's father, Laird Guinn has arrived to collect his daughter."

CHAPTER 4

One month later

"Come on, Cousin. Everyone will be doing it!" Aislinn flopped herself down on Blair's bed.

What everyone was doing was dancing around the fire tomorrow night. In the morning, the lassies would be rolling around in dew. Blair did not want to have anything to do with either activity. She'd only ever been an observer in the past, too busy trying to make sure Greer wasn't lured away by some shepherd feeling the need to sow his wild oats. It really was quite shocking to her sometimes that *she* was the baby in the family, when so much of her time was spent acting the opposite.

In fact, she was ready to return home to Dunrobin, but her father had gone off to meet with the king, and Liam had remained behind here at Ross Castle to deal with his new clan, in case in his absence they forgot who their new laird was. Since Lady Aliah and Lady Arbella had remained, Blair was stuck here, too. Which meant she currently did not see a way to escape her cousins, unless she could somehow disappear.

That was not likely to happen. Aurora and Aislinn were running wild and trying to drag Blair into their many schemes. Aunt Aliah was ragged from having to thwart most of their plans, and as of last night, she'd threatened to toss them both into convents very far away from each other after someone let spill that they'd seen them sneak out of the keep. Thank goodness, Blair hadn't been looped into any schemes again, not since the first time a month before.

Those two headed for a convent was probably a good idea.

"At least help us weave our flower crowns," Aislinn said.

With a great sigh, Blair felt her resistance wearing thin. There really was no harm in participating in traditional clan activities, was there? "All right, I'll help with the crowns, but nothing else. I dinna want to dance. I'm tired."

Tired of her cousins.

She felt horrible for even thinking it, but they were driving her up a wall, and she honestly wished she could hide from them under her bed.

"Tired? How do ye know ye'll be tired tomorrow already?"

"Intuition."

Aislinn shrugged and scooted off the bed. "We'll see. Aurora is waiting for us in the great hall."

Blair had barely been able to think, let alone do any of the things she enjoyed. Too much of her time was spent avoiding everyone in hope of avoiding her cousins. She'd not gotten to spend as much time with her new sister-by-marriage, Cora, as she'd wanted to because the twins were always there, causing mischief or talking too loudly. Blair was deathly afraid they would blurt out what the three of them had done in the middle of the night with the message in a bottle.

The last thing she needed was her mother threatening to send her off to a convent, too.

Down in the great hall, Liam's wife was with Aurora, as were her aunt and her mother. They all smiled at her and Aislinn's approach, though a small worried wrinkle marred her mother's brow. No doubt, she was wondering what had changed Blair's mind about being involved with the festivities she'd so far been removed from. Flowers and boughs hung on the doors, mantle and every other surface for the festivities that would take place the following day to celebrate the coming of spring. The rushes had been replaced and strewn with sweet smelling herbs, and every other surface had been scrubbed, giving the hall a refreshing and inviting fragrance that reminded Blair of home.

With the five golden-haired beauties beside each other, Blair felt more out of place with her dark locks. If she didn't look so much like her Aunt Heather, her father's sister, she might think she'd been found on the moors and brought into the fold as one of their own. Clearly dark hair was in their blood, and she just so happened to be cursed with it. Self-consciously, she touched her hair and wished it were cold enough outside to warrant a hood, but alas, with the coming of May on the morrow, spring was in full bloom.

The women rose from where they perched on benches.

"Let the gathering commence," her mother said, referring to their need to head outside and pick flowers for the crowns.

Cora slipped her arm through Blair's and started to lead the women from the castle. Her touch was slight and warm, and her smile inviting.

"I'm glad you decided to come down," she said in her smooth, soft English accent. "We've not gotten a chance to really get to know each other."

Blair smiled, glad that her sister-by-marriage felt the same way. Behind them, her two cousins were chattering away, and their mother was hushing them. Lady Arbella was whispering soothing words to her harried sister.

"I am too," Blair said.

The great keep door opened to a sunny morning, the air crisp and fresh with just enough of a bite to remind them that though flowers were starting to bloom, it was still possible to have one last winter storm. As they walked, several guards took up position around them at a distance that left them some privacy, but close enough to provide protection if needed.

With a *baa* of excitement, Blair's sweet pet sheep came loping across the bailey to greet her, relieving one of the stable hands who'd been chasing her.

"Would ye like to come, Bluebell?"

Her lamb rubbed her head against Blair's thigh, and she slid her fingers into the soft fleece of her back. Bluebell was a wee lamb about to go to slaughter for a mild deformity in one of her hind legs the year before. The Sutherlands were well known for their wool, and Blair's father feared the lamb wouldn't grow into a prized sheep.

When Blair realized the wee thing's fate, she'd rushed into the barn, tucked her up in her cloak and whisked her up to her chamber to hide her. When her father realized what she'd done, there'd barely been an argument about keeping the wee creature. In fact, she wasn't certain there'd been much arguing at all. Her father wanted her to be happy and was more than pleased to gift her with a pet.

She'd brought Bluebell to Ross, because she couldn't bear the idea of being without her.

"She is adorable," Cora murmured, rubbing her palm over the softness of Bluebell's forehead.

"Aye, she is."

They exited through the castle's main gate, marking the first time Blair had left the walls of Ross Castle since the evening she'd snuck out with her cousins. Their footsteps clicked on the wooden planks as they crossed over the bridge that spanned the moat, and they fell into whispers as they transitioned to the fields where wild flowers grew in bright, unadulterated colors of red, yellow, orange, white, purple, pink and blue. It was truly striking, and it gave Blair hope she hadn't felt a few moments before.

She dragged in a deep breath of the scents of flowers and sweet grass. With barely a cloud to mar the blue landscape of the sky, if it kept this way for tomorrow, they were in for perfect weather for the evening bonfire celebrations.

"Will you wake early with the maidens?"

Blair shook her head. She'd never participated in the morning rituals at Dunrobin Castle, and she did not plan to start now at Castle Ross. Just before dawn, the maidens would rise, and without dressing, they would run from the castle in just their night rails to this very field, and they would roll in the morning dew, scrubbing the moisture from the grass and flowers onto their faces. It was an odd ritual, to be sure, and there had to be a question of morality within it, but who was she to question a tradition, given its significance to her people?

Spring and all that it brought with it was a time of renewal, growth and fertility. The ritual, too, represented marriage matches that would be made, and hopefully, a blessing upon any maiden's womb for her coming vows.

Luckily, Blair's family knew her reservations and had never forced her to participate. And thank goodness. It was practically hedonistic the way the water soaked into the thin fabric of the night rails, clinging to the lassies' skin and giving the lads who stared a glimpse of their flesh beneath. No doubt, Aurora would wear her thinnest night rail for the ritual...

Nay, thank ye. I'm fine right where I am, bundled up. Unbidden, a shiver swept through her.

"Nay, 'tis not for me," Blair finally said.

"Why not?" Cora asked, with a little teasing rub of her elbow on Blair's ribs. "Have you a beau already?"

"Nay," Blair rushed, her cheeks turning red, as they did whenever anyone teased her. She was far too sensitive. She knew this, but it mattered naught—she blushed anyway.

"Oh, I did not mean to upset you."

Blair realized how tense she'd gotten and forced herself to relax, pushing out a small laugh. "Ye didna upset me, Cora." She patted her sister-by-marriage's hand. "I'm sorry." She shook her head, pursed her lips into a frown. "I've never done it before, and..." She snuck a glance behind her at her cousins.

Cora saw the line of her vision turn. "Ah. You're thinking the lads will be too occupied with the likes of them to pay you any attention?"

The heat in Blair's cheeks deepened. "'Tis not like that." She didn't like how selfish that made her sound, even if it was true.

"They do not stand a chance beside you, Blair. You must understand that."

Blair flashed her eyes toward Cora, her brow wrinkling. "What do you mean?" She was genuinely confused. Her cousins outshined her by far when it came to beauty. They were golden goddesses like her mother.

"You're too modest. You're gorgeous. And dark with an air of reserved mystery. The lads cannot take their eyes off you. Have you not noticed?"

Blair was stunned by this revelation, because she had indeed *not* noticed that at all. In fact, it seemed like every time she actually did pay attention, the lads were drooling over Aurora.

"When you decide you're ready for a beau, mark my words, your Da and Ma will have to fight them off."

Blair smiled at that, flattered and embarrassed all at once. "Ye're too kind to me, Cora."

"Not kind, just honest." She stopped walking then, gazing at the various flowers swaying in the gentle morning breeze. "Shall we?"

"Aye." Blair knelt in the field of flowers with the rest of the women, picking them down by the root so there was enough stem to weave together into a crown. She might have said she wasn't going to participate in the maiden washing, but she still picked as many bluebells as she could find—giving up a few to her hungry lamb—and hoped they brought out the blue in her eyes.

"My laird!" Raibert rushed into the great hall where Edan was finishing up breaking his fast.

Raibert's face was flushed with color, and his brows were drawn together with concern. He'd been out leading a patrol of their shores that morning, and given his state, it could only mean he had bad news.

"What is it?" Edan wiped the remnants of bread crumbs from his fingers and stood.

"Your housekeeper found this on the beach this morning when she and the kitchen maids were looking for mussels for supper. Ye must read it for yourself."

Edan took the bottle from Raibert's hand. Inside was a rolled parchment.

He narrowed his eyes, turned it over and tapped it onto his hand until the parchment came free. A message in a bottle? Was this some kind of bloody jest?

He unrolled the parchment that appeared to be fresh, not weathered and not wet. Someone had to have just dropped it on his shores, surely.

Inside, scrawled in beautiful feminine curls, was a message of only a few lines.

> *If ye're reading this, then ye've received my urgent message.*
> *Come and save me from the chains that bind my soul... I*
> *fear without ye, I shall perish at the hands of a most unjust*
> *captor.*
> *Fate has made ye my one and only knight.*
> *Ye'll find me at Castle Ross.*
> *I am called Blair the Not So Fair, and it is almost spring.*

Edan had to read the missive more than three times before he allowed himself to blink. What in the bloody hell was this?

"We must go to her," Raibert said. "It is as the Ross warriors claimed. The Sutherland laird is not who ye thought he was."

Edan shook his head. "This could have been written last spring. It could just be a childish prank. I canna take it seriously."

Raibert frowned. "But, my laird, what if 'tis nay? The parchment is fresh, not from last year. And given what the prisoners said about Liam Sutherland, how can ye not at least look into it?"

Edan stared down at the scrawled hand, knowing Raibert spoke the truth. If the lady was being held captive, he could not leave her to languish after having found her message. The Ross men had warned him that Liam was greedy, but to keep a woman against her will? He couldn't stand for that. If he didn't at least go check on her to determine if this were a jest or not, he wouldn't be able to live with himself if something were to happen to her.

When he'd questioned the Ross men before, once he'd withheld their food, one had broken down and said they'd lied, that for the love of a single woman they'd all made up the story about the Sutherlands, and he'd allowed them to live in chains, to eat. They were still below, as he'd gotten no new information. But perhaps the man had broken, and his confession of a lie was in itself a lie.

Ballocks! He'd gotten nowhere figuring out who was involved in his brother's death. If anything, he'd be able to speak with Liam Sutherland and clear up the rumors that his prisoners below stairs had started.

"Gather the men. We'll leave for Ross country within the hour." He prayed that if the missive were in fact a true call for help, they weren't too late, for spring was here, and spring had been near whenever the lass had written her missive.

But mostly, he hoped to shed light on whoever was responsible for his brother's death. He'd been looking for proof of wrongdoing, to lay the blame at someone's feet, and this mysterious bottle landing on his shores could possibly be the answer. But he didn't want to jump to conclusions. Making assumptions was a good way to put his men, his clan, in danger. Though he was still new to being laird, he wasn't completely naïve. He'd have to have a rock for a head to think that running off and accusing another laird of wrongdoing would get him anywhere.

How had the bottle gotten on the shores where the clanswomen had found it? Was it possible someone had planted the bottle there? Had it washed ashore? How very strange.

The hair on the back of his neck rose, and he stared down at his hand where he held the parchment, the lines curling into letters. Had someone here written it? Did they want him to go to war? Was it a test? A dare? An ambush from the inside?

When Raibert turned to leave, Edan called out, "Wait. First, gather the elders. I wish to speak to them in Connor's—" He shook his head, still finding it hard to believe his brother was gone. "My study."

"Aye, my laird."

Moments later, half a dozen men filed into the study, nodding in his direction with clear respect. In the month since Edan had taken his position as laird, he'd often spoken to the elders. He tried to gather their opinions on things as mundane as which field to plant in, or whether or not they should continue their increase of border patrols on the Campbell border. Chief Campbell had written back to say he'd not condoned any reiving and had in fact dealt swiftly by sending the men who'd participated to the stocks. The elders knew best. After all, they'd been here at Kilravock aiding his brother and father before him, when Edan had not. To not take their advice and superior knowledge into consideration would be a mistake. It was the same for a warrior newly knighted. If he went off on his own rather than following the king's directive or that of his captain, he would be a fool. Everyone could always improve themselves for the better by listening to those wiser. He hoped now to garner some information and advice on how to proceed with the missive and his suspicions regarding the new Laird of Ross, Liam Sutherland.

The problem Edan was that running a clan, seeing to their health, their bellies and all that was involved, was a lot different than simply being in charge of training men for war. He'd only been trained to prepare and lead men into battle and otherwise protecting a king.

With the men assembled and watching him expectantly, Edan leapt into his reasoning for their meeting. "I've asked ye here just now because something disturbing has showed up on our shores. Could be a hoax, a trap or a true call for help. It implicates Liam Sutherland once more in a dangerous scheme, and given he was already accused previously of being the man responsible for Connor's death, I canna let this summons go unanswered."

The men issued sounds of interest, but they allowed him to continue.

Edan held out the missive and read the contents aloud to the men. "My gut, as a protector, says we should save her, despite my misgivings about a possible hoax or trap. If we do nothing, and this poor lass perishes, the blame could be laid at our feet. I know my brother was more practical than I, and that because of his trust in ye, the clan was able to thrive. I feel we canna allow two such rumors to go unquestioned. I will have to go to Castle Ross."

Their grumblings grew louder, laced with affirmations in Edan's favor and anger that Liam Sutherland was once more being accused of something nefarious. Edan could allow one accusation to be brushed off, but two?

"I want to take a contingent of men to Ross country to confront Liam Sutherland. To demand access to Lady Blair to be certain she exists and is safe, and to demand he speak to me about his involvement, if any, in my brother's death. If I should determine he is responsible, I will demand he surrender himself to me."

"He will not surrender to ye," Murtagh said with a shake of his head. "Liam Sutherland is too proud. He's the son of the one of the most revered men in Scotland. He himself is a legend. He will fight ye."

Edan nodded, his lips thinned. "Aye, then so be it. If it comes to that, I will accept."

"With all due respect, my laird, but we have only just lost one laird—"

"Ye're suggesting I would lose," Edan cut Murtagh off. "Dinna let it come off your tongue so easily." His voice had held a note of sarcasm, but it was replaced with conviction when he continued. "I am honor bound to challenge the man who killed my brother."

The men nodded solemnly, knowing that to argue would be futile. "And the lass?"

"If we should find he is indeed holding her captive, I will return her to her family."

"Ye know a laird's duty is to marry."

Edan scowled. "Are ye truly suggesting that I would take a woman who'd been held captive and demand she marry me, rather than setting her free?"

Murtagh looked sufficiently cowed. "I'd not thought of it that way, my laird. Only thought for ye to capitalize on it."

"I'll marry when I choose, and it will be for the benefit of the clan and my bride." The last thing he wanted to do was get into an argument with the men about when, and whom, he should marry. They'd dropped enough hints over the last month about his duty to wed, and at every chance he got, Edan brushed them off. His life had already changed immeasurably, and he was not yet accustomed to where he was. "For today, I'm asking for your support, your guidance. Will ye give it to me?"

Murtagh glanced at the other men gathered. "We will support ye, aye. But ye'd best come back alive, laird. Your people need ye."

Edan nodded. He'd not been fighting his way to the top in the king's army for naught. Liam had a reputation as being the best knight in all of Scotland, but that wasn't a position he would hold for long. Edan was ripe to take that mantle.

"I'm going with ye, laird," Murtagh said.

"I'd be honored. Those of ye that remain, know that I am entrusting our clan, and my brother's legacy, in your hands while I'm away. There is still a chance that this message in a bottle was a trap meant to entice me away. Should that be the case, we'll need the proper precautions in place."

"Aye, laird. We'll have a messenger at the ready to bolt and find ye upon the road should we come under attack. The gates will be closed, and we'll double the guards on the wall."

"Good. Now, I've another question. Have any of ye heard whisper of a lass being taken? A family missing their daughter? Word travels fast within the clans. And I'm surprised we didna know of it before now."

The men mumbled nay, shaking their heads and turning from one to another. "Could be she's a Lowlander," Leith said with a shrug.

"Aye. Or her family didna want her," Murtagh added. "Maybe she was given to him as his *leman*."

Given to him as a mistress...like a piece of property. Edan found it hard to hold in his disgust at that notion.

"There is something else to consider," Leith mentioned. "The Earl of Sutherland will most likely side with his son. He's a formidable foe, as is the Laird of Dornoch, Liam's brother. If ye present too much of a threat upon your approach, ye may have more to contend with than simply facing Liam himself."

"Not to mention every other uncle, brother, or cousin of his," Edan added with a frown. "The bloody bastards control more than half the Highlands at this point."

"Which lends credence to what the Ross prisoner said about Liam wanting to gain control of the firth. More lands for their family."

Edan had never been close with Liam at Stirling. They'd never been given the chance. They'd fought in different regiments, were in charge of different men and sent on different missions. And even when they were both centered around the king's camp, whether in the field or at a castle, men tended to stick to their units. So while he'd heard of the man, he'd not interacted with him very much.

"A boon, my laird?" Raibert asked.

"Aye?"

"When we approach the gates, let us first negotiate."

"Of course. It never bodes well to prod a cornered bear. However, should we find that our suspicions are true, I can promise the likelihood that blood will be shed. And I dinna mean my own."

"We trust ye, and we'll support your decision."

Edan felt his chest swell with pride. He was starting to feel more like a laird and less like an imposter. Once he'd avenged his brother, he wouldn't have that nagging feeling he was not worthy of the respect of his clan. He would truly be their leader.

Connor deserved to be at peace in the afterlife, and every one of the Rose clansmen and women deserved the same in the here and now.

CHAPTER 5

B lair stretched awake before dawn, surprised at the energy flowing through her limbs. She'd not expected to feel this way. So alive, and...excited.

It was the first of May, and already she could hear the giggles from the bailey. The maidens who had gathered there were preparing for when the gates would open so they could flood out into the fields to roll in the dewy grasses.

And Blair was going to be among them.

It was reckless and went way beyond the comfortable walls she'd built up around herself, but after speaking with Cora, she realized it was harmless. And if she was going to make her parents see she was beyond childhood and ready to create a life for herself, perhaps this was a good step in getting there.

She still didn't believe a word of what Cora had said about standing out from her cousins as a contender amongst men. The Englishwoman was touched in the head if she thought Blair had anything on the fairy-like beauty of her cousins. But perhaps she'd end up taking a few lads by surprise. Not that she planned on having her parents pursue any of them in a marriage contract.

Blair swung back the covers and pressed her feet to the floor, ignoring the instant chill at the disappearance of her comfortable cocoon. She was already in her night rail, so there was no reason to change, but she did take her hair out of its braid, letting her long, wavy locks wrap around her shoulders and back like a dark cloak. She might be willing to roll around in the dew without a stitch on but her thin night rail, but at least her long hair would serve as a form of barrier to prying eyes, no matter how minimal, and perhaps afford her some warmth.

A lass had to have some standards.

Blair ran her fingers through her hair, splashed some cold water on her face and then tiptoed toward her door, not wanting to alert anyone that she was about. The last thing she wanted was for Aurora and Aislinn to come out of nowhere and pluck at her like she was a bairn and give her a reason to change her mind. They were the exact same age as she was and always had the ability to make her feel ten years younger. Well, not this morning. Today, she was going to start to live the way she wanted to be seen—like a woman. And she wasn't going to let anyone spoil this momentous moment for her.

The corridor was empty, but the noises from the great hall floated up the stairs. Even more lassies were gathering there, and she could hear Aurora's distinct tinkling laugh. Flirting with some guard, no doubt.

Blair hurried to the stairs, not wanting to be left behind. She reached the level below and was just about to step down onto the next flight when her mother's voice stilled her.

"Blair?" She sounded shocked, but also mildly pleased?

Blair swirled on the stairs, catching her hand against the stones before she tumbled down, and saw her mother, fully dressed, coming out of her chamber and onto the landing. Her eyes were wide with worry, perhaps looking for an injury that must have caused Blair to venture from her room.

"Mama." Blair flashed her mother a smile, hoping to ease her obvious worry.

Lady Arbella scanned Blair from head to toe, a small smile on her lips when she spotted no damage. "You're going out to the fields?"

Though it was posed as a question, it also sounded like there was a bit of wonder at the realization.

"Aye. I am."

Her mother nodded once and reached forward to tuck a lock of hair behind Blair's ear. "What changed your mind?"

Blair bit her lip, shrugged as if it wasn't a big deal that in all the years she'd been allowed to participate, she never had until now.

"Where is your crown?"

Blair pulled the ring of bluebells from behind her back and waved it before her in what she hoped was a nonchalant gesture.

"'Tis beautiful, darling. May I?"

Blair nodded, and her mother took the bluebell crown in her slim-fingered, graceful grasp. She lifted it and gently placed it on Blair's head, stroking her cheek as she did so.

"The flowers bring out the blue of your eyes."

Blair felt the heat rise to her face as she murmured her thanks. That was exactly what she'd hoped.

"Well, you'd best get going, my darling, else the rest of the maidens soak up all of the dew and leave none behind for you."

Blair laughed, imagining that her mother meant *lads* rather than dew, and her cousins rather than maidens. For she was certain that Aurora and Aislinn would have no problem in surrounding themselves with adoring and ogling beaus.

Whether or not Blair gained the attention of the lads, she was determined to enjoy herself and the freedom she was almost certain would wind its way over her limbs the moment she stepped outside and sank her bare toes into the earth. But she should let her mother know she was not interested in any of those in attendance, lest her parents take it upon themselves to find her a mate amongst them.

"I'm not wishing for any prospects here, Mama."

"But you *are* wishing for one."

Blair chewed the inside of her cheek and nodded. "I am."

"It's hard for me to see you for the woman you are." She smiled nostalgically. "You were my last babe, and I can still vividly see you curled in the crook of my arm, sleeping softly or cooing."

Blair leaned forward, wrapped her arms around her mother's waist and dragged in a long breath of her comforting scent. "Those memories will never fade, Mama. And they are ones I hope to create someday with a bairn of my own." Blair pulled back. "I'm ready."

Tears sparkled in her mother's eyes, catching the light of a nearby torch. "Well, then we'd best not keep the magic of our celebration waiting."

Blair thrust herself into her mother's arms once more and held her tight. "I love ye, Mama."

"I love you, too, my sweet lass."

Blair breathed in the familiar floral aroma of her mother, a scent that always calmed her and made her think of warmth and safety. One day, hopefully soon, she'd provide this same comfort for a bairn of her own.

At last, she pulled away, grinned to herself and then rushed the rest of the way down the stairs, feeling even lighter than when she'd woken. She'd not expected to have her mother's blessing. To have it was incredible, though she supposed her mother never would have said *nay*. She'd allowed Bella and Greer to participate in the celebrations, so why wouldn't she have allowed Blair?

In the great hall, she was met by a few shocked faces, but most surprised was her brother Liam, who knew well how much she had resisted the tradition over the years.

He approached her with a teasing grin on his lips. "What do we have here?"

Blair playfully swatted him, which he dodged. Then he whirled, taking in the few guards around the room.

"Who is he? Which one? Tell me, and I'll cut his heart out."

Blair rolled her eyes. "As I told Mama, the man I seek is not present. Ye'll only be wasting energy trying to sift through your men."

Liam looked skeptical. "Then where is he, missing out on this spectacular miracle of Blair Sutherland coming out of her shell?"

"He may not exist at all." Blair widened her eyes and pursed her lips to keep from smiling as she said it. Goodness, where had this teasing lass come from? She'd not even gotten a chance to dance in the dew, and already she was acting bolder, freer. "But if the magic of rolling in morning dew is to summon him, I'd say he'll be walking through your gates any day now."

"Ye wish, sprite." Liam tugged on a dark tendril, not hard enough to hurt, and winked. "Be careful out there." He slanted a glance toward their cousins.

"'Tis not I that needs to worry, brother, but the lads, I should think. I'm fairly certain the lassies in question dinna give a fig for their reputation."

Liam chuckled. "Ah, there she is, the wee sister I know well."

Blair rolled her eyes again. "I may have come down to participate in a ritual that is probably improper at best, but that doesna mean I have to give up all semblance of propriety."

"Perhaps ye should offer lessons."

Blair snorted at that. "I dinna think lessons will help those two."

As if on cue, her cousins let out loud squeals and rushed toward the main vestibule of the castle. "The sun is rising," one of them screeched.

"Time to offer ourselves up to the fairies," called the other, both of their voices so similar it was hard to discern who said what.

The great doors were wrenched open, and burgeoning sunlight filtered through, and with it a gust of spring morning wind. Goose-flesh instantly rose on Blair's skin, and she regretted her decision to go outside and roll around on the cold earth. A warm bath or climbing beneath a mountain of covers sounded oh so much better. Perhaps this new side of her that was testing the waters shouldn't include bodily harm, for surely freezing to death constituted such, did it not?

She glanced about the bailey for her lamb but did not see her. The stable lads must have been sure to keep her in her pen for the chaos that was about to ensue.

"Coming?" Liam teased, Cora grinned beside him, her eyes bright with love when she turned them on Blair's brother.

"Thinking about going back to bed," Blair murmured with a small smile.

"Too late, wee sister. I'm waiting to see who your mystery lover is." Liam teased, essentially saying he believed not one word she'd said.

Blair stuck out her tongue. "I've no lover, Liam." She glanced around quickly, suddenly weary of her reputation. "If anyone were to hear ye say such—"

But Liam cut her off with a loud chortle. "Relax, Princess. Your reputation is intact."

Blair huffed and hurried past him out into the dawn morning. She was wound up so tight, her spine was in danger of snapping. The stone steps of the keep were freezing against her bare toes, as was the wet bailey ground. Soft earth squished between her toes, and she stared down in awe, realizing it had been ages since she'd walked barefoot outside. Probably not since before her age was in the double digits.

The lassies ahead of her were running now, the wide gates yawning open and the fields in partial view from across the bridge. Pipers played a haunting lilt that rolled over her skin, drawing on her emotions. It always amazed her how the sound of the bagpipes and the various songs and rhythms could bring her feelings of joy, love, longing and sadness.

Excitement replaced some of the anxiety in her veins. With a smile on her face, Blair rushed through the gates to the fields, joining the other lassies who held hands and swung in circles, dew covering their bare feet and slicking up over their ankles to their calves.

Gooseflesh prickled up over her legs, and Blair's body shuddered. She rubbed at her arms, finding her toes curling in, seeking warmth.

"Ye can go back inside," Cora whispered. "Dinna fret, sister."

But Blair had made the choice to do this. To experience the unadulterated joy the other lassies, including her sisters, and maybe even her mother, had experienced. A rite of passage. By coming out here, she'd told her mother she was ready to take the next step as a woman and marry. If she retreated now and went inside seeking warmth, what would that say?

The other lassies seemed to have forgotten all about the cold now, thinking only of joy and how much fun it was to dance nearly nude in a field of flowers. Blair looked on them with acute envy, once more considering giving up. She had no one to dance with. No beau she wanted to impress. Perhaps this idea had been foolish and naïve of her after all. Not participating would in no way cause her parents to think anything about her, other than she'd come to her senses. Which was perhaps the biggest motivating factor for her to drop to her knees, the first of any of the lassies, and begin rolling in the morning dew.

The spontaneity of her actions swept a thrill through her veins. She swiped the dew over her fingers, rubbed it over her face, her lips, and then lay down and stared up at the sky as it turned from pink and orange to blue. She didn't roll anymore, just stared in awe.

There was a tiny part of her that regretted not having indulged in this hedonistic sport before. But the larger part of her heart was grateful. Experiencing it now, for the first time, when she'd been ready to call it quits, she had a different respect for it, a heavier appreciation, and perhaps even more enjoyment over it.

As she stared up at the sky that seemed to fight the sun for purchase, the ground beneath her rumbled, and she had the sudden wonder if the earth was laughing at her joy, or maybe the fairies were all stomping their feet, proud to have a newly converted maiden to play with.

But the rumbling continued, and the murmurs of the lassies around her grew concerned, as did that of the guards who were now shouting, pulling her completely out of her dreamlike state.

Blair sat up to see her brother's men running, grasping at lassies' arms. Liam had Cora's hand and was racing toward the gate, when he looked over his shoulder, eyes meeting hers where she still sat on the ground, confused. What was happening?

He motioned for her to get up, his shout lost in the chaos. Then he was pushing Cora into the arms of another warrior and turning to race toward her, shouting. Blair turned from him as the rumbling grew louder from the opposite direction. There she saw the answer to her question. Coming out of the horizon as though they were bred by the morning sun were several dozen warriors riding with the wind.

They were headed toward the castle, the newly risen sun sparkling off the weapons strapped to their bodies. She stared, both struck by their might, and in shock at seeing them at all.

Warriors.

Were they under attack?

They were not bellowing war cries, and neither were their weapons drawn in a warning. But they were mighty all the same.

All the warmth that had been in Blair's blood suddenly dissipated, and she scrambled to her bare feet, her gaze riveted on the bodies slowly growing closer. Who were they and why had they come? Ross men intent on taking their castle back? Boldly, she stared them down, willing them to turn back. Never would her brother surrender, and never would she want him too. A sense of rage and boldness enveloped her. Give her a sword, and she would raise it.

"Blair!" Liam's bellow cut through her courage, and she turned away from the advancing legion, recalling all too vividly that she stood there practically nude.

Coming to her senses, she started to run for her brother, who was cursing up a storm.

The guards had their weapons drawn, forming a line in the grasses as they urged the lassies to get behind them and to hurry back to the castle. Should the riders turn out to be enemies, they would reach the guards first. Her brother wasn't wearing his sword and held only a dirk in his hand—a misstep she was certain he would berate himself over for days to come.

Archers were already knocking their bows upon the walls, prepared to let them fly as soon as they were given the go-ahead.

Blair ran as fast as she could, feeling as though the quicker she went, the more distance was put between her and where she needed to go. And then she was with her brother. He grasped her arm and pulled her along, shouting words she couldn't understand, because all she could hear was the pounding of her heart, staccatoed by the horses behind her.

As soon as her feet hit the wood of the bridge, the guards on the wall bellowed for the men on horseback to halt.

They bellowed the order again and again, their voices rising with urgency, and then she, the last of the maidens over the bridge, fell to her knees in the muck of the bailey, panting, feeling as though she might throw up. Warriors scrambled to cross behind her, and her brother lifted her, tugging her out of the way.

The portcullis chains cranked as it was lowered, and then the gates were slammed shut, a bar as thick as a tree trunk placed in the iron braces to keep the enemy out.

It had not yet been confirmed whether the men outside their gates were enemies, only that they were advancing on them with enough weapons strapped to their bodies to be bloody. They were unannounced, and apparently unrecognized, which suggested they were indeed enemies prepared to lay siege.

"Are ye all right?" Liam asked, his concerned gaze searching her face.

Blair only had enough time to nod before a man's voice could be heard from the other side of the wall.

"Sutherland!" The bellow was filled with rage and sent a cold tremor of fear racing over Blair's skin and up her spine.

One thing was for certain, this did not seem to be a social call.

Beside her, Liam stiffened, met her fearful gaze and said, "Go inside the keep with the other women."

Blair swallowed hard, nodded and started to walk toward the keep steps when the next words she heard stopped her in her tracks, one foot still slightly raised in the air until she *thunked* it hard on the bailey ground.

"Show me the lass called Blair the Not So Fair!"

What? Nay... It couldn't be... She'd burned that missive! Watched wide-eyed as it caught flames and disintegrated into ash. The bottle she'd thrown out to sea had been empty. So how in Hades was a man standing on the other side of the gate bellowing the made-up name she'd penned and then burned? Her gaze bore through the keep door, willing Aurora to come out and explain. Her cousin could be the only reason this was happening. And yet not all the blame lay at her wayward cousin's feet. For it had been Blair who'd written it in the first place.

All the blood rushed from her face, pooling somewhere down on the ground. And now war was upon them, just as she'd suspected when she'd jestingly scribbled the words on parchment.

"Blair?" Liam murmured behind her, his tone guttural.

She turned slowly to face her brother, feeling faint as his questioning eyes met hers. He would think she'd betrayed him. She *had* betrayed him. Even if it was unknowingly.

"This is all my fault," she muttered, staggering backward, her heel catching on the stone steps. She fell hard, her bottom pounding against the edge of a stair as she slid down onto the stone. The fall was jarring, but not nearly as jarring as having heard her words tossed over the walls of Ross Castle by an enemy warrior.

Liam stared at her; horror written on his face. Confusion mixed with horror as he shook his head. "I dinna understand. What did ye do?"

CHAPTER 6

They'd come over the hill, while the fair maidens dressed in white had rolled amongst the heather, their shifts dewy and clinging to their forms like a second skin.

When Edan and his men were spotted chaos ensued. Women and men started to run.

One lass among them all had stood out as she boldly faced Edan and his men, the sleek darkness of her hair striking against her white night rail and sun-kissed skin. It was enough to cause Edan to hold his breath. What woman simply stared, spine straight, shoulders squared, looking prepared for battle when an army advanced on her?

Had she been stunned or ready to cut him down?

Saints, but he'd probably never know, and yet he couldn't get her out of his mind. Even now as he tilted his head toward the top of the twenty-foot wall, taking in the men who glared down at him, images of his approach flashed in his mind.

Every last one of them had scrambled over the bridge, and the gates had been closed tight, the resounding thud of a heavy wooden bar being put into place echoing in the stillness of the dawn air.

Up on the wall, men pointed their arrows toward Edan and his men, the sun glinting off the tips of sharpened steel. Truth be told, he was grateful they'd opted not to shoot before finding out why he was there.

"Show me Liam Sutherland," Edan demanded once more.

At last, his demand was met by the familiar, yet not well-known, face of Liam peering over the wall down at him.

"How dare ye advance on my castle," Liam roared, narrowing his eyes. "Who the hell are ye? What the hell are ye doing here? And why in bloody hell are ye asking about Blair the Not So Fair?"

Edan had to force himself not to smile. Liam was making it hard not to like him. He had to remember this man may have caused the demise of his brother and might be holding a woman captive. Though seeing how freely the sprites just danced and rolled in the fields had Edan growing ever more skeptical about this last bit.

"I see ye dinna recognize me, though ye've not cause to remember me other than we served the king at Stirling together until ye took your place here. I am Edan Rose, recently named laird of my clan. I've a number of matters to discuss with ye, Sutherland."

Liam waited a moment before saying, "And how do ye bloody well know my sister's name? And by what reason would ye have cause to insult her?"

That gave Edan pause, and he frowned. Blair existed. And she was his...*sister*? And insult her? Perhaps by calling her plain?

Whatever the cause might have been, it was obvious the missive could not be taken seriously. Or at least, the likelihood was very slim. Edan gritted his teeth. What kind of game was someone playing? Edan didna believe in coincidences, and the fact that he'd been lured here at all under two suspicious accusations was making the hair on the back of his neck stand on end. However, no matter the circumstances, or how false they may be, Edan needed to talk them over with Liam to be certain, one way or another.

"We can address the issues shouting over the wall, or ye could invite me in," Edan said, his voice strained. "I didna come to war with ye." *Unless ye give me cause.*

"Ye think I'd invite ye in after the way ye arrived? How do I know I can trust ye?"

Edan grinned, trying to break some of the tension. "Ye've no cause to distrust me or my clan." *Unless ye murdered my brother.*

"Rose ye claimed?" Liam's face bunched in confusion. "I've got no dispute with Clan Rose."

Annoyance simmered low in Edan's gut, and he tried to tamp it down. "Have ye heard of my brother, Connor Rose?"

Liam's face was blank over the wall and Edan's neck was going stiff from staring the twenty feet up at him and trying to decipher his emotions. "I'm afraid I didna know him personally."

"He died." The words dripped painfully from Edan's tongue, and he watched for any change in Liam's stance, but there was only sorrow.

"I'm verra sorry for your loss, but I dinna know what that has to do with me or my clan."

"This is nae your clan," Edan baited, aiming to see if he could make Liam break. Such a statement would be enough to send some men to battle. What kind of man was Liam Sutherland?

Liam frowned now and let out a growl, his chest visibly puffing even from this distance. "Nae my clan?" he bellowed. "I suggest ye take your army and shove off, Edan Rose, else I tell my archers they're free to let loose a few arrows."

"I like your conviction." Edan was impressed.

"Is that it, ye've come to lay siege to the castle? To take your piece? The king granted me the title and the lands. I earned it by my loyalty and my duty. If ye're who ye say ye are, then ye should be following the king's edict, unless ye've become a traitor to your country."

Edan kept himself calm as he replied, knowing he'd goaded just this reaction from the man. In any other situation, he might have been angry. "I've fought for the king since I was a wee lad, Sutherland. This"—he pointed at the long scar on his face—"I received saving the king's life. And trust me when I say, I dinna need a piece of your land or your title. I've lands and a title of my own. Lands and a title that should have belonged to my brother, but he was cut short of his life. Which is the second reason for my being here."

Liam was quiet for a moment, the anger slipping from his face to hide behind a blank slate. "Tell me straight, Laird Rose, and let us not continue to bandy words. Why are ye here?"

"Again, I request we speak face-to-face, instead of shouting over the walls. Once more, I give ye my word I've not come to bring war to your feet." He chuckled. "If I had, would ye nay see more of my men?" There was no need to tell Sutherland he and his men could take on a vast army with their low numbers.

Liam pondered his choice for a moment. "All right. Only ye, though, and divest yourself of your weapons."

"Ye think I'd enter your castle alone and without a way to defend myself?" Edan chuckled. "Come now, I'm nae a fool."

"Ye came here. I didna invite ye."

"Aye, but the matter of my visit makes it imperative I've a way to protect myself."

"Then we must speak as we are, for I'll not leave the safety of my walls, and ye'll not enter what ye think is the danger of mine."

Liam was correct. They were at an impasse; neither of them trusting the other, and with cause.

"Agree. Tell your archers to lower their bows and have your men turn their backs. I'll have mine do the same to give us the illusion of privacy."

If Liam thought the request was off, he didn't say so. He nodded to his men, giving the order. The arrows were lowered, and his men obliged their laird and turned their backs on Edan and his men. At the same time, Edan made good on his word.

"Your backs," he ordered, and his men shifted their horses backward, issuing more than a few grumbles of their own.

This move was a show of trust on both their parts, however slight. For at any moment, one or the other could have his men turn and fire shots and their leader would not be protected. And the men would be unprepared. They were in essence, lowering their defenses.

"Now, we are alone," Edan said with a subtle laugh, which Liam returned. "And I'll get straight to the point. My brother, Connor, was murdered a little more than a month ago. And I've four prisoners who swear they did the deed on your orders." He purposefully left out the means by which his brother's life was taken, so he could see if Liam would make a mistake.

Liam looked stricken now, brows firmly drawn together, lips pressed. When he did speak, it was through bared teeth. "I'm no murderer, and I dinna like the insinuation of such."

"And yet ye stand accused."

"By ye and your mysterious prisoners. What makes ye think they tell the truth if they were the ones who carried out the murder?"

Edan grimaced. "I didna take them at their word at first, which is why I didna come sooner. It is only recently I felt it imperative I seek ye out."

"What changed your mind?"

"The missive in the bottle."

"What missive?"

"From Blair."

By now, Edan had memorized its contents, and so he recited it to Liam. "*If ye're reading this, then ye've received my urgent message. Come and save me from the chains that bind my soul... I fear without ye I shall perish at the hands of a most unjust captor. Fate has made ye my one and only knight. Ye'll find me at Castle Ross. I am called Blair the Not So Fair, and it is almost spring.*"

As he spoke, Liam's face grew darker and darker with rage at each word. "Is this some kind of jest? Do ye seek to insult me, Rose? I think 'tis time ye left, afore I have my men shoot a hundred arrows into ye."

"Allow me to speak with her," Edan said.

Liam laughed at that. "Ye've stormed my castle on the words of murdering outlaws and a mysterious letter my sister would have never written. Ye've risked your life and that of your men on falsehoods."

Now it was Edan's turn to grow angry. A slow burning started in his chest. This was why he'd asked the elders to speak with him. This was why he was certain he was not cut out to be laird. And this was why he knew he was not worthy, that though his men stood with their backs to him, they would hear all that Sutherland said, with his mocking tone, showing how very much a fool Edan was.

"If the lass wrote falsehoods that have brought an army to your gates, should ye not speak with her about it?" Edan said.

"I'll not subject her to such, especially not at the request of a stranger. She's an innocent, and ye play a dangerous game."

"All the same, it was her name. Who would have written the missive in her name, if she'd not penned it herself? Why in the span of a month has your name, and the deeds ye may have done, touched my ears? Even if false, Sutherland, ye must admit the coincidence is nay a coincidence at all."

Liam's frown deepened. "We will settle this easily, Laird Rose, and then ye'll get the hell off my lands."

"How do ye propose that?"

"Let me see the missive."

Edan gritted his teeth. If he let Liam have the missive, he could destroy it, and if he didn't then they would never know the truth.

He would have to risk losing this piece of evidence in order to gain answers, which he was willing to do in order to put this fiasco to rest.

"And what of the accusation of murder?"

"I dinna know your brother, nor would I have had any cause to murder him. I'm an honorable man, Rose. I dinna go about plotting the murders of men."

"There is a rumor going about that ye wish to control the Moray Firth, that the garnering of Ross lands was only the start."

Liam shook his head and chuckled. "Ye know I'm just a soldier like ye, Edan. I was not born to be a laird. I earned it. And this land I was granted, this title, it was not easy to take. Why would I risk that? Why would I risk my family, my clan, my king's trust?" He shook his head. "Would ye?"

"Nay," Edan said gruffly, finding it irritating that Liam was pointing out ways in which they were similar when he'd come here to face down a possible enemy. To bring his brother's murderer to justice. He was coming up empty, because as much as he wanted to have found the man responsible, he believed Liam.

"The bastards who came to your castle, who rot in your dungeon, are no men of mine. We face our foes; we dinna cower behind walls. If they claim to be Ross men, then they are deserters, for all the men who've pledge allegiance to me remain behind these walls. Ye have my word as a loyal subject of King Robert the Bruce."

Edan drew in a long breath, most of the last vestiges of his suspicion shattered. "I believe ye wouldna, for I wouldna. But that doesna discount that these men, and possibly others, are trying to name ye as a traitor and murderer. I'll agree to show ye the missive."

Liam nodded to one of his men and said something Edan couldn't hear. Then he turned back to him. "We are going to open our gates, raise our portcullis partway and lower our bridge. One of my men is going to come out to retrieve the missive. Dinna approach. Dinna have any of your men turn around and dinna attack my man, else an arrow will pierce your heart faster than ye can draw breath."

"Aye, ye have my word."

"Good." Liam waved his hand, and moments later, Edan could hear the creaking of the pulleys as the bridge was lowered and the portcullis raised only halfway.

He scanned the wall, taking in the number of guards and the arrows pointed directly at his heart. Trusting that none of the archers' arms would get tired and accidentally let an arrow fly, Edan fixed his gaze on the single man walking over the bridge toward him.

Perhaps the same age as Liam, with hair the color of fire, the man made quick work of the bridge with long strides. When he reached Liam's mount, he nodded.

"I'll bring it back to ye," he said.

Edan acknowledged the man and handed him the bottle that held the missive.

The warrior eyed the bottle and winged a brow. "What's with the bottle?"

"How it arrived." Edan didn't give him any further information than that.

The man bobbed his head and as soon as he was back beneath the portcullis and it had been lowered, so too were the arrows pointed at Edan's heart.

The minutes ticked by for what felt like hours. He wanted to turn around and ask Raibert what he thought of the way things were evolving, but he didn't want to endanger his men by one of them turning to look at him as he spoke. So instead, he took the time to scan the castle tower, noting it was perhaps five or six stories high with thin arrow-slitted windows and crenellations on top that housed one—nay, two —guards.

Liam shifted on the ramparts and waved the bottle in the air to show he'd received it, and Edan waited patiently as he uncorked it and dumped the small missive into his hand.

He stared down at the parchment for longer than it took to read it, which told Edan he was reading it over and over just as he had. And it told him something else—Liam recognized the hand.

At last, Liam muttered something to his men, and then called over the wall. "I invite ye in, Laird Rose, along with your men. We'll dine in the great hall. I trust ye've not had a chance yet to break your fast?"

"Not yet," Edan said with a curt nod. "We thank ye for your hospitality."

Liam grunted down at him. "Ye've Blair the Not So Truthful to thank for that." The words were perhaps not meant for Edan to hear, as they were muttered, but Edan heard them all the same as they floated down to him from the ramparts.

So it was as he suspected, and the lass had indeed written the missive.

The creaking of the pulleys was heard once more, and Edan directed his men to approach with caution.

"Are ye certain we can trust him?" Raibert said. "'Haps 'tis is a trap, just like the one the men laid for your brother."

"We'll be cautious, but I suspect if 'tis were a trap, he'd not allow all of us to enter his walls fully armed. He's extending his trust to us as well, for he doesna know with certainty we will nay attack once we cross the bridge."

"True enough." Raibert glanced up at the ramparts, and the men whose bows a moment ago had been knocked and ready to kill but were now slung docilely over their shoulders. "Ye think his sister wrote the missive?"

"Aye."

"Why?"

Edan shook his head. "I didna have sisters, so I dinna know."

"I had sisters," Raibert said, "but I never paid enough attention to know if they did anything so reckless."

Reckless, aye, 'twas. But if Liam's sister was a wee lass, there could be some measure of forgiveness, nay?

The bailey was lined with warriors, some in Sutherland colors and others wearing the Ross plaid. Liam crossed toward them dressed in both—a plaid that looked to have been fashioned out of both colors, with Sutherland pleated around his hips and Ross colors swung over his shoulder.

Edan dismounted and handed his reins wearily to a wee stable lad who stared at his scar with terror. Liam approached, arm outstretched, and Edan didn't hesitate to grip the extended offer and show of respect. The man's grip was strong, and they held on to one another longer than necessary as if to show just how strong they both were.

"Welcome to Castle Ross," Liam said, his tone as ironic as his words, since the day before, Edan had considered challenging Liam to a fight until he'd come to his senses and realized questioning him would be more appropriate.

Liam handed Edan the bottle with the missive inside. His face was blank, eyes hard. "I believe this belongs to ye, Laird Rose. Though if ye burned it and forgot about it, I'd be in your debt."

"I take it ye recognized the hand."

Liam gave a curt nod. "Aye."

"Then consider my visit one of neutrality, as I intend to see it returned to the rightful owner. Allow her the chance to explain and perhaps burn it herself."

"I'll not allow ye to harm her, and the Earl of Sutherland, our father, would likely deny ye the chance to greet her."

Edan frowned. "I've never harmed a woman in my life. And if ye deny me the chance to meet her, allow me to at least lay eyes on the woman who believes herself not so fair and yet worthy of rescue."

Liam grunted. "I'll think about it. And what of your previous accusation?"

"On hold for now."

Liam's eye twitched, and Edan was certain the man was not happy with that. He wouldn't be either. He'd not said he thought Liam responsible, but he hadn't said he didn't think so, either. And that had to sting a little, especially after Liam had offered him and his men a place at his table.

"I mean no offense, Sutherland," Edan said, extending an air of camaraderie. "I hope ye understand my position. If it were your brother..."

"I'd be the same way." Liam shook his head and swung out his arm, showing Edan the way inside. "As much as it pains me to have such an accusation thrust at me, I fully understand your reservations, and I do intend to help ye get to the bottom of it. Let us go inside."

Edan looked behind him at his men, who had all dismounted and were eyeing the guards around the bailey warily.

"Come," Liam said, his voice full of authority, and the men glanced at Edan for approval.

Edan nodded to his men and walked beside Liam into the castle. In the great hall, none of the maidens he'd seen dancing on the moors were present, but servants scurried back and forth preparing the long trencher tables for a feast. The scents of the impending meal made Edan's mouth water. He'd barely eaten since leaving his castle the day before.

"Please, make yourself at home." Liam flagged down a female servant. "See that our guests have some ale afore the feast begins."

The servant nodded and then snapped her fingers at a few lassies holding tankards, who made quick work of pouring them cups and passing them out.

A lovely blond woman approached and slipped her arm through Liam's. He looked startled to see her in the great hall, as though he'd not expected her to be present. How curious. Edan studied her. She was beautiful, elegant, and watched Liam with respect and clearly love. His wife, if Edan had to guess.

"Who are your guests?" She smiled at them, though it did not reach her eyes. Though her gaze scanned over his scar, she did not falter, nor did she stare.

Edan tried his best to hold in his surprise at both her decorum and her accent. Liam's wife was a *Sassenach*. Interesting, given the man was known for his duties of governing the border for the king. How had he come to marry a woman he should ostensibly hate? Though, just by looking at her, with her kind eyes and beautiful smile, Edan could guess.

"Laird Edan Rose and his men. This is my wife, Lady Cora, Mistress of Clan Ross."

She glanced up at her husband, then swept her eyes over the men, assessing. "Welcome to our home."

"My thanks for your hospitality, and I do apologize for frightening any of the maidens with our hasty approach. I assure ye, my lady, frightening lassies is not a hobby of mine." Edan bent at the waist, brushing a kiss over her extended knuckles.

A slight blush colored her cheeks, her lashes dipping. "I'm certain they will be pleased to hear it from you, as they'll be joining us for the feast."

Again, Liam jerked his gaze down, as though he'd been wanting to change this part of the evening festivities. Perhaps he did not want the maidens to mingle with the newcomers, and had Edan been in his boots, he would have felt the same way. Alas, Edan was glad for Lady Cora's intervention, for it meant he would indeed have a chance to lay eyes on the woman whose missive had brought him here.

"I would request that your men disarm themselves," Lady Cora said, her eyes scanning his heavily armored men. She swept her arm out to indicate the Sutherland and Ross warriors. "You see, they are not so armed inside our walls. And we assure you that you'll be safe here. But to see a man sitting at the table with his sword still strapped to his back may give some of our ladies a bit of a start."

Edan inclined his head. Was this Liam's plan all along? Have his wife disarm them so he wouldn't think too much of it? He eyed the other warrior a moment, trying to make the assessment, but Liam kept his thoughts close. "We will honor your request, my lady." He nodded to his men, who set down their ales and strode outside to leave their weapons in the bailey, and he did the same.

The bailey was quiet. Those who resided in the castle eyed them warily, and it made his skin crawl a little to be so closely watched, as though he were the nightmare that haunted children's dreams. He tried smiling a few times, but it felt more like a grimace, and judging by the way it had some women fleeing, it looked that way too. A grimace plus his scar was mighty intimidating.

Once they were back inside, Lady Cora had once more disappeared, and Liam stood by the hearth, a frustrated look on his face. So when they were outside divesting themselves of their weapons, had he convinced his wife the women should not dine with the men? Edan couldn't fault him if that was his decision. After all, what did Liam really know of him other than the word he'd given?

When Liam spotted him, he motioned Edan forward with a short gesture of his hand.

"The women will be down in a moment, as will my sister."

Edan raised a brow, taking the cup of ale Liam offered him. He sipped the lukewarm brew.

"'Tis not what I want. But without my da here to provide his opinion, I find myself in charge of my sister's fate. Perhaps it will do her good to see what her folly has wrought. I will say nothing to her of the missive and see if she doesna confess it herself."

Edan said nothing.

"I need not say that one wrong move on your part, and I'll have your head."

"Ye need not. 'Tis understood."

"Then while we wait, tell me about these men who claim I sent them to murder Connor."

CHAPTER 7

Blair's teeth were still chattering, and the prickles of a chill remained along the lengths of her arms, no matter how much she sought to warm herself. She'd long since divested herself of the damp, dew-covered night rail. She'd stood before the hearth until her skin turned pink from the heat, dressed fully in her hose, chemise, gown and boots, and then put herself back before the thriving hearth.

She shouldn't be shivering, and yet she was. An ache had developed in her jaw from trying to clamp her teeth closed to stop the chattering.

This, she reasoned, was because of the man she'd seen flying over the hill on horseback. The one who'd led his men on what looked to be a siege of her castle, and the fact that he'd so loudly called out her name.

But not just her name. Nay, he'd called out the moniker she'd given herself in a letter that she'd burned.

When she'd come inside, she'd looked for her cousins, but they were nowhere to be found. Hiding, no doubt, for they had to have been the ones to copy her message and send it out into the firth. *Cowards.*

The stranger was in the great hall. She wished she'd gotten a better look at him, for she could barely piece together his features from the distance at which she'd seen him. All she knew was that his hair was dark, and he was very, very large.

The clang of battle did not ensue, nor any shouts of pain. So they had not been attacked. And now all was silent.

She'd strained to hear what was happening, leaning slightly out of the window. Had begged her maid to seek out information from the guards who might know, but Liam's words with the stranger had carried on the wind, and none of the guards were talking. Her mother had stopped by to check on her and make sure she wasn't too trauma-tized by the incident, but Blair's few subtle questions had revealed nothing. Her mother had no information about who the man was, or why he was here. And thankfully, she had not been informed that he'd called out for Blair.

A soft knock sounded at the door, and Cora entered, eyes filled with compassion as she swept her gaze over Blair. She knew the truth. Had to. Else why would she wear that expression?

"You look as though you've seen a ghost," she said.

"I feel as though I might have." What was the use in keeping it in when Cora would already know the truth—that he'd asked for Blair by name. Liam told his wife everything. Theirs was a marriage Blair would very much like to emulate.

"What do you mean?"

Was it possible that Liam had not said anything? Blair cocked her head to the side, wrinkling her nose. Cora sauntered casually to the window and stared out, watching something below that gave her a measure of pleasure, based on the small smile on her lips.

"The warrior...he called my name," Blair said softly.

"Oh, aye," Cora murmured, glancing over her shoulder at Blair before returning her gaze to the bailey below. "I did hear about that. Odd, is it nay? Do you know him, then?"

Blair shook her head, forcing her heavy feet toward the window. What was it that had Cora so intrigued? And how was it possible that Liam hadn't told her about the missive? Was it possible the stranger had not revealed where he'd gotten her name? "I've never met him before. I dinna even know what he looks like."

"How do you think he knew your name?" She was still peering very pointedly at the bailey. "And he was very...tall."

Aye, Blair could tell that by the way he almost dwarfed the men who rode beside him.

But she was still mesmerized by the fact he might have kept the evidence about her missive a secret. Goodness... Her mind was whirling. She'd burned that letter! How was this even happening?

Blair bit her lip, not wanting to answer Cora's question and feeling heat climb to her cheeks, along with a solid pain in her temples. Other than her, Aislinn and Aurora were the only ones who knew about the message in the bottle, and if they told what they knew, they'd have to admit to much more than simply being aware of the missive.

Cora turned her attention back to Blair, whatever she'd been looking at in the bailey no longer holding her interest.

"A coincidence?" Blair said with a shrug of her shoulders. "Maybe I heard wrong."

"We all heard him. Did we *all* hear wrong?" Cora's attention was now firmly on Blair, her eyes narrowed, and her arms crossed. She looked the way Blair's mother did when she was trying to get the truth out of Greer.

Blair sank onto her bed, flopping back and covering her eyes with the heels of her hands, impervious to the wrinkles she was putting into her gown.

"You said it was your fault. What did you mean?" Cora's voice was soft, but there was an edge to it.

Whatever stalling tactic Blair tried to employ—which she was admittedly without talent for—Cora would break through.

At any moment, she expected her mother to come into the room, to demand answers after having finally heard what happened, but for some reason, she'd not yet come.

"I'm too embarrassed to say," Blair finally answered.

Cora sat down beside her and took Blair's hands away from her eyes. "I held a secret for a long time that endangered my family, and maybe even yours. Telling the truth is always best if the chance of strife can be avoided."

Blair let her hands fall and blinked teary eyes at Cora. "My mother will never forgive me, and my father will think me a lass of less morals than my own cousins."

Cora's eyes widened at that, and she let out a laugh. "Less morals than Amorous Aurora?"

Blair let out a loud groan. "Is that what she's being called? Och, but that is so awful."

"Aye, I feel bad for the chit, but I think she may have kissed every eligible bachelor in the keep, and the maids see all. Liam has much to tell their father when he returns."

"Her mother has threatened her with the convent, too."

"Both of them. Might do them some good. I was housed in a convent once many years ago. 'Twas not overlong, and I was not a lass of ill morality, but I did hold secrets, and having time to reflect on them made me a better person."

"I did something terrible," Blair said, suddenly feeling the need to confess. "And I am nay normally terrible. Or maybe I am." She shook her head, wiped angrily at the tears that had started to trek down her cheeks. "I have always prided myself on doing the right thing, and the one time I slipped—this happened." She spread her arms out, in essence encapsulating all of the troubles at the castle currently.

"Perhaps we can fix it. The men are being amiable now. No blood has been shed."

"Amiable? How?"

"They are divesting of their weapons in the bailey as we speak. I came up to get ye."

"Get me?" Blair shook her head so hard her newly wound knot came undone to whip tendrils against her cheeks. "Nay, I canna."

Cora gave her a sympathetic look. "I understand your reservations, Blair, but we must always face our fears. Especially when the man came specifically to Ross to find ye. How was it he knew ye were here?"

Blair squeezed her eyes shut again. "'Tis impossible, and yet it has happened. Only by the grace of an evil tricking hand."

Cora sucked in a harsh breath. "What has happened, Blair?"

Misery encompassed her. She needed to talk to someone, couldn't hold this in. Not if she was going to face the men downstairs. "I wrote something. It was silly. A game, really. I never thought anyone would actually find it, else I wouldna have done so. I burned it... Or else, I thought I burned it. I can remember very vividly tossing it in the fire, and yet, he has found it."

"You think sorcery?" Cora looked very worried now. "Such things dinna exist, Blair."

Blair sighed, knowing that indeed, it had been a very *live* and *unmagical* being that had dealt her this hand. "Nay. I think Aurora."

"How?"

"'Twas she and Aislinn who encouraged me. I thought I tricked them by throwing an empty bottle into the firth and burning the missive, but either they switched it, or they copied it, and now it has fallen into the wrong hands."

"What did it say?" Cora asked softly.

"I dinna remember exactly. I wrote in riddles."

"Try to remember..." she urged.

"It was something about needing to be saved from the chains that bound me, from a captor who kept me prisoner."

Cora gasped, her hand fluttering to her throat, realizing that in her idiotic missive, Blair had essentially accused Liam of holding her captive. "Why?"

"It was a game!" Saints, but she felt wretched. "And not at all what I meant. I am not a prisoner here, nor am I chained. It was...fiction, a metaphor. I was trying to be like Bella."

"She has tossed messages out to sea?" Cora looked doubly horrified.

"Nay..." Blair stood abruptly, lacking air, needing her brother. "I must speak to Liam. He has to understand I didna mean to bring a siege to his castle."

A soft knock had them both jolting, their gazes fixed on the door.

"Blair?" It was her mother, voice full of concern.

Blair jumped from the bed, swiped at her tears and rushed to the door. She opened it quickly and grasped her mother to tug her inside and shut the door swiftly again.

"This has all been a mistake, a terrible mistake," Blair rushed. "I need to go home, to Dunrobin, now! Mama, please." She ignored the desperation in her voice, ready to get down on her knees to beg her mother.

Lady Arbella shook her head somberly. "We cannot leave just yet, my love. There is a feast."

"I dinna want to feast. I want to go home."

Lady Arbella's smile softened. "And earlier today, you wished for a husband."

"What?" Blair said, exasperated.

"You did—do you not recall what you said to me on the stairs earlier?"

Blair thought back to the stairs, the way her mother had looked at her, and the way she'd so lovingly placed the bluebell crown on her head. Where was that, anyway? She'd lost it on the field.

"You said you were wishing for a lad, and then to your brother you said he'd be walking through the gates any day now. I thought you were expecting this?" Lady Arbella looked truly perplexed now. "It was rather unconventional of you, and I am not at all pleased about it, nor will your father be, but alas, it has happened. Where did the two of you meet? How did he know to come?"

Blair thought her head might explode. Just pop right off her neck. Her mother didn't sound like her mother at all.

With a huffed breath, she let out a long sigh and a groan, and rushed to the window to see if the men were still there. They weren't, and their horses had been safely tucked into the stables.

"Let me escape," she whispered on the wind.

"We are wanted in the great hall," Lady Arbella said. "That is what I came to tell you."

"Oh, I feel like a terrible hostess," Cora said, rushing toward the door.

"Do not fret, my dear," Lady Arbella said, "they will not start without you."

The shivering returned with a vengeance, and then just as swiftly, Blair got a hold of herself, squared her shoulders and bit down hard enough to break a stone, if it had been between her teeth.

Cora was right. It was better to be honest, and Blair had always told others to face their fears, to be strong, to be truthful. That was what she needed to do as well.

Even if it scared the bloody wits out of her.

Good God... What were people going to think? Given all she'd said, they would think she'd planned this.

Well, she hadn't, even if she was inadvertently responsible. All she had to do was go below stairs, tell this man—whoever he was—that it was all a mistake, a silly game. And apologize to Liam.

Then she'd excuse herself, request an immediate visit with the priest and demand her penance. She was certain to pay dearly.

With her head held high, she exited the chamber and approached the stairs. She ignored the way her knees attempted to wobble, and that she had to hold on extra hard to the roped railing.

The closer they drew to the great hall, the louder it got. When she finally reached the door, feeling the presence of her mother and Cora behind her, Blair found it hard to draw breath. Even still, she pushed forward, searching the crowd for her brother, her eyes landing on one man in particular. Goodness, but he was tall. Like a mountain or a tree in their great hall... He was brutally handsome in a way she couldn't describe, because he shouldn't be so.

His hair was as dark as hers, and his eyes a storm-filled gray, made meaner by the slash of a wicked scar that started on his forehead and ended in the middle of his cheek. He wasn't smiling. Nay, his wide, perfectly shaped mouth sat in a set line; his dark, stubbled jaw tight. Ordinarily, she would look away, intimidated by his sheer presence. Saints, she might even run. If she were smart, she would, for certain. But she didn't. She didn't even look away. Her feet remained rooted in place as he approached her. Heart pounding, she gripped her skirts to absorb the slickness on her palms, but also because she needed to hold on to something, to focus herself, instead of falling in a wretched puddle.

Up close, he was even taller, and she had to practically crane her neck to look up at him. He was broad enough to block out the great hall in front of her, leaving only enough room for her to look at the sweep of his muscled chest and shoulders, the thickness of his neck. The squareness of his jaw and line of his nose, marred by a bump where it had broken probably more than once. And that scar... A jagged line that spoke of danger, bravery and survival. Rather than detract from his striking visage, the scar added to it.

She found herself staring at him, wide-eyed but not afraid, rather... awestruck. When her eyes traveled to his, a flicker of vulnerability passed through them. Quick enough that if she hadn't been studying him, she wouldn't have noticed it. And the longer she held his gaze, the more intensely he stared, and the more her heart started to pound in a way she'd never felt before. Almost a fluttering. And her breath...it was coming erratically, as though she were drowning in the depths of his gaze and the power that emanated from him.

"My lady." His voice was a deep caress that sent her already pounding heart and irregular breathing into a tailspin. Her mouth went dry. Was she dreaming? Because in the story she'd made up, a warrior, powerful and handsome would come to her rescue and take her away for a life of bliss...

The warrior bent at the waist, managing to be elegant at the same time he was formidable. How did he move his body so effortlessly? When he straightened, his words rumbled out of his chest, nearly vibrating through her. "I am Laird Rose."

Blair opened her mouth to speak, but no words wanted to push forth. Heat suffused her face. She licked her lips. Cleared her throat. Rushed to offer him her hand. Finally, her voice decided to make itself known. "I'm Lady Blair."

The hint of a smile crossed his mouth, drawing her attention to the tantalizing curve. "Ah, the infamous Blair." He took her hand in his, warm and rough against her skin, and brought it toward his mouth. Eyes on her, his lips hovered over the flesh of her knuckles, heated breath fanning over her skin, making her feel like she might just fall in a pool of skirts and thrumming skin. "But I daresay whoever has called ye Blair the Not So Fair, has not done ye justice, for ye're verra beautiful."

Heat slapped hard against her cheeks, and her heart skipped a beat so violently she could have been shoved.

No one had ever called her beautiful. And from the look in his gaze, he was very serious. Laird Rose did not appear to be a man with a penchant for lies... She could tell from looking at him, at his demeanor, that he was a man who considered honor above all things to be of the utmost importance.

Which gave her pause. Because how would he feel when he found out the truth of the missive?

"Ye flatter me, my laird."

"I tell the truth."

As she suspected... Was he emphasizing the word truth? Or was that all part of her imagination?

Blair swallowed around the lump in her throat and delicately tugged her hand away from his, only aware just then that he'd still held it. "It was a pleasure to meet ye, my laird." Saints, but she had to get away from him, if only to draw in a decent breath. She started to walk around him, to find her brother, or anyone really who didn't make her heart pound as he did.

But as she passed, his long fingers slipped around hers once more, and she didn't resist when he placed her hand on his arm. Zounds... the muscles bunching beneath his shirt had her heart pounding harder. Was this why Aurora went wild for the men as thickly muscled as Laird Rose?

"May I escort ye to the table?" But he wasn't asking. In fact, he was already walking, leading her toward the trestle table up on the dais at the front of the great hall where her brother and their family always sat.

She should be irritated that he wouldn't wait for her answer, but truth be told, she would have said aye, because within seconds of spotting him across the hall, she was fairly certain she would do anything he asked. Which was extremely dangerous...

"Thank ye," she murmured, for what else could she say?

When they reached the table, he led her to a seat, pulled it out for her and took the one right beside her. It was then she noticed the extra chair. This man had been invited to dine at the head table.

What was happening?

Her mother sat down on the other side of her, but Liam had yet to make an appearance. It would seem her brother wanted to prolong her torment. Aislinn and Aurora whispered behind their hands, their eyes shifting from Blair to the man beside her in an obvious way before they took their seats on the other side of him.

Well, that was a saving grace. At least they might distract him from talking to her.

A pang of discomfort sliced through her gut, and for a moment, she wanted to shove a good several feet of space between her lad-hungry cousins and the interesting new laird. Oh, dear... Was that jealousy? She'd never experienced it before, but if pressed to identify the burning in her gut, the irrational desire to put herself between Laird Rose and her cousins, to...claim him for her own... Aye, she was indeed jealous.

Blair sat ramrod straight, not even allowing her spine to touch her chair.

And then her brother entered the great hall and headed straight for their table, avoiding her gaze the entire way. Goodness, she'd never seen Liam without a smile on his face, though she was certain there were times. He was always so jovial, especially when in the presence of his family and his lovely wife.

It would appear, however, that her torment was going to continue.

Blair couldn't decide if she was more uncomfortable with the fact her brother wouldn't look at her, or with the fact that everyone seemed perfectly all right with the man sitting beside her. Not two hours ago, they'd all been running for their lives.

Was she the only one confused?

Gazing out over the people slowly taking their places at the tables, she could see the wary glances between the Ross-Sutherland people and the newcomers. There were about twenty of them, all tall and rugged like their leader. They sipped their ale and kept their gazes on the warriors in the room, as if expecting a brawl would break out at any moment.

She didn't blame them. She felt the very same way.

This was madness, wasn't it?

The whole left side of her was thrumming with heat—his heat.

Blair shifted her gaze to her brother as he pulled out a chair for Cora on the opposite side of Lady Arbella. When he was seated, the servants brought out dishes of roasted venison and carrots, freshly baked bread, mountains of freshly churned butter, mutton pie, mushroom and herb pies and stewed greens with turnips.

Normally, Blair would have picked delicately at her food, but eating was a distraction now from the seemingly mad world she'd been dropped into, so she cut off large pieces of meat and asked for a double scoop of butter for her bread—though she did avoid the mutton pie as she was not a fan of eating animals she deemed pets.

Indeed, curled up in the barn with the hounds was her beloved Bluebell. The ivory fleece of her body was soft as a cloud, and black on her face was marked with one large white ring around her eye. She had the disposition of, well, a lamb.

"Riders!" The call from the doors of the great hall had everyone stilling in their seats, and before Blair could even take a breath, Liam had his dagger at Laird Rose's throat. Laird Rose barely moved, as though he didn't recognize the threat of a blade that could end his life.

The Sutherland men followed suit, drawing their weapons, and every Rose warrior in attendance found a steel dagger at their throats.

The lump of bread in Blair's mouth was dry and heavy. She couldn't summon the strength to chew. The thought of swallowing made her want to gag. If she weren't so stunned, she might have spit it out, or at least taken a sip of wine to help her swallow, but as it was, she'd turned halfway in her chair, eyes trained on the cut-from-marble profile of Laird Rose. The muscle in the side of his jaw flexed and his scar went gone white, but those were the only indications he was aware there was a blade at his throat.

"Who comes?" her brother growled.

Laird Rose pressed his hands flat to the table, eyes steady, face firm.

"I dinna know. My party is all accounted for. Do ye think we'd so readily surrender our weapons, and allow your blades at our throats if we planned for an attack?"

Liam did not remove the knife as he nodded at one of his guards. "Go and see."

His man leapt from his position and rushed from the great hall.

"What have I done?" Blair murmured, fingers inching up toward her throat.

What was supposed to have been a childish game and fanciful bit of whimsy was turning out to be a momentous mess that she would never live down.

In fact, someone in this room might not live at all.

CHAPTER 8

Edan kept very still.

The trust he and Liam Sutherland had tentatively formed was in danger of being broken very quickly. He had no idea who was riding on the castle, but it was extremely unfortunate timing for him. Because if it was a foe, Liam would never believe that Edan wasn't involved.

He'd be lucky if Liam didn't just kill him right now before waiting to find out who approached.

No one would blame him—not even Edan himself.

He would, however, not go down without a fight. Nay, if Liam attacked him, Eden would use the knife and fork beside his trencher to first jab Liam in the eye and then between his ribs. They'd both go down, Edan's death a surety and Liam's life hanging in the balance.

Dinna move, he told himself, his fingers itching to grasp the eating utensils and see this moment through.

Beside Edan, Lady Blair had grown very still as well. Edan had enjoyed watching her shovel bite after bite into her mouth to avoid conversation or eye contact with him. The way she'd pause every few moments just to stare. She fascinated him. The lass had not been scared or disgusted by his scar at all. Instead, she'd regarded him rather boldly and with something akin to awe, which he found impossible. Not a single woman had looked on him like that after he'd fallen beneath the sword.

And damn if he hadn't been enjoying that. But all joyful thoughts were gone now that the steely edge of a blade touched his neck, a hair's breadth away from drawing blood.

"Dinna do anything hasty, Sutherland," Edan said in his calmest voice. "I swear I know not who approaches."

Liam only grunted, the veins in his neck pulsing. Sweat beaded at Edan's temple and slowly trickled down the side of his face.

"I dinna believe in coincidences."

"Neither did I until a few days ago," Edan countered softly. "But look where we are now."

"I was a fool to have let ye in," Liam growled.

"Nay, friend." Edan emphasized their bond. "We are both warriors for Scotland, followers of the same king. I believed ye when ye said ye didna kill my brother. Mayhap we can still work together to find out who did."

He was negotiating, and not well, but he hoped to solidify the trust he had in Liam, to get the bloody dagger away from his neck.

Again, Liam grunted. He didn't pull the dagger away, but no longer was Edan's skin warming the blade.

What felt like an eternity later, the guard Liam had sent to the gates returned. "'Tis the Earl of Sutherland returned, my laird."

The entire great hall let out a collective sigh—Edan included, though his was not audible. Liam withdrew his dagger from Edan's neck, and his men did the same to the Rose warriors. Liam slapped Edan on the shoulder and gave a short, almost embarrassed laugh.

"Apologies, Laird Rose. Tension is higher in the room than anticipated, aye?"

Edan did not smile. He rose from his chair, his face not revealing anything as he did so. "Completely understandable, given our introduction. However, I would have hoped our earlier understanding would have held some merit, that ye might have asked afore ye put a knife at my throat. And I'm sure ye'll understand now, why my men and I will have to excuse ourselves?"

Liam fixed an even gaze on Edan. "I would prefer ye stay, Rose. Greet my da, the Earl of Sutherland. Maybe he will have information regarding your brother."

"With all due respect, Sutherland," Edan's throat tightened when he spoke, "ye held a dagger to my throat without question. Who's to say the next rider willna have ye doing the same?"

"And ye rode upon my castle on the word of criminals and a silly chit."

Lady Blair gasped, and Edan felt a sudden pang of guilt. He wanted to protect her, which was not his place. If her brother wanted to call her silly, which he very much thought himself after the confusion, then so be it. Why should he care? God, why *did* he care?

"All the same, 'tis probably best we left."

Just then, the Earl of Sutherland entered the great hall to cheers from all the Sutherlands present. His wife, the lovely Lady Arbella, stood from her chair and glided across the hall to greet him.

When Edan glanced toward Lady Blair, her chair was empty. He caught sight of her edging around the room, trying to make her escape.

His first impulse was to go after her, to demand answers. To question why the hell she would pull a stunt that could have ended in bloodshed. In fact, he shoved his chair backward, hard enough the scrape of the legs against the floorboards of the dais echoed up into the rafters.

The Earl of Sutherland's gaze fell on Edan then, and the smile that filled his face fell before recognition hit. They'd met more than once at Stirling, and Edan had always held the earl in high regard. In fact, as a lad, he'd looked upon the man as a sort of idol. Every wee sprite in training wanted to be Magnus Sutherland, Edan included.

"Sir Edan?"

"Aye. Laird of Rose, now."

"Ah." The earl's face shuttered. "I did hear about your brother. My condolences to your clan."

Edan gritted his teeth to keep from asking what the earl had heard.

That was better suited to a private conversation, rather than under the scrutiny of the entire great hall.

He approached the earl, bowed as was due the man's placement in their realm, and accepted the earl's nod of approval.

"What brings ye to Castle Ross?" Magnus asked.

Edan shifted his gaze to Liam, who looked grim. The man clearly did not want to be the bearer of news regarding his sister's deed, nor that Edan had suspected him of being behind Connor's death.

"A misunderstanding," Edan offered. "We are on our way back to Rose lands."

"What misunderstanding?" the earl asked, ignoring Edan's blatant request to be dismissed. The way Magnus was eyeing him, and the tone of his voice, suggested he would not allow Edan to leave until all had been revealed.

Edan respected the man immeasurably, which made it even harder to say what he did next. "I'll leave that to Liam to discuss with ye, my laird."

The earl gave a very short shake of his head. "Nay, I'd hear it from ye."

Bloody hell. "Then perhaps it would be best if we spoke in private." Edan scanned the room in case his meaning wasn't clear.

"I agree." The earl no longer looked placid. A hardness had come into his eyes. He didn't like that Edan hadn't been willing to share, and probably more so that his son hadn't either.

Edan had witnessed the man on the battlefield, though he hadn't had the honor of fighting in his unit. Still, he knew he'd never want to be at the end of Magnus Sutherland's sword.

Edan nodded to his men to remain behind as he followed the earl out of the great hall with Liam at his side.

When they reached Liam's study, the earl paced toward the window and stared out as the clouds slowly rolled in, darkening what had started out as a beautiful spring morning. In the distance, the mountains loomed, their icy caps grazing the sky. The scent of salty sea air filtered on the breeze that was picking up speed.

"Storm's coming," Magnus said. "Looks like it will be a bad one. Ye and your men had best stay behind."

Edan raised a brow that said he knew the man was stalling. "We are not unused to storms. We're Highlanders."

Magnus chuckled. "Good answer." Leaning back against the windowsill, he crossed his arms over his chest, still filled with muscle despite his age. Streaks of silver ran through his gold-ginger hair. How had Blair come by her lustrous raven locks when both her parents were fair? "Now, let's quit the small talk and tell me why ye came. What was the misunderstanding?"

Edan felt alike a lad being scolded for some deed he had not committed. Taking up a similar stance by the door, arms crossed, eyes steady, he explained to Magnus about the death of his brother, and what the prisoners had confessed. "I didna act immediately, as I knew the reputation of the Sutherlands and their relationship with the king. I would never take the word of an outlaw over that of a man of honor. I couldna believe that any of ye would try to murder a laird in order to gain his lands."

"Ye'd be correct," Magnus said without hesitation.

"I've continued looking into the death of my brother, and I've come up empty so far. Then we received a strange missive." He shifted his gaze to Liam. "From your daughter, Blair."

Magnus uncrossed his arms and took a step forward. "What kind of missive? How do ye know it was her? How does she know ye?" The last question was growled as if Edan had spent time climbing walls and sneaking into Blair's chamber in order to defile her with no one the wiser. "Have ye taken advantage of my daughter?"

Standing his ground, Edan explained, "She signed her name. And I had no knowledge of her afore I received the missive. I swear to ye, on the lives of my clansmen."

"I read it. 'Tis her hand," Liam offered. "I take full responsibility for her having sent it under my watch."

Magnus cast his son a glance. "Did ye have knowledge of the letter?"

"Nay."

"Let me see it."

Edan pulled the bottle from his sporran and crossed the room to hand it to the earl.

He waited patiently as Magnus read the missive—over and over from the length of time it took him.

"This is her hand," he mused. "But I dinna understand. Have either of ye spoken to her about this?"

Liam and Edan both shook their heads.

"This is unlike her." Magnus sounded as perplexed as Liam looked.

"Aye. Blair is normally verra reserved. This makes no sense." Liam ran a hand through his hair. "Besides the obvious fact that she is not a prisoner here and never has been."

"And so after receiving this message, ye rode on the castle?" Magnus asked.

"Aye. We made the assumption that if Liam was willing to hold young lassies chained as she says, that perhaps he was willing to poison a man."

"Ye came to attack the castle." Magnus's words were not a question but a statement. "To steal away my daughter."

"Nay, I'd not steal her. Only rescue her if she was being ill-used. And would not attack unless provoked to do so. We rode hard, out of anger, aye. But I only planned to challenge Liam as the murderer of my brother and captor of women if given reason. I first wanted to speak with him."

"This is madness." Magnus blew out a breath, shoved the missive back in the bottle and placed it in his own sporran.

Edan didn't ask for it back, as he was certain he would only be denied, and he didn't plan to challenge the older man for it. The longer time went on, the more he wanted to simply go back to Rose lands. If Liam wasn't responsible, Edan still needed to figure out who was, and the longer he was away, the more vulnerable his clan was to attack and further treachery.

"Well, then I guess ye know what to do now," Magnus said with a heavy sigh.

Edan narrowed his gaze. "Aye. I had planned to leave as I

mentioned," he drawled out. "I ask Liam to accept my apology for disturbing his people, and for any fear we may have caused. That was not our intention. I'd be honored to call the Sutherlands an ally of the Roses."

"Aye. I hold no grudge against ye, Edan. I'd have done the same thing, truth be told," Liam offered. "I hope we can call each other allies, as we each hold pieces of the firth, and no matter how big or small a clan, they're always stronger when they stand together with their friends."

"Aye, allies," Magnus murmured.

"'Haps we should be more than allies," Liam said, crossing his arms over his chest and glancing between his father and Edan.

Both Edan and Magnus turned, narrowed eyes on the other warrior.

"It would seem my sister got what she asked for," Liam said, nodding toward Edan.

Edan raised a brow, still not fully understanding—and not sure he wanted to.

Magnus's eyes widened, as the meaning of Liam's words dawned on him.

"Pardon me?"

"Ye can leave, Laird Rose, but mayhap ye should be taking my sister with ye."

"Liam, nay," Magnus said. "We canna offer her up in marriage without consulting her."

"Ye're the only sire in all of the Highlands who allows his daughters to choose their husbands. She nearly brought a battle to our doorstep, and Laird Rose here was clearly intent on rescuing her. I see nothing wrong with the two of them marrying."

Edan let out a short laugh, certain he hadn't heard correctly. "Begging your pardon, my laird?"

"She asked to be rescued," Liam shrugged, "and here ye are. Ye must see the logic in it."

"Ye do have a point," Magnus mused. "I'd have to speak with her, and your mother of course, but I canna see the harm in arranging a marriage between the Rose clan and the Sutherlands."

Edan shook his head, feeling the color drain from his face. "Aye, I would have rescued her, but then I'd have taken her somewhere safe, like a convent. I didna come to take home a woman."

"Not just any woman, but a *wife*," Liam continued as if Edan hadn't spoken.

Magnus nodded. "A solid plan."

His mouth fell open so wide if it had not been attached to his face, it would have likely hit the floor. They were *not* jesting. Judging by the look on their faces, they might be willing to go to battle over this.

Battle or not, Edan had to state his own intentions. He was a laird after all, not simply a warrior in an army where he was required to follow orders. "Nay, I most certainly did not come to take a wife. Lady Blair is a lovely lass, and I'm certain will make a man a fine wife, but begging both your pardons, I am not that man."

Magnus crossed his arms again and fixed Edan with a hard stare. "Are ye already betrothed?"

Edan cleared his throat, feeling himself waver slightly on his feet. How the hell had this happened? "Nay."

"Do ye find my daughter repulsive?"

"Of course not."

"Then ye'll need an advantageous marriage as the new laird of a small clan, especially with your brother having been murdered. Ye have unseen enemies. Ye need allies. I'm offering ye one, son. Consider it. 'Tis the truth, my daughter might not even have ye."

Edan gritted his teeth. "I'm not under your command," he felt compelled to remind Magnus.

"That is a fact."

Edan gave a short nod, feeling his stomach start to unknot. "Then we understand each other. I'll be going back to Rose lands now. *Without* a wife." Without waiting for a response, he headed for the door. Outside, a flash of light rent the sky, followed by a loud crack of thunder and then the flood of rain pounding the earth. He paused. *Bloody hell.* Fate was sending him quite a twist now, wasn't she? Riding in a storm as wild as this was going to be a torment, not to mention treacherous on some of the rises. Who knew how long it would last? Could be an hour. Could be three days.

With a heavy sigh, he glanced over his shoulder. "With your permission, we'll build camp outside your walls until the storm is over. Hopefully, we'll be off your lands by morning."

"Granted," Liam said shortly. "But know ye're invited to stay longer. Join us for the celebrations tonight."

With a curt nod, Edan stalked from the room, his problems only seeming to grow.

৩৬৩

BLAIR SANK BACK into the shadows of the corridor, watching as Edan stalked from her brother's study. Normally, she left the snooping to her sister Bella, who'd grown quite adept at it, and on a few occasions dragged Blair along with her.

Unfortunately, she'd not been able to garner much from the conversation that had taken place behind the closed door. Their voices had been muffled, their tones fading in and out with the sounds of revelry still going on downstairs. Soon the bonfires would be built beneath great tents, despite the storm raging anew, and when the sun was replaced with the moon, the fires would be lit.

Blair had not been brave enough to press her ear to the door to hear exactly what they said. Aye, she'd stepped close a few times before backing away, afraid that someone might see her, or worse, that those inside would yank open the door, and she'd die of mortification.

Tucked into an alcove and completely covered by shadows, she held her breath. Laird Rose really was an incredible looking man. Though she'd been busy shoveling food into her face to avoid him, she hadn't been able to stop sneaking glances. His dark hair hung in lanky chunks around a sharply angled face, giving him a savage, wild look, and yet he'd been able to keep such rigid control. Dark lashes framed his gray eyes, shading them from view most of the time, and that long, noble nose had a lump at its crest. The scar had turned a shade of white

97

when the knife had been at his throat. Facing death, he still looked formidable.

Formidable and in control, and yet with a wildness underneath that he kept locked away.

A contradiction that spoke to her soul. For she longed to be wild and yet had to keep a tight rein on her actions.

Blair bit her lip. She ached for a thrill, to be as tempestuous as the wind.

She started from her thoughts when Laird Rose closed the door tightly, turning the grimness of his countenance toward the shadows where she stood. He was completely still, seemed to be staring right at her, but she knew he couldn't see her. It was too dark in the alcove, exactly why she'd chosen it.

"I know ye're there," he said in a barely audible tone. "Show yourself."

Blair didn't move.

He edged closer.

She pressed her back to the wall, her lungs stinging from having held her breath for so long. Her heart pounded at the idea of being caught—*by him*.

"Come out," he growled, stopping halfway to her.

If he'd had a weapon, he would have drawn it, she was certain. This jerked her from her silent stupor. Because even though he didn't have a weapon, she knew how dangerous he was, and judging by the look on his face, he was ready to do battle.

Blair stepped slowly from the shadows, keeping her eyes locked on his. At the sight of her, his eyes widened in the torchlight, lips parting then shutting. She'd have bet coin that it took a lot to shock this man —and yet she had.

"Why do ye hide there?" he asked, his brows furrowing.

"I wanted to hear what ye were saying." No point in lying. She met his gaze boldly to see what he thought about that honest statement.

He swept a look of appreciation over her, and a slow grin filled his handsome features. "Your family seems to think writing that missive was unlike ye. Yet from what I've seen of ye, from the windswept moor, to your greeting in the great hall, to now where ye hide in the shadows, I'm not surprised."

Heat rose to her cheeks. It was true. Since meeting him, she had not been acting like herself, and yet she felt more alive than she had in years. "Oh?" she asked, wanting to hear more. Wanting to keep him talking, because the sound of his voice was doing things to her insides that she didn't even know were possible.

He stepped closer, crowding her space, taking away some of the air meant for her to breathe. Zounds, but he was so incredibly tall. She could curl up into him, thread her fingers in his wild hair—wait... What? Curl up into him? Touch his hair? Where had these thoughts come from?

"Ye stood on that field of flowers in naught but a night rail looking like ye wanted to do battle with me."

Blair felt like gasping, panting. She tried hard to surreptitiously draw breath as she said faintly, "I had no weapon."

"I'm not certain ye would have needed one."

She cocked her head, confused by that statement. "Every warrior needs a weapon."

He reached out, his fingers curling on a loose bit of her hair. Every fiber in her being reached forward, wanting that touch on her skin.

Good God! What in the world was happening to her?

"Not everyone needs weapons forged in steel, lass."

Blair's mouth parted in shock, in...something. Her body felt as if every inch was prickling, and only the touch of his fingers could soothe her.

His gaze dipped toward her mouth, and she had that fleeting moment of her breath being lost to her once more, and the desire to kiss him came strong. She clenched her fists at her sides, bit the inside of her cheek, hoping the painful reminders would rein in whatever this wildling was that wished to be set free.

Years of reservations and practice at being a lady seemed to have little effect on her now. Nay, indeed, she was ready to do whatever he wanted...

She willed herself to take a step back, put distance between them to break the spell. This was madness. Need palpated her insides, pummeling her, almost. Her spine hit the wall, and with the step she took back, he followed, filling her space once more. There was no getting away from him. Instead of being upset by that, she was bursting with...merriment.

"What chains bind ye?" He reached behind her, tugging at the lace that held her hair tightly coiled at the nape of her neck. It slowly unwound down her back and around her shoulders. He threaded his fingers through her long mane, and she was fairly certain she was about to faint. "There," he murmured, his warm breath fanning her face. "I have set ye free, wee dove. Fly now."

Blair couldn't have moved if her life depended on it. "I am not a bird," she whispered. "I dinna fly."

"Walk away then, unless I take your vow for me to be, what was it? Ah, aye, your *one and only*. What if I were to take your words to heart and kiss ye on this verra spot?" Again, his dark gaze fell to her lips, and she found herself swaying forward before she violently tossed herself back against the wall.

Aye, she wanted that very much... But she couldn't. Shouldn't... Or could she? Should she?

"But my da and brother could come out at any moment," she offered, hoping he would be the sensible one since she seemed incapable of leaving the prison of his arms and her desire. "Anyone could see." Even as she said those words, the wildling inside shouted that she didn't care. To kiss him, kiss him now, before it was too late, and he withdrew the offer.

She'd heard the stories of what had happened when her da had caught her Aunt Lorna and her husband in a heated embrace before they were married. Laird Rose wouldn't survive the beating, and she'd not be able to survive them being parted.

With a heated hand on her hip, he nudged her deeper into the alcove before pressing his large palms on the stones on either side of her face. His hard body pressed to hers, pinning her in place, and every part of her wanted to moan with wicked glee.

"Ye didna hear what your da said in there, did ye?"

Blair couldn't seem to make her tongue work. She shook her head, confused about why he'd ask. Why he wasn't kissing her already? Though his face was shadowed now, she could see he was grinning. The wicked glint made her knees weak. She kept her hands at her sides, afraid if she touched him, she would be lost forever. She should run. Truly, she should slip out from where his arms caged her in against the wall and bolt to her room. Bar the door behind her. Forever.

And yet she was frozen for a second, that wild part of her hoping he would make good on his unspoken promise and kiss her.

"I shouldna be here," she whispered.

"Neither should I," he answered.

She touched him then, pressing her hands against the solid wall of his chest. But she didn't push. Instead, she felt the beating of his heart pounding beneath her palm, the way his muscles dipped and swelled, curling beneath his skin with power and danger. Her breath hitched.

"What if I did come here for ye?" he asked gruffly. "What then?"

Her throat wasn't working, her tongue refused to form words. She swallowed, willing herself to speak. "It was just a game. A play on words. I burned it; ye should never have seen it."

"Your words had the power to almost bring two clans to war."

He didn't seem to have heard her say she'd burned her missive, but it didn't matter, because she was having a hard time even concentrating on words. Why did his body have to feel so...good?

"Is that what ye meant about me not needing a weapon?" she managed.

"Nay." Zounds, the way he drawled out the word lit her body as though he'd stroked her.

"What did ye mean then?" Her voice was husky now, throaty, strangled almost.

"This." He dipped his head, allowing his lips to brush gently over hers.

CHAPTER 9

S aints, but his lips were warm, soft, and she felt herself melting into him. Sensations whipped inside her, sparking flames along her flesh. Her nipples hardened, and she gasped as her entire body came alive at the touch of his mouth on hers.

This was what troubadours, bards and poets meant when they spoke of a kiss being life-altering. Because it was truly *wonderful*.

Blair leaned into Laird Rose's kiss for perhaps only half a second more before the very *Blair* side of popped back into control. She yanked away, hitting the back of her head on the stone wall as she shoved him with all her might.

Laird Rose didn't stumble as she would have had she been on the reciprocating end, but he did let her go, did back away and give her room to breathe.

"Are ye all right? It sounded like ye hit your head." His voice was all confusion and concern, which only added to her mortification.

"Perfectly good," she lied and then felt perfectly mortified all over again. Perfectly *good*? Who said such things? "If ye'll excuse me, my laird."

Lord, if she didn't sound nonchalant, as though her lips were not still buzzing from the feel of his mouth against hers, and her cheek was not still searing from the stroke of his fingers.

Without waiting for his reply, she slipped past him into the corridor and ran toward the stairs. She leapt onto the first one and took them two at time, her lungs and thighs burning from the exertion. She gripped her skirts in her fists to keep them away from her feet. When she reached the level with her chamber, she didn't stop until she was inside, and the door was at her back. She bent over, gasping for air, her stomach churning and threatening to toss up every massive bite she'd consumed at the feast.

Had she really just kissed that man?

Well, theoretically, nay. *He'd* kissed her. But she'd allowed it. Encouraged it. He'd warned her he would if she didn't leave, and yet she'd stayed. Because she'd wanted him to. And he wasn't just a man. He was something else altogether. Godlike, she thought, which made her feel foolish, even as the enamored part of herself gave a hard nod of "aye."

Blast it all, but his warm lips on hers had been divine; his breath on her cheek heaven-sent...

This was what all the fuss was about. This was why Aurora couldn't stop kissing every lad she came across.

But Blair had to wonder, did every man kiss like Laird Rose, or was that something singular to him? Blair stood up straight, ran her fingers through her hair, eyes squeezed shut as she let out a loud groan.

"My dear, are you all right?"

Blair jumped, her eyes going wide. Lady Arbella was perched on the edge of the bed, staring at her as though she'd grown eight heads.

Taking a deep breath, Blair swiped the frustration off her face and worked for an expression of complacency. Dear heavens, her lips still tingled. Could her mother see them tingling? Was there a change in color? They felt swollen, thoroughly kissed. Oh saints, but she was certain to be found out! Despite the panic warbling through her head, Blair managed to say rather blandly, "Quite all right, Mama."

"What happened?" Her mother stood and approached her,

squinting her eyes as she studied Blair's face. "Your hair has come loose...and your face... You look different."

Blair touched her locks, feeling the softness and wondering if Laird Rose had noticed how silky her hair was—and wondering what had happened to her hair ribbon. Was it still curled in his fist? On the floor in the alcove outside her brother's study, where someone would find it and report that she'd been there?

"It got caught." Her throat was so tight she'd nearly burped the words out in an effort to make them come.

"Caught?"

"On something. A torch post, maybe?" She was a bad liar. Years of telling only the truth, and condemning storytellers, left her without the skill needed to give her mother a good fib.

Lady Arbella didn't naysay her, though her expression suggested she wanted to. "What is going on with you, my dear? You have me worried. You're not acting like yourself."

Blair thought back to those private moments in the alcove, how Laird Rose had thought her spirited behavior suited her, and how her family thought the opposite. And that was because for most of her life, she'd worked to fit a mold that was so unlike her sisters. She wanted to be a living saint, and now she'd had a taste of what it meant to be wild and...she *liked* it.

With that realization, she promptly burst into tears, covering her face with her hands and falling against her mother, who wrapped her arms around her and cooed soothing words.

"Did someone hurt you, my darling?"

"Nay," Blair wailed. "Only myself."

Lady Arbella stroked soothingly down Blair's back, standing there solidly as long as it took for Blair to cry out all her sorrows.

When she was finally spent, she pulled back and met her mother's gaze. "Mama, I dinna know who I am anymore. I am not me, and yet I am."

"What do you mean?" Her mother stroked her hair away from her face and searched her eyes.

"I have spent so many years perfecting what I thought a lady should be, who I should be, and now there is this part of me that wants to be free."

"Freed from the chains." Her mother's words caused Blair to stiffen.

"Aye. How did ye know?"

"Liam shared the contents of the missive with me before supper. I did not have the time yet to ask you about it. 'Tis why I am here now."

"Oh." Blair shook her head. "I am so stupid."

"Nay, my darling, you're not." There was no hint of derision in her mother's voice, only concern and love.

"It was a game, but the playing of it was..."

"Fun?"

"Aye. But, Mama, ye dinna understand. I burned that missive. I never sent it. I dinna know how Laird Rose got it. The only thing I can come up with is that one of my cousins switched out the missive, that she stole it and sent it herself."

"Why would she do such a thing? Come now, there must be another reason."

Blair shook her head, miserable. "'Tis all my fault. I told her my dreams of a husband. She must have thought she was helping."

Her mother pressed her lips to Blair's forehead. "Mayhap that is what happened. There is nothing we can do about it now but face the consequences, which seem to have been set aside. Do not worry over it, my darling. Your da and Liam will handle it, and Laird Rose will be on his way."

Aye, he'd be on his way, and the very idea of that set her mind to reeling with regret. She didn't want him to leave. In fact, every part of her was yearning to run outside, to find him in his camp, and tell him that he was right, that he knew her better than she knew herself, and that she wanted him to kiss her again, every day, for the rest of their lives.

Blair let out a shuddering breath.

"Do not worry, my dear. All is well. You'll not be punished for your dreams. Every lady has them. I did, too."

Her mother's words mollified her slightly, but they did nothing for the need she felt to bring Laird Rose back into that alcove. "And did your dreams come true?"

Her mother laughed. "In a manner of speaking. I always wanted to be with a gallant knight, and when I was headed to Scotland and stolen away by a wild Highlander, I thought my life was over. Instead, my gallant knight came to me in another way." She took Blair's hands in her own and squeezed. "You see, my darling, the things we really want —sometimes they come to us disguised as something else. So you must ask yourself what you really want."

Blair drew in a deep breath. "I dinna know."

"That's all right," her mother said. "Sometimes we do not know what we want until it's right in front of us."

Or until he's kissing ye...

⚜

LADY ARBELLA SUTHERLAND had been married to the love of her life for nearing thirty blessed years. In all that time, she'd known pleasure, pain and true joy, along with a few moments of sorrow. She'd kissed the scraped knees of each of her beloved children and held them close as they grew older and bloodied limbs became broken hearts.

She knew each of her children well. Could read them, and most of the time, she could decipher what they might do next in a situation— something that had helped her greatly when they were growing up and getting into mischief.

Of all her children, however, she had the hardest time figuring out Blair. She had suspected it was because Blair couldn't figure herself out, either.

Blaire was the youngest of five, and her older siblings were very set in their ways and secure in who they were and very much in the spotlight. This had probably given one who may be just a little confused about their place in the world even more to worry over.

Arbella's thoughts about Blair seemed to be confirmed now. Poor lass was confused and had gotten herself into quite a predicament. But Arbella had no doubt she'd be able to pull herself out of it. Blair was quite intelligent. Perhaps more so than any of her siblings. It was how she'd been able to embody so many different parts of herself.

Arbella suspected her daughter had been embracing as of late a side of herself she didn't often express. The part that was more like Greer, her sister who caused mischief. Arbella would have to think of a few ways to subtly help her daughter fully out of her shell.

She closed the door to her borrowed bedchamber to find her husband leaning one arm against the mantle and a hand on his slim hip. Even after thirty years, the sight of him still sparked excitement within her. He was just as handsome as the day he'd ridden across the battlefield to scoop her up, even if his hair was peppered with silver and a few wrinkles lined his eyes and mouth.

"I must beg your forgiveness," he said. "I may have done something ye will not approve of."

Arbella's heart flipped. There had only been a few times in their marriage when he'd said words like those, and every time, he was right: she did not approve.

"Tell me." She didn't take another step into the room, needing to root her feet against the floorboards, to lock her knees in place and keep herself upright.

"I suggested, rather strongly, that Laird Edan Rose marry our daughter."

Arbella's stomach tightened, and the color drained from her face. "Magnus—"

"I know, it was foolish, and I never should have done so without speaking with ye first. Without speaking to Blair first. I gave her older sisters choices when it came to marriage, and when the opportunity arose, I went with it."

Arbella pressed her lips together firmly, afraid that whatever she might say would start a war between them. To say she was angry would be an understatement. "How could you do that? We do not even know this man."

"I know him. He's a loyal vassal to the Bruce. A damned good fighter. Saved the Bruce's life; that's how he got the scar on his face. I'd trust him with my life. But it doesna matter, as he refused."

Despite the glowing accolades, she was still irritated. They'd promised to talk with each other about each match made for their children before attempting to make the match, and with Blair being the last to wed, she especially wanted to be a part of it. "It *does* matter."

"He has refused."

"What if he changes his mind?"

"Then we shall deal with it at the time."

"What if he is cruel to her?"

"He wouldna be. I'd not give her to a cruel man."

"But what if he was?"

"I'd kill him."

"But how would you know? What if he got to the deed of killing first?" Arbella shook her head, pressed her fingers to her temples and tried to quell the hysteria that was quickly growing. "I'm sorry. I shouldn't question your judgment, nor should I revert to believing every Highlander is violent. My old maid Glenda still gets into my head sometimes."

Magnus sighed. "Nay, 'tis my fault. It was foolish; I know that. I'd not have let him take her if Blair declined. But the fact that he refused shows me he is a good man."

He did have a point, but she wasn't going to give him credit for it.

"You're lucky, Magnus Sutherland, because if he had and decided to make war over your taking back the offer, I'd have taken a sword to you myself."

"And I'd have knelt down afore ye and let ye do the deed."

All the fight went out of her as he approached and tugged her into his strong arms. "What is she doing?" he whispered. "I'd take Greer's spearing Roderick MacCulloch over inciting war for her brother as Blair has done."

"She says she burned the missive, Husband, that Aurora must have played a dirty trick on her and switched the parchment. She had no idea this was coming."

"Aurora," Magnus groaned. "Blane's daughters will be the death of us all."

Arbella shook her head. "My sister certainly has her hands full..."

What on earth were Aliah and Blane going to do about their wayward daughters? That was a problem that would need solving another day. "We must remember, there was no war, and we must be grateful for that. It would appear that this Edan Rose is a bit more thoughtful and focused than some men might have been."

"Aye. The king praised him greatly when I was at Stirling, saying he'd done well in battle, had led his men to victory, and that not having him at camp would be a loss now that he'd gone home to take on the duties as laird since his brother's passing."

"What do you make of him accusing Liam of being behind it?"

Magnus shook his head. "I havena even had the time to contemplate it. I've been so engrossed in our daughter's confusing behavior."

"She wants things that conflict with one another."

"What do ye mean?"

"She wants to be set free, to marry, to run a household, to be in charge of something. Yet at the same time, she wants the protection of being the bairn in the family, the stoic one who never does any wrong and is coddled because of it."

"What do we do?"

"I think you were onto something saying she should wed. Perhaps it is time we let her grow up."

Magnus tucked Arbella against his chest and pressed his lips to her forehead. "It was so much easier with Greer and Bella. They had a clear path, even if they were both obstinate about it. Blair has somehow remained elusive."

"Aye. I canna believe she's going to be twenty-one in one month's time." Arbella wrapped her arms around her husband's middle. "I told her tonight she needed to ask herself what she wanted."

"What did she say?"

"She doesna know. But...I think she does."

"How so?"

"When I was waiting for her, she burst through the door, face flushed and clearly frustrated. She looked like..."

"Like what?"

Arbella shook her head, certain that if she told her husband what she thought, he'd round up every lad within one hundred miles and stick them in the stocks.

"Arbella?" Magnus drawled out, raising a brow she knew to mean he would drag it out of her, no matter how hard she tried to hold it in.

"Her lips... They were swollen, red, like she'd been thoroughly kissed."

Magnus stiffened, thunder rolling over his face. "What the devil?"

"Aye. I think perhaps that is why she's been acting so strange. Maybe she has already found someone."

"I will kill him for not stepping forward and asking permission before putting his mangy paws on my daughter."

Arbella laughed softly. "Oh, Husband, I'm fairly certain our Blair'd not let anything mangy or paw-like touch her."

"She has a pet lamb."

"True enough," Arbella conceded. "Still, I believe she must have some standards."

"I will take your word for it, and we'll get to the bottom of whoever it is that's been kissing our daughter in secret."

CHAPTER 10

Edan stalked past the clansmen piling wood high for their bonfires beneath makeshift tents being used to ward off uncooperative weather. Outside the castle walls, more tents had been erected for him and his men to be housed overnight. Rain spit down on them, soaking their hair and dripping from their noses, but the people wouldn't be stopped from celebrating the arrival of spring, storm be damned.

He shook the rain from his dripping hair, feeling quite damned himself.

His lips were still hot from the feel of Blair's lush mouth on his. He'd had no intention of kissing her when he'd caught her spicy scent in the corridor and heard her soft intake of breath from the alcove. Wee spying chit.

When he'd told Magnus Sutherland he had no intention of wedding his daughter, he'd been speaking the truth. And yet the moment he'd caught sight of her large blue eyes staring up at him, felt the softness of her locks entwined in his fingers, the sensual curl of her lips, the way she'd boldly stared instead of running, he'd been lost.

There was something mysterious about Blair that drew him to her.

A part of her that seemed caged and begging to be let out. A lass in good need of kissing.

And ballocks, had he given her that kiss. If she'd not been a maiden, the daughter of a powerful earl who'd just offered her to him in marriage, Edan wouldn't have stopped at kissing. Nay, he would have tucked them even deeper into the alcove, stroked his hands up and down the length of her curves, slipped his fingers beneath her skirts and caressed her until they were both panting with carnal need. He would have brought her to the height of pleasure again and again.

Even now, his blood still pounded with lust, and he found walking unbearable, given the tightness in his groin. He gritted his teeth against the need. How had one silly chit been able to do this to him? Bloody hell, but he'd wanted to bury himself deep inside her from the moment he'd seen her whisk into the great hall, her cool gaze settling on his. To press her against the stones, wrap her long, luscious legs around his hips and drive deep into her silky cavern.

To possess her utterly. To slip through that mysterious exterior and find out what made her heart beat beneath. To make her heart beat for *him* and no other.

Every other lass he'd met in his life had been eager to please, eager to show off her talents, her beauty, her desires—that was, until his once-handsome face had been carved up by a *Sassenach*. But not Blair. She seemed to want to stick to the shadows. To watch him, study him. She was not afraid. If anything, she looked intrigued. Keenly interested. And damn if he didn't like it.

He thought he'd nailed it when he'd told her he understood the meaning of her letter. To be freed from the chains that held her soul... Why the bloody hell did he feel like he could be the one to free her?

Why did he kiss her?

Blood and bones, he wanted to kiss her again.

He stomped his feet into the earth as he walked, as though he'd pound the ground into submission when he couldn't seem to do the same with himself.

Idiot. He was a bloody idiot.

"My laird," Raibert said, addressing him as Edan entered the center of camp. The men had erected their own canopy above a fire, where several sat around roasting a goose and drinking from a tankard. "Compliments of the laird."

Edan nodded to his guard, knowing he would want a full report. He indicated for Raibert and the men to join him in his larger tent where they might be afforded more privacy. The rest of the men, who were busy with setting things up or resting, were gathered into the tent as well. With whiskies in hand, the men sipped while Edan explained his meeting with Magnus and Liam—leaving out the part about the marriage proposal.

"We've been forgiven for our intrusion and confirmed as allies, though that friendship is tenuous, and I suspect only granted because of our mutual respect for the king and service to His Majesty. They have invited us to join them for the celebrations this evening."

The men nodded, grinning, happy to be able to celebrate and flirt with the lassies, drink whisky and feast, rather than be stuck on the road during a storm. Edan was glad he could give them something to make them happy. No one wanted to travel in the rain on a night they could be dancing and making merry.

"I trust we'll not be called out by any of the Sutherland-Ross fathers," Edan said, eyeing his men. "A wee bit of flirting is all well and good, but nothing that would have a lassie's da coming at ye with a club."

His men chuckled, rubbing elbows and reminiscing about the time one of the men had to run nearly five miles before he got away from a lassie's da and was only allowed to return when it could be vouched that a mere kiss was all that had taken place.

"And what of Lady Blair?" Raibert asked the question all the men had been wanting to hear.

"Innocent of any wrongdoing. Just a misunderstanding."

Raibert narrowed his eyes.

"I'll not hear anything else on the matter," Edan insisted, knowing that when they were alone, Raibert would not let the matter rest. "That is all. Go and make merry, but not too much, for we will be leaving in the morning, storm or nae." Edan dismissed his men, and they filed out of the tent, all except Raibert, who lingered near the opening as Edan had guessed. The man had become indispensable to Edan, something of an advisor, having worked so closely with Connor before his murder.

Edan eyed him, refusing to say what he knew Raibert wanted. He didn't want to talk about it, not now. He wanted to go swim in the loch and work out his frustrations. If Raibert wanted to know the truth of the matter, he was going to have to work to get it out of Edan.

"Was that all, my laird? What of the lass?"

Edan let out a long sigh and shook his head. "As I said, 'twas all a misunderstanding."

Raibert crossed his arms over his chest. "A misunderstanding is taking a man's place at the table, not knowing he's been sitting there for the past decade. A misunderstanding is when ye ask for roast goose and ye get a gorse pie. A misunderstand—"

"Enough. I know what a misunderstanding is. She says she didna send the letter."

"But she did."

"Someone did."

Raibert squinted his eyes. "She is bonny."

"That has nothing to do with it."

"If she were a man, ye'd not let her off the hook so easy."

Edan grunted. "Aye, likely. But if she were a man, we'd fight it out with fists and blades. In the Highlands, a man has to fight his battles and be trusted by his fellow warriors and laird to not turn tail, lie or misunderstand that when a sword is coming at him, he needs to fight. A man's place and attention to duty can mean life or death. Such is not always the case with women." Even as he said it, he knew it sounded like folly. No matter the case, man or woman, the type of misunderstanding in that missive was a matter of life and death. And if he were honest, he bet that Blair would take him up on a fight. Edan let out a frustrated growl.

"Ye like her."

He gritted his teeth now. "I'll nae answer that."

"Confirmation."

He more than liked her, if the heat still rushing through his blood was any indication.

"I kissed her." Raibert's eyes widened at Edan's words. "After her father offered her to me in marriage and I declined."

Raibert's eyes widened, and he let out a whistle. "Ye didna accept and still ye kissed her? Hardly seems fair."

Edan scrubbed a hand over his face. Damn the rain, he needed to swim.

"Why did ye say nay?"

Edan shrugged. "I didna come here to take a bride."

"Nay?"

"Nay," he said firmly.

Raibert grunted. "What man rides hell bent for leather over a mysterious missive only to walk away when all looks well? What man kisses a lass and forgives her such a transgression, and then walks away?"

"This man." He rolled his eyes.

"Too bad, my laird. She'd have made a bonny wife, and someone else is nae likely to pass up the opportunity. Myself included."

Edan growled, leaping forward to curl his fist around the collar of Raibert's *leine*. "Ye'll nae touch her." Bloody hell, he couldn't imagine anyone else touching her without rage filling his blood. No one else should be able to sample the delicacy that was her kiss. Lips that tasted of the finest fruit, a tongue like honey. He could have feasted on her all day.

Raibert held up his hands in surrender, a smirk on his face, as though he'd provoked Edan on purpose. "All right. All right. But, my laird, 'tis a fact, ye need a wife."

"Not yet." Edan let his clansman go, feeling the walls of the tent closing in around him.

Raibert shook himself with a laugh. "I know ye're not keen to hear it, Edan, but now would be a good time."

"I've only just become laird and figured out most of what I'm supposed to do in such a position, and ye'd have me add a woman to the mix?"

Raibert shook his head and crossed his arms over his chest, his stance indicating he wasn't going to budge, either physically or in his words. "Providing heirs to your seat, sons and daughters to populate our clan, is half of what ye're supposed to be doing."

He hated how right Raibert was. "Then I'll be choosing a wife who is suitable for our clan."

"Why isna she? Her da is one of the most powerful earls in Scotland, and both of her brothers control a large portion of the firth—allies for us on the waters."

"I already told him nay. I canna simply march back inside and tell him I've changed my mind after realizing the advantages."

"Pardon my saying so, my laird, but ye can, and ye'd be fool not to." Raibert did not ask to be dismissed and ducked out of the tent, shaking his head. Had it not been Raibert, who'd helped him so much over the last couple of months, Edan might have called him out for speaking to him that way, for turning his back.

Had he been wrong in declining the offer? Beyond how much he wanted her?

Nay. His gut instinct had been to decline, and he had to trust his gut, didn't he? Maybe not. The lass would be hugely advantageous to his clan, to himself as a laird, to have such allies to call upon should he need to.

Not to mention he was lusting so badly after Lady Blair that he felt like a green lad straight out of leading strings. It was almost as though he'd never been with a woman before, the way he was fantasizing about undressing her, revealing every inch of her flesh like he was discovering a woman's body for the first time.

Edan tossed back the rest of his whisky, feeling the fire of frustration racing through his blood.

He needed the chill waters of the firth on his back. That seemed the only way to calm himself down, else he would go storming back into the castle and demand that Blair be his.

BLAIR ALLOWED her maid to help her dress for the evening bonfire celebrations, but thus far, she'd refused to leave her chamber. Outside, the rain had given them a short reprieve from her tears, but Edan Rose and his men were still camped beyond the walls—and worse, her maid had let slip how excited she was for a chance to dance with one of the men.

They were staying.

She'd hoped they were leaving.

Once the storm came to an abrupt stop and the sun beamed down on them, drying the messy grounds, Blair had thought maybe, just maybe, they would depart.

But nay, no such luck for her. And now that she knew they were staying—that *he* was going to be out there—she couldn't leave her chamber.

She'd spent the whole day thinking about what she wanted, as her mother had suggested, except Blair was fairly certain the thinking she'd been doing hadn't been what Lady Arbella had in mind. Nay, because Blair had spent all day thinking about that kiss, and how much she wanted another one.

The way his lips had slid sensually over hers. His breath on her face. The touch of his hand on her hair, as he'd tugged free the ribbon, that somehow felt like he was setting her free. The way his larger body had pinned her to the wall. The way his muscles felt beneath her fingertips, the pound of his heart against her palm. The very heat of him. The power. The sensations that whipped through her body, even now making her hot and...*needy.*

She wanted to feel it again, his kiss, his heat, his body. The power that her own body leeched from him in that kiss.

And if she went outside to dance and feast around the bonfires, she was certain to feel that tingling in her blood that made her bolder. The same tingling that had tunneled through her limbs and propelled her to run through the night toward the firth where she'd tossed in that silly empty bottle. Only this time, she might kiss Laird Rose right in front of everyone, and her family would know her for the wanton not even she had realized she was.

Blair leaned against the cool stone of the window casing, hoping for some relief for her heated skin. She stared down at the fires that raged below, and the laughter and singing and music floated up toward her, tugging at her, enchanting her.

Everyone looked to be having such a good time. Their bodies rocked in the light of the orange flames; their voices raised in song and elation. She wanted desperately to enjoy it, too.

Just as she'd not participated before this year in the maiden's morning dew rituals at Dunrobin, she'd also been hesitant about dancing round the fires. So pagan it had always seemed. But now, when she gazed upon them, she realized it was a celebration of being alive. Each time at Dunrobin, she'd stood off to the side. Reserved, preferring to watch rather than participate, and now she found her fingers drumming a tune against the stone, and her soul swaying to the music of the pipes.

Maybe if she just went down and stuck to the shadows. Watched tonight as she had any other night. Held tightly to the new part of herself that seemed without control. Avoided Laird Rose. Aye, that was the most important part. If she caught sight of Edan Rose, she had to run away from him, as she should have done before he kissed her—else she'd run into his arms.

Nay, this was a bad idea. She shouldn't. She should stay in her room and work on her needlework. Mending shirts. Darning socks. And even as she listed off the many things she should be doing, Blair's feet shifted toward the door, as if by their own accord. Her hand reached for the handle, and she watched, as though it weren't her own fingers lifting the cool iron. Resigned to her fate, she shuffled down the corridor and took the stairs as slowly as possible. The scent of roasting meat filtered through the castle. The closer she drew, the louder the music, the more joyful the sounds of celebration. The more her heart pounded. The more she felt like she was sucking in her breaths through wool.

And then she was outside, the cool crisp air of the evening met with the heat of the fires. Lasses danced around the fires holding hands. Men drank from mugs while children leapt about chasing dogs, and she spied a few couples that had sneaked off into the darkened corners—one of whom Blair was certain was Aurora and the guard from the postern gate.

Blair could no longer judge her cousin's escapades, given she'd indulged in one herself just that morning. And though she was loath to admit it, she was secretly hoping for another dalliance right now.

Cora danced toward her, her blond locks swaying free, and her gown a beautiful deep green with a swath of Sutherland/Ross plaid across her middle. She gripped Blair's hand and tugged her toward the fire. "Dance with me, Blair."

How could Blair refuse her? The haunting melody spoke to her soul, and before she could deny her, she felt her feet moving, her hips swaying. As soon as she was in line with the other women, the flood of excitement pulsed through her limbs. She danced and laughed, intoxicated by it all. When she finally managed to get away, sweat slicked down her back. Blair took a proffered mug of spiced wine and swallowed a sip quicker than she should have. The warmth slid down her throat to make her belly tingle.

Blair swayed a little to the music, scanning the crowd as she moved around the fire.

So far, she'd spotted several of Laird Rose's men, but not the tall, striking warrior himself. Her gaze kept floating toward the tents set up for him and his men. Had he barricaded himself over there, as she'd done in the castle?

Was he afraid of what would happen should they meet again?

Well—she was, too, but that hadn't made her stay in her chamber, now had it?

Without hesitation, and definitely without thinking, Blair slipped into the shadows and glided unseen toward the main gate. The music faded behind her; the soft sound of her footfalls muted by the noises of those celebrating. With a glance up at the guards on top of the wall, who were chatting and drinking ale, she hurried undetected over the bridge toward the tents. Some of the Ross men who hadn't joined the festivities were sitting on overturned logs around their own campfire, passing a jug of what was most likely whisky as they jested back and forth. She paused to study their lighted profiles, but none were Laird Rose.

He was most definitely hiding. She grinned, feeling a flicker of excitement ignite inside her. Oh, but what fun it would be to tease him for trying to avoid her.

Then her smile faltered. She wasn't going to tease him. In fact, she sobered, what was she even doing here? What if he wasn't hiding at all and had instead found another lass to kiss?

This was foolish. They barely knew one another, and to tease a man she didn't know after only having shared one kiss seemed incredibly naïve, did it not? Once more, she'd let the willful part of herself do the thinking.

Shaking her head, Blair turned to leave. If she hurried, no one would spot her, and she'd not have to explain to anyone the wayward direction of her thoughts. But before she had taken two steps, she paused mid-stride. There he was, lit up by the light of the fires and the moon. Heaven help her.

Blair nearly swallowed her tongue at the sight of him walking back toward the tents *without* a shirt on. He wore trews that sat dangerously low on his hips, barely tied at all, and the very muscled length of his powerful torso was exposed in all its glory. He shook wetness from his hair with his hand, causing the muscles on that arm to bulge with the vigor of it. Blair's gaze scanned his nakedness and a chest that dipped and curved in the moonlight, as though he'd been forged by the heavens. She was completely mesmerized, lapping up the very sight of him. She'd witnessed men without their shirts on before. And certainly warriors with physiques that were just as strong. But there was something about this man that had her breath catching and her knees going weak.

Thankfully, he'd yet to spot her. His gaze was aimed toward the castle as he walked. Was he thinking about joining the festivities? Was he thinking about her?

Oh goodness, if he saw her here, she'd be mortified!

And he was only getting closer. She didn't have time to bolt away; he'd notice her for certain then. The only thing left to do was hide and pray he walked on by. Then she could slip back to the castle, where she would barricade herself in her chamber. Blair ducked into the first tent she could find and waited for his shadow to pass.

And waited.

The darkness of his shadow paused just outside the tent where she hid. She clapped a hand over her mouth, holding her breath. *Go, keep going!*

But he did not keep going. In fact, the shadow reached for the flap of the tent. With dawning horror, Blair realized her mistake. She must be in *his* tent.

She pressed her hands to her mouth to keep from gasping. Maybe, by some miracle, he'd be distracted and would go over toward his men and have a sip of whisky, allowing her enough time to escape. For if he were to find her, what would he think of her being in his private tent? Alone! At night! She could have melted right into the earth.

Blast it, Blair! What the hell were ye thinking?

His fingers curled around the edge of the tent opening and then stopped. It seemed to take forever before he opened it fully to stare at her, as though he'd known before even looking that she was there. Time seemed to stand still as his gaze locked on hers, a tiny lift to one corner of his lips. Water dripped from his hair, down his nose, his neck, his chest. She jerked her gaze upward, realizing she'd let it slip. He truly was an incredible specimen.

Edan ducked inside the tent, taking up the expanse of the opening, the top of his head brushing the soft roof. The flap dropped down, encasing them both in near darkness, save for the light that seeped through the side walls.

"My lady," he drawled. A line of firelight that came through a crack in the walls of the tent slashed across his mouth. His lip quirked further, as though he found this humorous.

If she weren't so mortified at how forward she was being, she might have also found it funny. But as it was, she was currently hoping the ground would open up and swallow her whole. Or that he'd drop into sleep from exhaustion, and she could leap over him and run away.

"I'd ask what ye were doing here, but I think I already know." He took a step toward her, and her heart dropped somewhere near her boots.

Zounds... What did he think?

Her tongue felt twisted; her throat dry. She couldn't form words and so only shook her head.

"Nay?" Oh, why did he have to draw out his words like a caress? Every utterance from his mouth stroked a path down her body all the way to her toes. "I'm wrong, lass?"

Miraculously, she found her tongue. "Wh-what do ye think I came for?"

The slow grin lit by the slashing light on his face was enough of an answer. And her belly did a flip of excitement at the wicked thoughts such a promising grin brought her. Aye, she did want to kiss him.

She shook her head, both to him and to herself. "I only came to see where ye were, as the celebration is...is... There is a feast... And ye were not there..." Everything she was saying was weak and not at all the true reason for her having snuck into his camp.

He was only a foot away from her now, and she was finding it harder and harder to breathe. He smelled fresh like the firth, and his hair was damp. Relentless rivulets of water dripped onto the bare flesh of his chest, demanding she follow their path with her eyes. Her body was getting hotter. The hairs on her arms, and even those on the top of her head, seemed to be rising and reaching for him.

She kept her gaze locked on his, afraid that if it traveled southward, she would not leave this tent a maiden, for the dark look in his gray eyes promised so many wicked things—including the deflowering of her very carefully guarded maidenhead.

"I should go." Her voice was low, breathy.

"Aye, ye probably should." His tone was equally husky, filled with a desire she felt in every inch of her being.

She didn't move.

"My lady..." He stepped closer, leaving only a few inches of air to separate her from what she so desperately wanted—his mouth on hers.

She willed her feet to move, but they didn't budge. And like in her chamber when she'd tried to stay behind, to refuse participation in a night filled with hedonism, her body seemed to have a mind of its own. Desires it was intent on fulfilling. She tilted her head back and stared up into his shadowed eyes, her lips parting, and a soft breath leaving her.

"Ye want me to kiss ye." It was a statement, not a question. And oh, how true it was.

"Aye." The word slipped from her mouth on a sigh. "But I shouldna."

"Aye. Ye shouldna. And I shouldna." He stepped closer, his heat radiating in the air between them. "But as we've already done so once, what would one more time matter?"

That was exactly what she'd been thinking. *Saints...* She was going to need to do extra penance for this. And it would all be worth it.

Laird Rose reached large, warm hands forward, slipping them up her arms as he tugged her nearer and closed the distance between them. Her skin felt singed where he touched her. Her heart joined the staccato rhythm of the drums outside, maybe beating faster. The wet heat of his chest pressed against her gown and left little bits of dampness that reached through the fabric to touch her skin. Water that had been on his bare flesh was now on her own. His lips brushed hers so gently they could have been a feather. The soft kiss was a tease. It made her heart leap, her pulse throb against her throat, and she whimpered with need, laying her hands to his warm skin ever so lightly. She jerked back, recalling his near nakedness. Kissing was one thing, but to touch him?

Edan let out a low growl in his throat, wrapped his arms around her waist and hauled her flush to him. His lips claimed hers in a kiss that sent her head spinning. Her curves molded perfectly to his hard body, and still she didn't know what to do with her hands. She could barely even think about it, as his kiss overpowered all thought. He slanted his mouth over hers, his tongue teasing the seam of her lips, dipping inside to run along the edge of her parted mouth when she gasped.

This kiss was very different from the one they'd shared outside of her brother's study. This was... This was as though his mouth was making love to hers. As though he'd staked his claim. And in answer, she tasted him back. Tentatively at first, she slid her tongue over his, and then with frissons of excitement lancing through her, she moved her tongue against his in earnest, bold strokes filled with passion.

Zounds, but she was coming undone. How could she ever go back to life as usual after having been kissed this way?

Blair wrapped her arms around Edan's neck, finally figuring out what to do with her hands, wanting to touch. Her fingers tangling in his damp locks, certain that after tonight, after this, she was never going to be the same again.

CHAPTER 11

L ady Blair felt more delicious in Edan's arms than when he'd
kissed her that morning in the alcove.

Edan wasn't certain if it was because he'd been wanting
to kiss her ever since, or if it was because upon reaching his tent, he'd
caught her scent. At first, he'd thought he was drunk. That perhaps
somehow the firth had been filled with whisky, and he'd drunk enough
to sate ten men. For what would she be doing in his tent?

When he'd slowly peeled back the flap and revealed her inch by
inch, she been standing there with a look of desire and bewilderment
on her face that had been both endearing and sped up his heart,
sending his blood shooting southward. He'd also, for a flash of a
moment, wondered if she'd been sent there to kill him. The assassin in
her brother's great scheme.

But the thought was fleeting and overpowered by his desire to
kiss her.

This was a lass who knew what she wanted, and yet she was afraid
to take it unless presented with the offer. And Edan was more than
willing to offer a kiss. Ballocks, he was in trouble, because truth be
told, he was willing to present her with a whole lot more.

It was one thing to kiss her lightly in an alcove, to walk away before his tongue could brush over hers and claim her. But this... This was madness. This was a kiss filled with passion and desire. The very primal heat of him yearned to lay her out on the ground right now and take what they both wanted. To claim her for his own in truth—again and again.

But he'd denied her father's offer this morning.

Why on earth had he done such a thing? Because with her in his arms right now... He wanted her. More than he should. Edan needed to pull away. To tell her to go back to her chamber and lock the door. To tell his men to pack up their camp and prepare for a long night upon the road. Instead of doing any of that, he ran his hands through her silky dark locks, wrapping a long tendril around his finger.

Somehow this chit had managed to wrap herself around his insides and clung there like a barnacle on a *birlinn*. Yet even as he thought it, he knew it wasn't true. He'd resisting seeking her out all evening. It was why he'd gone to the firth for a swim. He'd needed to cool the fever building inside him. He'd needed to put distance between them.

"*Mo chreach,*" he murmured against her mouth.

She whimpered in answer and tucked herself closer.

Edan's shaft was rock hard and pressing hotly to his trews, quite in danger, in fact, of pushing its way out of the loose ties and terrifying the woman altogether. He really needed to let go. To force her to leave...

A few seconds more of kissing... That had to be enough. *Had* to. Edan ran his hand down her spine, hovering around her hip, and resisted the urge to slide lower to grip her rear so he could tuck her pelvis against his hardness. He slid his hands back up to the middle of her back to keep himself in check.

When those few seconds passed, Edan knew he was in real trouble. Because he couldn't let her go. Didn't want to. The desire to take her home, for her to be his, was so intense, it sent a burning heat through his chest.

Stop! Get control, man!

He cupped her face in his hands and slowly ended the kiss. Both of them were panting. With his forehead pressed to hers, his eyes open, staring into her blue gaze, he whispered, "Marry me." Then he swallowed hard, not having expected those words to fall off his tongue.

Blair gasped and stepped backward enough that his hands fell from her face. She swiped a hand over her forehead, pressed her fingertips to her lips. "Ye're only saying that because we kissed. It doesna have to be—"

"Marry me, Lady Blair." His voice was soft, and he sauntered forward, even as she stepped backward. "Ye said yourself, I was your one and only knight." He meant it to be a tease, referring to her missive, but his words were gruff and full of need.

"Nay, I canna." She shook her head, swiping hair from her face that stuck to her lips.

Edan paused, her words sinking in. "Why not?"

She ceased her fidgety movements, her face toward his. "I... I dinna know ye."

"We know each other better than most whose marriages are arranged. There is something between us, lass. Ye'd not have come to my tent tonight if there wasna. Ye would not have allowed me to kiss ye for a second time today."

"Aye..." She shook her head again, clearly confused. "Something has come over me."

He knew exactly what it was, because it had come over him, too. "Desire."

"Aye." She touched her lips, and he resisted the urge to pull her into his arms again. "And I canna marry ye simply because I want to keep on kissing ye."

He chuckled. "Some would say ye should marry me because of that."

In the darkness, she cocked her head, and he could almost picture the look of curiosity on her face. "What of other things?"

Edan slid his gaze over the shadows of her body, remembering the feel of her luscious curves, the way her chest rose and fell at a rapid pace against his. "Other things?"

"Other things that are not kissing."

Mo chreach, but his head was going places it shouldn't if he was going to let her leave with her maidenhead intact. "Like...making love?"

She gasped. "Nay!" Her delicate fingers came to her throat, and he wished to reach out and press his fingers there to feel how her pulse leapt. She seemed flustered now. "I meant, such as conversations about things ye like, or what ye dinna like."

Edan tried not to stare at her, as confused as he felt. What could she possibly mean? No one had ever asked him such things, and he'd never put those questions to another, either. Having gone to be fostered at such a young age and rarely coming home, he'd not observed many married couples. Was that something they did? As he studied her silhouette, he was struck with a strong desire to know such things about her.

"I would know what ye dinna like and what ye like. As my wife, I would seek only to give ye pleasure." He was certain of it.

"And your clan?" She sounded worried. "What will they say?"

Now that was something he knew for certain. "They will rejoice in our union." They'd been asking for him to wed, and Raibert had already given his blessing. The clan would be thrilled by the alliance.

She bit her lip. "This is all very sudden." She sounded nervous now, and she kept running her fingers over her lower lip.

Edan brushed her arm with the backs of his fingertips, which made her jump a little at the contact. He chuckled. "Dinna fash, lass. I vow if ye give me a chance, ye'll not regret it. But I'll not beg ye. If ye wish to be mine, then know the offer stands. If not, I ask ye not to come back to my tent again. The desire to kiss ye is too strong." His words were perhaps not the most romantic, but a man could only take so much, and her hesitation was starting to cause some of the potent power of her kiss to drift away, leaving vulnerability in its place. An emotion he rarely experienced and was most certainly not enjoying.

Blair nodded. "I should get back to the castle." She took wide steps around him, avoiding meeting his gaze, and a painful thump thudded in his chest.

He had a feeling this might be the last time he ever saw her, for why would she not say anything more about his offer?

She ducked out of his tent without a backward glance. When he came out behind her, she'd disappeared into the shadows. The lass was good at that. If her scent didn't linger behind her, he might have wondered if she'd been there at all.

He stared into the distance, watching her huddled figure cross over the bridge and through the gate. If he were a more selfish man, Edan would go to her father and tell him that he accepted the offer to wed his daughter; perhaps even go so far as to say he'd already taken liberties and brace for the beating that would certainly come afterward.

But Edan wasn't a selfish man. He admired her. Aye, he wanted her to be his. He wanted to kiss her, make love to her, share a life with her. But she was right, they barely knew one another. And he wasn't going to force her into something she didn't want. Not when she was so confused. Not when she might have regrets about it after. The last thing he wanted was for his wife to regret having married him.

Edan shook his head as he headed for the campfire. He grabbed a jug of whisky from Raibert and drank deeply.

"How was your swim?" Raibert asked.

Edan grunted. "Not long enough."

BLAIR RAN ALL the way back to her chamber, her breath heaving once more as she burst through the door, just as she had that morning. And just like that morning, her mother was sitting on her bed, patiently waiting for her. Though this time when Arbella spotted her daughter, she only nodded and said, "Ah, so I see you've found what you want."

"What?" Blair asked, confused.

"Where were you?" Her mother arched one delicate and perfectly shaped golden brow.

"Outside. Dancing with the others." Blair waved her hands around in the air as if to dust away the falsehood on her lips. The lie felt deceptive to her own ears, and she knew her mother would pick up on that without a moment's hesitation.

"Well, your bedchamber has a lovely view of the gate, and the tents beyond, and I've a good eye."

Ah, so her mother had seen exactly where she'd been. That stopped Blair cold. Her arms fell at her sides, her blood ran cold, and her feet suddenly felt entirely too heavy.

"Nothing happened," Blair lied again, and was certain it showed on her face. Not to mention her lips still tingled from the way Edan had kissed her.

"Lies do not become us, dearest."

Blair sighed and sank back against her chamber door, her heart feeling as though it were in her throat. "I was with...someone. A man. A verra handsome man."

"Who?"

"Laird Rose." Blair sighed, resigned to telling her mother, even though she'd tried to hide it at first.

Her mother looked shocked at that. "Truly?"

"Aye."

"Huh. Well"—she stood—"then perhaps we should have a conversation with your father?"

Blair shook her head vigorously. "Nay, Mama, please. I dinna want Da to know." She chewed her lip, hearing Laid Rose's voice in her head asking her to marry him, and her heart skipped a beat. She didn't even know his first name...

"What happened?"

Her mother's question snapped her back to the present, and Blair considered hiding the truth, but she could tell by the way her mother was looking at her that she already knew what the truth was. "A kiss, that is all." But again, she sounded as though she only spoke a half-truth, and her mother raised a brow. "And he asked me to marry him."

"And what did you say?"

"I said it was too sudden. That I didna know."

"Why did you go to his tent?" The question was softly spoken but jarring enough in its bluntness.

Blair shrugged out of her cloak to buy herself some time to try and think of what her answer could be. Slowly, she walked to her wardrobe and hung the cloak inside. "I was curious." That was the truth.

"About?"

"Him."

How could she tell her mother she was curious about whether or not the kiss from that morning had been as powerful as she'd made it out to be? How could she tell her mother that she was curious to touch him once more?

"I'm sorry," Blair whispered. "I know ye must think me horribly immoral, and I will go to confession first thing in the morning and accept whatever penance is given."

Lady Arbella laughed softly. "My darling, I do not think you immoral. There is pleasure in kissing. To be curious is only natural. Especially when the kissing is with a handsome warrior."

She chanced a glance behind her, seeing that her mother looked only amused. "Ye're not mad?"

"Nay. I might be if ye decided to take up kissing with every lad in the castle, but to have kissed one man twice..." She shook her head. "I canna be mad at that."

Blair gasped. "I didna tell ye we kissed twice."

Her mother touched her cheek and stroked softly. "My sweetling, you forget I was once young. I could tell by the way you looked this morning that you'd been kissed."

Blair sighed and hugged her mother. "It was wonderful."

"And he asked you to marry him?"

"Aye. And he said he would seek only to please me, Mama." She pulled away and stared at her mother. "He is kind and strong, and I believe I would be happy with him."

"So why do you hesitate?"

"I dinna know. I've been so confused lately." Blair frowned, thinking about all the wild thoughts she'd been having. The longing to be set free. If she married Edan, would she be set free or only imprisoned once more?

"Did he tell you about his conversation with your father?"

"Nay."

Arbella sighed and tugged Blair toward the bed where they both sat. "Your father offered your hand to Laird Rose this morning. Laird Rose declined."

"What?" Blair's stomach soured. It would seem the man was playing games with her. Why?

"He said he'd not come here for a wife."

"And then he asked me to marry him?" She shook her head, all the elation of the moments they'd shared sliced by an imaginary dagger.

"Aye."

"I dinna understand... Was it because he felt obligated for having kissed me?"

Lady Arbella shook her head. "I cannot say why he changed his mind, my dear, but plenty a man has kissed a woman and not offered marriage. I think he meant it."

"But he said nay to Da... And Da offered without asking me first?" She wanted to be offended by that, but the part of her that knew it was her father's right to do so didn't argue.

"The point is, my darling, he would not agree this morning, and something has changed his mind. I'm guessing that something is *you*."

"Why didna he mention it to me, then?"

"My guess would be he wanted you to agree to marry him, not to be forced."

Blair leaned back against her pillows and stared up at the rafters. That made sense.

And she'd hesitated, at which point he'd said he wasn't going to beg her. She could understand the man had to keep his pride, and she'd never wish for him to beg her anyway.

"I'll ask you again, my dear. What is it you want?"

Blair smiled, glancing down at her fingers that not too long ago had been threaded in his wet hair. She pressed her hand to her belly, trying to quell some of the flopping, to no avail. "I want to keep on kissing him."

Arbella smiled and ducked her head as she let out a soft laugh. "Then I think ye know exactly what to do about it."

"Aye. I'll speak with Da first thing in the morning." Was she really doing this? Laird Rose was really going to be hers?

"Good. I'm certain you'll have his blessing, and you already have mine." Her mother stood, bent down and gave her a kiss on the forehead. "Sweet dreams, my darling. On the morrow, you'll be a betrothed woman."

The slow unraveling that had begun when she thought he'd played her for a fool coiled back up, bouncing around inside her. A betrothed woman... Her whole future ahead of her.

Sleep was the last thing that came to Blair that night. Nay, all she could think of was what a future with Laird Rose would bring, and the pleasures of his kiss.

CHAPTER 12

When dawn broke the following morning, the dark ashes from the bonfires steamed, though they no longer burned. Bodies lay huddled under woolen plaid blankets, and dogs licked at their owner's faces.

Edan went in search of the stable master to let him know they'd be preparing to leave shortly, and to have their horses fed a hearty breakfast of oats to prepare for the journey.

The stable was quiet, save for the light scuffing of a hoof or a snort.

Edan cleared his throat to alert the master, or any lads, of his presence. What he didn't expect to hear was a woman's voice answering him, "Who is there?"

Why did it sound like Lady Blair? Edan quickly and quietly traversed the dirt-packed path between the stables toward the back, where he found Blair sitting in the hay with a large lamb taking up more than the entire expanse of her lap. The soft white creature had a black face and boots and was licking Blair's face with all the affection he might expect to see from a puppy. The sight was endearing, even if it was unexpected.

Blair was giggling and stroking her fingers through the thick fleece. When she spotted him, she stilled, and her face flushed a pretty pink.

She was even more lovely like this than she was in the moonlight. A shy smiled covered her face. It looked at first like she might look down, but she seemed to force herself to meet his gaze.

"My laird," she said softly.

Edan leaned against the barn wall, arms crossed over his chest as he watched. "I take it ye like lambs?"

"Aye," she giggled. "This is Bluebell."

"Your pet?" He raised a brow.

"Aye." She ducked her head behind the lamb's face, pressing a kiss.

"And I suppose this is why ye didna eat any mutton yesterday."

"Indeed it is."

Why was he so fascinated by this? "She seems to like ye quite a bit."

"How could ye tell?" The playful grin on Blair's face was enough to make his own smile broaden. *Mo chreach*, but he was enchanted by her.

"Well, if not by the way she's licking all over your face, it would be how comfortable she is draped over your lap." He refrained from mentioning how he wouldn't mind taking the place of the lamb.

"I've had her since she was only a few weeks old. Do ye have any pets, my laird?"

"None as loving as yours."

"Nay? Your horse doesna love ye?"

"He respects me."

She winged a brow at that. "And have ye no hounds? Doesna every warrior have a hound?"

"I've never had a home to raise one in."

"But now ye do."

"Aye."

She grinned. "Perhaps I will get ye a wee puppy then, my laird. Someone to lick your face."

This time, his lip curled mischievously, and he couldn't help but say, "'Haps I've already found someone I want to lick my face."

If possible, her face went ten shades of red, and once more, she ducked behind her lamb's body to hide herself.

Edan cleared his throat, shifted on his feet and then kneeled in the hay to rub his own hand through the soft fleece. "Indeed, I may need a Bluebell of my own." His words and gesture had the desired effect, and she peeked out from behind her lamb's head. "I came to tell the stable master to ready mine and my men's mounts for departure."

Her mouth formed a circle of surprise, and a little wrinkle formed between her brows, but she didn't say anything.

He'd told her the night before he wouldn't beg, that he wouldn't ask her more than once. Yet if he didn't, he'd spend the rest of his days wondering if she would have agreed to be his had he only set aside his pride and opened his mouth. "That is...unless I've a reason to stay."

She swallowed hard, the "O" of her lips disappearing as she closed her mouth.

A tug in his chest had him reaching for her and taking her hand in his. He brushed the pad of his thumb over her knuckles. "What say ye, lass?"

"I see no reason for ye to leave just yet," she whispered.

Hope soared inside him, and he flicked his gaze over her face, trying to gauge if she was saying what he wished for.

But she kept ducking her head, hiding her eyes from his regard. Edan stroked his free hand over Bluebell's pelt, unable to let her go. Blair wouldn't look at him, but her eyes followed the path of his hand. He touched two fingers to her chin and bid her look up at him.

"Marry me," he said again, then winked. "And I, too, shall lick your face."

Blair burst out laughing and tossed a handful of hay at him. Edan chuckled, tugging straw from his hair, enjoying this playful side of her.

"Always so serious, my laird. I would not have thought ye one to make such jests."

"I may surprise ye more often than not, my lady, but I promise ye, I make no jest about marrying ye. Say aye and come away with me."

"I dinna even know your given name." She pursed her lips, looking perplexed.

"Edan, lass, call me Edan."

"'Tis a pretty name."

He raised a brow. "'Tis the first time I've ever heard that word used to describe me."

She reached forward, her hand pausing in mid-air. Her beautiful, big blue eyes met his. But she clammed up then, as though not giving herself permission to speak her mind or to touch him as she'd wished.

Edan took her outstretched hand and drew it to his lips. "Marry me."

An audible sigh left her, her mouth opening and closing, throat bobbing as she swallowed. Edan waited patiently, but when no words seemed to be forthcoming, his heart sank. She didn't want to marry him, or else she was in shock.

He hoped for shock. Withdrawing his hand from hers, he stood. "I'll see ye in the great hall to break our fast, and I hope ye'll have an answer for me then." And then he headed in the direction of his horse, giving her the space she needed to sort out her thoughts.

He wanted her to want him. To choose him herself, and not because she felt she had no other choice, or because he'd asked her enough times that she'd finally submitted. And he wasn't going to kiss her again until she said aye.

If by noon she'd not yet come to him, he would be on his way back to Rose lands. It made no sense for him to stay, and his men back home would be wondering what had transpired. Luckily, they were only a day or two's ride away, depending on the weather. If he'd come on a *birlinn*, it was only a few hours across the firth.

Edan's mount greeted him with a knicker and a bob of his head, thrusting his dark muzzle toward Edan's outstretched hand. He was wrong when he said his mount only respected him. The beast did like him, loved him even, and the feeling was mutual. He stroked a hand over Burn's soft muzzle and face, rubbed down his neck.

"How did ye sleep?" he murmured, pulled out a carrot from a nearby bucket and passed it to Burn, who crunched with pleasure.

Behind him, he could hear the clop-clop of the sheep hooves against the stable floor. When he turned around, it was to see that Blair must have slipped unheard from the stables, because her sweet lamb was all alone. Bluebell slid her body along his side, and he patted her head and picked out a carrot for her, too, which she gleefully took and ran back toward the hay where she'd been sleeping.

Edan left the stable and made his way to the great hall, seeking out the Earl of Sutherland. He found the man standing and speaking with his son by the mantle. Lady Blair was not yet present, though her two cousins were standing in the corner of the great hall, whispering and pointing at him.

Had she been talking about him? Was that too much to hope for?

"My laird," Edan said with an incline of his head toward Magnus and Liam.

"I trust ye enjoyed your evening?" Magnus asked.

"Aye, my men and I owe ye our gratitude for your hospitality." Edan cleared his throat and took the ale a passing servant handed him. He downed the contents in one long swill. "I was wondering, my laird, if I might have a word with ye in private?"

The older man nodded without hesitation and passed a glance toward his son, words exchanged between them in looks only.

He followed Magnus up the circular stair until they entered the same study that they'd used the day before. Once the door was closed, Magnus went to a sideboard and poured a dram of whisky, drinking it down before offering one to Edan, even though it was morning.

Edan shook his head, wanting to remain perfectly level-headed. "I wanted to discuss with ye—"

"I know what ye want to discuss, but perhaps now I've changed my mind."

Edan swallowed, his words disappearing for a moment. What the devil? "Perhaps is not a certainty, and I'll take my chances. I've gotten to know your daughter better since we spoke yesterday."

"How much better?" Magnus narrowed his eyes at Edan as though he knew exactly what had happened between them. He set the small pewter cup down on the table, far more gently than his white-knuckled grip would have indicated.

"We've spoken on several occasions. And I believe I made too hasty of a decision yesterday in rejecting your offer to marry her." And dammit, he prayed the lass was going to find him before noon and tell him she agreed to wed. "I would verra much like ye to reconsider, if she's willing."

"Why do ye want to marry her? And dinna spew at me reasons of an alliance, because I already know that. I want to know why ye think ye're worthy of my daughter's hand." The older man's gaze was hard, assessing as he raked it over Edan. He felt much the same as he had that first time he'd met the king. A wee lad who should have been home cuddling with his mother, but instead thrust into a world of political intrigue and violence. The king had paused, wondering why he should consider fostering a weak-looking lad. And from that moment on, Edan had made certain he went above and beyond to prove he wasn't ever weak. To prove he was worthy.

Worthy. There was that word again that had the power to bring Edan to his knees. He'd been trying to prove since he'd first drawn breath that he was worthy. Worthy of parents that abandoned him to the king's court. Worthy of a king who'd been forced to raise him. Worthy of replacing a brother he barely knew other than what an incredibly honorable leader he'd been. Worthy of a woman he found he couldn't stop thinking about.

The time for wondering had to come to an end. Hadn't he proved himself enough? "I have served the king well since I was but a lad. I will protect her with my life. I will make her happy."

Magnus seemed unfazed. "I dinna need ye to recite your vows to me, lad. I need ye to tell me why ye cherish her enough to wed her for all the days of your life."

Edan drew in a deep breath and decided to bear his soul. If he were the father of an incredible woman, he'd want to hear the truth. To know that a man cherished his precious prize. "She has captivated me like no other. Where others find her to be indecisive, I find her to be definitive. She is a strong and intelligent woman, one whom I'd value at my side to help me rule Rose lands, to grow our clan together." There were other reasons, but those he didn't think the earl would want to hear, such as how he longed to hold her in his arms and hear those little whimpers of pleasure as they crossed over his lips. How he wanted to tease her, and see her face light up with pleasure, hear the surprising tinkle of her laughter, and uncover all the mysteries of her soul. "I am fond of her," he added. "And I believe she is fond of me."

Magnus grunted and poured himself another drink, this time not offering one to Edan. He didn't blame the older man. He supposed when he had children, it would be hard a thing to say goodbye.

"I have heard many good things from the king about ye, enough so that I can say ye're a good man. There is also the fact that ye impressed me yesterday when ye said nay in regard to my proposed betrothal. Understand that Blair is a verra special lass. Not only is she my youngest daughter, but I believe her to be the most cunning, and should ye ever cross her, I dinna doubt she'd thrust a dagger through your heart—and mine would be next."

Edan swallowed, though he couldn't help a small smile. "I dinna doubt ye, and I'd expect nothing less."

"I will have to speak to my daughter before I can offer ye my blessing."

"I would only wish to marry her if she is willing," Edan repeated.

Magnus nodded and poured yet another drink. "Was there anything else?"

The man was going to be drunk before they even had breakfast. "Only that I admire ye, my laird, for indulging her with Bluebell."

Magnus grunted a laugh. "I expect ye'll do the same."

Edan grinned, recalling how Blair had actually been the one to promise him a wee pet. "I will spend the rest of my life making certain she is well pleased."

Magnus grunted. "Good. Now, if ye'll excuse me."

The older laird didn't move from where he stood, and so Edan took his cue and left the study. As soon as the door was closed, he caught the scent of Blair in the corridor.

He couldn't help a soft chuckle. "Are ye hiding out here again, lass?"

She let out a soft sigh from the alcove where he'd first kissed her. "I find I'm getting rather good at all this subterfuge. 'Haps I should make my ploy to spy for the king." She stepped out of the shadows, stunning him once more with her dark beauty.

"'Tis a dangerous thing for anyone, especially a woman, but I think ye'd manage if that was your pleasure."

"Ye were speaking to my father." She glanced toward the closed door.

"Aye."

"About what?" Her gaze flicked back to his, hoping for an honest answer, and no doubt expecting he'd skirt around it.

"I told him that I wished to marry ye, if ye'd have me."

She cocked her head. "And what did ye say?"

"That he'd speak to ye about it."

She nodded. "What would ye say if I told ye I came to speak to him on the same matter?"

Edan's chest swelled. "I'd say ye'd have made me a happy man."

"I didna say that I agreed."

A dagger to the heart, that was. "Do ye jest, my lady? I fear if ye're not mine, I'll be an unhappy man the rest of my days."

She smiled and reached forward. This time she didn't hesitate and pressed her hand to his heart. "Though the circumstances of our meeting were... Let's just say, I'd have planned differently."

He nodded.

"I have never met another man like ye, my laird." Beautiful blue eyes searched his face.

She took his breath away. He wanted to hear her call him by his name from this day and forever more. "Call me Edan, sweetling."

"Edan." His name rolled sensually of her tongue. "I wish to marry ye."

He pressed his hand over hers and brought her knuckles to his lips, enjoying the flash of pleasure that coursed over her face.

"I've never heard words that gave me more pleasure."

He wanted to kiss her, to draw her in, but at that moment, her father opened the door and glared daggers at their joined hands.

"Rose," he growled at Edan. "Get your hands off my daughter."

"Da," Blair said, her voice melodic. "I wish to marry this man."

Magnus let out a long-suffering sigh. "I expected as much."

Blair's laughter had Edan smiling, and even Magnus, as gruff as he'd been a breath before, had merriment dancing in his eyes.

BLAIR WATCHED EDAN WALK AWAY, his shoulders straighter than
when he'd first approached her father's study. When he was out of
sight, she slipped into the chamber to speak with her father. He was
standing by the sideboard pouring a dram of whisky. Before he could
sip, she hurried forward, pressed her hand over top of it and asked, "Is
that for me, Da?"

Magnus raised his brows. "Do ye need it, lass?"

Her da had indulged each of his daughter's believing they all had a
place in the world; however they saw fit. He'd bought her bows and
oars so she might try her hand at the skills her sisters possessed. He'd
allowed her to ride as often as she wanted, even the warhorses that
most lassies wouldn't dare mount. He'd allowed her to sip his whisky
when her mother wasn't looking, and to learn to read before she was
fully adept at cutting her meat.

"I think so." She pressed a kiss to his cheek.

"So ye want to marry, aye?"

"I do."

"And ye think Laird Rose is the man to see it through?"

"No other has ever interested me."

"That says quite a lot."

"I thought so."

"What if I'm not ready to part with ye?" he asked.

Blair sipped the whisky and screwed up her nose, nearly choking on
its potency before she tossed it back the rest of the way. The liquid
burned a path down her throat and warmed her belly.

"I would say the same, Da. I'm not ready to part with any of ye, but
I am ready to be a wife, and I find myself to have taken a fancy to Edan
Rose. He is a good man. I think I can make him happy, and I'm certain
he will make me feel the same way."

Magnus nodded. "'Tis what a father hopes for. What I dinna understand is the missive, lass."

She bit her lip and shook her head. "I dinna know how it got into
his hands. I thought I destroyed it... I think one of my cousins felt the

need to act on my behalf. And I forgive whichever one of them did so. But I fear I shall never trust them again for taking away my choice, even if it has brought me happiness."

"Aye. We are lucky the foolish actions did not lead to war."

Blair looked toward her feet, feeling ashamed. "I'm sorry, Da."

"Och, dinna fash. We all make mistakes. But I must know that your decision to wed Laird Rose doesna stem from guilt."

Her head shot up, and she shook her head. "Oh, nay, Da, I really do care for him."

"Well then, we've a wedding to plan."

She wrapped her arms around her father, squeezing her eyes shut and listening to the familiar beat of his heart.

He pressed his hand to the back of her head, stroking down her hair. "I love ye, sweet lass."

"I love ye, too, Da."

"I suppose I should make the announcement afore I finish this jug of whisky and canna walk straight."

Blair laughed. "I've never seen ye not walk straight, Da."

"I've never had to give away my youngest daughter afore, either."

She glanced up at him then, taking in the crinkles at his eyes and the slight sheen of what was likely tears. "Ye're not giving me away. I'll always be your daughter."

He pressed a kiss to her forehead and then cleared his throat. "Aye, always."

They made their way down the stairs to the great hall, where everyone was slowly trickling in to break their fast after having attended Mass.

Blair met her mother's eyes and grinned with pleasure. She then sought out Edan. He stood at the back of the great hall, leaning against the wall, his muscular arms crossed over his chest. She flashed him a smile, which seemed to have the power to make him thrust off the wall as though the stone were burning him. He started to move forward through the crowd, and with every inch he drew nearer, the more tingly she felt.

And then he was there before her, and her father was saying loud enough for all to hear, "Congratulations are in order. Laird Rose has asked for my daughter's hand, and she has agreed to the union." Then more quietly, he said, "It is my opinion we should perform the ceremony here, before ye head back to your castle."

Edan grasped her father's arm and shook it as he gave his thanks, then he took her hand in his and brought it to his lips. "Ye've made me a verra happy man, lass."

Blair grinned. "And I am a happy woman."

Her mother approached next, tossing herself around Blair in a great hug before doing the same to Edan.

Cora and Liam joined them, as did her Aunt Aliah, Uncle Blane and her two cousins.

Cheers went up all around the great hall, reverberating through the rafters.

Blair's belly was buzzing with excitement. She slipped her hand in Edan's and smiled up at him. This was a new adventure she was about to embark on, and one that promised to be full of surprises and pleasure.

"If ye'll excuse me one moment." She let go of his hand and hurried toward Aurora and Aislinn. "I suppose I have the two of ye to thank for my happiness."

"Nay, Cousin," Aurora said, "'twas all your own doing. We thought ye'd gone addled when we read the missive. And to think he actually came!" They fanned their faces with their hands and laughed as if it were all a great jest. "Aye, thank goodness I had the forethought to switch out the vials. I knew ye'd not go through with it. Indeed, when I slipped the vial into a satchel of goods being exported over the firth, I never thought it would actually arrive anywhere. Dear me, we thought he was going to massacre the lot of us when he rode over the moors."

Blair smiled wanly, nodded and then backed away from them, wishing she'd not said anything at all. To hear them laugh in jest at the danger they'd caused... She was certain she could never hold them in her respect again.

CHAPTER 13

Blair sat with Cora, her cousins and the other ladies on a hill after a walk to gather more flowers for the great hall. It had been decided she and Edan would wed on the morrow. Only her mother and aunt were missing from the crowd, as they worked with the castle servants to prepare for the big day. The men in the field below were training, and from where the women perched, it was easy to pick out who was who.

Edan and Liam engaged each other heavily in sword play, which had Cora and Blair grasping hands. The clangs from their blades reverberated up the hill and through their bodies.

"It is a testament to their skill that they do not kill each other," Cora murmured, as though she were trying to reassure herself of that fact.

"Aye. They are both verra skilled indeed." Watching Edan was causing her breath to hitch in ways she'd not imagined.

Edan's body moved in fluid, powerful motion. He matched her brother in breadth of shoulder but towered over him by several inches. Despite his added height, from what she could see, neither had an advantage over the other. For all the civilities they had to keep, this seemed to be the one moment they were able to unleash their control

—to a point. Neither would kill the other or hack off a limb. But she wouldn't be surprised if they ended up drawing blood.

It would seem the ladies were not the only ones interested in the mock battle and display of might. The other men had slowly stopped their own training to watch, her father included. He stood off to the side with his arms crossed over his chest.

Part of her wondered if her father had put Liam up to the challenge, to see if Edan was worthy of her in marriage. To see if Edan could protect her. Blair almost laughed at that. The man had ridden from his castle upon receiving her message in a bottle, intent on saving a woman he didn't know. To think he wouldn't protect her now that she was to be his wife was preposterous.

"Edan is very skilled," Cora said in her delicate English accent.

"Aye." Blair was discovering this now, too, and admiring greatly the way in which he controlled his body as though it weighed no more than air. The power he must have...

Of course, thinking of his strength brought the memory of his arms around her, the muscles of his chest beneath her finger tips, the corded bunching she'd felt of his shoulders. It was amazing to her how very different her body was from his. Where his body was hard, hers seemed soft. Where he was broad, she was slender, and where he was slender about the hips, she was wide. Made for each other, they fit together like the pieces of a puzzle when she was in his arms. And, oh, how she wanted to press her softer parts to his harder ones.

She sighed, leaning her head on her hand, her elbow resting on her knee. The sound of her contentment drew the attention of most of the women present. A few laughed faintly, and others outright teased her for watching her future husband so intently. Color rose in Blair's face, but she couldn't help observing him.

"I could watch them all day," Cora mused. "In fact, there have been days I did just that."

Blair smiled. "I could do that, too."

She was glad that Cora would only be a day's ride or so away. Her oldest sister Bella was the farthest, Niall's lands being more northern than Dunrobin, and Greer was closer to Dunrobin as well, though on the southern border. She missed her sisters and her brother Strath, whom she hadn't seen in the longest time. Mayhap this year they'd all be able to get together at Yule again, as they had in years past.

Messengers had been sent out to her siblings, but she didn't expect they'd be able to reach Castle Ross before she was wedded and on her way to her new home.

The thought of a new home had her heart doing little palpitations. She turned to Cora, seeking sisterly advice.

"What was it like when ye first came to Castle Ross...as a new bride and mistress?"

A soft smile covered Cora's lips as she glanced down toward the field where all the men were fighting. "It went better than I expected," Cora said. "Took the people a little while to get used to us being here, more so because I'm English, but they did accept me."

"Aye." Blair did have the advantage of being Scottish. And Edan and Liam were similar in that they were both not the original lairds, though Edan was at least brother to the old Laird of Rose. Liam had had to win over a clan that had gone against their king in the name of serving Ina Ross and her vile husbands—both of whom had been English. "Do they ever worry that ye'll...turn your back on Scotland?"

Cora pursed her lips and a flicker of hurt flashed in her eyes. Blair instantly felt terrible for what was implied, even though that wasn't what she'd meant.

"When I first met King Robert, he asked me the same thing. I am loyal to my husband and to his country, which is Scotland. I hope that one day our two countries will be at peace with one another, but that does not mean I'll ever betray Liam, or the trust King Robert has bestowed upon me."

"I didna mean it like that. I'm so sorry." Blair touched her shoulder, realizing that though Cora and Liam had been married for some time, the subject was still a wee bit touchy.

"Liam has had many hurdles to cross," Cora said, toying with an amber stone pendant. "And now this latest rumor that he might have had something to do with Edan's brother's death." She shook her head. "It breaks my heart that anyone would think he could do such a thing."

"Mine too. I know that Edan wants verra much to find whoever is at fault and see they are punished, that my brother's name is cleared. I'll do my best to convince those at Kilravock that he had nothing to do with it."

"I know you will." She stroked her hand over Blair's, where it still rested on her shoulder. "You're a good sister."

"So are ye."

The men on the field caught their attention once more as cheers went up. Edan and Liam were shaking hands, their bodies slick with sweat and great big grins on their handsome faces. Blair felt her insides warm with love for her brother, and a giddy excitement for the man who would become her husband.

Blair studied Edan, mesmerized by the strong lines of his face, and the dark hair the clung with perspiration to his forehead. Lord, but he was gorgeous.

She couldn't wait to marry him tomorrow, and then be able to kiss him, touch him, whenever she wanted, every day for the rest of her life. The priest had been called, and her mother, aunt and several women of the castle they'd employed were hard at work preparing her trousseau and a new gown for her to be wed in.

Through all the excitement, there was still the lingering dark cloud of Edan's brother's murder, and the fact that someone had tried to pin it on Liam.

She'd not been lying or exaggerating when she'd told Cora she would do whatever it took to convince the Rose clan that her brother was innocent.

❦

BLAIR BARELY SLEPT ALL NIGHT. Flutters in her belly and tingling in her limbs kept her awake. As dawn burst in through the window, she leapt from bed and rushed to the basin to splash cold water on her face.

Today, she was going to get married.

Her cousins, who'd shared her bed the night before, roused slowly, stretching, and Aislinn whined, "Why are ye awake already? Should ye not sleep in as ye'll likely be up all night?"

Up all night? Blair wrinkled her nose and picked up a brush to run it through her hair. Having barely slept last night more than an hour, she was certain she would sleep like a bairn tonight. Besides, tonight she wouldn't have to worry about an upcoming wedding. The deed would be done, and she could rest easy.

"We've hours yet to get ye ready," Aurora murmured and patted the bed. "Come back to bed, ye've left a cold spot."

"I barely slept a wink, and I'm wide awake. I could get married right now."

"Nay," they both said in unison groans. "Your hair isna done."

They both climbed begrudgingly from bed to help her get ready, practically dragging their bodies across the floor, as though they'd been called to the stocks.

The morning went by in a whirl, and when Blair finally did make it downstairs with her mother and father at her side, she barely saw any of the faces they passed on the way to the kirk. Her hands shook, sweat trickled down her spine, and she couldn't feel her feet. Her breaths were coming quickly, and she was fairly certain if she didn't find a chamber pot right then and there, she would throw up all over the beautifully embroidered gown made for her. The blue of the fabric was a near match for her eyes, and tiny bluebells were embroidered into the cuffs, hem and neckline—all of which would be ruined by the unsightly clumps of regurgitated porridge.

And then she saw him.

Standing on the stairs of the sacred building was Edan, his gaze riveted on hers. Gone were his trews, replaced by a Rose clan plaid of muted red, green and blue. His *leine* looked crisp, and his boots polished. So neatly put together—all save for that wild dark hair that waved gently with the breeze. Seeing him standing there, she was suddenly no longer full of nerves. She picked up her pace now, practically dragging her parents to the altar.

Blair heard the priest ask if she came to wed willingly, and she heard herself say, "I do," but the rest of the words uttered were a blur.

The only thing she remembered vividly was a stormy-gray gaze holding hers captive, and the slow grin on his lips before he leaned down and claimed her mouth in front of one and all.

His lips slid over hers softly, much like he had kissed her in the alcove. Tingles raced over her skin, and he was pulled away much too quickly, leaving their kiss brief and filled with promise.

The rest of the day was packed with celebration, dancing and bonfires. Pipers serenaded them, and they kept being whisked off in opposite directions, until they were finally brought together once more at the feast.

Edan fed her bites of their meal as they sat side by side, but she wouldn't have been able to tell anyone what was served, only that food had never tasted so good. And neither had wine. Her cup was never empty and being nervous and needing to do something with her hands, she may have imbibed a bit too much.

When her eyes started to get droopy, Edan stood beside her and lifted her into his powerful arms. He was so warm. His heat sank into her, and she smiled lazily up at him, tracing her fingers along his jaw and then the scar over his eye.

"Ye're so handsome," she said, her words a little slurred.

He grinned down at her. "And ye're a wee bit sauced."

She giggled. "Is that why I feel so sleepy but also like laughing?"

"Aye. Say goodnight to everyone."

"Goodnight everyone," she shouted and then planted a kiss on his stubbled cheek.

The crowd cheered and started to chant a bawdy song, but Blair wrapped her arms around Edan's neck and rested her head on his shoulder, completely oblivious to it. He carried her up the stairs, and her mother followed, stopping Edan on the stairs to ask if she could prepare her daughter for bed, but Blair shook her head.

"Edan can help me, Mama." She passed her mother a wistful smile. "All will be wonderful."

Lady Arbella glanced toward Edan, who nodded. "All will be well, my lady. And if we've need of ye, we shall have ye fetched."

"Take care of my daughter well, Laird Rose."

"Upon my life, my lady."

When they reached Blair's chamber and barred the door, Edan set her down and slid his palms along her cheeks. "Alone at last," he murmured.

"Aye."

And then he kissed her so thoroughly her knees buckled. He caught her up against him, carried her to the bed and laid her gently upon the mattress. Blair felt a bit like she was floating. Her entire body was tingling with anticipation of what was to come, all the kisses from Edan would be wondrous, and perhaps she was suffering from a wee bit of nerves.

But the way Edan's gaze roved over her body, hunger clear in his features, made her own need for more kissing light up inside her and squelch the nerves that threatened.

"Ye're so beautiful," he murmured, looking incredibly serious when he said it.

How could he find her as such when she was so different than everyone else? "Dinna tease me, Husband, for I am Blair the Not So Fair."

Husband. She thought it sounded funny on her tongue, and so she laughed and slapped her hands over her mouth as she hiccuped.

Edan grinned down at her, teasing in the crinkle of his eyes. He bent forward and kissed her again as he pulled the blankets up around her. "Beautiful and intoxicating."

"Intoxicated," she corrected.

"Aye," he chuckled.

This time when he kissed her, she drifted off to sleep.

EDAN SLOWLY UNDRESSED, chuckling to himself over the lass drunk and asleep in bed a few feet away. His *wife*. Drunk as a warrior after a battle, and all kitten purrs and soft touches. She thought him handsome...and herself not beautiful. He shook his head. How the tables seemed turned in that respect.

He glanced over at her, arms flung over her head, mouth slack, and soft snores puffing against the sheets. A brute might have doused her with cold water to wake her and take what was now rightfully his, but Edan wanted Blair to enjoy every moment of their first time together. Hell, he wouldn't be able to enjoy it unless she did.

And so he slipped into bed beside his snoring wife, tugged her supple body into his arms and dreamt about making love to her instead.

Upon the morrow, he'd see to it she was sighing with pleasure instead of sleep.

CHAPTER 14

Blair peeked shyly at her new husband as they rode toward his home at a pace that could only be described as stops and starts. Whenever Edan seemed to be getting into his own head, the pace would quicken, and then he'd appear to remember she was there and slow down. It was dizzying, but not so dizzying as the thoughts running amuck in her head.

Had they made love last night?

She didn't feel sore...and there hadn't been any blood on the sheets. But the last thing she remembered was him sliding into the bed beside her and kissing her. A lass ought to remember her wedding night, and Blair was ashamed she had not even an inkling of recollection.

Oh, what shame!

When she'd woken that morning, Edan had already been gone from their chamber, and she'd been too mortified to ask. Married only a day, she was already failing as a wife.

She couldn't seem to find her tongue and was unable to hold a conversation with the man in question. She even taken to counting the hairs in her mare's mane to keep from looking at him.

The ride to Kilravock was not overlong, and they arrived in the very late afternoon, an hour or two before sunset. She'd barely paid attention to where they were going. All of the sudden, the castle stones were looming up in front of her, and they were hurrying through the gate. The clan had been informed of their arrival by a scout and were waiting for them in the bailey. A cheer to their laird's return went up while they cast curious glances at Blair.

Her face grew hot, and then hotter still when Edan appeared beside her, reached up to grasp her about the waist and took her down from the horse. His hands were warm, and as whenever she was near him, her insides tingled and pulsed.

Surely if she'd made love to her husband, she would remember it?

Edan took her hand in his and led her through the throngs of people toward the steps of the keep. When they reached the top, he turned them about to face the crowd.

"My wife, Lady Blair Rose."

Blair smiled out at the crowd, still a little bit in shock she was a married lass and now mistress to an entirely new clan. For the most part, she got on well with everyone she met, as she tried more often than not to be amiable. Her new clan would be no exception. However, she did notice a few of the clanswomen in the crowd did not offer her a smile in return. One woman looked downright sour.

She brushed aside the sting of their greeting, for there were plenty of others who seemed pleased to meet her.

"Come, my sweet, I'll show ye to your chamber." Edan squeezed her hand as he murmured the words.

"Mine? Do ye not mean ours?"

He looked at her, perplexed. "My brother and his wife had adjoining chambers, as did my parents before them. The lady had hers, and the laird his."

"My parents share a chamber, as do my brothers and sisters with their spouses."

Edan narrowed his brow. "The king does not share a chamber with his wife."

"And while ye're a powerful man, ye're not the king." She couldn't help but retort, and then bit her tongue just after the words were out of her mouth and she awaited his reaction.

Edan surprised her with a grin and a slow wink. "Ye wish to share my chamber?"

Oh saints, she wished she could remember last night!

"Aye." Though she wanted to glance toward her feet, she kept herself from doing so. She meant to live every day as a wife who did not cower in front of her husband. A wife who was not embarrassed, even if she was. A wife who could always look her husband in the eye, even if she couldn't remember a single thing about her wifely duties. "But if ye prefer..."

He gave a subtle shake of his head. "I would verra much like to be closer to ye." His voice scraped along her spine, sending shivers of anticipation racing over her. Nay, they certainly had not made love yet; she would know.

"My laird." The sour-faced lady hurried up the keep steps, sweat trickling down her temples, her fists bunched around the fabric of her skirts. "Shall I fetch her ladyship a bath?"

Edan glanced down at the woman quizzically, and so Blair nodded in answer. "Aye, that would be lovely."

After having grown up in a regiment of men, it would seem he was not yet aware of the things a lady wife might desire. A bath was a luxury, one she didn't indulge in often, as it required quite a lot of work from the servants. They would need time to heat the water, carry up the tub, and then to empty the tub, bucket by bucket. But in this case, after having traveled for the whole of the day and feeling very nervous about any marital duties she would most assuredly be required to perform today, she could use a warm bath to relax herself.

She smiled kindly at the sour-faced woman, who still did not return the gesture. Blair accepted the challenge, determined to win the woman over.

"Aye, my lady. Give us a bit to put it together." She sounded tired, weary even.

"And your name is?" Blair asked, trying to keep her voice cheerful.

"Mrs. McQuinn, but ye can call me Agnes. I'm housekeeper at Kilravock."

There was something in the way that Agnes was staring at her, as if waiting for something, but Blair couldn't be sure what it was. Strange, truly. She studied Agnes a little harder, but as soon as she started to scan her face, the sour woman snapped her fingers at a few lassies behind her, who leapt as though instructed by a military leader.

As they filed past Blair and Edan, they curtsied to their laird and offered him kind smiles, but they eyed Blair warily with tentative smiles and then scurried after Mrs. McQuinn. Though she thought it odd, as none of the women at Dunrobin, or even Castle Ross, had acted thusly toward her, Blair brushed it off. They had just lost a mistress they'd only just gotten used to, and now had another to become familiar with.

So he brought a little Sutherland whore back with him? She had to pinch herself to be certain she wasn't sleeping, for this was too good to be true. How could she have every possibly dreamed all of this up? Her plans would need a bit of tweaking, but that was nothing hard. Oh, zounds, but it was hard not to laugh with glee or clap outright with joy at the hand she'd just been dealt.

She shook her head, watching the Sutherland chit, and gleefully planning all the ways in which she was going to make that bitch suffer.

EDAN TOOK Blair's hand in his and led her inside and up the spiral stairs to the third level, where he opened a door to the chamber on the left. They entered into a small solar. On the right was a door that opened to reveal a bedchamber, and on the left was the same.

"This one is mine," he said, leading her toward the chamber on the right. "Ours," he corrected with a flash of a smile.

She smiled at his correction and followed him into the chamber that was quite plainly appointed and very masculine. A large four-poster bed dominated the far wall. The posts were carved in swirling knots that resembled those often found on Pictish stones, and at the center of each post was a harp in various forms. One was on the back of a mermaid, another being played by a warrior, the third showed the strings as arrows, and the fourth was being strummed by a lady. The details were intricate and beautiful, and she couldn't help but reach out to stroke her fingers over the designs.

"'Twas commissioned by my grandfather," Edan said. "There is a matching one, albeit slightly smaller in the other chamber."

"It is verra lovely."

"Aye. And so are ye." His eyes were on her, and even though he didn't take a step closer, she felt his heat all the same, a warmth that scaled up her neck and over cheeks. He mesmerized and enchanted her with his words.

His gaze settled on her lips with the same intensity as it had when he'd kissed her the day before in her chamber at Ross Castle. That part she remembered.

She flicked her own gaze toward the bed, wanting to ask him what had happened that night. *Did they...?* She licked her lips and glanced back at him, feeling her palms grow slick.

Edan did move closer then, silently shifting forward until she really did feel his heat on her skin. He touched two fingers to her chin and tilted her face toward his. He leaned down and brushed his soft mouth over hers. Blair's body immediately reacted with frissons of excitement dancing over her limbs.

She leaned in, wanting to feel his hard body against hers. To taste what she'd missed the day before. She wanted to ask him to make love to her again, or for the first time, whichever it was.

"Will ye—" she started to ask but was cut off by a sharp knock on the door of their solar.

"Your bath has arrived," Edan murmured, pulling away with a sigh to go and let in the servants.

A long line of them filed into the solar carrying a large wooden tub, linens, sweet smelling soaps and buckets of water. They didn't enter the laird's chamber, however, and went straight into the lady's dwelling.

Blair didn't correct them. She pressed her hand to Edan's arm when it looked like he might. "'Tis all right for now," she said, feeling marginally relieved that she might have some privacy while bathing. "They dinna need to know where I sleep at night."

Edan grinned, winking down at her in such a sensual way that she shivered.

"I'll leave ye to your bath, my lady. I need to have a word with my men to gather reports of what has gone on since I left."

He pressed a tender kiss to her forehead and then disappeared through the same door as the servants.

When she entered the lady's chamber, the tub had been filled halfway with water and set up with linen inside. No maid had been left to assist her, which was just as well, for she would have said she could bathe on her own.

A linen towel for drying was draped over the side, and herbs were floating on the top of the water. There did not appear to be a cake of soap. She opened the wardrobe and the chest at the base of the bed but found none. But a quick peek in Edan's chamber found a ball of dull-smelling soap beside his wash basin. It would have to do for now.

Blair stripped quickly out of her clothes, grateful for the tub, and determined to rest in the warm water just long enough to ease her nerves, but not overlong that the servants might think her lazy. First impressions were important, and she desired that they would know her as a good role model rather than a pampered lady.

Standing naked before the tub, Blair lifted her foot to step into the water, submerging just a few toes before she shrieked and leapt back. The water was ice cold. Nay, it couldn't be. Who would have offered their lady a cold bath? Perhaps it had only been so hot she thought it was cold...if that were even a possibility? Blair dipped her finger into the herb-strewn water and frowned. It was indeed so cold it must have been pulled straight from the well and brought up to her chamber without having gone near a fire.

Tears sprang to her eyes at the cruelty of it. Was it possible there had been some confusion? But Blair knew there could not have be. Whoever had strewn in the herbs would have swirled them about the water, and before instructing her it was ready, the temperature would have been checked. There was only one person who had told her it was ready: Agnes McQuinn.

Blair immediately thought of her sour, pinched face. She'd done it on purpose. Offered her lady something nice, only to take it away. This was a direct insult, to let her lady know just how Agnes felt about her —which was wholly unfair, given Blair had only just arrived and had not been here long enough for anyone to form a grudge against her. Blair stood up straight, stiffening. What had she ever done to deserve such treatment?

She turned around to find the hearth empty of a fire, though there was a stack of logs in the grate. Using a lit candle on the mantle, she held the flaming wick to the logs until they caught in several places. At least she could warm up after her cold bath—which would not be one of leisure. For she had decided she would wash, though she would not be submerging herself in the water. The last thing she wanted to do was let the offensive housekeeper know she'd upset her. And she certainly didn't want to bother Edan to take up her cause with the petty servants. Soon enough, she'd win them over. She had to.

Blair returned to the tub, stepping into it so as not to make a mess on the floor. Given how vindictive Agnes was, she wouldn't be surprised if the woman sent up sweet servants to clean up any mess Blair made, if only to get them to hate her. Saints, but the water was frigid. Gooseflesh rose along her limbs, and she was certain it wouldn't be long before her teeth chattered.

She dipped her hands in the cold water and splashed it on her face. She used a small square of linen to wash with the bland soap, certain now they'd purposefully not provided her with any. Good thing she'd washed her hair the day before on her wedding day, or she'd have to dunk her head in the freezing water, too.

After she finished scrubbing, Blair stood before the fire until her skin turned pink with warmth. She then dressed, replaited her hair and headed down the stairs to find the kitchens.

It was nearly evening, and Agnes would at this point have already conferred with the cook about what to serve for supper, but she could at least introduce herself and let them know that she would be speaking with them first thing in the morning to discuss meals.

Blair passed through the great hall, smiling at those who stared at her openly, and gaining a few smiles back. But several sniffed at her and had the audacity to raise their noses before turning their backs.

She tried not to bristle at their rude behavior, but she was finding it rather difficult. The smell of cooking grew stronger, and she followed it through the back, halting on the threshold of the kitchen when she spotted Agnes in a deep huddle with the cook. The hearth gave off scents of roasting meat and baking bread, and on the long trestle table down the center of the kitchen, onions, root vegetables, garlic and herbs were all in the process of being chopped. They'd yet to notice her standing there, and Blair caught snatches of their conversation, which cut like a dagger.

"There's one thing for certain," Agnes was saying, "she's no Lady Rose."

Blair's eye widened, feeling the sting of the insult deep in her chest. Heat once more filled her cheeks. But with her back straightened and her voice steady, she said in a manner she'd often heard her mother speak to a wayward servant, "Ye see, Agnes, that is where ye're wrong. For I *am* Lady Rose, and so I shall remain."

The two women jolted at the sound of her voice and turned to face her.

Cook looked quite a bit more apologetic than Agnes, who only stared at Blair with a blank expression. "I trust ye enjoyed your bath, my lady?"

Of all the nerve... "'Twas...invigorating." Blair brushed away what she knew was meant to be another dig and stepped into the kitchens. She ignored Agnes, which she knew would only make the woman angrier, but at the moment she did not care. Blair faced the rest of those in the kitchen. Scullions, spit-boys, undercooks and dish-washers all faced her, their gazes shifting toward Agnes as though they worried about whatever their facial expressions might give away. "I am Lady Blair," she said, head held high. "New mistress of Clan Rose. I wanted to introduce myself to ye all. My mother, the

Countess of Sutherland, is on good terms with her kitchen staff, as I wish to be with all of ye. We'll meet each morning to discuss the days meals."

Once more, their gazes shifted, but this time to Cook.

"I know change is hard, and ye've all been through so much already. I'm so verra sorry for your losses. I dinna intend to take anything away from your memories, but I do hope that we will all create new ones and make Laird Rose's mealtimes those of enjoyment and leisure." This was how it was at her home. Mealtimes were the moments in which they all relaxed and enjoyed each other's company. She very much wanted to create the same atmosphere here.

"At Kilravock, the housekeeper is in charge of setting menus with the cook," Agnes interjected. "That is my duty."

Blair finally glanced toward Agnes, who not only still looked sour, but there was a challenging rise of her eyebrows as well.

"I understand," Blair said, pausing as she eyed each one in the kitchen, wondering just how long it might actually take to win them over. It seemed Agnes ruled with an iron fist.

"Good, we've an understanding," Agnes said.

"Oh, nay." Blair's tone was soft, but firm, and she held her hands tightly before her to keep them from trembling. "Ye misunderstand me. I said I understand, but I'm afraid we will have to allow for changes. I would be more than happy to confer with ye, Agnes, and then ye confer with Cook, but I verra much intend to be a part of the process."

Blair had not raised her voice, nor used a cruel tone, and yet the gaped mouths of those present might have suggested otherwise. It was so quiet one could hear a pin drop.

Agnes was turning nearly purple in her rage.

"I'll take your silence for agreement. Thank ye all so much for the warm welcome," Blair emphasized the word warm to point out she had not enjoyed the cold bath. "I look forward to the meal ye're preparing for our supper."

Several of the understaff nodded and murmured, but they were cut off with a sharp look from Agnes. Blair didn't stay to hear what rebukes the housekeeper might offer, as she very much felt like she could vomit.

She hurried, more like fled, from the kitchens through the great hall to the outside. A moment with Bluebell to bury her nose in the sweet animal's fleece would set her to rights. She easily found the stables, but her sweet sheep was not present. Blair walked up and down, peering in every stall, but there was no sight of her lamb.

The stable master, an older gentleman with a tanned and weathered face, approached. "My lady?"

"I am looking for Bluebell, my sheep. The laird told me she'd be housed here."

The man gave her an odd look. "Nay, my lady. I've not seen her."

She thought Edan had said Bluebell would live in the stables, but perhaps she'd had heard wrong.

Blair wondered out of the stables and poked her head in various huts and other structures until she found her lamb in a barn filled with livestock being fattened up for slaughter. A keening cry left her lips as she rushed forward to grab hold of the braided rope collar she'd fashioned herself, startling the lads who were tending the animals.

"Bluebell does not belong here," she cried. "She is my pet."

The man in charge of the livestock and the lads looked at her as though she were addled, but she ignored them and led Bluebell out of the barn and into the bailey.

She marched her lamb over to the stable, shoved open the door and stepped inside. "I'll need a stall," she said to the stable master, who passed her the same look as he had before. "Bluebell will reside here and be treated as well as the laird's horse."

The stable master blustered in horror, but Blair would not be cowed.

"My lady, I'm afraid it would be quite impossible—"

Blair was close to tears. With one hand fisted at her side, she straightened as much as she could. Since coming here, she'd met with nothing but unfriendliness and antagonism, and she was only a few minutes away from breaking down. "My husband, your laird, has already agreed to accommodate Bluebell. Ye're going against his orders."

The stable master frowned. "I have yet to hear the order myself, my lady."

So it would seem he was going to argue this with her, too. Blair bristled. She'd had quite enough. "Then go and find him."

The stable master looked ready to spit, but Blair's nerves were already overflowing from her cold bath and the confrontation with Agnes in the kitchen. The mistreatment of her precious pet was the last straw.

Fortunately, Edan strode into the stable right then, his narrowed gaze flicking back and forth between her and the stable master.

"What is the problem, Master Arthur?" he asked gruffly.

Master Arthur gestured wildly at Bluebell. "The lady seems to be under the impression ye gave permission for livestock to be housed with the horses."

Livestock! "Bluebell is *not* livestock." Her eyes were starting to sting, signaling tears would be coming soon.

"I did," Edan said, staring hard at the stable master. "In future, my lady's requests shall be granted without my permission required."

"Aye, my laird." Master Arthur turned red in the face, but not from anger. Instead, he looked at Blair with genuine regret, the first of which she'd seen from anyone today. "Apologies, my lady. We shall take verra good care of your lamb."

"Her name is Bluebell."

He pressed his hand over his heart. "She will be as my own."

Blair watched, forcing her tears at bay, as Bluebell trotted happily beside the stable master down the walk until he found an empty stall to place her.

"All is well?" Edan asked.

She nodded, though right now it felt very much like not all was well.

CHAPTER 15

Edan had been on his way back to the keep to see how his wife was settling in after gaining a report from the gate master, when he'd spotted Blair walking determinedly out of the barn and toward the stables with her sweet lamb in tow. She'd looked visibly upset, though the line of her jaw was set in purpose.

He'd been of a mind to let her figure things out on her own when he'd seen a few of the women who helped about the castle gathered in a trio and pointing toward the stable. Blair didn't see them, and Edan didn't like what he was able to deduce from the scene.

It would seem his order for Bluebell to be taken and given housing with the horses had been ignored. Instead, she'd been stuck with the livestock—which would have been disastrous, had anyone decided lamb was on the menu.

Good God, she never would have forgiven him, and Magnus Sutherland would very likely have descended upon Rose lands like a wolf on its prey.

The fact that the lasses were having a good fit of giggles over it had Edan wondering if the wrong placement of the lamb had been done on purpose. He'd not dealt with any lasses while growing up, other than the few who'd flirted with him and those he'd stolen a kiss or enjoyed a tupping with, so he had no idea how the feminine mind worked.

As a lad thrust into the king's army, he'd gone through his own fair share of cruelty and teasing in order to fit in. Did women have something of the same? Well, it didn't matter. He'd not allow his wife to be tormented, and he certainly wasn't going to allow her sweet pet to be murdered, especially after having made a promise to her to see to Bluebell's well-being.

Edan had marched into the stable and set things to rights. Now, he stood outside of his mount's stall, listening to Blair's soft murmurs after she'd insisted on seeing to Bluebell's comfort herself. Having given her privacy to do so, he could see that she was seeing to her own as well. The sheep seemed to have the ability to calm her.

What he was supposed to do with a wife, he had no idea. There hadn't been any training on it. Aye, he knew he needed to bed her, and he would this very eve and hopefully every eve after, in order to gain heirs, but what else did one do with a wife? He knew not the first bit of business about a mistress's place in the castle, and so he'd determined to leave that to the housekeeper.

Edan held out a palmful of fresh oats toward his horse, who gingerly lipped the kernels from his hand.

Housekeepers worked very closely with the lady of the castle to keep everything set to rights, and thus, Agnes would know more about the running of it than he would, or at least the way it had been run. As lady of the castle, Blair was free to change anything she wanted. He had men to train, fortifications to see to, crofters and clansmen to care for. There were taxes that had to be paid, revenue to be calculated and a myriad of other confusing details he was still trying to learn himself. His brother's steward had been as helpful as he could be, but Edan still felt rather hopeless.

He was a knight, a warrior, and he knew how to take orders as well as dispense them. In a battle, he could kill a man with no weapons, and taking on three at a time was easy, even with the damage to his eye.

The elders were pleased he'd come home with a wife, no doubt relieved they would not have to pester him anymore into marrying. They were especially happy with whom he'd aligned their clan.

His warriors were equally pleased and eager for him to send out an invitation to Magnus, his brothers, and every one of their sons for a tournament. The Rose clan warriors prided themselves on being proficient with their weaponry and fighting skills, but to put it to the test in a tournament was always a pleasure, and for the most skilled of Scotland's warriors to now be aligned with their clan was a boon.

Blair should be able to figure things out on her own. As a lady born and bred to be mistress of a castle, she would indeed have what she needed in hand.

Even still, he would have to keep his ears and eyes open for any hints of her or Bluebell being abused.

"She is settled," Blair said, approaching from the direction of Bluebell's stable.

"And are ye?" He raked his gaze over her, from the flush of her face down to the booted toes peeking from beneath her skirts.

"Aye."

"Then we should go into the great hall for supper. I'm starving."

She smiled, though her expression was guarded as she nodded her agreement.

Edan narrowed his brows, taking in the slightly forlorn look of his bride. "Ye would tell me if ought was amiss, aye?" he asked.

"Of course." She touched his elbow, drawing his attention to her long, slim fingers and making him consider what it would be like for those elegant hands to be on his bare flesh.

Och, but supper couldn't be over soon enough. He was ready to take her up to their chamber right now and make her his. To pleasure her all the night through. With his thoughts having turned decidedly southward, he took her hand in his and headed back toward the castle keep. The sooner they ate, the sooner he could take her above stairs and make her his wife in truth.

The great hall was full of bustle, as clanswomen worked to set the tables and hounds were shooed outside. Trenchers, and even a few flower centerpieces too, had been set on the long trestle tables. They were trying to make it special for their lady, and that pleased him well.

He led Blair toward the dais, where their two chairs were in the center. Several other chairs had been placed on either side for the clan elders. The scents coming from the kitchen were incredible, making his mouth water. He pulled out Blair's chair, and she murmured her thanks as she sat and placed her napkin primly on her lap. She looked guarded. Not her usual self, and certainly not the same as she'd been at Castle Ross. But he suspected it was because here she was not surrounded by her family.

The housekeeper approached, giving a slight curtsy in their direction as she held out a jug of wine. The rest of the cupbearers poured ale or wine for those in attendance. Edan would have normally done so for himself, but he suspected Agnes was trying to make a good impression on her new mistress.

Edan indicated she could pour the contents into their goblets. She started first with his and then moved to Blair's. As the red liquid decanted into his wife's goblet she stiffened, and he could only think that perhaps it was because she'd had a bit too much the night before.

But Agnes saw fit to pour her wine to the very top, until Blair said, "That is plenty."

Agnes startled, seeming to have forgotten what she was doing, because her hand jerked back with the jug, and a large splash came out of it to slap against Blair's cheek. His wife gasped, as did the housekeeper, who set the jug down and grasped for a napkin. She reached over the table to help dab at Blair's face, tipping her wine goblet in the process—but quick with his reflexes, Edan snatched it and uprighted it before more than a few drops could fall on the table.

Blair's nostrils flared as Agnes reached for her again. "I've got it," his wife said more sharply than he'd heard before, but then she quickly softened her voice, adding. "My thanks for your attempt to help."

She wiped the wine from her face, her cheeks flaming red, poor lass.

Beneath the table, he squeezed her knee, hoping to ease her

worries, but she jerked toward him, seeming surprised at his show of comfort.

"Do ye want to wash your face, lass? I will tell them to wait in serving supper."

"Nay," she hurried. "I dinna want to make anyone wait for me. Besides, ye said yourself how hungry ye were. I'll be fine. I've wiped it good enough for now."

"If ye're certain?"

She dragged in a long sigh, blinked her eyes a few times, as if trying to find the answer. "Aye. I'm certain."

"At any time, ye just give me the word, and I will take ye upstairs."

Blair nodded, a tight smile on her face.

Mo chreach, but the lass was having a troubled time of it today. If anything else were to happen, he wouldn't be surprised if she sent a missive to her da to come and get her, just as Connor's wife had.

Edan signaled for the meal to be served, and as the trenchers came to the table, he took his time choosing the choicest cut of meat for his wife, and the thickest slice of bread. She wrinkled her nose, however, and he realized too late that the meat being served was mutton. Gritting his teeth at his error, he quickly removed the mutton from her trencher and put it on his own.

"Mrs. McQuinn," he called, "is mutton all that is being served this eve?"

"Aye, my laird. Does it not suit?"

Blair placed a hand on his arm, and when he glanced down at her, she gave a slight shake of her head.

"Is her ladyship not pleased with the meal? When she visited us in the kitchen, she said it smelled delicious."

Blair stared at the housekeeper; her expression unreadable. "A personal preference, nothing more," she said.

"Is it because we didna slaughter the one ye brought for us? I can be certain 'tis done tomorrow; we simply did not have time this afternoon."

"Nay!" Blair all but shouted at the same time he did.

"The lamb ye are referring to," Edan said, "is not to be harmed. She's a prized pet of her ladyship's."

Agnes McQuinn looked confused but nodded all the same. "I shall see if we've any leftover rabbit stew from luncheon. Will that suffice, my lady?"

"Aye," Blair nodded. "Thank ye."

He could have sworn he heard Agnes ask under her breath if her ladyship had a prized pet rabbit too, but she'd wandered off before he could ask. He supposed even if she had said it, it would do no good to call attention to it if Blair hadn't heard. He'd have to speak with the housekeeper separately to make certain she was not deliberately trying to offend his wife.

"Please, my laird," Blair said, "tell the people they can eat."

It was then he noticed the whole of the great hall staring in their direction. No one would normally eat until the laird and his lady first had a bite.

"Eat!" he said jovially.

But he would wait, even despite Blair encouraging him. "This is our first meal together as man and wife in our castle. I'll not do it alone."

A moment later, a steaming bowl of stew was brought out by Mrs. McQuinn. She smiled triumphantly. "As hoped for," she said, and had the intelligence to look at her lady with genuine pleasure, which of course pleased him.

She set the bowl down on the table exuberantly and it tipped forward, spilling a stream of brown broth over the lip of the bowl, onto the wood of the table and into Blair's lap. Despite her leaping back out of the way, the broth rained down on the lap of her gown like a waterfall.

"Oh, dear me, not again," wailed Agnes.

Blair flashed angry eyes on the woman, which were quickly shuttered, and her frown was replaced by a bitter smile. "'Tis quite all right." She took her napkin, already stained with wine, and dabbed at the ruined gown.

"My laird." Agnes turned pleading eyes on Edan. "I swear 'twas an accident. I am so sorry. To think in all my years working in fine households, I've never had so many accidents in a year as I've had today." She dropped to her knees; hands clasped as if in prayer. "Please forgive me."

"Stand." Edan had no choice but to believe her. "I'm certain my wife will agree that ye're simply overcome with having a new lady present. All is forgiven but see to it yourself that her gown is washed clean on the morrow."

"Aye, I will." She crossed her hands over her heart and scurried away.

Blair sat motionless, her face red and her lips thinned and white. She was clearly furious.

"I dinna think she did it apurpose," he murmured, settling his hand on her leg once more. "But if we find out she did, ye'll have first hold of the flog to her back."

"Aye, ye're probably right." Blair's tone was quite clearly filled with cynicism. She glanced down toward her bowl. "I've no spoon, but if we call her back, she might hit me on the head with it."

Edan chuckled, squeezed her leg gently again, and motioned one of the cupbearers forward. "A spoon for my lady wife."

"Aye, my laird."

A moment later, spoon in hand, Blair was eating, and so did he. He watched the way she delicately brought the spoon to her lips, taking the smallest of bites. She pulled small hunks of bread and dipped it in the broth, eating that as well. However, she did not finish, and sat back in her seat with a hand to her belly when her bowl was not even halfway eaten.

"Was it not pleasing, sweetling?"

She grimaced. "Aye, verra delicious. I am simply full."

"Shall I escort ye upstairs?" *Mo chreach, please say aye.*

"I think I should like a moment of privacy." Her face had taken on a paler shade.

She was worried about the marriage bed. *Dammit.* He'd no experience with comforting virgins, but he would do his best to ease her worry. Perhaps a few moments alone, and then he would show her she had nothing to fear and only pleasure to look forward to. Well, after the initial bite of pain, and he would do his damndest to make certain it was over quickly.

He took her hand in his and brought it to his lips, kissing her softly. "I'll be along shortly, my love."

"Take your time." She stood, her face going another shade paler, and then she hurried from the great hall as though the Devil were on her heels.

Ballocks, but he felt like a monster. His bride was fairly fleeing from him.

❦

BLAIR BARELY MADE it to her chamber before she threw herself toward the chamber pot in the lady's room and vomited everything she'd sipped and eaten at supper. She heaved and heaved until the muscles of her stomach hurt, and then she heaved some more, until she felt she would die from the pain of it. She fell weakly to the floor and curled in a ball. She shivered at the stabbing within her gut and sucked in heady breaths of air, praying Edan would not come up yet. When at last the cramping in her belly subsided enough that she could move, she rolled onto her back and used the skirt of her ruined gown to wipe at her face.

The stew had not tasted bad, but clearly, it had not agreed with her.

Oh, she was so very glad she'd made it back to the chamber before she made a mess of herself in front of everyone. Good God, the way her husband had looked at her, like he wanted to kiss her, as she was trying to hold in the contents of her stomach.

She flopped an arm over her eyes and drew in a shuddering breath. Any moment, he was going to be up here to take her to bed, and here she was, ill on the floor.

A soft knock sounded on the outer chamber. Blair did not invite whoever it was inside, for if it had been her husband, she was certain he would have simply strolled in. She rolled to her side again and stared at the two trunks that had been brought in from their journey but had yet to be put away. The chests did not hold all of her things, but they did hold everything she'd brought with her to Castle Ross.

"My lady?"

Blair recognized the voice of Agnes McQuinn. She pushed up to sitting, feeling another wave of nausea roll over her. She wanted to slam the door in the fetid woman's face. She'd done all of those things on purpose. Blair was no fool, even if her husband was oblivious. Of course, he knew nothing of what had happened earlier in the day to lend credence to the truth. Why hadn't she told him? But even as she asked the question, she knew the answer. The man had enough to worry over trying to solve his brother's murder. He need not be bothered with petty problems.

The housekeeper came in, took one look at the chamber pot and clucked her tongue.

"My lady, are ye unwell?"

Blair glowered up at her, the accusation that the woman had tampered with the stew on the tip of her tongue. But it had not tasted bad, and the illness could be a result of nerves and exhaustion, or even an ague from her cold bath, so she kept her mouth shut.

"I came to gather the gown and get ye ready for bed myself, seeing as how ye've no maid quite yet." Agnes wrung her hands in front of her and actually looked contrite. "I must offer my sincerest apology, my lady, for our earlier conversation and my blunders at supper."

"And my bath?"

"Your bath?" She had the nerve to look confused.

"Never mind, ye know what ye did." Oh dear heavens, she gagged again, but nothing came out.

"Please, I beg ye, forgive an old woman for her blunders." Agnes was hardly old, only maybe ten or so more years older than Blair herself. "I promise to make it up to ye. By this time tomorrow, ye'll be singing my praises."

"Ye're bold to think so," Blair muttered, allowing Agnes to help her to her feet. She swayed and unfortunately had to cling to the wretch.

"I'll take good care of ye," Agnes murmured.

And surprisingly, she did. She helped Blair into a night rail, brushed out her hair, gave her a rinse for her mouth and wiped down her face with sweet-smelling water from where the wine had splashed.

"Her ladyship here afore ye loved this herbal rose water for her face. What say ye?"

"'Tis verra pleasant."

Agnes clucked her tongue again. "Good. I shall make certain ye've plenty."

The housekeeper was, it would seem, trying to mend the ill start they'd had. 'Haps she'd realized her antics at supper had been a bit too much, enough so that Blair could cause a stink that got her dismissed.

In any case, it was nice to be pampered. It reminded Blair how much she missed her mother. Agnes tucked her into bed and Blair was so exhausted she didn't argue that it wasn't Edan's bed. Through a foggy haze, she heard Agnes greet her husband in the solar adjoining their two chambers.

⚜

THIS WAS ALL TOO EASY, truly. How simple it will be to place the blame on someone else. Goodness, they are making it entirely too simple. All of them. Idiots.

And this wee brat... Ha! She is an embarrassment to all women, thinking she's one of us. I should have put more of my specialty into her stew. Let her retch a little longer.

It makes me laugh that the laird has taken so long to figure out nothing. Perhaps I'll add him to my list, too. But in the meantime, I've others to frame, and someone else to kill.

She hid her smile as she slipped out of sight and back to her sleeping quarters. Once there, she reached beneath her cot, where she found a very special jar painted black as tar, the color of death and her dreams.

CHAPTER 16

The sound of Edan's boots on her bedroom floor echoed in the chamber, waking Blair. She'd lain abed for over day but felt much recuperated now.

"Ye're awake." He smiled down at her as he entered her chamber.

Blair propped up on one elbow and fidgeted nervously with the cuff of her night rail.

"How are ye feeling now?" He came close to the bed and pressed the back of his hand to her forehead. His brow was wrinkled as he looked down at her. "Ye dinna feel feverish anymore."

"I'm feeling much better actually." And that was the truth of it. She'd been able to purge whatever had caused her stomach upset, along with the rest of her stomach contents the day before, and the night before that, and rested without issue all night long, and throughout this morning. Agnes had brought her some porridge, and an herbal tea that made her feel divine. She'd had a bath—warm this time—and then gone back to bed for a small nap.

"What do ye think caused it? Was it the food?" The latter he asked quite slowly, as if the notion only dawned on him as the words came out.

She bit her lip and felt her face flush, not wanting to implicate anyone if it weren't the case, for Agnes had been so kind to her, and the woman was already skating on thin ice with their laird. "Perhaps it was only nerves."

"Ah," he said softly and sat down beside her on the bed. "Ye need not be afraid of me, lass."

"I'm not afraid of ye."

"That is good." A small smile curled his lips. "I thought 'haps your nerves about...the bedding sent ye rushing off, until ye gained a fever and remained abed all day yesterday."

"I'm not afraid of the...bedding." The way he spoke it was almost the answer she needed to know whether they'd lain together before.

"I promise I will be as gentle as I can be with ye, lass."

She yearned to lean into him, to feel the press of his lips on hers. "I have no doubt." Then before she lost her nerve, she rushed out, "Did we...at Castle Ross, after the feast..."

He chuckled and tapped her on the tip of her nose. "Ye passed out like a drunken shepherd, sweetling, and so I put ye to bed."

"Oh." She breathed a sigh of relief. "I thought mayhap I was a terrible wife for not remembering."

Edan leaned in close to her, his gray gaze locking on hers. "Trust me when I say, when we lay together, it will not be something ye forget."

A flutter started in her belly and worked its way upward, causing her breasts to feel heavy and ache. So strange the way her body reacted to him. And how very much she liked it.

He leaned forward and brushed his lips on hers. "I'm sorry. I should leave ye to rest. Ye're only just recovered and must be exhausted."

But she suddenly felt very much alive, and the only flutters in her belly now were of anticipation. "Nay... I want to... I want to go to your bed."

"We could stay here." He traced his fingers along the length of her arm, and gooseflesh rose in the wake of his touch. "Seeing as how ye're already abed."

The lightness of her night rail had her feeling very exposed, nearly naked. She was very much aware of his strength so close, and how he could rend the fabric with one tug. Oh, the thought of it sent a shiver racing from her breasts to the point between her legs, and she shuddered.

"Ye're not well. Ye're shivering." His brow wrinkled again, and he tucked the blankets closer around her.

"'Tis not from feeling unwell, Husband. Just the opposite."

She thought the slow grin that curled his lips appeared very primal, indeed. His gray gaze singed her flesh. She had no idea what exactly he was thinking, as her experience in the bedchamber was nonexistence. But that look—and the promises it made—had her heart skipping a beat, and heat thrumming in her limbs.

"Then with your permission…" He tugged at the laces of her night rail.

"Ye're my husband; ye need not ask permission."

"I will all the same, from this day until death do us part." His voice was low, gravelly, sensual, and his breath skated over the skin he bared slowly to his view.

He tugged the laces of her night rail open, exposing her chest all the way down to the center of her stomach, though her breasts were still barred from view by just a few inches of thin fabric. Her breath came faster, and the heated rake of his eyes was as sensual as his light caress. She had the sudden rush of a thought that she *wanted* him to expose her flesh; she *wanted* him to see her fully naked. To touch her.

He leaned in again and captured her lips softly. The kiss was gentle at first, just a slide of his lips over hers. He tasted of whisky and spice and smelled of the fresh outdoors and leather. He licked along the seam of her lips and slipped inside when she parted them, curling the length of his tongue over hers. Slick velvet heat caressed her. Goodness, but she was losing her breath altogether. She touched her tongue to his, her heart pounding as she recalled just the way she'd kissed him in the tent. She sank into him as he touched her, laying featherlight strokes on her hair, her neck, her shoulders. He reached around the back of her, sliding his fingers down her spine and shoulder blades. Then he traced a path from her shoulders to her elbows, swirling in the creases before following the downward path to her hands, where he laced his fingers in hers. That simple act of holding hands was so incredibly sensual, Blair thought she'd never be able to do so again without first thinking of his kiss.

He brought their joined hands up to his shoulders, unlaced their fingers, rested hers there and then took hold of her waist and pulled her even closer to him. The fabric of her night rail dipped open, and a rush of air touched the skin that had yet to be exposed, and then the rougher fabric of his *leine* was pressed to her chest, and she swore he could probably feel her heart beating against his own.

Edan lifted one of her legs, placing it over his lap and causing her shift to rise up over her thigh. If their faces weren't locked in a kiss, she was certain he would see the dark curls between her thighs. The very idea of him looking at her there sent a swirl of nerves racing through her. At the same time, it sent a frisson of yearning to that very central point.

He slid a hand up her leg and over her knee, pausing there to draw light circles that made her gasp. No man had ever seen her bare leg, let alone touched her. When she'd thought about the marriage bed, she hadn't believed it could be so...*tantalizing*. Edan touched her everywhere, stroking, igniting something inside her that was powerful and overwhelming.

When his fingers shifted upward, skating over her inner thigh, she made a move to clamp her legs closed, which was impossible since she was on his lap. .

"'Tis all right," he murmured against her lips, and then his fingers were delving higher and sweeping gently over the damp curls that hid her woman's flesh, and she found herself scooting closer—*wanting more.*

She suddenly desired his touch on her most intimate parts... Goodness, but it was...intoxicating. He slid the pad of one finger over her folds, touching a sensitive knot of flesh that made her gasp with pleasure. He stroked again, around in a circle, over and over until she could barely breathe. His tongue dove into her mouth, teasing the tip of her tongue before retreating and swirling in the same rhythm as his finger.

Blair tightened her hold around his neck and held on as he swept her up into clouds of pleasure. And then, with the pad of his thumb still stroking that hot little bud, he dipped another of his fingers inside her just the barest of an inch. More pleasure spurred her toward something. She wasn't certain toward what, but she knew she needed more of it. Her hips tucked forward in silent plea, and his fingers inched deeper and then out, swirling wetness over her folds. Oh, this was so very wicked, she was certain. What was he doing? Why did she crave more?

His fingers worked magic on her, stroking, dipping, teasing, pleasuring. And like the wanton she was certain she was, Blair lapped it up with every stroke of her tongue on his.

She cried out when her body burst into a thousand shards of decadent bliss, and she clung to him, both surprised and eager for more.

"Aye, lass," he murmured against her lips. "That's it. Let go."

Oh, gone she was. Her breasts were tender, nipples aching points, and between her thighs was pulsing and slick, and although she'd just experienced the pinnacle of pleasure, she greedily wanted more.

Edan laid her gently back on the bed at the same time he undid his belt and wrenched the fabric of his plaid away. He hooked her knees over his arms and guided them to wrap around his waist. The very heat of his hard body touched to her center, and she gasped in shock and pleasure.

"I want ye, lass. I want ye so bad..."

Lips pressed to her neck, he murmured of her beauty, the silkiness of her skin. He skimmed kisses over her collarbone and her breasts, flicking his tongue over her nipples.

Blair moaned softly, arching her back. The same pleasure, the same need she'd felt with his fingers on her built, however impossible it seemed. And then he was kissing her again, rubbing the heat of his hard body against her, sliding the tip of his arousal against her. She'd not even seen what it looked like, but she could feel it, hard and hot pressed to her center.

And then he was pressing forward, his hands gripping her buttocks as he lifted her and thrust inside.

Pain erupted, and she cried out at the invasion of his body into hers. Fingers dug into his shoulders; eyes wide. He'd said it would hurt, and he'd not lied. How could something that was so pleasurable moments ago feel so... She wiggled beneath him, trying to ease the feeling of fullness inside her, and Edan groaned.

"Please, lass, dinna move. I'm so sorry." His forehead fell to hers, his tongue flicking over her lip before he captured her for a kiss that made her forget about the pain.

Blair remained still as he instructed, trying to ignore the discomfort, to find pleasure once more in his kiss. Which she did...quickly forgetting anything but pleasure. When he started to move, slowly at first, she continued to remain still, but there was pleasure in his movements, made greater when she lifted her hips to meet his thrusts.

Saints, but she liked the delicious sensations of his body sliding in and out of hers. The bed creaked with his movements, muffling the sounds of their bodies' slickness, and drowned out only by their groans and pants of pleasure.

"*Mo chreach*," he groaned against her ear. "I canna wait."

Instinctively, she knew what he meant. He wanted that burst of pleasure that had knocked the breath from her before, too.

"Aye," she answered, wanting to hear him find his pleasure.

His pace quickened, and when he cried out, his entire body seemed to shudder over her. Blair smiled into the crook of his shoulder. Pleased she could give him the same pleasure he'd given her.

When the shudders of his body subsided, he rolled away from her, went to the wash basin and dipped a cloth into the leftover rose water. He brought it back to the bed and slid it between her thighs, which still pulsed.

She shivered, surprised her body still wanted more.

"Lass...that was beautiful," he murmured, pressing her thighs apart. "But I fear I finished too soon."

"Nay, it was beautiful, as ye said."

He grinned. "But ye didna find your pleasure a second time."

"Neither did ye."

He winked down at her. "My wife shall find hers twice."

"What?" she whispered, as he slid lower on the bed and pressed his mouth to where he'd just washed her.

Blair nearly came off the bed as the heat of his tongue stroked over her pulsing flesh, and the sensations he'd created in her a moment ago came to life once more.

"Delicious," he crooned against her flesh as he tasted her, devoured her.

Blair bowed her back, legs fallen open and hands thrust in his hair as he brought her once more to that place where she knew not breath or heartbeat, only rapture.

BEFORE DAWN HAD a chance to sneak her pink light through the fur skin covering his wife's window, Edan reluctantly dragged himself from her bed. It was an effort to disentangle her warm limbs from his, and she made a soft whimper of protest before rolling over and curling up in sleep once more.

As much as he wanted to stay abed, there was much work to be done since he'd been gone. A missive had arrived from the king requesting the prisoners he'd been holding be transported to Stirling. The king would discern if they were involved with the other syco-phants from the former Ross clan, fighting for their laird and assassi-nating leaders aligned with the Bruce. It would appear his brother was not the only one to have been murdered.

And so, after washing and dressing, Edan took one last look at the bride who had surprised the hell out of him and left the chamber. He needed to round up his prisoners and he needed a message delivered to Liam Sutherland, who was also working on clearing his name. The Sutherlands needed to know that the ring of traitors extended far beyond what they'd originally thought.

CHAPTER 17

S un filtered through the bedchamber window, and Blair smiled as she stretched, eyes still closed as she relived some of the moments from the night before. Edan had been so gentle with her and seen to her pleasure again and again. Either he was special, or women tended to keep secret how wonderful the marriage bed could be.

Now she understood the looks she'd seen Cora giving Liam, and the way her own sisters stared at their husbands. Her whole body ached, but not in a way she didn't like. And any of the sickness she'd felt before Edan had come to her chamber was completely gone.

She sat up, tossed back the covers and blanched.

A red stain marred the sheets from their lovemaking. Her virgin's blood.

Embarrassed, she made quick work of stripping the bed and balling up the linens. One of the maids would still likely see the evidence of their consummation, but at least not so blatantly on display.

Blair shivered in the drafty chamber. She'd not needed a fire to warm their chilly room the night before, because the heat they'd created together had been plenty. But without Edan's big, warm body surrounding her, the draft in the room overpowered her. She tiptoed over to the hearth and was going to light the fire when she realized she'd be better off simply dressing and going down to where there was an even larger fire in the great hall's hearth to break her fast.

She washed quickly, truly enjoying the scented water Agnes had left in the basin...and then she shivered. Not from cold, however, but from the scent of the floral water drawing her memory back to the night before, when Edan had pressed his mouth to the very heat of her.

Just the thought of it had frissons of need coursing through her and pinning her in place. Her nipples tightened, and she shivered. Aye, that was incredible.

Who'd have thought that the Blair who followed the rules and did everything she was supposed to, Blair the Peacemaker, would also be Blair the Lusty Bride.

She chuckled to herself and then brushed out the knots in her hair created from the friction of her head moving against the mattress as they'd made love. She replaited it, tied it off with a pretty blue ribbon and then opened her trunks to pull out a gown.

But the trunks were empty, filled only with an extra pair of boots, several chemises and her cloak.

She frowned and moved to the wardrobe, where she found her gowns all hanging, save the one that needed to be cleaned. She dressed quickly in a light blue gown, wishing she had a strip of Rose plaid to tie in the center. She'd have to make certain to get some later.

Descending the stairs, she passed two maids heading up to the bedchambers to clean. They gave her surreptitious looks, whispered something and hurried past.

Blair frowned. It sounded very much like they'd just called her a "whore." But how could that be? She had to have heard wrong. Of course she'd misheard; there was no way on this earth they would call her such, because she wasn't, and also because of the extreme disrespect such an insult presented.

In the great hall, Edan was nowhere to be found. Given that his side of the bed had been cold that morning, she guessed he'd long since broken his fast, before getting to work on his laird's duties.

Her stomach growled, but it did not appear that breakfast was being served, else she'd already missed it. She headed toward the kitchens, planning to grab a crust of bread and try again with Cook and those present. She was determined to make this work, for them all to get along as well as her mother did with her own kitchen help. But inside, the servants eyed her with suspicion and what looked like censure.

"Good morn," Blair offered, smiling warmly.

Only one smiled back and was quickly elbowed by Cook who stood beside her.

"Might I have a bite to eat?"

"Breakfast has already been served," Cook said. "We serve it when the laird wakes."

Blair was taken aback. Had the cook really just refused to give her something to eat? Perhaps they thought she expected to be served in the great hall. She continued to smile, hiding her shock. "'Tis all right. I dinna need to be served. I'm plenty capable of serving myself."

"As we know," someone muttered. "*Whore.*"

Blair whipped to the right, certain now that she had heard what they whispered. Her face grew red with embarrassment. Had they heard her and Edan making love the night before? That seemed the only reasonable notion for such an insult. Suddenly, what she and Edan had shared felt shameful. She swallowed around the lump in her throat and forced herself to speak. "Beg your pardon?" Her voice was calm, though it held an underlying note of steel.

"We know why ye married our laird," piped up the woman who'd called her a whore so outright.

She was young, perhaps even younger than Blair herself. Pretty, with freckles around her cheeks, and her hair the color of freshly churned earth. Her lips, however, were not pretty and formed a sneer that had the power to turn her whole face ugly.

"Ye carry his babe. Gave yourself to him afore ye were wed."

"Aye, we'll not serve a whore."

"Soon enough, the laird will see ye for what ye are."

Hateful words came at her from all sides.

Blair narrowed her eyes. Why on earth would they think that?

Then she knew—the night before when she'd been sick, Agnes must have assumed it was because she was pregnant. All of them must have thought as much.

Well, they would know soon enough when they saw the sheets. Now she wished she'd left them proudly on the bed, brandishing her a maiden until last night.

Agnes came into the kitchen then, clucking her tongue and the words of the scullions ceased. "What's this?" Her voice was sharp in the direction of the servants. "Dinna criticize our laird's choice in a wife. Besides, the bairn will be born legitimate. And we canna starve the laird's bairn." Agnes reached into a basket and produced two bannocks. "Here. One for ye and one for your bairn."

Tears threatened the backs of her eyes, stinging. Agnes, who'd seemed so kind the night before, who'd said she wanted to turn a new leaf, was behind these rumors? Even now as she held out freshly baked bannocks in Blair's direction, she had the nerve to smile sweetly.

Without a word, Blair whirled from the kitchen and fled their vile slurs and the offer of food. As she rushed toward her chamber, she could hear their laughter and knew Agnes was indeed no friend of hers. Every cutting remark sliced into her chest. What had she done to deserve such anger? Such hatred? Who were these women to think they could treat her that way? Had they treated the last laird's wife so cruelly?

How was she going to survive this?

Up in her chamber, Blair fought tears as she paced the solar, fists clenched at her sides.

"My lady?" A chamber maid around Blair's own age stepped out from her bedchamber, the sheets clasped in her arms. "Are ye all right?"

The lass looked genuinely concerned, her warm brown eyes welcoming as she gazed on her.

"Should I get his lairdship?" she prodded, setting down the bundle of sheets.

"What is your name?" Blair asked.

"Willa, my lady."

Blair regarded the sheets and nodded toward them. Willa's gaze followed hers, a slight blush coloring her skin. The proof she was no whore was right there.

"Ye didna have to strip the bed, my lady. 'Tis my job."

Blair sucked in a shuddering breath, trying to force her emotions at bay. All her life, she'd longed to belong. To find a place, to find herself, and just when she thought she could start anew, to truly be herself, she was running from the shame of what people would make her into.

Willa cast her gaze toward the ground. "Are ye in need of...women's linens, my lady?"

Ah, so she thought the blood on the sheets was from her monthly.

"Nay, last night...we... I...," Blair's voice wobbled. It wasn't as though she could come right out and say that she'd been a maiden until last night.

"There was blood..." Willa's voice trailed off, and then her mouth formed an "O" and she glanced at Blair in understanding. "Och, I see." She beamed a smile, and again Blair was taken aback by a friendly face.

Was this going to be a trick as Agnes's show of warmth last evening had been?

"Begging your pardon, my lady, but I am ever so pleased," she gushed. "I knew what they were saying couldna be true."

That was enough to make Blair want to cry all over again.

"I'm in need of a lady's maid," Blair said. "I dinna want to interfere with your duties as chamber maid, but if they can spare ye, I would like to offer ye the position."

Willa gasped and dropped into a curtsy. "My ma would be so proud, and I'd be honored."

"Who is your mother?" Blair asked, praying it wasn't Agnes.

"She's gone now to her maker," Willa explained. "But she was the housekeeper here before she took ill."

"Oh. When was that?"

"Around the time the old laird married a year or so ago. She brought several of her own staff with her, and Mrs. McQuinn was one of them. She's been housekeeper ever since and endeared herself to everyone."

"It is uncommon to have a housekeeper in the keep who has not always been a clanswoman, is it not?" Blair asked, knowing the answer already.

"Aye, but the servants love her, and it was her ladyship's request."

"Why didna Agnes return with the lady when she went home?"

"She begged his lairdship to stay. Said she'd found more of a home here at Kilravock than she ever had with her own clan. She married one of the laird's men, too, ye see. Taking his last name."

"Ah." And those words could be true. Agnes seemed to have formed quite a band of servants, mostly women, clinging to her every word and directive. Enough so that they were willing to torment their own lady.

But perhaps she had not gotten her claws into one—and if Blair could gain an ally in the old housekeeper's daughter, she just might be able to turn things around for herself here.

"Willa, it seems I've not gotten as good a start here as I would have liked. I need someone I can trust."

Willa's eyes widened, and she nodded. "I know it, my lady. And I swear to ye, I was not part of any of the tricks that have been had on ye."

"That is good to know."

"I will talk with the others. 'Twill not bode well for them to go against the mistress of the castle."

"Ye need not say too much yet. Agnes seems the sort who will only gloat in knowing I'm fully aware of her intentions to sabotage me." Blair walked toward the window of the solar and stared out at the landscape, wondering if she'd catch a glimpse of her husband training. "I'd rather know what Agnes hopes to gain. I am married to the laird, and our marriage canna be annulled. Ye've the evidence there in your hands. I'm not a... I'm not what they say I am."

"And I'll be sure they know that. But beyond that, I will try and figure out any plots against ye."

Blair let out a long sigh. "Thank ye, Willa." She didn't want to voice any of her other concerns. But she'd be a fool not to think there was something quite nefarious in Agnes' plan to disrupt the household.

It felt personal, as though Agnes wanted to hurt her, and Blair couldn't for the life of her figure out why. What she did know, instinctively, was that she needed to watch her back.

"Oh, and my lady, have ye yet told your husband?"

Blair shook her head. "I know I should, but he's already got so much to worry over with the death of his brother and becoming laird."

"Aye, but he could help ye."

"Ye dinna think he will be upset, and believe that I've been causing trouble?"

"Och, nay. But if ye want, I can tell my brother, and have him relay it to Edan."

"Aye, perhaps coming from Raibert, it will be better received."

She felt foolish, but one of the reasons she'd been so nervous to tell Edan herself was that she worried over whether or not he'd just think her a troublemaker. After all, they'd met under circumstances which though weren't her fault, theoretically, she was responsible.

"What a mess," she murmured.

Willa patted her on the back. "Dinna fash, my lady. We'll get it all sorted out."

⚜

EDAN'S SWORD clashed against Raibert's in the field. They were covered in slick sweat, their *leines* long since removed, leaving them to fight in their trews like most of the other warriors.

But Edan's heart was not in it. He found his gaze wondering back to the keep, and his thoughts sliding toward the night ahead with his beautiful bride. *Mo chreach*, but he wanted to call an end to the training so he could go back to their bedchamber and worship her body all over again.

"My laird," Raibert asked, a bit of humor in his voice. "I nearly took your other eye out just now."

Edan stilled. "I've a lot on my mind."

"Might it have to do with your wife?" Raibert frowned.

"Aye."

"I heard what the ladies did to her. Willa was quite distraught over it last night."

Willa was Raibert's sister. They shared the croft that had been their parents before they died, and now the two of them kept it up. Their mother had been the housekeeper all of Edan's life, until she'd passed some time a year or two before, just after their father had fallen in a skirmish.

Raibert's words sank in then, and Edan frowned. "What are ye talking about?"

"She didna tell ye?" Raibert stabbed his sword into the earth and Edan did the same.

"Tell me what?"

"The cold bath. The rude comments."

Edan shot a glance toward the keep towering over the castle walls. Anger heated in his chest. What the bloody hell was Raibert saying? "Her bath was cold?"

"Aye. And Willa's fairly certain Mrs. McQuinn spilled things on your lady wife apurpose."

"Why would she do that?" Edan's grip tightened on the hilt of his sword.

"Willa doesna lie."

"I'm not accusing her, Raibert. I only want to know why she thinks these things happened?"

"I dinna know. She was marching about the croft last night, and I could barely get a word in." Raibert wiped the sweat from his brow.

Edan tugged the sword from the earth. "Why did ye wait so long to tell me?"

Raibert held up his hands in surrender. "I thought ye knew."

Edan's frown deepened, and he pointed the tip at the man and then jabbed it back hard into the ground. "I didna." Why didn't Blair tell him her bath had been cold? Did she prefer cold baths? If the women had been unwelcoming, cruel even, to his wife... Why had she put up with it without telling him?

Saints, but did she think he didn't care? After all, last night he'd told her he didn't think that Agnes had spilled the stew on purpose.

And then there was the mix up with Bluebell, which he now believed to have been malicious.

"Will ye take over from here? I need to go and see my wife."

"Aye, my laird. We'll not expect to see ye again until the morrow," Raibert teased, which sent up a raucous bit of bawdy jesting amongst the other men.

Edan would have grinned at the newly wedded jest, but he was too angry. Then he realized that for the first time, the men were all working together cohesively and treating him as their laird, so he tossed back at them, "Dinna come knocking, lads. Leave sustenance at the door."

With his men laughing and cheering behind him, Edan marched back up to the castle, not bothering to put his shirt back on. He had one thought only—making sure Blair was all right.

His wife wasn't in the great hall or kitchen, and she wasn't in their shared rooms either. He did find her, however, with Bluebell in the stable, which was perhaps the first place he should have looked.

She glanced up at him, startled. Her gaze skimmed over his bare chest, and a flush of color rose in her cheeks. Was she remembering the first time she'd seen him like this, when she'd snuck into his tent? Lord, she was beautiful sitting in the hay with her wee lamb. A rush of emotion welled in his chest, a strong desire to protect her. Just as he had then.

"Edan," she murmured. "I didna expect to see ye until later this evening."

"We need to talk, lass."

Her eyes widened, and she looked surprised. "All right."

He held out his hand to her and tugged her to her feet. "Let us walk."

"Would ye mind if we brought Bluebell?"

He smiled down at the lamb, rubbing her head as she leaned against his leg like a hound. "Nay."

He took Blair's hand in his as she attached a leading string to her pet. They left the stable and headed for the gate and out to the River Nairn, just a short walk away. Trees lined the water, providing shade and some modest privacy. The water lapped softly at the shore, grasses waved in a gentle wind and birds chirped from the branches of the trees. He'd come here often as a lad, tossing rocks into the water with his brother. Swimming. Fishing. There were fond memories here that he hoped to someday share with his own bairns.

Bluebell munched on some flowers, one of which Edan plucked and offered to Blair before she could chew it up. "She wanted ye to have this," he teased.

Blair laughed and tucked the yellow flower behind her ear.

"How are ye...adjusting?" he asked, hoping she would tell him all that had gone on.

Edan studied her face. The smile from a second ago faded, and her eyes dulled as she looked out toward the water. The forlorn curl to her lips was a punch to the gut. "As well as anyone can in a new place, I suppose."

He didn't doubt Raibert's trust in his sister, but Edan hadn't known Willa enough to say whether or not what she'd said was true. However, seeing the way Blair's shoulders had slumped now had him believing.

"And the servants," he hedged. "Are they being welcoming?"

Her gaze shuttered completely then, and she sucked in her lower lip, but not before he saw it tremble.

"Blair," he murmured, pulling her in for an embrace and putting his arms around her . With her face tipped up, he locked his gaze on hers. "I would know if they are nay treating ye well."

"Willa has been verra kind to me. I offered her a place as my lady's maid."

He smiled, swiping gently at one of her tears. "Good. She was verra concerned about ye. Told her brother Raibert some things last night that have me concerned, too. Have the other servants been cruel to ye?"

She drew in a ragged breath, her body giving a slight tremble. She'd kept so many pent-up emotions. "Some have, but I dinna know why."

Anger lanced him anew, and if he hadn't been holding her, trying to ease her ache, he would have marched into the bailey sword drawn and demanded satisfaction. "I will see that it stops."

"I dinna want to cause a fuss," she said, her fingers splaying across his bare chest and making his heart skip a beat. "I think it must be hard for them to get used to a new mistress so soon."

"They dinna need to get used to ye, lass. They need to treat ye with respect. By playing tricks or spewing unkind words, they dishonor ye and me, and our clan."

She pressed her cheek to his chest. "I want them to like me."

"I dinna know how they couldna. Ye're the kindest, sincerest lass I've ever met. They are fools not to like ye."

"I dinna recall my sisters having this issue. Even Cora seems to be having an easier time of it."

"I'll speak with them."

"I dinna want ye to solve my problems for me, Edan. I want to solve them myself."

"I can well understand that, lass."

"Please dinna say anything just yet."

He ground his teeth, unable to make that promise. It was in his nature to protect, and she was his wife. If he didn't do something about it, he'd be a monster. Yet he understood her desire to gain the respect of the women herself, rather than because they were forced into it.

"We'll do it your way for now, lass, but if I dinna see improvement by tomorrow's eve, or if I witness any other blunders as at supper last night, I'll have words with them."

Blair pressed her lips right over his heart and kissed him. The heat of her mouth on his bare skin was enough to make him groan inside, and his body was instantly alert to her presence. Her floral scent, the soft brush of her hair against his wrist where her plait fell down her back. The curves of her body pressed to his. Her breath on his skin.

He tilted her head up, kissed her thoroughly, hungrily, and would have laid her down on the grass right then and there and made love to her had Bluebell not taken that moment to attempt to make a snack out of Blair's gown.

Blair shrieked in surprise as the sheep gnawed on her gown with innocent eyes. With a laugh, his wife tugged her skirt from her lamb's mouth and examined the damage. There was only a wearing in the fabric where the lamb's teeth had grinded against the wool.

"She is jealous," Blair said, winking at her husband in a way that stole his breath. She was also always so serious; when she became playful, she was stunning.

"Aye," he chuckled, then more seriously added, "What can I do to make up for the unpleasantness that has been your start at Kilravock?"

Besides beat some sense into the clan. He'd thought he was going to have a hard time fitting in, being laird, filling the vast shoes his brother had left behind. He'd never even thought that his wife would have to do the same. Had Lady Mary, his brother's wife, dealt with the same? She'd left in such a hurry, he wasn't certain they'd spoken more than a few words, and certainly not enough for him to get an idea from it.

Edan knew war and he knew protecting, but he was not so educated in politics and the inner workings of a clan, or women for that matter. He supposed he could try and rule them as he did his men in the Bruce's army.

Some of the things he'd established at Stirling had been initiated here thus far, such as breakfast before dawn, followed by correspondence and then training until the nooning.

They started back to the keep, hand in hand. A loud gurgling sound came from the direction of her midsection, and Blair glanced at him, her cheeks turning bright red.

"Was that your stomach?" he asked.

"Aye," she said miserably. "I was abed when they served breakfast."

"Ye still could have eaten."

She shrugged. "'Tis almost the nooning. I can wait." She stroked his arm. "Honestly, 'tis nothing."

Edan studied her a moment, but she gave off no appearance of distress. He leaned a little closer. "How are ye feeling this morn?"

Her cheeks turned a deeper shade of red, but a soft smile covered her lips as she kept her gaze on the ground while they walked. "Perfectly well. Not a moment of sickness at all. I think it was but a touch of nerves and the food disagreeing with me."

"I am glad to hear it." He tipped her chin toward him. "And from making love?"

She tripped over her skirt then, and he caught her up in his arms. She was so flushed he wondered if it was a fever. Ballocks, but he was a monster! The lass should be in bed resting.

"Perhaps ye are nay well after all, sweetling. I should not have taken ye to bed... *Mo chreach*, but I hope ye can forgive me."

She laughed and patted his shoulders. "I am perfectly well. I merely tripped in shock."

"Hmm." He wasn't certain her believed her, but he didn't want to argue the fact. All the same, he wasn't about to overexert her. Edan lifted her up into his arms.

"What are ye doing? I can walk."

"But I'd much rather carry ye. I canna have my wife falling at my feet. I'll get a big head."

She laughed at that, kissed his cheek and pressed her forehead to his shoulder. Edan carried her all the way to their rooms, scaring one of the servants from inside who carried a basket full of fabric, probably for laundering. He took her into his chamber, ducking beneath the doorway.

"That reminds me, Edan, I'd like to mend your shirts and hose."

"The lass has probably just taken them." He narrowed his gaze. Why would she want to repair his clothing?

"I shall request then that they allow me to do it." Her tone was matter-of-fact.

"If it pleases ye, but ye need not bother, as we have servants to complete the tasks."

"It would please me overmuch."

He settled her on his bed, loving the sight of her dark hair spread out on his clean white sheets. Images of her naked, writhing beneath him had him instantly hard. God, she was stunning, and she didn't even realize it. He would go slow, so as not to overexert her. "Speaking of clothes... I need to get ye out of yours."

She wrinkled her nose in confusion, and so Edan kissed her, dipping his tongue into her mouth to toy with hers so she understood exactly what he meant. She sighed into his kiss and pressed herself hard against him. He needed no further answer from her and swiftly covered her body with his.

"Wait," she said, her hands on his chest, her eyes filled with worry. "Does a lady do such things in the middle of the day?"

"I'm certain she does." He kissed her neck, sliding his hand beneath her skirts, her silken thighs meeting his calloused palms.

"I wouldna want any of the clan to think me...wanton." Her legs spread as she said it, and he dipped a knee between them, pressing his thigh against her warmth.

"No one would dare," he murmured, tugging on her lower lip with his teeth.

She quivered beneath him, but then suddenly, she was stiff as a board.

"What is it?" he asked.

"They will," she said firmly.

Edan pulled back to look down at her, seeing the worry etched into her features. "I will cast out anyone who dare names my wife anything other than a saint."

She bit her lip and looked on the verge of tears.

Edan rolled to the side, now even more confused than he had been before. He tugged her to her side too, so that they were facing each other.

She pressed the heels of her hands to her eyes and drew in a shuddering breath. "I'm sorry. 'Tis my duty to provide ye with heirs, and here I am worried over a bunch of nonsense."

"Lass, I wasna making love to ye because I want heirs. Aye, heirs will come, but I brought ye to bed because I want to touch ye. Because I want to hear those little sounds ye make in the back of your throat when I pleasure ye." He stroked the side of her face, hooked his fingers in one of hers and drew her hand away. "If ye truly dinna want to..."

"I do. That is the problem," she said, tears slipping down her cheeks.

"There is no shame in desiring your husband."

That seemed to calm her, and she cast her watery blue eyes at him. "Ye're right."

"I will nay force ye, and if ye're still feeling tired from yesterday…"

She relaxed, and he consigned himself to the idea of walking away from her lush body and beating the hell out of himself in the cold river to calm the heat in his own.

Suddenly, she sat up and looked down at him with a face full of determination. "This is ridiculous."

"What?"

She leapt from the bed, pacing back and forth in front of him, tangling her hand in her hair, and then tugging it free. Edan watched her, feeling even more at a loss to the workings of the female mind than ever before.

Her bright blue eyes were vibrant. "All my life, I've tried to be someone else, tried to live up to the standards everyone else had set for themselves. I'm good at most things, but I'm not great at any one thing."

"I doubt that, lass. I'm certain ye're great at anything ye set your mind to."

"See, but that's the thing, Edan. I havena set my mind to anything." She tugged on the ribbon that held her hair in a ruined plait. "Perhaps that is the problem. I've been too worried about what people think rather than doing what pleases me, what pleases ye. Mayhap, I'll just do what makes me happy."

"What makes ye happy, lass?" He was genuinely curious.

"I like helping people. Not because I think 'tis the right thing, though I do, but because I really enjoy it. And…" She came back toward the bed and knelt down beside him on the mattress with her knees tucked under her. "I like kissing ye."

"Then I say ye kiss me now, Wife, and help put me out of my misery."

She laughed at that, and then leaned down over him, her dark hair unraveling around their faces, blocking the view of the room. "With pleasure."

CHAPTER 18

They spent the rest of the day in each other's arms, discovering what made each of them gasp and sigh, until Blair was delirious with happiness and completely sated. Her limbs felt like they were made of pudding, and her cheeks were starting to hurt from grinning so much.

Her stomach growled loudly, reminding her she had yet to eat that day, and by now it was well into the middle of the night. Somehow, the day had slipped by in a wave of bliss where hunger did not exist.

"Ye're hungry. I need to feed ye after sapping all your energy." Edan drew a circle on her belly and then kissed the center.

"Will ye let me make ye something?" She bit her lip, hoping he'd say aye.

"Make me something?"

"Aye. In the kitchen."

"I didna know ye had skill with cooking." He sounded surprised, and she was pleased to show him something she was good at.

"Aye. I used to cook with my mother when she would take over the kitchens at Dunrobin."

"It would be my honor to taste whatever ye make me, lass."

"Let us not waste another minute, else I lack the energy."

Edan pulled on trews that accentuated the muscles in his rear and also outlined his manhood, which she'd finally been able to see and found herself quite enamored with. Goodness, but she loved the shape of him. The man was exquisite perfection. He didn't wear a shirt as he waited for her to dress, and she wondered if he'd put one on at all. She tossed on her gown, not bothering with a chemise. Why be formal when they would be quite alone?

"Hop on my back," he said, turning around and crouching. "I shall carry ye down the stairs in the dark so ye dinna trip on the hem of your gown."

With a laugh of delight, Blair leapt onto his back and wrapped her legs around his waist. They certainly were behaving like children, but she didn't care. She was having fun, perhaps for the first time in her life, eschewing all the mantles she'd donned and accepting herself for who she was—which she still had to discover quite a bit.

Down in the kitchen, Edan lit a candle and shooed the spit-boys from where they slept in front of the hearth out to the great hall with a promise of an extra ration in the morning. Though they had to be concerned over the laird and his wife taking over the kitchens, the lads said not one word.

Blair made quick work of finding the flour, butter, eggs, cheese and some leftover pork from the day before. She made a simple dough, rolled it out on the work table and then spread butter over it. She then cracked open the eggs into a bowl and whipped them, sprinkling them with some of the cheese she'd sliced and diced. She stole a few hunks to quell the rumbling in her stomach and pressed another to her husband's lips, grinning saucily as he took not only the cheese into his mouth but her finger.

She spread the egg mixture onto the dough, and the pork onto one side.

"Why not both sides?"

She shrugged. "This is how my mother always made it. The side without the meat was for her and my sisters and I, and the side with the meat for the men."

"Do ye nay like pork either?"

She tilted her head. "I dinna dislike it, not like mutton. But my mother doesna eat any meat, and neither does my sister, Bella. I suppose I'm somewhere in between."

"I'd be happy to share my side."

She started to roll the dough and ingredients into a long cylindrical shape. "And I'm happy to share mine."

After rolling the dough, she sliced it into sections and placed them in a pan before setting it into the hearth to cook. Edan sat on a stool watching her, eyes dipped and lazy. His gray gaze had the power to make her knees go weak, and most times she forgot all about his scarred eye. She sauntered closer to him, pushed between his spread thighs and brushed her lips on his. She stroked her thumb over the scar and pressed her lips to his brow.

"Does it ever pain ye?"

"Sometimes." His hands slid over her hips, down to her buttocks. "How long do we wait?"

"Not too long, if we're lucky."

"I know what we can do in the meantime." The gray of one eye disappeared behind a slow wink as his lips curled devilishly.

"I dinna want to leave in case it burns."

"Who said anything about leaving?"

"Oh," she breathed out, understanding dawning. He meant to make love to her right here in the kitchen. *Saints...*

Edan gave her no time to think, leaning in to kiss her fully on the mouth.

He lifted her up and placed her buttocks on the hard surface of the work table, skimming his hands up over her thighs. Oh, how very wicked this was. And how much her body yearned for him to touch her. To spread her wider and sink inside the way he had the night before. Tingles of anticipation alit her flesh. Her nipples were hard little stones, and she whimpered as she tilted her head to the side, silently begging for him to kiss her neck.

"What if someone should come in?" she panted, as he skimmed his mouth over her flesh.

"No one would dare."

And she knew this to be true. He'd dismissed them all and firmly shut the door. Anyone who entered would be doing so at their own peril.

As vast as the keep was, for as many people that had access to this particular place in the structure, right now, they appeared to be all alone.

"I've never made love in a kitchen," he murmured, his breath fanning seductively over her skin as his lips, featherlight, teased up the column of her neck to her ear. He tugged at the laces of her gown until both of her breasts were exposed to him.

"Ye willna be able to say that in just a few short minutes." Boldly, she reached between them to grip the hardness of his arousal that pressed thick with wanting against his trews.

Edan let out a low growl, his hands slipping beneath her rear as he slid her forward, closer. He spread her legs wide, hooking them over his arms. Blair's head fell back with pleasure at the carnal need and his primal prowess. With his mouth capturing hers, he made quick work of untying his trews, allowing her to grip the hot, silky length of him. The heavy weight of his velvet member in her palm was a sensation she was sure to never get enough of.

"Put me inside ye, love," he murmured against her lips.

Blair slid the plush tip of him over her slick folds, shivering at the sensual feel. As soon as she placed him at her entrance, he thrust forward, instinctively knowing that was the right spot. His shaft slid through her fingers, against her palm and deep inside of her, and when he retreated, the slickness from her body, covered his hardness.

With her legs wrapped around his hips, her mouth sliding over his again and again, she used the muscles of her belly to balance upright. When the pleasure was too intense and she could no longer concentrate on that, she held tightly to his shoulders and let him take her to heaven.

Blair cried out, her moan of pleasure stifled by his kiss, as he swallowed her passion and answered with a guttural groan of his own. Their bodies shuddered, radiating pleasure, stealing their breath.

Blair collapsed back, the flour on the table top soaking up the sweat slickened over her exposed flesh. But she didn't care. She'd just experienced earth-shattering pleasure with the man she loved.

Loved?

When had that happened?

She couldn't put her finger on it. And right then, she wasn't certain she wanted to. Because her husband was kissing his way down to her breasts, his tongue dipping out to circle each hardened nipple. He roamed lower, pressing his heated tongue between her thighs, and she was crying out with pleasure once more...

BLAIR SLEPT LATE the following morning, stretching languidly in bed, her body sated, and her mind full of hope and possibility. In the oasis of Edan's arms, the world felt right. There was no murderer trying to frame her brother for the deed, or the fear that whoever it was might go after Edan next. In his embrace, there was only delight, passion and the delicious prospect of all the future held.

This was what she'd wanted when she thought of a husband, of starting a family. Blair flattened her palm to her belly, pressing on the flesh beneath her navel to see if she could feel the little knot that Bella had showed shown her when she was first with child. She didn't feel anything yet. When did one start to feel a bairn?

She supposed it wasn't this quickly, but she couldn't wait to feel that tiny bump, to give Edan a child, to hold her own bairn in her arms and gaze into its eyes, knowing she'd given it life.

With a sigh, Blair tossed aside her covers, a grin still on her face. Edan had slept in her chamber, only slipping out before dawn with a kiss on her lips and a promise to see her later that day.

Blair checked the solar that connected their two rooms but did not see Willa. No matter, she could dress on her own. She washed up and donned a fresh chemise, then opened her wardrobe to eye the few gowns hanging inside. Today felt like a blue day. She plucked the gown that reminded her of a summer sky and stepped into it, only to find she could not pull it up over her hips. What the devil?

She gave it another tug and heard a tear as the seams fought against her. With a frown she tugged again, but the blasted fabric wouldn't budge.

Stepping out again, she tried pulling it over her head, but couldn't even get the sleeves to fit over her arms, and she ended up stuck for several moments as she struggled to remove it.

Blair stared in horror at what had been her favorite gown. It did not seem to fit her at all, as though it were never even hers. She glanced at the other gowns in her closet, and after trying each one, she found that they too had all shrunk overnight.

She'd not eaten too much the day before—in fact, she'd barely eaten at all save for the savory dish she'd made Edan. That was not enough to make everything in her wardrobe too small—even if she'd stuffed her face. *Impossible!*

It was then she noticed the light-yellow gown had a brown thread at the seams. She never used brown thread.

On close examination, it looked as if every gown had a coarse brown thread at the seams. She had only ever used a finer, lighter color. Someone had taken in all of her gowns.

Blair sank to the floor in a dejected heap, the discarded gowns all around her. Tears blurred her vision, but she tried to force them away. A horrible trick had been played on her. But why? Who would do such a thing? Who had the time to spend taking in all her gowns? Her thoughts roved to Agnes and the other ladies who'd treated her so cruelly since she'd arrived. Did they really hate her so much?

Blair's belly knotted, bile rising up her throat. She swallowed hard around the burn. The very idea they would try to hurt her made her want to retch, but to do so was only allowing them to win.

She considered staying right here for the rest of her life, but that would only show whoever had done this that they could beat her. And they couldn't. She wouldn't allow it!

Luckily for her, whoever had decided to take in all of her gowns had not removed Blair's own sewing kit from the chest against the wall. She pulled out her needle, thread and thimble and set to work on the blue gown. She only had time for one gown if she was going to make it to the kirk in time for Mass before breaking her fast. She would have to do the rest later.

Blair worked as fast as she could, not caring for the beauty of her stitches like she normally did, and rather only for function. If she didn't come down in time, she'd have to explain why, and that would only give whoever had pulled this trick something to laugh over when they saw her absent. Anger boiled inside her, and she missed the gown, stabbing her finger. A bright droplet of red pooled on her fingertip, jolting her from her angry thoughts.

When she finished, rather than replacing her sewing kit in the chest, she hid it in the back of the wardrobe in Edan's chamber just in case someone took it upon themselves to look. No one would dare go rifling through the laird's things.

She tossed the rest of the gowns into the wardrobe and tightened the laces on the blue gown from behind, a trick she and her sisters had learned when they were little to dress faster and not have to wait for their maids to go play. Truth be told, it had been Greer who'd taught them all the trick because she so often wished to sneak from the nursery chamber to eavesdrop on others.

With her hair freshly coiled into a plaited knot at the nape her neck, Blair pasted a cheerful smile on her face that felt as much of a lie as it was. When she reached the bottom of the stairs, Willa was there, looking surprised to see her.

"Oh, my lady, a lovely choice of blue today. I wasna expecting to see ye. The laird sent me to wake ye. I'm ever so sorry I wasna there to help ye get ready."

"Dinna fash yourself, Willa," Blair said. "I'm plenty capable of getting ready on my own."

"Aye, my lady, but ye're mistress of Kilravock and the lady of the castle—"

"'Tis quite all right," Blair said, not wanting to bring attention to herself and her gowns any more. "Where is my husband?"

"He awaits ye in the great hall, my lady."

Blair found Edan in the great hall, leaning an elbow on the hearth as he stared at the flames. He was all alone, the hall surprisingly empty of people. Just the sight of him, tall and lithe and powerful, took her breath away. His hair looked windswept, as though he'd just gone for a ride, and there was color on his face giving credence to that same line of thought. He was striking, mesmerizing. The breadth of his shoulders was the stuff of heroic tales, not to mention the corded muscles that bulged in the sleeves of his *leine* and the taut curve of his calves, visible in plaid and boots.

"My laird," she said quietly, crossing the great hall toward him.

Edan turned to her with a devastating smile that had her steps faltering. He lurched forward, catching her as she fell against him, a laugh escaping her lips. Lord, she was clumsy around him.

"Are ye all right?" he murmured.

"Would ye believe me if I said your smile caused me to trip?"

Merriment danced in his gaze, and she only had eyes for him. How was it possible this man had the ability to take her breath away again and again?

"Ye'll give me a big head."

"Well, in that case, I shall keep it a secret." She righted herself, smoothing a hand down her skirts.

"How did ye sleep?" He swept his gaze over her face, her body. As he roamed down the length of her, Blair felt the heat of his stare fuel desire inside her, desire that was mirrored in his eyes.

"The best sleep I've ever had," she murmured.

"Me as well."

She wanted to suggest they go back upstairs and *sleep* some more, but she knew that with all that needed to be done, to ask would be improper. Already, the castle had to be abuzz with how they'd confiscated the kitchens *after* having spent the entire day locked up in their chamber. Perhaps that was the reason for the cruel trick of taking in her gowns.

"What is wrong?" Edan asked, his brows furrowing.

Blair worked to swipe the emotions from her face. "Nothing, why?"

"Ye got quiet. And ye're frowning."

She wanted to press her finger to the wrinkle between his brows and smooth it out.

"Och." She waved her hand, letting out a fake laugh she hoped he didn't pick up on. "I was merely wondering if anyone might have fed Bluebell her breakfast."

"We can go and see."

"Thank ye, but it can wait until after Mass. I dinna want to keep everyone waiting."

"When ye didna come down right away, I told Father Thomas to give blessings to the clan and we'd join him after."

"Oh." What would they think of her now? *Nay!* She had to stop worrying about that. If Edan had given his blessing, all would be well. Even still...the longer she kept away from normal tasks, the greater the divide would grow between her and the people.

"Ye're disappointed."

"Nay," she lied. "I dinna want to keep everyone from their day." And that was true. She only wished she'd been able to sew faster, then they'd be at the kirk with everyone right now.

"They will thank ye for not making them wait, lass. Spring is full of long, hard days of work."

Blair latched on to that. "I wish to help."

Edan glanced at her in horror. "In the fields?"

Blair shrugged. "I am not unaccustomed to working."

"Your da had ye in the fields?" Edan looked appalled.

Blair cracked a small smile. "On harvest days, we often went to the fields to help. My da believes in one clan, and everyone helping the clan to thrive."

A light shone in her husband's gaze them. "That is an incredible idea. I admire your father for being such an excellent leader. Then we shall go and help one day, too."

Blair's smile widened. "Your people will love ye for it."

"I will let them know they've ye to thank." He stroked her cheek, and she leaned into his touch.

"I need no gratitude." But it wouldn't hurt for them to realize she was one of them, and she had their best interests at heart.

Blair couldn't help but wonder if a lot of the prejudice against her was that they truly believed her brother was responsible for the murder of their laird. Part of her aim was for them to see that she and her family were kind, trustworthy. It was going to take a lot of work, she knew. But Blair was not afraid of work. She'd spent her whole life striving for perfection and applying herself in this manner would be no different than any of the other tasks she'd taken on.

At home, Blair was the peacemaker, too. She always had a kind and encouraging word for those around her. And yet here at Kilravock, it seemed she was doing everything *but* making peace. In fact, right now all she wanted to do was scream and rant at whoever had decided to destroy her dresses. If she ever found out who it was... It would be best to kill them with kindness and ignore their cruelties. To get to the bottom of why they would treat her thusly and solve the issue.

Edan lifted her hand to his arm and guided her out of the keep, down the stone front stairs into the bailey and across the way to the stable.

As they passed those in the keep, Blair smiled and inclined her head to every person she saw, even if they avoided eye contact. She wanted to make good connections, as well as search out their faces for anyone who might stare at her gown a little too long, but she found no one. Either they were all very good at hiding their guilt, or none of them were the culprits of such a cruel jest.

She suspected it had to have happened when she and Edan were in the kitchens. They'd been there for hours, and it would have taken that long to do it, likely with more than one person, too.

When they entered, the stable master greeted them as he directed the hands to mucking out the stables and feeding the horses.

"Your wee lamb has made many friends," he said.

"That is delightful." Blair clapped her hands with excitement.

The stable master grinned. "Aye. Slept with a few lads last night, and she's already partnered up with his lairdship's warhorse this morning. She's a flirt, she is."

"Och, dinna sully her reputation," Blair teased back.

At the sound of her voice, Bluebell came trotting around the corner with an excited bleat.

Blair squatted to wrap her soft lamb in her arms and pressed a kiss to her nose.

"We're taking good care of her, my lady," the stable master said. "Soon she'll be ruling the stable alongside me."

Blair laughed at that; certain Bluebell would indeed take up that position.

"I'll have an extra jug of whisky delivered to ye for our thanks," Edan said. "Ye deserve it for making my wife happy, and her wee lamb."

"I'd do it without the whisky, but all the same, I'll be happy to accept."

Edan clapped the man on the shoulder, and then led Blair to the kirk, where Father Thomas waited on the front steps, looking nervous.

"Father," Edan said.

"Laird Rose. My lady." He bowed his head but did not step aside for them to enter.

"I'm obliged to hear your bride's confession afore allowing entry." The man shuffled on his feet, shifting his eyes nervously.

Blair felt a knot growing in her belly, having an idea of what this was about—one of the many sins the womenfolk of Clan Rose seemed to think her guilty of.

Edan stiffened beside her, and she could fairly feel the anger rolling off of him. "Ye'll allow us entry into my kirk, or I'll have ye sent away and another priest in your place."

"My laird...I must hear the lady's confession."

"Ye mean your lady, my wife, Lady Blair Rose. Never refer to her as the lady again."

"Apologies, my laird, but she's not given her confession."

By now, Blair's face was so blazing hot, she was certain it resembled a stain of blood on her cheeks. Those in the vicinity of the kirk had slowed their movements in order to better hear and see what was happening.

"Ye tread on dangerous ground, Priest," Edan growled.

"'Tis all right," Blair said softly, squeezing Edan's arm. "He is right, I have not yet given my confession to him, and I would be more than happy to do so."

Father Thomas nodded warily.

"Where should ye like to hear my confession if ye'll not allow me inside?" Blair continued.

"He'll hear it inside the kirk without argument," Edan growled.

Father Thomas reluctantly agreed, and Blair followed him inside, feeling like the greatest of sinners when she knew the sins on her conscience were mild compared to others. As she followed him into the dimly lit kirk, she couldn't help but wonder what rumors had been placed in his ears for him to offer her a less-than-welcoming greeting.

The priest took her to the pew in the front of the kirk. He sat on the bench, bidding her kneel before him, which she did without argument.

He said a prayer, crossing himself, and then bid her give him her confession.

"Bless me, Father, for I have sinned. It's been several days since my last confession. The day of my wedding to be exact." She bit her lip and then drew in a deep, steadying breath, trying to prepare herself to speak her sins aloud to a man of the cloth, who would no doubt judge her harshly given his predetermined notions of her tarnished soul. "I am guilty of lust, Father. For when I look upon my husband, I...I think of things no woman should."

"What things?" His tone was bland, surprisingly without judgement.

Blair's eyes widened as she stared at the priest's feet. She couldn't answer that... Yet he prompted her again. "I think of him...without clothes."

"Go on."

This was humiliating... "And myself without clothes."

"Ah, ye speak of the marriage bed." The man sounded almost relieved.

"Aye, Father." She too was relieved, but only because he'd not made her go into more detail.

"Did ye have these thoughts afore ye wed?"

"Nay." *Saints!* That was a lie! She'd just lied to the priest. Perhaps she could find solace in her lustful thoughts and that Edan had been clothed when she'd imagined him kissing her...

"Did ye share your body with your husband before ye wed?"

"Nay, Father."

"What other sins have ye committed?"

Blair's hands shook, and she kept them folded tightly in her lap. "I wished ill on the person who took my lamb to slaughter."

"Wished ill?"

"Aye."

"Death?"

"Nay!" She startled, looking up at him, suddenly realizing exactly what the women must have told him. That she was responsible for Edan's brother's death, that she was a harlot. "I am not a murderer or a contemplator of such things. Nor am I a whore, Father."

He crossed himself, avoided meeting her gaze, and then he crossed her, too. "Those who wish ill on others, be it causing death or harm, are sinners. Pray that no injury comes to anyone, else the blame will be on your head, and the fires of Hell will be your eternal resting place." He barely paused to take a breath as he continued. "A woman's place is not to enjoy the marriage bed, but to provide children. Ye must serve a penance. Ten Hail Marys. Abstain from meat for three days, and when your husband demands his rights, close your eyes and think of God."

Rather than feel absolved from her confession, Blair felt...*worse*. As though she were a demon seed corrupting Edan with the pleasure they'd both shared. As though she'd actually been the one to harm the old laird when she'd never even met him. She swallowed hard, waiting for the priest to rise before she did. A moment later, Edan was there beside her, his large warm hand engulfing her own. They faced the front of the kirk, both kneeling on a cushion, but she heard none of what was said. Only the pounding of her heart and the fear that she might actually be wicked.

BY THE TIME they left the morning mass, Blair was so quiet, still and solemn that Edan had grown quite concerned.

"What's wrong?" he asked as they walked out of the stone chapel. "What did he say to ye?"

She smiled meekly at him and shook her head. "I'm just in my own world today, I'm sorry. Let us break our fast, and then I've some things I need to get to today."

"Aye, me as well."

But still, something wasn't sitting well with him, and no matter how many times he asked, she didn't elaborate. They ate their luke-warm porridge in silence, and when the meal ended, she begged he excuse her and rushed from the great hall without waiting for his reply.

Something had happened with the priest; he'd bet coin on it. And whatever it was had left her feeling less than herself.

He wanted the lively, teasing woman back. Edan sat back in his chair and crossed his arms over his chest. One of the women servants came and cleared away his breakfast. He waited until he no longer could for Blair to appear once more, but she did not.

There were missives to read, judgments to render, men to be trained and crofters to be spoken to about the harvest. He planned to make good on his promise for them to help out as Blair wanted.

When he stood, there was a commotion coming from the kitchens. Not exactly shouting, but most definitely raised voices that drew his concern. As he edged closer, he could hear the soft-spoken words of his wife, though what she said was indiscernible.

Cook, however, was going on about meatless meals and that it was absurd to expect the lot of them to eat no meat for three days.

"I wish to abstain from meat, Cook. I'm not asking ye to have meals prepared for everyone that are without, only mine." Blair spoke with dignity and in a quiet, soothing tone that was meant to stroke egos, but seemed to be doing the opposite for Cook.

"Ye have brought your strange customs upon this house. How can I serve ye different meals than everyone else? 'Twould be like saying ye dinna like my cooking."

"It is not that at all, and perhaps it would be best then if my meals were served in my chamber."

"No meat for three days?" This was the voice of Agnes. "Only one reason ye'd be asking about that."

Edan cocked his head in curiosity. He really should make his presence known, but he wanted to see how his wife faired with her people —just as she'd requested.

"What's that?" Cook asked, sounding incredulous.

"She's been given a penance. A *lusty* penance." Agnes sounded rather smug, but what shocked Edan was the round of hissing he heard amongst those in the kitchen.

The hissing stopped, followed by a moment of silence. Edan couldn't help but wonder if he'd missed something; perhaps his wife killing them all with one glower.

But then she spoke again, her voice full of calm pride. "Aye, I have been handed a penance. Penance for wanting my husband. And if desiring to extend the line of Rose men by growing a bairn in my belly is something I should be punished for, then so be it. It is far less a sin than what I have been dealt by the lot of ye. Prejudice, unkindness, cruelty. Since the moment of my arrival, ye have made it clear that I am unwelcome and undeserving, and through no fault of my own, for I have only showed ye kindness and tried to know ye better. Ye may wish to be rid of me, but I'm not going anywhere."

Edan wanted to rush in then, to scoop her in his arms and flog every last one of them. These were the rumors that Willa had told Raibert about, the ones Blair had tried to make out as nothing. He couldn't stand for it. Wouldn't. Aye, she'd given them a piece of her mind, but he needed to add to it.

But as he stepped forward, Blair appeared before him, bumping into him, her shaking hands on his chest. Blue eyes brimmed with tears, and her face was flushed.

"My laird," she said, clearly embarrassed, but also loud enough to let those in the kitchen know that their interaction with her had been overheard. The collective gasp and scurrying of feet as they made quick work of returning to their duties echoed in the dark corridor.

"We need to talk."

She looked toward the ground, nodding meekly.

"Come." He took her hand and led her outside to the stables. Silently, he lifted her onto his warhorse, not bothering with a saddle. He pulled on a bridle, and leapt up behind her, steering his mount through the gates and in the direction of the firth's beaches.

This was not what he should be doing as the new laird, avoiding his work in order to comfort his bride, but what other choice did he have? He was her husband, her protector, and she needed him.

CHAPTER 19

Blair closed her eyes and drew in a deep breath of the salty air. Though it was nothing compared to the North Sea and Dornoch Firth upon which her family's castle of Dunrobin sat, the Moray Firth was close enough for the smell of salt to carry.

Edan dismounted, tugged her down with him and held her in his arms. The familiar scent of him surrounded her. She wanted to sink against him but doing so made her feel all sorts of things she'd been told were wrong. How could they be? He was her husband. Wasn't she supposed to want him? Hadn't she seen the same looks she gave Edan mirrored on the faces of her sisters? The same look she'd seen on Aurora's face too, and Blair had judged her. This made her feel a bit like a hypocrite, for she hadn't judged the guards who so eagerly agreed to embrace her cousin, but she had harshly wished her cousin would be sent to a convent, where nuns and priests would likely shame her as Father Thomas had just done to Blair.

It wasn't fair. Edan made her happy, and she wanted no other. How could this be wrong?

"Tell me," he said, and though it was not a request, neither was it a demand.

Blair sucked in air through her nose, closing her eyes for a moment, a gentle breeze washing over her skin. What was there to say? Too much...

"Father Thomas asked me if I'd given myself to ye before marriage." She bit her lip and stared at his chest. "I know I did not in the sense he meant, but I did seek ye out. Let ye kiss me. Perhaps what they are saying about me is true."

Edan stroked his fingers over her cheek and then tipped her chin back so that she was looking up at him. "What are they saying?"

How could she tell him? What if he said they were right? Blair bit her lip and started to shake her head, feeling the crush of those nasty rumors deep in her heart. But the one person who'd been on her side was her husband. She could count on him, trust him, she was certain. Hadn't he come for her, to protect her, before he'd even known who she was? "They've called me a whore. The priest said I should not enjoy the marriage bed. That I should only think of God."

Edan scoffed. "Lass, if ye're not enjoying the marriage bed and only thinking of God when I touch ye, then I'm not doing it right."

Blair looked up at him sharply, her mouth forming an "O" of surprise. Edan cupped her face, his thumb stroking over her cheek.

"'Tis perfectly natural for ye to want me. It doesna make ye a whore for wanting to kiss me afore we were wed. Physical attraction between two people is completely normal and should not be shamed. I dinna like that the priest was trying to shame ye, love, and I dinna like that the women were doing it to ye, either."

"I dinna understand." She shook her head, thoroughly confused. "Why would everyone try to make it out like I am sinful? I got the sense Father Thomas was searching for something, hoping I'd confess to more than what I did. Almost like..."

"Someone filled his head."

"Aye." She looked up at him then, meeting his eyes. "That is exactly it."

"I'll have no more of it." He stiffened, the muscles in his chest bunching beneath her fingertips.

"Wait. Dinna do anything just yet."

"Och, I dinna plan to just yet. First, I'm going to make love to my wife before God and all, so they might know that when the two of us are together, it is heaven on earth."

Blair's belly did a flip, and she shook her head, but he stilled her protests, silencing her with a kiss that made every inch of her heat up. Edan swept her off her feet and laid her down on the sand, covering her with his body. And he made good on his promise then, showing her that pleasure, while it was not an earthly thing, neither was it a sin. It was something much more beautiful, much more profound, than either of them could have imagined.

"Agnes, I should like to prepare baskets of food to bring the ill, as well as mothers in childbed."

"That would be a lovely thing, my lady." Agnes was still smarting from the tongue-lashing Edan had given her upon their return from the beach, a verbal whipping the housekeeper then had to give out to the clanswomen who served in the keep.

No one had yet come forward to apologize about her dresses, but Blair didn't expect any of them to, least of all Agnes, who she suspected of either being in charge of the trickery, or at least participating in some way.

Well, Blair wasn't going to let anything get her down. She was still glowing from all the attention her husband showered up on her on the beach, her skin still tingling, and her rear still stinging just slightly from the sand.

A brand, she would think of it as such. Edan's mark on her. A shiver swept over her.

"Are ye well, my lady?"

"Perfectly." Blair found herself humming as she filled up a basket with freshly baked bread, cured meat, cheese, fresh-picked berries and various herbs that could be used in tisanes to cure the numerous ails of the people. When she was finished, she hoisted the hefty basket in her arms and marched out to the bailey. At the last second, she decided to take Bluebell with her. She attached her to a leading string and then made her way toward the village. She asked along the way to be taken to the new mothers' crofts first. Outside of their small croft, she tied Bluebell to a post and then knocked.

A tired-looking young woman, with her ginger hair falling in ragged tendrils around her face, opened the door.

"My lady."

"I have come to visit ye and your bairn."

"Och, not mine, but my sister's."

"Oh, I see."

"Come in, my lady." She stepped back, allowing Blair entry into the dusty, dimly lit hut.

The main room was small, appointed with a cot on one wall, a table in the center, and shelving and a workstation on another. Near the small window, a brazier held a fire and overtop of it a pot of something, stew perhaps.

Lying on the cot, sweat covering her body, was the new mother. The sister who'd answered the door stood beside the soaked mattress, holding the bairn who cried as though in pain. Blair's heart lurched at the scene.

"Her milk's not come in, and she's got a fever," the sister explained, face drawn with worry.

"Has the midwife been to see her?"

"Aye. Says she's got childbed fever." She shook her head and swiped at a tear.

Blair's throat constricted. Not many mothers lived through that. Blair wasn't an expert in herbs or midwifery, but she knew enough to offer a little bit of comfort.

"Has the midwife offered her anything for her fever? A tisane or poultice?"

"She bled her."

Blair nodded, knowing this was often the remedy for most illnesses, though she was skeptical it would work, especially for a woman who had not healed from the bleeding that came from having the bairn. "Will ye try this? 'Tis a tisane for fevers and infection. It may make her feel a little better." She pulled one of the small herbal sachets from her basket and laid it beside the meal she'd placed on the small table in their cramped hut.

"What is it?"

"Rosemary, thyme, chamomile, ginger and willow bark. I dinna know if it will help her, but it is used often for infections and fevers at Dunrobin, and so I thought it might help those here, too."

The woman eyed her warily, as if she didn't trust her. "I'm not certain I should give it to her."

"I can make it for ye if ye want. Or hold the bairn while ye make it."

Exhaustion etched the other woman's face. "Haps if ye held the child. There's no wet-nurse for him, and I've not yet had a child, else I'd feed him. Mayhap if ye want to try the goat's milk and the rag again, he'll eat. He doesna seem to want it from me."

Blair set down her basket and reached for the bairn, whose cries had grown weak. His eyes were closed, his face pale and thin, the blue lines of his veins showing visibly on his forehead and cheeks. Not like what the bairns she'd seen before had looked like, with pink in their cheeks.

She located the bowl of goat's milk and the rag beside it on a small table near the bed where the mother lay, silent and sweating. She dipped the rag into the milk and held it to the bairn's lips, rubbing back and forth and cooing for him to open. He made a little noise, moving his lips slowly, searching out the rag. She dipped it again and placed it on his mouth. He sucked hungrily. And when he wrinkled his brow, she moved to dip it into the milk again, repeating the movement over and over until the bairn drifted off to sleep, a little color back in his face.

"How did ye do that?" the woman asked quietly, peering at the sleeping bairn.

"I dinna know."

"Did ye have younger brothers or sisters?"

"I am the bairn in my family," Blair smiled. "But I often went with my own mother to visit new mothers in our clan."

"That is admirable of ye."

Blair found it odd that this woman mentioned it was admirable for the leaders of the clan to take care of their own. The Rose clan was thriving, so it was clear they were taken care of somehow, but all thought it odd for her to be so involved. "It is the way it should be. The way I intend it to be here. What is your name? I feel remiss in not asking for it sooner."

The woman flushed with color. "Och, my lady, ye dinna need to feel that way. I am Helen, and my sister is Frances."

"And the bairn?" Blair glanced down at the sleeping infant in her arms.

"He is named for his father, Alan."

"A strong name."

"Aye." Helen smiled sadly down at the bairn, then walked over to her sister with the steaming tisane in a cup. "Franny, open please. Drink."

When she didn't respond, Helen dipped her finger in the cup and put a drop of tisane on her sister's lips. The woman shook her head and moaned.

"Please, Franny. Drink for Alan. The bairn needs ye."

This time, Frances's yellowed eyes blinked open, her mouth parted. She tried to take a sip, sputtering at first. Helen held her head up with a hand beneath her neck to help ease her with drinking, which seemed to help.

"After she drinks, she should be washed, and another poultice placed on her..." Blair felt herself blushing, as she slid her gaze toward Frances's womb.

"I understand. The midwife did do that yesterday."

"I dinna want to step on your midwife's toes, Helen, but in Dunrobin, we did this several times a day. The infection seems to breed in the nether regions, and when cleaned often, it doesna have enough time to grow worse."

Helen bit her lip and nodded. "I will see it done."

"I'll come back tomorrow and check on the lot of ye. Where is Alan the elder?"

"In the fields, my lady. He'll be there late, doing the work for the three of us." As she spoke, she continued to help her sister drink until Frances refused another sip.

"He sounds like a good man."

"He is."

Blair settled the swaddled bairn in the wee basket fashioned into his bed and quietly left the small hut, her heart sad for those inside. It was rare for a woman to survive childbed fever, but she would pray all the same.

She visited several other crofts, distributing more food and herbal tisanes, taking the small children out to play with Bluebell and giving their mothers a moment to rest, until the sun was starting to set. Though she was exhausted, a smile covered her face. As she made her way back to the keep, she made a list of all she would need to gather on the morrow to bring during her next round of visits, but her joy was stopped short when she reached the bailey and a hysterical woman shouted and pointed at her.

She recognized her as the wife of one of the men she'd visited who had a fever and what appeared to be an infection of the lungs. He'd been coughing up blood, his breathing rattled. His wife had told Blair that Father Thomas had already been by to give the last rites, for they didn't expect him to live much longer.

She was shouting *horrible* things.

"The food she brought us was rancid! Poisoned, like done to our laird. As soon as I fed him her poison, he started to vomit, and then... and then...he *died*!"

Blair stilled, her hand coming over her heart, her basket dropping at her feet. The one part of her wanted to rush forward to offer this woman comfort in her grief. She'd just lost her husband. Blair couldn't imagine would that would be like. She couldn't bear to lose Edan, not when she'd finally found someone in this world who seemed to understand her.

But worst still, this woman somehow thought Blair was at fault... Clearly, she wasn't; the man had already been in the throes of death when she arrived, but that didn't make it any better. Not when people in the bailey were staring at her, shaking their heads and whispering behind their hands.

"She'll kill us all!" the woman screeched.

Blair covered her mouth, her hands shaking as she tried to hold in her sobs.

One of the warriors, perhaps a cousin or brother, came up, grasped the woman and tugged her into his arms. He led her away, trying to calm her.

Blair stood rooted in place; the accusing looks of everyone around her boring through her like nails in a coffin. How could it be that they thought her capable of such a thing? She shook her head. "I didna. I wouldna. I was helping—" She cut herself short and hurried toward the keep steps, acutely aware of those whispering that she'd been sent by her brother to kill them all. That they shouldn't let her near them, that they should take care of her first.

"My lady," the stable master held out his hand, and she passed Bluebell's tie over to him.

Distraught, Blair ran up the steps, realizing at the last minute she'd left her basket in the middle of the bailey. She turned around to get it but then stopped. She was in mid-sob, tears streaking down her cheeks, and she didn't want anyone to see her looking like that. Not when they would only judge her as guilty, her sobs that of someone remorseful for what they'd done.

⚜

AT THE SOUNDS of the screeching in the bailey, Edan called a cease to the training he'd been doing with the men in the field. The sun was already starting to set, and the lot of them were exhausted anyway. A sense of dread filled him, and without knowing yet what was happening, he was certain it had something to do with his wife.

The poor lass couldn't seem to get away from trouble. He'd been so worried about them finding him worthy, but now it was his wife he was more worried about.

When he reached the bailey, most of the commotion had died

down, but there were more than a dozen people willing to tell him that Blair had been accused of murdering James, the warrior who'd taken ill with a lung infection some weeks before.

"This is ballocks," he told Raibert. "How could they possibly think her at fault?"

Raibert was scowling just as hard. "It doesna make sense. The man was already dying. Given his last rites even."

"Aye. They are looking for a way to blame her. A way to blame her for Connor's death, I warrant." He confided to his clansman about what Blair had told him happened with the priest.

"What are ye going to do?"

"I will speak to the people. But first, I must find my wife."

Raibert nodded. "I'll find out who else she visited today and see if they'd be willing to step forward when ye call the clan, to bear testimony to her goodness."

"Thank ye."

"Ye need not thank me. 'Tis my duty to ye and the lass. Ye're my family, my laird, and she your wife, which makes her my family, too."

Edan nodded, running a hand through his hair. "I thought it would be hard to gain the people's respect after my brother's death, but I never thought I'd have to deal with this."

Raibert pursed his lips in concern. "Aye. 'Tis not right."

Edan left Raibert in the bailey to go in search of his wife. He entered the solar betwixt their chambers to find her chamber door shut tightly. And when he tried to lift the handle, he found it barred.

He tapped softly at the wood. "Blair?"

There was a rustling behind the door but no answer.

"'Tis Edan, love, will ye let me in?" He asked, rather than demanded, she open the door, understanding that in her vulnerable state—a state completely out of her control—she might want some measure of control herself.

There was more rustling and then a thump against the door as she lifted the bar. She didn't open it, though, and so he tapped once more. "Does that mean I can come in?"

A miserable sounding, "Aye," came through the cracks.

Edan opened the door slowly, scanning the chamber to find her face-down on the bed they'd shared. The place that had been filled with much happiness and pleasure was now drenched in her tears. He shut the door behind him and approached the bed. He sat on the side and stroked a soothing hand down her back.

"I heard what happened."

"I didna kill that man."

"I know ye didna. Raibert knows it. And likely, most of the people know it, too."

"Why would she accuse me of such? The priest was leaving when I arrived, having just given last rites."

"Aye, love. James's been dying a long time. In her grief, his wife is looking for someone to blame."

"But why me? I did nothing but try to offer her comfort."

"Some things people do or feel canna be explained."

Blair blew out a ragged breath and rolled over to face him. Her cheeks were flushed, her reddened eyes swollen and damp, and her nose was running. Edan stroked her tear-stained face with the pad of his thumb, and then he reached into his sporran and pulled out a small square of linen that he used to wipe her nose.

"I am not a bad person. One mistake, and now I am seen as evil."

"What mistake?"

"The stupid missive in a bottle."

"Aye, but without that one mistake, we would nay be wed."

"That is debatable. Ye might have still ridden on Ross Castle to seek out my brother."

"Mayhap, but who's to say I would have fallen for your charms? Ye'd not likely have come to seek me out in my tent."

"Is that the only reason ye married me? Because I came to your tent?"

"Lass, I decided I wanted to marry ye the moment I stepped out of your brother's study to find ye lurking in the shadows." He took her hand and pressed it to his heart. "Something in your soul speaks to mine."

Blair smiled at him; an image he didn't think he'd ever get used to seeing. She was so incredibly beautiful.

"I feel the same way."

He leaned down and brushed his lips over hers. "I dinna want to see ye sad. I'd wage a war, if it would make ye happy."

"I only want your people to know I care for them, that I consider them to be a part of my family now."

"They will. We will see to it that they do."

"How?"

"I am going to speak with them."

She started to shake her head, and her hair, already loose around her face, batted back and forth. "I dinna want to make it worse, to call attention to myself."

A sharp knock sounded at the door.

"What is it?"

Raibert entered, his face full of panic. "There's been another death. This time...it is clearly poison." His eyes shifted to Blair, who sat incredibly still on the bed. "James's wife, the one who accused ye. When I went to call them all to the bailey for ye, she was dead inside her hut.."

"It wasna me," Blair said, her voice growing hysterical. She clutched to Edan fearfully.

Bloody hell! Someone was going to a great length to prove his wife was a murderer.

He took her shaking hand in his and brought it to his lips. "We know, lass, but the people will think it is ye, especially with her accusation before."

"Someone is trying to frame me." Blair's eyes were wide with fright, and she was starting to tremble all over. "I wasna even here when your brother was...killed."

"Aye."

Raibert cleared his throat. "Ye need to come now, my laird. Ye need to address them. They're gathered outside. And 'tis probably best for your wife to remain here, where she'll be safe in case...someone decides to act out on their own."

"One of them is killing their own. The Sutherlands had nothing to do with Connor's death. The prisoners lied." He scrubbed a hand over his face. "What the bloody hell is going on?"

Blair let out a wretched sob. Edan still held her hand in a strong grip. "We will figure out who has done this, my love."

"We need to work together," she said through her chattering teeth.

"Aye."

"Starting now. I canna remain behind. I must go with ye to face them. If they think me hiding, a coward, they will only think all the more that I am guilty."

Edan drew in a ragged breath. The last thing he wanted to do was expose her to the raging mob that was gathering in the bailey. But she was right. "All right."

Raibert frowned but nodded his agreement.

"Allow me a moment to compose myself." She swung her legs over the side of the bed.

Edan stood with her and approached Raibert. "Have the guards line the bailey. I'll be down in a moment. Every last man, woman and child should be present."

"Except the ill," Blair called. "Some of those I saw today canna get out of bed."

"All right, save for the ill."

Edan watched his wife splash water on her face, replait her hair and then leave it to lie down the length of her back rather than twisting it into a knot. The look caused her to appear less severe. With the evidence of her tears still reddening her eyes and the sad turn of her mouth, she looked the picture of innocent sorrow. He knew it wasn't a ruse, knew that deep in her kind heart, she was bleeding for those who'd died, and those who thought her capable of murder.

With her hand in his, he led her down the steps toward the bailey, where they would face the crowd together, not for the first time.

They looked like a mob. Angry faces glared up at them, their stances hostile. Toward the front was a woman holding a bairn, who looked on Blair with pity, and near to her was a man with much the same expression, accompanied by several others. These must be the people that Raibert had found to testify of her kindness and care. Willa stood among them as well.

Blair's fingers trembled against his, her palm slick with sweat.

"Dinna fear, sweetling," he whispered. "An angry crowd feeds on such. Show them your strength."

She straightened her shoulders, stiffening beside him. Her chin came up, and she looked directly at the crowd, rather than at her feet.

"There have been many accusations levied against my wife, your lady."

"Murderer!" someone shouted.

Raibert started in their direction, but Blair called for him to stop. "Please," she asked.

Raibert looked to Edan, who wanted his guard to beat the bloody pulp out of the man who would call his wife such a sinner.

"Lady Blair is no murderer. And I'm ashamed that we should have to stand here and claim her innocence to her people, those who should be supporting her. What is your claim? That a dying man died? That she somehow poisoned my brother from afar? She is not responsible. And poor James's wife—what's to say she didna poison herself in her grief?"

He was laying the seeds of doubt; he could tell from the way the angry grumbles lessened, and people's faces turned from rage to confusion. But there were still some who would only believe that Blair was guilty.

"To take one's own life is a sin! She'd not have done that! Murderer! Murderer!"

"I will nay tolerate accusations of murder against my wife. If ye would believe that James's wife was murdered, then we will add her death to my brother's and continue to investigate. But know this, the one responsible is here today. Gathered here with ye where ye stand. Who among ye had cause to kill James's wife? Had cause to kill my brother? Who among ye would wish to pin such on my wife? Ye want her to be guilty because ye dinna want to believe that one of your own could do such."

"She is a Sutherland! The Sutherlands are to blame!"

Edan shook his head. "We would blame someone so far? Not even think to blame the Campbells, who've been reiving our lands? Ye search because ye want it to be her. But ye're wrong. Anyone who continues to lay the blame of death at my wife's feet will be punished. I willna tolerate it. We canna take the words of one or two hysterical people as gospel. We must seek out the truth in all its forms. We are not a mob who'd believe a rumor, but good and just people."

Angry murmurs went out through the crowd.

"From the moment my wife arrived, her welcome has been less than comforting. Those who've been cruel to her know who ye are. Know that I, too, am aware of the cruelty ye've bestowed on her. I'm ashamed that such is happening within my own clan. Out of the whole of Scotland, our clan—our home—this is where we should feel safest. Not where we should worry about discord, strife and disharmony."

Beside him, Blair was still looking out at the crowd, tears tracking down her face, but she didn't look weak as she cried, she looked strong. Stoic, even.

Edan hoped that his brother's wife hadn't been treated as badly as Blair, that his mother, and his brother's mother, had been accepted with open arms.

"Are there any among ye who might step forward and testify to my wife's kindness?"

A hush fell over the crowd, but then the lass holding a bairn stepped forward. "I will." She turned to face the crowd and told them about how the bairn in her arms, her sister's bairn, had not been eating. That she'd been trying to feed him for days but that as soon as Blair held him in her arms, she was able to coax him to suck the goat's milk from a rag, and he'd finally fallen into a sated sleep. That her sister, who has been suffering from childbed fever, had seemed to sleep peacefully for the first time after Blair's visit.

The man beside her stepped forward to tell everyone how Blair had come and sang to his children, tried to comfort him while his wife lay in a fevered state, and that the food she'd brought had been delicious and from the laird's own kitchen.

More and more people stepped forward to share their own stories, including Willa, who said that when she thought she might no longer have a place in the clan, she'd been given the highest honor of serving the lady of the castle.

As people stepped forward, it seemed like more and more came out of the woodwork. The stable master spoke of her sweet Bluebell, and that no one with a cold bone in their body would have saved a wee lamb and spoil it as Blair had. Even Raibert praised her kindness and spoke how the people at Ross Castle respected her, how she was the daughter of one of the most powerful men in Scotland, a favorite of the king—and to disrespect her was as good as disrespecting their sovereign.

Edan wasn't so certain he'd go so far as to say that, but it was a good place to start.

The angry faces that had greeted them upon their exit of the castle softened. And Blair was no longer shaking. It seemed she'd found strength in the words of those who spoke of her character.

Edan's chest swelled with pride as he stared at his wife. And to think, he'd turned her father down at his first request. As he watched her, as he listened, as her hand in his grew still, he realized with a stunning clarity that he was in love with this incredible woman. That he was the luckiest man in the Highlands.

CHAPTER 20

Though Blair wanted nothing more than to take her meal in her chambers, Edan said they needed to eat in the great hall to show their strength. Strength was not exactly something she felt at the moment.

Even still, she knew he was right.

"My lady," Willa said, as she rinsed the lavender scented soap from Blair's hair, "there is something I must tell ye."

Blair used a linen to wipe the water from her face and turned in the tub to face her maid whose worried tone matched the wrinkle in her brow. "What is it?"

Willa bit her lip and looked away. "I shouldna have said anything."

Blair placed her hand over Willa's, where it rested on the side of the tub. "Please, Willa. Ye can trust me."

Willa blinked her eyes rapidly as she looked up toward the rafters, as though she were trying to keep herself from crying. "I know, ye're so kind."

"Please, tell me what has ye so upset."

"'Tis about the previous lady, Mary Guinn. And Agnes."

"Guinn?" Alarm bells were going off in her head now, for Guinn was the name of the clan who'd ridden on her family after the daughter of the laird had spurned her brother Strath so many years ago.

"Aye." Willa cocked her head, watching Blair with curiosity. "Mary Guinn was married to Connor."

Mary. She was Jean's sister. Knowing exactly who she was had Blair's mind racing. She licked her lips as she thought it over. Was it just a coincidence? Or was this vengeance? "And?"

"Her maid, Agnes, married McQuinn, one of the old laird's men. Well, she... I heard the two of them talking afore Lady Mary left. Mary said she thought the Sutherlands should pay for the humiliation her sister suffered. I dinna know what she was talking about, but it seems like something ye should know."

"What are ye saying, Willa?"

"Only that it seems... It seems like perhaps Lady Mary and Agnes might have... Och, I dinna know. 'Tis all too much for my small brain. I'm a maid! I dinna know much about the ways of such things, but it struck me as something I should tell."

"Why did ye not tell anyone afore now?"

"I was scared. Scared of Agnes. But now that James and his wife are gone, with her death especially suspicious, I couldna keep my tongue any longer."

Blair sank back against the tub, the warmth of the water a startling reminder of the cold she'd been greeted with by Agnes.

"Do ye think Agnes stayed behind to carry out her lady's...orders?"

"I couldna say, my lady." She ran a comb through Blair's hair. "But if she were planning to blame the Sutherlands and get away with it, seems like leaving Agnes behind to take care of her dirty work would be a good plan."

"What of the men who were captured?"

Willa sucked in a breath between her teeth. "I was hoping ye'd not ask me about them, my lady."

"Why is that?"

"To speak of it is a sin." She dropped the comb as she said it, then fumbled to pick it up.

"Trust me, Willa, please. Whatever ye know and relay to me isna a sin, but a duty to your laird. Ye canna be punished for doing your duty."

Willa stilled, eyes toward the rafters as she thought that over. "Ye're right. The men... They were Lady Mary's lovers."

"All of them?" The words slipped out before she could pull them back, and visions of her cousin Aurora came to mind. She couldn't say she was surprised, given Mary's sister, Jean.

But instead of feeling condescending toward the women, she was sad. Sad that they felt the only way they could garner attention was to seek out physical contact with multiple men. Did they not understand they could be valued on their own merit? For who they were, for the skills they possessed?

"Aye, my lady."

"Thank ye for sharing this with me," Blair said quietly.

"I would do anything for ye, my lady."

Blair finished her bath, and Willa helped her dress and fix her hair in silence. When she was finished, she searched for Edan in their solar and then his study. She hoped to find him before they supped, but he was not in either of the rooms. She'd have to wait to share this news with him until after they'd eaten.

As she guessed, Edan was in the great hall, talking with Raibert and several of his men. The trestle tables had been set up, and people were pouring in to eat. Before she'd come down, Blair had nightmares of the people boycotting a meal with her. She was pleasantly surprised to see them all filing in with smiles on their faces, some more wary than others.

"My lady," Edan said, separating himself from his men to sweep a low bow as he took her hand and pressed his lips to her skin. "Ye're a vision."

Blair couldn't help but giggle at his gallantry. "I thank ye."

Rather than let go of her hand, he tugged her forward and brushed his lips against her forehead. With his arm still draped over her shoulder, he led her to the table and pulled out a chair for her to sit.

As the meal was brought out, she was surprised to find that Cook had followed her request for no meat in the supper. Instead, they were served a hearty barley and turnip stew with freshly baked bread and butter, followed by slices of cheese alongside berry tarts. The meal was delicious, and when she saw Cook peering out from the doorway to the kitchens, Blair smiled and mouthed *thank ye*. Cook nodded back and then ducked away, clearly having only come out to see if the lady approved.

When the meal concluded, Blair whispered to Edan, "Can we go upstairs? There's something I need to discuss with ye."

"Aye, love."

He stood, pulled back her chair, and with his hand in hers, they bid the clan goodnight and headed upstairs. Halfway up the second flight, Edan made a sound that had Blair whirling round. He wavered on his feet, slapping his hand against the stone.

"Are ye all right?" Blair asked with concern, reaching for his arm which felt warmer than usual.

"Too much whisky." He laughed and shook his head when she tried to loop her arm through his. "Had a few drams afore ye came down." He motioned with his hand for her to continue on in front of him. "In case I fall, I dinna want to take ye down with me."

"Edan, if 'tis that bad, I should call Raibert or one of the other men to help ye up the stairs."

"Nay, sweetling." He sounded breathless, and his face had gone pale, droplets of perspiration forming on his brow.

"Edan." Her voice came out sharp and terrified.

Even as she reached for him, he swayed once more. He started to go backward, but she managed to tug him forward, so he dropped to his knees on the stairs rather than tumbling backward.

"Raibert! Help!" she shrieked.

At the sounds of her screams, men came running from what seemed like all directions.

"What happened?" Raibert demanded, lifting Edan up onto his shoulder.

Her husband slurred inaudible words, and Blair felt very close to fainting. She blinked rapidly, shaking her head, fanning her face.

"I dinna know. He was dizzy. Said he'd had too much whisky. But he didn't look... He was pale, sweating... He started to fall, and I pulled him forward before he toppled down."

"Poison," someone said behind her. "Is it not obvious? *She* did it."

"Nay, I didna. *Nay!* I would never!" Blair's tone rose in pitch as she combatted grappling hands and vicious accusations.

"Seize her!" someone else shouted. "She's tried to murder our laird!"

They tore at her hair, her gown, her flesh.

"He may have been blind to her evilness, but we canna be, else she kills us all!"

Blair's vision grew dizzy herself as she tugged against the grappling fingers. "'Tis not true! I love him. Raibert, please!" But her husband's guard had already disappeared up the stairs. The hands were tugging harder, so much so she could no longer balance on her own two feet, and she fell into the pinching pulling hands.

"If 'tis poison, he needs help. Dinna let him die! I can help him!" She was shrieking now, panic setting in. Right now, they were likely going to take her out to the firth and drown her. "Have ye frankincense or mugwart? Lovage? Boil them in vinegar. Something that is an antidote to poison, please! At least make him vomit! For the love of all things hol—"

But her words were cut off when someone hit her hard with something over the head. Her words slurred, and she tasted blood in her mouth as she bit her tongue. Her vision blurred completely, and the sounds from all around dulled into one long hum.

Blair woke sometime later, her head pounding with pain and her body aching. Her fingers scratched against cold, wet stone. She was in a dank cell that smelled like death. She pushed up on her elbows, trying to rise, and found Raibert on the outside of the cell staring in at her.

"Ye're awake," he said, but his voice was not friendly.

"Edan?" she asked, wiping her hair from her eyes.

"Alive for now."

"Did they use an antidote?"

"Why do ye care?" Raibert scoffed.

Blair stiffened, coming more alert. "What?"

"Ye poisoned him."

He thought her guilty? She shook her head. "Nay, I didna, ye have to believe me."

Raibert's gaze did not waver. "Then who did?"

She pressed her palms to her temple, squeezing her eyes shut and trying to make her vision steady. "Agnes."

"Agnes? The housekeeper?" Raibert clucked his tongue. "What has she got against the laird?"

"Not against the laird."

"Then who?"

"Me." Blair knew she wasn't making sense. Even to her own ears, she sounded guilty.

"Why would she not poison ye, then?"

"She wants me to suffer."

"I might have believed ye before, after what Willa told me the women were doing to ye."

"Aye, that was all true." She pushed to her knees and tried to stand, but she stumbled back down. Sitting back on her heels, she pressed her hands together in prayer. "Please, Raibert, ye must know I'd never hurt Edan. I love him with all my heart."

"And yet this willna have been the first time ye've tried to deceive, tried to start a war."

"Nay," she said breathlessly.

"I know about the missive in the bottle."

"That wasna me. A mistake..."

"Just like this?"

"Nay, Raibert, please listen." She licked her lips, her mouth so very dry. "Agnes was a Guinn. The Guinns have a vendetta against my family."

"Seems rather farfetched."

"Aye, but Willa heard—"

"Dinna bring my sister into this."

Blair pressed her lips together, keeping herself from retorting that he'd been the one to bring her in first. "Agnes was overhead speaking with Lady Mary, who said the Sutherlands had to pay."

Raibert let out a long breath and shook his head. "Just tell me why ye did it? My laird is a good man. A great man. And he cared for ye greatly."

"Raibert." She choked on a sob. "I didna hurt him, I swear it. 'Twas Agnes. And if ye dinna stop her, I dinna know who she will hurt next."

Raibert was silent for a long time, his gaze steady on her, though he didn't let any of his emotions show.

"I will speak with Agnes."

"Ye believe me?" she asked desperately.

He shook his head, sorrow in his eyes. "Nay. But even a small knot of doubt must be unwound."

Then he walked away, leaving her in the dark.

INCREDIBLE.

This had all been so much easier than she thought. In fact, the idiot laird had gone down much faster than she expected. She thought he would need several meals filled with her poison before her special treatment would take. But as it turned out, he wasn't made of stronger stuff. Well, he'd probably live, since he'd not had the proper dosage. That was all well and good. She'd only done it to place the blame on another. Nay, she was getting ever closer to her true target's great demise.

She shivered, excitement thrilling through her limbs.

And the lady... Oh, but it had almost been sad to watch her shriek and scream. It was obvious from her reaction that she wasn't guilty. That she really did love their laird. But the people were too caught up in the accusations to see the truth. Sweet Blair could have been halfway across the world, and they'd have still blamed her. That was the way with mobs. One small word shouted over and over was enough.

She wondered if she could get them to turn on one another? Probably. But it was so much fun to have the finger pointed at Blair.

What a dumb name that was: Blair. Blah. Ugly and so very masculine. What were her parents thinking, giving her a man's name?

Well, she supposed it matched her. She was mannish with her dark looks and overlarge limbs.

How was it that the laird found her at all appealing? Well, soon it wouldn't matter, anyway.

But goodness, she was having a lot of fun inciting everyone to terror. Now they would think they were all safe with Blair locked up in the dungeon. Too bad they had no idea who was really responsible. And it wasn't as if anyone would listen to the rantings of a prisoner, even if Blair did figure it out. Which she wouldn't. How could she?

She sat back on her cot, tipping the jug of whisky she'd pilfered from the cellar into her mouth and smiling at the burn as it went down her throat. *Fire.* Was that how her victims felt?

She let out a little laugh. Years from now, they would still never know it was her. For what reason did she have to kill? No one would ever believe that it was simply for the thrill of it. That she liked to watch the life drain out of a body, that she needed their souls in order to survive.

With another tipple of whisky, she let out a long sigh. She supposed it was time to go help the laird get back on his feet. She couldn't risk him dying and ruining her plans, for if he were no longer laird, she wouldn't get to kill Blair. Nay, the rabble would see to it first, and that absolutely could not happen.

The lady was hers to get rid of.

CHAPTER 21

E dan's insides felt like they were on fire as he bent over the side of his bed and emptied everything from his body into the chamber pot below. Willa handed him a cloth, and he swiped it over his mouth and tossed himself back against the pillows. Earlier, Agnes had been attending him, but he hadn't seen her in hours. He was feeling more like himself now. Eyes hazy and voice scratchy, he asked, "Where is my wife? Where is Raibert?"

Willa shook her head, her face full of sorrow as she broke into tears. She pressed her hands to her face, sobbing as though something awful had happened. Edan's heart seized.

Good God, had Blair been poisoned, too?

"Where," he demanded, swallowing hard against the throbbing in his throat from bout after bout of vomiting.

Willa ceased her sobbing for a moment to answer. "She's below, my laird. And Raibert is questioning Agnes. He thinks she may have been the one to...to..."

Edan muttered a curse. "Below where?"

"The dungeon, my laird."

"What?" There was enough force behind the word to be a bellow, but it only came out a croak, and he gasped at the pain of it.

"Aye, they have all gone mad, taking her below as if she were actually responsible, but I told Raibert, I think 'tis Agnes. She has been ever so cruel to my lady, and now this?" Willa started to shake and covered her face again as sobs wracked her.

"Ye think 'twas Agnes?"

"Aye. My laird, ye must save Lady Blair afore they get to her. They will kill her." Willa was balling in earnest now, loud wails, and she swiped her hands furiously over the tears. "Please, my laird."

The maid need not have begged, for Edan had already tossed back the covers, thrown his legs over the side of the bed and pressed his feet to the cool floor. He tried to stand but fell back to the bed, his body weakened. "I canna stand."

Willa crossed herself and started murmuring a frantic prayer.

Edan rolled his eyes with annoyance. "I am not going to die. Help me out of bed."

Willa looked pained, her gaze darting toward the door. "I'll go and get someone."

"Willa, now."

She nodded, reached for his arm and put it around her shoulders. He was luckily still dressed, though he smelled like death itself. But there was no time to freshen himself, not when his wife was suffering. They made it a few steps before he stumbled to the ground, catching himself with his hands before his face smacked into the wooden planks. Pain ricocheted from his knees and wrists.

Bloody hell, that hurt!

"My laird!" Willa screeched.

At her scream, several guards rushed into the room and lifted him from the ground.

Gritting his teeth, he demanded, "Take me to my wife."

"My laird, she is in the dungeon," one of the older men argued. "She did this to ye."

Despite the pain in his throat, Edan let out a roar. "Nay, she didna, ye bloody fools. And if ye dinna take me to her right now, I'll kill the lot of ye with my bare hands."

The men knew he'd not the strength to make good on his threat, but they allowed him the moment anyway. One of the men lifted Edan's arm around his shoulder and led him down the several flights of stairs to the castle's dungeon. Every step was an effort, but he pushed on, imaging his wife's torment and all of the ways he'd have to make it up to her.

The stink of the dungeon hit him full force. The air smelled of death and torment, damp and musty. No place for a lady. No place for anyone with a soul as innocent as hers. They rounded the corner at the bottom of the stairs, and the torchlight shone into the cell that the bastards he'd kept prisoner for a month had occupied.

Blair was on the floor, facing the opposite direction, curled into a ball and shivering.

"Blair," he groaned.

She rolled toward the cell bars and sat up, a gasp on her lips as she spotted him. A bruise marred her face where it looked like someone had hit her. He thought he'd felt rage before, but it was nothing compared to the fury that lanced him at the sight of his wife having been mistreated. Whoever had done that to her was going to pay for it.

"Open this door," he demanded to one of the guards, who wasted no time in doing so. His voice was coming out stronger than it had above stairs.

Edan found his strength to walk and stumbled into the cell. He dropped to his knees beside Blair and tugged her into his arms.

"Oh, my darling, I am so sorry," he murmured against her ear. "I'm so sorry." He choked with emotion, and she wrapped her arms around him.

"Ye're alive," she said, sobbing against him. "Is it really ye?"

"By the grace of God and Willa. She made me a tisane that helped force the poison from my body. But ye, my love, ye have suffered so much. I'll never forgive myself for letting harm come to ye."

"Dinna worry over me. I am so grateful they were able to save ye."

"Guards, take us back upstairs." He wanted to carry her himself, but considering he could barely lug his own body, it was best if they had help.

The guards were silent, their faces grave as they carried Edan and Blair back upstairs. Edan insisted they take them both into his wife's chamber. In the light of the candles and the sun streaming through the windows, of which the coverings had been pulled back to air out the fetid smell, Edan could make out the terror etched into Blair's face. She stared at the guards, back at him, and back to the guards, fear in her eyes. Lips pinched closed, as though she were afraid to say anything and have them toss her back in the dungeon. Good God, but he couldn't let her be afraid.

Lying on the bed side by side, Edan ordered everyone out.

"But my laird..." Murtagh hedged, his own brow wrinkled with concern.

"Get. Out." Edan spoke through gritted teeth, trying hard not to bellow the directive. So help everyone if he had a sword...

As soon as they were alone, he pulled Blair into his arms. She was stiff and appeared to be holding her breath.

"Lass, breathe, please. I'll not let them hurt ye." He stroked her back, kissed her temple, uncaring of the dirt on her face from the dungeon.

Slowly, she started to loosen her muscles, but with it came an uncontrollable tremor and sobs that shook her harder, fat tears that wet his shirt.

"I... I thought ye'd die. They thought I did it. I told them what Willa said about Agnes, but I dinna think they believed me."

"They are questioning her now, my love."

He tugged her closer, never wanting to let her go, the very idea of how close he'd come to losing her enough to make him wage a war against his own. In the short time he'd known her, Blair had become a part of him. He couldn't see a future without her. Didn't want to. He loved her so damn much.

And he needed her to know that.

He stroked her hair and whispered against her ear, "I love ye, *mo chridhe*. I love ye so much. I'll never let them hurt ye."

Rather than smile up at him as he expected, she cried all the harder, her own limbs tangling around his as she clung to him. God, what torments had they put on her while he was too sick to know where she was?

They fell asleep in each other's arms, both of them emotionally and physically exhausted. When he woke some hours later, it was to Willa and Raibert gently tapping his shoulders.

"My laird," Raibert said. "Willa has brought the two of ye something to eat, and the servants have carried up tubs and hot water for the both of ye to bathe in. Where would ye like us to put them?"

Edan couldn't remember the last time he'd had a bath. He usually swam in the loch or sea, or a burn if nothing else was available.

"None for me." He couldn't leave her, even if it was to get clean.

"But, my laird..." Raibert wrinkled his brow, clearly uncertain how to proceed.

"Put them both in my chamber then. And leave us to ourselves. I'll tend to my wife."

Neither of them commented, though Willa looked concerned. She'd grown quite fond of Blair, and likely wanted to know for herself that her lady was all right.

"She'll be safe with me," Edan assured the maid.

Alone once more, he gently woke Blair by kissing her tenderly on the lips. One kiss. Two. And she started to stir. He stroked her face until she blinked open her beautiful eyes. A soft smile played on her lips before it fell as reality returned to her.

"Edan," she gasped.

"My lady love," he said, smiling. "A bath awaits ye."

Her brow wrinkled. "But..."

"Ye're safe. I vow it."

She pressed her palm to his cheek. "I love ye, Edan. I didna get a chance to tell ye before, and when I thought I'd never see ye again, I regretted not spilling my heart to ye. I love ye so much."

He'd not expected the words to puncture into his chest as they did, to make him swell with pride and an ache to consume her, but they did.

"Never has a man loved a woman more, I'm certain. I'd go to the ends of the earth, fight everyone who stood in my way. I want only to make ye happy. God, I love ye so." He kissed her again languidly and then gently tugged her from the bed. "Come now, afore the water gets too cold."

"Where is the bath?" She glanced about the chamber, her gaze coming back to his in confusion.

"I had them set them up in my chamber."

"Them?"

"Aye." He took her hand and led her out of her chamber, through their solar to his own chamber, where two large tubs had been filled with steaming water. Linens lined each. Folded neatly on the bed were more linens for washing, drying and two small balls of soap.

"We're to bathe...together in the same chamber?" She raised a brow.

"Aye. Are ye all right with that? I have already seen ye naked, lass." He winked, hoping his teasing would take away some of her worry.

She blushed a pretty pink, her lashes fluttering. "I am not embarrassed."

"Then allow me to help ye undress."

He disrobed her slowly, kissing her neck, shoulders, trailing his fingers up and down her arms, over her spine, not caring at all that smudges of dirt lined her skin. She was his, and he was hers, and he'd love her in any form. He kissed her knees, and when she was finally standing nude before him, he led her to the tub and held her steady as she lowered herself into the steaming water with a sigh of pleasure.

He went to the table, poured them each a glass of wine and brought her one.

"Will ye not bathe?" she asked, taking a sip of wine, a sigh on her lips.

"I intend to."

She raised her brows and wiggled them a little, a clear indication she intended to watch him disrobe. Thank the saints, a bit of her good nature was returning after the ordeal.

Edan felt himself flush and took a long gulp of his wine. Since when had he ever been nervous about being undressed by a lassie's eyes? The very idea was laughable, and yet here he was.

He handed her a ball of soap and a linen square to wash with, then faced her as he slowly stripped off his *leine* shirt and trews—all of which ought to be burned. From having undressed her, and the challenging looks she'd given him, he was hard, rock-hard, and straining for her touch.

Blair licked her lips, her eyes on that solid appendage. "I think this bath is big enough for two," she said, her voice coming out a little crackly.

Edan swallowed the rest of his wine before coming closer to her. "If I get in that bath with ye, there will be more happening than simply washing." He took hold of his engorged shaft and stroked up the length of it.

Blair's eyes widened; her desire clear on her face. "Oh, sweet husband, I count on it."

Edan needed no other enticement. He climbed into the tub facing her, their legs entwined. They washed each other, stopping to kiss until they were both breathless, and then washed some more, stroking the soap and cloths tenderly, tauntingly over each other. He kissed her breasts, suckling on her taut pink nipples, and she kissed his chest, sliding her fingers lower into the water to grip his arousal exactly the way he'd done a moment ago.

Good God, if she kept that up, he'd finish before they'd even started.

With that notion in mind, he tugged her so that she straddled him, pressing the tip of his cock at her velvet heat and thrusting up inside her. The water sloshed in the tub at their movements, but they were both oblivious to it. They were caught up in the moment of their bodies becoming one. The magic of making love.

Edan gripped her hips, showing her how to move, keeping the pace steady even when she gasped with pleasure, seeking to ride him harder, faster.

"Not yet," he crooned, "too soon." He took her nipple into his mouth, sucking hard until she cried out with pleasure and tugged the hair at the nape of his neck.

She felt incredible. Her body wrapped around him like a warm, silken glove. He clutched at her buttocks, round and plush, soft and supple. He was trying so hard to stay in control, to drag out their love-making as long as possible, but the little crooning noises she made, her warm breath against his ear, her breasts bouncing against his chest...

He couldn't hold back any more. Edan pounded upward, allowed her to take the pace from slow and controlled to fast and frantic. Her moans grew louder, and then he was moaning in answer, clutching her arse, grabbing the back of her neck and tugging her forward to kiss him. He thrust his tongue into her mouth, letting all his passion unleash into her.

A second later, she was shuddering over him, and he swallowed her cry of release with his own...

Blair choked out a moan that was a half-sob as they clung to one another. He felt that every bit into his soul. He didn't want to imagine what would have happened to her, had he not woken when he did...

CHAPTER 22

Two days later, after taking much-needed time to recover and rest, Blair and Edan emerged from their chamber. During that time, it seemed Raibert and the elders had come to the conclusion that Agnes was indeed guilty of trying to poison Edan. They were sure she'd poisoned Connor before him and was responsible for the other suspicious deaths. The basket that Blair had left in the courtyard when she'd run inside had been found in Agnes's chamber, and it looked as though she'd been preparing to use it against Blair.

While they were both happy to still be alive, the exit from their chamber was not to return to life as usual or to start over. It was to preside over the official accusation and judgment of Agnes's guilt.

The entire atmosphere of the castle seemed to have soured, growing thick with tension.

Edan's jaw flexed, and his muscles were tight. Blair longed to stroke her hands over his body to ease the tension, but if two days in bed making love had not been enough to calm him, neither would rubbing his shoulders. Agnes's life was in his hands now, and she knew that would not be an easy thing to come to grips with. It was different than in battle, where death faced you head on and demanded an answer.

When it was multiple words against another, what made handing down a harsh sentence feel right in one's mind?

Her father had had to do the same thing over the years. Some of those accused were pardoned, but those with more serious offenses were executed. It couldn't be an easy task.

Edan paused at the great main doors that led outside. The muscles of his jaw were flexing and unflexing in the dim light. Blair reached for his hand and squeezed it. He glanced down at her, face grim.

Blair nodded, as though to say it was all right, but her throat was too tight to actually speak the words.

In the courtyard, Agnes had been removed from the stocks, but she was on her knees, arms shackled behind her back. The woman's hair was bedraggled and blowing all around her red-splotched, tear-stained face.

At the front of the gathered crowd, a man stared with a pained expression at the housekeeper. Blair had a feeling this was her husband. What terrible thoughts must be going through his mind right then? If the laird was in agreement with her guilt, would that guilt then shift to him? Was his wife going to die? Would he be next?

Blair's heart ached for the man. It even ached a little for Agnes. What had gotten into her; what hatred had stolen her heart that would make her want to kill so many people out of spite?

Edan let go of Blair's hand and made the motion for everyone to follow them inside. Agnes's husband stepped forward to help her stand, but Raibert made a motion with his hand, and the man stepped away. Blair's heart lurched at the expression of pure anguish on the man's face.

Saints, but how was she going to make it through this? Agnes's punishment was not only going to be a consequence for her, but so many others, too.

Inside the great hall, Edan took his place in his chair, and Blair moved to stand behind him, to place her hand on his shoulder as she'd been taught to do by her parents.

"Nay, sit beside me." He motioned to a servant, who was quick to bring over the chair by the hearth for her to sit in.

Blair nodded slowly, keeping the smile from her face that he would want her to be seated at his side, rather than perched behind him. This was no time to gloat. Her father did the same thing with her mother, but she'd been taught this was unusual and not to expect it. Edan really did love her. Not only that, he respected her.

The clan gathered, seemingly divided. Blair felt the hostility from half of those in attendance, as they did not even try to hide their glowers. She worked hard to ignore it, to look only to those she knew trusted her and believed her innocent. She just wanted this to be over. Willa gave her an encouraging nod as the crowd parted, and Raibert brought Agnes to the center of the great hall. She started to go to her knees, but Edan stopped her.

"Ye may stand, Agnes."

The housekeeper looked relieved as she wavered on her feet, steadied by Raibert. Tears spilled down her cheeks, and she looked terrified. Not exactly the face of someone Blair would have thought was capable of murder—especially so many. She expected the woman to be raving, spitting mad.

Cruel people shouldn't have the ability to appear frightened, since they had not the forethought to stay themselves from brutality.

"Agnes McQuinn of Clan Guinn, ye stand accused of multiple murders. How do ye plead?" Edan asked.

Blair sat ramrod straight beside her husband. He, too, sat tall. She prayed for mercy, her heart hurting as she looked on the woman.

"I am innocent, my laird, I swear."

Low hisses of disapproval went through half of the crowd—the half that was on Blair's side. The other half stomped their feet, causing several guards to step toward them with bared teeth, warning them to calm or take their leave.

"Do ye deny cruelty to your mistress?" Edan asked, his voice calm.

Agnes's gaze darted to Blair, pleading for understanding, and pinning Blair to her chair. Blair thought herself a good judge of character normally, but Agnes was confusing her, for if she were to go with her gut instinct, she'd think the woman innocent. It was hard to look away from the housekeeper, and so Blair worked instead on keeping her face a steady, blank slate, all while her mind whirled in confusion.

"My lady, please, I beg your forgiveness for the petty trick I played and the rumors I started, the way I antagonized ye. I am guilty of that, but not of murder, not of harming ye or the laird, I swear it."

"Trick? As in a single trick?" Blair responded, trying to keep her incredulity low. "Ye played more than one on me, Agnes."

Agnes cocked her head in confusion. "The bath, my lady. That is all, I swear it. If ye speak of spilling the wine and the stew, I didna do it apurpose, I swear it! I was not feeling well that night, not balanced on my feet."

"And what of my food making me sick my first night? My altered gowns?"

Blair eyed the woman, but she looked completely confused about the other things Blair referred to.

Agnes shook her head. "I am sorry for anything else ye might have perceived wrongdoing in, truly I am, but I didna alter your food, or your clothes, my lady. Someone is setting me up. I wouldna ever kill anyone." The woman's eyes widened. "I am innocent! Someone has entrapped me!"

Blair felt even worse now, that sense in her gut returning. Was Agnes telling the truth?

"Do ye deny taking Lady Blair's basket from the courtyard and placing it in your chambers?" Edan asked.

"Aye, I didna take it. It wasna me!" Agnes was growing hysterical, shifting her head from side to side, looking at the people as though one amongst them might stand out to her as guilty. "Who of ye is trying to frame me?"

"The way ye stand accused of trying to frame my wife?" Edan growled. "She was taken to the dungeon, accused of trying to murder me, and there ye stood quiet all the while."

"I thought her to be guilty," Agnes murmured, swiveling her head back toward Edan. Her eyes widened as she realized that was the wrong thing to say to her laird.

Edan leaned forward, the wood of his chair creaking beneath his weight. "Ye wanted her to be seen as guilty so ye could get away with it. We found the poisons in your room."

"I dinna know anything about poisons. I've not the stomach for killing." Her mouth opened and closed like a fish out of water as she searched for more to say.

"Ye lie." Edan's voice was low, and from what Blair knew of her husband, it was a warning. Judging from the reactions of everyone else in the room, they were of the same thought. "The evidence is overwhelming. We've testimonies from more than one who says ye wished ill on me and my wife. What I dinna understand is, why my brother? Why the people of your clan? How did ye get the men previously accused to testify for ye?"

Agnes shook her head, sobbing now, her words unintelligible.

"How much did my sister-by-marriage pay ye?"

"Mary?" Agnes looked stunned again. "She didna have anything to do with this."

"So ye admit that ye did?"

"Nay! That is not what I meant."

"Did she leave the poison with ye? What do ye get out of it?"

Agnes's knees buckled then, and she dropped forward. Her husband rushed to her aid, battling off the men who tried to stay him. But he wasn't in time. Her knees crashed, and she wavered forward. Raibert lifted her, but she shook her head, preferring to kneel.

"Easy, McQuinn," Edan warned her husband, but waved away the men from trying to pull him back so he could be by his wife's side. The man tugged her to her feet. She buried her sobbing face against his neck.

"I'd not kill anyone," she said over and over again. The way her voice broke tore at Blair's heart.

"What say ye, McQuinn, of your wife's charge?"

He shook his head, trying not to scowl at his laird, though it was obvious as he shifted his gaze up to the rafters. "I think her guilty of unkindness toward her new mistress, aye, but not murder, my laird. She's not wicked, just a spiteful woman."

Agnes sobbed harder, and her husband cooed something in her ear that reminded Blair of the way Edan had comforted her just days before.

The whispers rushing through the crowd of gathered clan members sounded like the rustling of wind just before a storm. Blair was completely torn. This woman who stood cowering and sobbing was either an incredible actress, or she had not done the deeds she'd been accused of. Indeed, Blair found so much similarity in the way in which Agnes was acting, and the way she too had shouted her innocence that it startled her.

Blair pressed her hand on top of Edan's and glanced at him. She had so much to say, and yet she couldn't say a single word for fear of what everyone would think. Edan glanced down at her, gaze locking on hers. If only she could share her thoughts with him. She mouthed the word *mercy*, and hoped he understood her.

Edan turned back toward Agnes McQuinn. "The evidence that ye were involved is irrefutable. But according to a witness, we have reason to believe ye didna act alone. Tell me who has helped ye, who put ye up to it, and I will show ye mercy."

"What kind of mercy?" her husband asked.

Blair waited with bated breath, hoping her husband would not say that his type of mercy was a quick death.

"She may return to Guinn lands."

"Banishment?" McQuinn asked.

"Aye. And I'd grant ye my blessing to go with her."

McQuinn squeezed his eyes shut; clearly the choice was a tough one. Let his wife live and be banished himself or let her die and he remain with the family he'd known all his life.

The couple whispered, with each of them shaking their heads in turn.

At last turning from her husband, Agnes faced them head on and said loud and clear, "Lady Mary Guinn, wife of your late brother."

Blair's shoulders dropped. She'd been so sure that Agnes was innocent, and yet the way she'd so boldly tossed out the name... It made sense why Mary Guinn would target her, but why Connor beforehand?

"Why?" Edan asked.

Agnes looked terrified, glanced at her husband. "I dinna know."

"Try harder."

She jerked her gaze back toward Edan, eyes wild as she searched the room as though searching for an answer. "Mary was unhappy. She was certain the laird was going to...get rid of her."

"Why would my brother do that?"

"Because..." Agnes was no longer crying, and the red-splotched cheeks were becoming pale. She looked ready to faint. "Because...she'd not yet gotten with child. She was becoming ill. Feared he was trying to kill her."

"And so, she sought to off him first." It was not a question Edan asked.

"Aye."

"Why then did she leave ye behind?"

"She knew I was happy here." Agnes glanced up at her husband. "That I'd found my place."

This sounded like the most honest thing the woman had said yet.

"So why then would ye go against your clan?"

Agnes turned to face her laird, agony rippling over her features. "As Mary said, any enemy of the Guinns is an enemy of mine."

"What do ye mean by that?"

Agnes shook her head, as though she didn't really know.

"I need an answer."

Agnes's gaze slid toward Blair, pleading for...forgiveness. Then she slid her gaze away. "The answer is easy, my laird. Your lady wife is a Sutherland."

Blair let out the breath she'd been holding as harshly as she would have if someone had punched her in the gut.

The blame of what was happening was once more on her shoulders, and this time she couldn't shout out her innocence. Blair might not have done the killing herself, but she was responsible all the same. She had to tell Edan what had happened between the Guinns and her family.

"To be clear, a feud between the Guinns and the Sutherlands has no bearing on this clan. My wife had no feud with Mary Guinn or her family. To say and believe such is blasphemy."

Blair winced. Edan had no idea...

"Go and pack your things, McQuinn. Ye and your wife will be accompanied by my guards so as to be certain ye dinna try to escape, nor attempt to harm anyone further."

McQuinn's face flushed, and he shuttered his emotions, but Blair had seen them flash for an instant, a whirl between shame and anger.

Edan dismissed everyone from the great hall abruptly and then sat back with a heavy sigh in his chair.

"I've need to speak with ye," Blair said urgently, twisting her hands in her lap.

"Come with me to my study. I've some missives to write."

She followed him to his study where he pulled out parchment, ink and quill.

"Who will ye write to? Laird Guinn?"

He shook his head. "What did ye want to speak to me about?"

"'Tis about the Guinns..."

He stopped what he was doing and met her gaze, eyes narrowing. "Aye?"

"They may have cause to be angry with me." She bit her lip. "A few years ago, I was the one who found out about Jean Guinn and her lover. I told my brother to go and find her when I knew she was with another man. They were betrothed, ye see. And I could not abide by her cuckolding him. After he found her with a lover, he took her back to her clan, shamed. War broke out shortly after."

"Ye think this is your fault?"

"Aye." She folded her hands in front of her and glanced down at the ground. "I will understand if ye'd wish to send me back to my da, and I'll not deny ye, should ye attempt to annul our marriage."

Edan let out a long breath. "I'm not sending ye anywhere, and I'm not annulling our marriage, Blair. I love ye, I told ye that. And what happened between your brother and his betrothed was not your fault, nor the battle after. She was the one who broke the promise between them. Any grudge that Mary Guinn had on behalf of her sister is ridiculous. I'll not hold ye responsible, and I'll raise my sword to anyone who dares."

"Ye're not mad?" Blair peeked up at him through her lashes.

"Not even a little bit." He said it straightforwardly, and that was exactly what she needed—no nonsense for her to try and wade through.

"Oh, thank God." She rushed around the table and threw herself against him. "I was so worried."

"Ye need not have been. Is that what ye wanted to tell me while we were in the great hall?"

"Part of it, aye. I had also wanted to say I thought Agnes innocent, but then when ye offered her mercy, she changed."

"Aye, I thought so, too. But I'm still not certain." Edan shook his head. "'Tis the only reason I'm letting her go, because I canna be sure."

"What will ye do?"

"I've need to write the Guinn chief and put the question to him. Tell him what's been happening. I'll send it ahead with a messenger, and we'll set out tomorrow to return Agnes. If Mary did have something to do with my brother's death, I am honor-bound to see her punished."

"Will ye write my brothers? My da?"

"Aye. Straight away. 'Tis a four day's ride north to the Guinns. I should return within a fortnight or less. I'll not stay long, I swear it."

"And what if he wishes war upon ye, as he did my brother, Strath?"

"I will attempt to negotiate, but ye know I'm a warrior, lass. Battling is in my blood. I need to avenge my brother, protect my clan and protect ye. I've got to get this put behind us, else for the rest of our days, there will be those in the clan who think ye responsible."

Blair nodded, knowing he was right. "I willna sleep until ye've returned to me."

"Och, lass, after a lengthy journey such as this, ye'd best be well rested, for I plan to make love to ye the whole day and night through."

Blair smiled, feeling color rise to her face as he dipped to kiss her.

CHAPTER 23

Blair stayed near the main gate, watching as Edan and his men rode into the distance until there was nothing left but her imagination and what would happen when they got there. Inside her boot was the dagger he'd given her for protection, should she need it. She turned away slowly, facing the crowd of onlookers. Everyone appeared as weary and drained as she felt. She had not been afforded a moment of peace since she'd been at Dunrobin Castle, and that had been months before.

Smiling and offering kind words to those she passed, she made her way to the kitchens to gather a small bundle and then went out again toward the village to check on Helen, Frances and the wee bairn, Alan. She wanted to thank Helen for stepping forward and telling the clan that she was a good person.

She knocked softly on the croft, and when it was opened by Helen, she found Father Thomas inside, praying over Frances.

Her throat caught, and her hand flew to her mouth. Oh, God! She was too late. Blair stared at Helen with sorrow, but Helen smiled, her face lighting up with hope.

"She is better, my lady. Father Thomas came by to bless her and the bairn."

Better… Frances was better, not dying!

"Oh, thank God," Blair said, feeling the breath she'd been holding leave her body and her heart start to pump once more.

Father Thomas nodded to her, "Lady Rose."

"Father."

He ducked from the croft, thankfully, as Blair still felt wary of him since he'd made her feel so ashamed of herself for things that Edan told her were quite normal. She wondered if when Edan returned she should talk to him about seeking a new priest for Rose kirk. Someone who seemed interested in building up the clan's members and not tearing them down. There was an air of bitterness at Kilravock. Perhaps part of it would dissipate with Agnes having gone. But if not, the man who was supposed to lead them toward bettering their souls might be the next step.

Blair set the package she'd put together for them down on a table, which included some cheese and fresh biscuits.

"My lady." The croaking voice came from where Frances lay on the bed. Her wee bairn slept soundly in her arms, looking pink and tiny and happy.

"Frances, I'm so verra glad to hear ye're better."

"Thank ye so much for what ye did for me, and for my bairn." She glanced down sweetly at her sleeping bundle. "Nay doubt without ye, neither one of us would be here."

Helen smiled gratefully at Blair. "I dinna know what I would have done without my sister."

"I feel the same about my own." Blair reached forward and took Helen's hand and then grasped Frances's with her other. "Ye're both verra lucky to have each other. If ye're ever in need of anything, dinna hesitate to ask."

Blair made her way back to the bailey and then to the stables to check on Bluebell. She was curled up asleep in a bed of hay beside a napping stable hand. Blair grinned, putting her hand over her mouth to stave off a laugh.

"He was up all night delivering a foal," the stable master said in a quiet tone. "Your Bluebell is keeping him warm."

"She seems to have found several friends here, has she not?"

"Aye, my lady. The sweetest thing. Almost as though she doesna know she's a lamb."

"I'm glad she's happy."

At the sound of Blair's voice, Bluebell perked up. She stretched, let out a *baa*, climbed to her feet and trotted over to give Blair a wet lick on her cheek.

"Would ye care to walk, sweetness?" Blair crooned, and Bluebell answered with an enthusiastic *baa-baa*. "We'll be back."

Blair clucked her tongue, and Bluebell trotted beside her out of the barn and toward the gate. A stroll in the fields, mayhap even down by the firth sounded perfect. She wanted to breathe in the salty air and think of her husband, her family. To give a prayer of thanks for the good fortune she had right now.

"My lady, ye should stay within the walls," one of the guards advised at her approach.

Blair paused, ready to give in, but then the defiant streak that sometimes caught hold of her loomed up. "Did my husband give that order?"

"Nay, my lady."

As she suspected. Well, she'd stick to the fields where those on the wall could still see her. "I should like to walk outside the walls. Allow me an escort then, if ye think my safety is a concern."

The guard nodded, though he clearly did not want to consent, and he waved a warrior to follow her.

She walked through the gate and over the bridge toward the fields, where she plopped down to pick some flowers while Bluebell grazed.

The guard paced in a wide circle, his gaze out toward the horizon.

"What are ye looking for?" she asked.

He did not glance back as he answered. "Campbells. And anyone else that shouldna be here."

"Ah." Blair plucked another flower and stared at the buttery yellow petals. She'd heard the clan had a problem with the Campbells reiving, but since she'd been here, there'd been none of that.

Bluebell delicately plucked the yellow flower from Blair's hand, lipping it into her mouth and chewing with exuberance. There she remained in silence for a while, other than the few words she murmured to Bluebell, plucking flowers for her lamb. All the while, the guard looked so strung up she thought he'd snap. Perhaps it was best to put the guard out of his misery by calling their walk and flower picking to a close and heading back to the castle.

Rather than take Bluebell back to the barn, however, Blair led her into the castle, snapping her fingers and uttering a command to settle the hounds who raised their hackles at the sight of a lamb inside the keep.

Up the stairs they went to her shared rooms with Edan. She flopped in a chair before the hearth in the solar, and Bluebell curled up on the tapestried rug and went to sleep. With Edan gone, it would be lovely to have her sweet Bluebell with her.

Two days passed in relative peace. The people went about their duties, and while Blair helped in the kitchen and with visiting the bedridden, Bluebell tended to her stable hands as though she were the one in charge. In the evenings after supper, Willa attended Blair in her chamber, though she worried about her brother, Raibert, being away, which only caused Blair to worry about Edan.

The men would be more than halfway to their destination by now, which meant soon they would come back home.

"With both of them gone, the castle is defenseless. I know we've the elders and the other warriors here," Willa babbled on, "but 'tis not the same."

Blair nodded mutely, knowing the dangers but not putting voice to them. At home, she was certain her mother would not have allowed such a conversation to take place, with a servant worrying the lady of the house, but Blair couldn't fall into that line. Willa was her friend, and the lass was clearly distressed over it.

"I'm sorry, my lady, I dinna mean to worry ye."

"Ye're only voicing my own concerns. On the morrow, I'll speak with the elders in regard to the security of the clan."

"Look at wee Bluebell." Willa giggled, changing the subject as she glanced toward Bluebell, who lay curled in a fleecy ball at Blair's feet. "So docile and sweet."

"Aye, she'd not hurt a fly."

"She's like a bairn to ye, aye?"

Blair nodded, stroking her fingers through the fleece, while Willa stroked a brush through Blair's hair. "I dinna know what I'd do without her."

"Hmm." Willa hummed and then clucked her tongue. "Och, my lady, I nearly forgot. I found your sewing kit in the laird's wardrobe. Someone must have misplaced it."

"Oh." Blair frowned. Willa was looking through the laird's wardrobe? But why? She wasn't in charge of his laundry. Blair turned around to take the sewing kit.

Pain ricocheted off the side of her head, and she fell from her chair, vision blurry, the taste of blood on her tongue. She blinked her eyes, trying to focus as Willa loomed over her.

"My goodness, my lady, what are ye doing down there?" But there was no worry in Willa's tone, and the menacing look in her eye was enough to warn Blair that they'd all been so very wrong.

❧

THEIR JOURNEY to Guinn Castle did not go quickly. It rained for many of the days, and Edan worried about what was happening at home. Agnes protested her innocence only once, but then clammed up at a word from her husband.

But still, her protests, even after having been shown mercy, gave Edan pause.

They arrived at the castle on a gloomy day, and rather than be locked out as Edan expected, the laird who'd received their message allowed them entry right away.

Mary Guinn met them in the great hall, her face drawn full of concern.

Edan hardened at the sight of her. According to Agnes, she had killed his brother. And all those days ago, when he'd told her she could stay with the clan and she'd denied his kindness, he never once thought she was the reason he'd be standing here now. That she'd needed to escape her guilt.

"We received your messenger," Laird Guinn said, appearing beside his daughter. "And 'tis glad I am that ye came so we might clear this up."

Clear this up... As if his brother's death was only a misunderstanding. "I'm listening," Edan said, the hardness in his tone not lost on the Guinns.

"Daughter." Laird Guinn glanced toward Mary, giving her permission to speak.

"I am innocent of what ye suggested in your missive." Mary eyed him levelly, and he sensed sincerity in her tone. She was not hysterical, nor insistent, but composed. "I should have told ye before I left, but I was scared. The reason my da was already on his way to take me home was because someone was trying to kill me."

"What?" Edan bristled, shock rippling through him.

"Aye. And I'm fairly certain 'tis the reason I was never able to conceive."

Someone had tried to kill her...before they'd killed Connor. "Explain."

"At first, it was just that my...flux...was..." Her face brightened, and she bit her lip, stopping her words altogether.

Edan too felt his throat dry a little at the talk of women's issues with someone other than his wife.

"'Twas not normal," her father interjected. "And more than once, she was certain she was miscarrying."

"Aye. I told Connor, but he thought I was just being overly suspicious and thought I was perhaps a bit hysterical over not getting with child, even though I had at least three times."

"Let me try to understand this," Edan said. "Someone was poisoning ye, causing ye to lose your bairn? Who would do such a thing?"

Tears filled the woman's eyes. "I dinna know. But soon after, I grew verra ill whenever I ate. I would throw up the food and be abed for days. Connor thought me of a weak disposition. He couldna believe that it was poison, but I knew it was, for when I would sneak down to the kitchens at night and eat what I could find, I was never ill."

Edan thought of Blair on her first night, how she'd been ill when served stew instead of mutton.

Mary shook her head. "My da came to get me because of what was happening. I've not been ill since I got home. But after Connor, and what ye said has been happening, do ye not see that I am innocent?"

"Why did ye not tell me?"

"I was afraid." Her composure cracked for a split second before she contained herself once more. "I'm sorry."

"Agnes stands accused as your accomplice," Edan said. "She confessed."

"Then she lied." Mary searched the great hall for Agnes. "Where is she?"

"In the bailey."

Mary turned to her father. "Can we bring her in?"

"Aye."

Agnes was fetched to come inside, and as soon as she saw Mary, she ran for her, arms outstretched. Edan stepped between them in an attempt to save Mary from Agnes's attack, but Mary shoved around him. Instead of attacking her, the two women embraced.

"What the devil?" Edan growled.

"I feared leaving ye, begged ye to come with me."

"I couldna leave McQuinn." Agnes turned to face Edan then, her face full of regret. "I lied to ye, my laird. Mary was not involved, and neither was I. But coming here seemed the only way to escape a death sentence for something I didna do, and the only way to convince ye of the truth."

Guilt ate at Edan's gut. This was why he'd had doubts, because she wasn't the one. Which meant he'd left his wife at home with the enemy. *Bloody hell!* She could be suffering at this very moment. Edan fought the urge to leave. He needed a few more answers.

"Then why the cruelty to your lady, my wife?" Edan asked her.

"I was not in charge of Lady Blair's bath. And by the time I found out what happened, I took the blame as housekeeper for not having checked. After that, I thought to blend in so I could find out who might be at the heart of the cruelty. I hoped to put a stop to it, to save your wife, rather than allow what happened to Lady Mary start all over again."

"Why did ye not say so?" he asked. "If ye'd only spoken the truth, we'd not be here. My wife would not be in danger now."

"I couldna figure out who it was, and by the time ye were accusing me, it was too late. The evidence was against me, I knew it. I only wished to appeal to your mercy, which ye did show me, in hopes I could reveal the truth to ye."

Edan clenched his fists. "So ye've no idea who it might be?"

Agnes shook her head. "The only one who would have had access was Willa, but the lass is too sweet for all that."

"Too sweet," Edan said, his stomach coiling. He turned to Raibert. A flash of shock and pain showed in his eyes before he shuttered it. Did he think his sister capable? Incapable? Soon enough, they'd find out. Not another minute could be wasted here when Blair might be in trouble. "We have to go. Now."

"Aye, my laird." Raibert's voice was tight. He knew what his laird was suspecting. But he didn't place any blame with Raibert, for he could not have known, could he?

"Can I come back? Will ye nay banish my husband?" Agnes said. "He's only ever been loyal to the Rose clan."

Edan let out a harsh breath. "Aye." Then to Laird Guinn, "I thank ye for your hospitality, and for allowing me to speak with your daughter."

"Can we send ye with provisions?"

"We've enough. Thank ye."

Edan hurried from the castle. If he thought the journey here was long, the four days back were going to be agony as he worried over whether his wife would be alive when he got there.

BLAIR WOKE IN THE DARK. Hard, cold earth beneath her body. For a moment, she thought she'd been buried alive, but the space around her was too vast when she held out her hands. Not even a sliver of light came inside. And it was damp. Cold.

She could hear the scurrying feet of rats, feel their noses sniffing against her body, and as she batted them away, she wondered how long it would be before they decided to feast on her despite her protests.

Where was she?

This was not the dungeon. Not a cave. Maybe she was dead. Maybe this was Hell, and Father Thomas had seen her banished here.

She pushed to her feet, wobbling and swaying against dizziness. Her head pounded.

She reached up, touched a place on her forehead that hurt like the devil, and her fingers came away hot and sticky.

Blood.

What had happened?

She'd been in her chamber getting ready for bed, talking to Willa, petting Bluebell.

And then Willa had hit her hard on the head with...something. A candlestick.

So how had she ended up here? In this dungeon that wasn't a dungeon?

"Hello!" she called out to no one, and only the rats answered with a quick scurry.

Blair held her hands out in front of her, shuffling forward, not knowing what she might kick until she came to a wet and grimy earthen wall. She was definitely underground somewhere. She slid her hands along the wall, walking slowly around and around, never really certain if there was a beginning or an end, but determining wherever she was must be circular.

Choking on a sob, she collapsed to the ground and pulled her knees up to her chin. A great shudder rocked her. She reached for her boot, remembering the knife Edan had given her. She'd not even had time to pull it. But it was empty. Willa had taken it.

She was going to die in here. Without a doubt.

She had no idea how long she'd been here already, but she guessed only a few hours. Her head wound still bled, and while it felt crusty around the edges, the center was warm and slick.

Hours... And there was still at least a sennight, give or take a day or two, before Edan would return. By the time he did, she would have perished. Wouldn't she? How long could one last underground without food or water?

"Oh, Edan," she whispered. "I'm so sorry."

She was sorry for luring him into this marriage that had been doomed to fail from the start.

"I'm sorry, Mama and Da." For not trying harder to be the good girl she'd strived to be, for not listening and paying attention.

Oh, God... Where was Bluebell? What had Willa done to her?

That only made Blair sob harder. The one friend she thought she'd made here at Kilravock had been her worst enemy. And now everyone, including her sweet lamb, was going to pay for that mistake.

CHAPTER 24

The miles of road between Guinn country and Rose did not disappear quickly enough. At long last, the top of Edan's tower keep came into view. Rather than breathe in a sigh of relief, the anxiety he'd felt for the whole of the trip kicked up a notch, causing his heart to pound without mercy until he feared his ribs would crack.

They rushed over the moors, but with every glide of his mount, he could have sworn the distance remained the same. A trick of the mind, to be sure. Then he was pounding over the lowered drawbridge and thundering into the bailey.

Rose men and women stared up at him startled, their eyes full of alarm and wariness. Several rushed off, as if he were an invader and not their laird. Was it because of the way he'd entered—or something else? Because his brain was throwing scenarios at him that had him reaching for his sword.

The hair on the back of his neck standing on end.

"Where is my wife?" His voice was a near growl, and even Raibert, who'd ridden in beside him, had his hand on the hilt of his sword as though they'd just entered an enemy's bailey.

Murtagh stepped forward, his expression resolute. "She'll not be coming out to greet ye, laird."

Edan bristled. "I asked, where she is? What have ye done with her?"

"She awaits ye and your judgment. She's killed again, my laird."

Edan let out a bellow that had children and animals alike running. Women cowered, hiding behind men if they were near. But Murtagh puffed his chest, ready to do battle with his laird on the matter.

"How dare ye," Edan said. "How dare ye lock her up for a second time when it is nay she who has done these crimes. We've only just come from Guinn lands, where my brother's wife told me she begged her father for rescue, because someone tried to kill her first. She'd thought it was Connor, trying to kill her off for not having his bairns, but nay, it was one of ye. And I'll have your head."

But for now, he needed to get his wife out of her imprisonment.

"Raibert," Edan growled, knowing that his guard and the other warriors they'd brought back would take care of those who wished to go against him.

As soon as he took a step toward the keep stairs, Murtagh drew his sword.

"Dinna make me kill ye, old man. Ye're wrong. We've heard proof of it."

"She'll kill ye, and the bloody lot of us," Murtagh bellowed. Several of the other men saw the elder had pulled his sword and went to do so themselves.

"Your laird has spoken," Raibert shouted back. "We've all heard testament from the Guinns, and that no fault was had by them. How can ye go against the truth? Do ye hate her, do ye hate your laird so verra much? Traitors every one of ye that would dare to raise your swords to your laird."

Should they not immediately retreat, the men were sealing their fate. To pull their sword on Edan was to sign their own death warrants.

It was up to Murtagh who'd issued the challenge against Edan to begin with.

"Put it away, Murtagh, and listen to reason. Else, die here today."

Murtagh bared his teeth, his knuckles white on the hilt of his sword. "Your da would be ashamed of ye." But he put the sword back.

Edan tried not to let the painful words get to him. "Methinks 'tis ye who ought to be ashamed for condemning an innocent woman."

He didn't wait to see Murtagh's reaction or to hear his reply. He had only a desire to find his wife.

When they'd locked her in before, it had been in one of the cells of the dungeon where the Ross warriors had been housed some weeks before. But this time, with them feeling certain she was the one to have gone on a killing spree, Edan would bet his life they put her in *the hole* to rot.

The hole of Kilravock was nothing more than a dank pit in the rocky ground with a solid iron disk overtop to keep anyone tossed inside down there, and without light. He'd been gone for a little over a fortnight, and there was no telling how long she'd been down there.

Edan gripped the iron, hauling it away with a roar. The guard on duty handed him a torch, his eyes filled with regret for having been the one to stand there.

Edan gripped the torch and held it down into the darkness, lighting up only a portion of the dungeon, but not enough. Edan didn't see her.

"Blair," he called. "I'm coming to get ye, my love."

He waited for a response, but there was none. He turned to the guard, wondering for a moment if he had gotten it wrong. "She is here?"

"Aye, my laird." Anguish sounded in his tone. "Though I've barely heard a peep all day."

"How long has she been down there?"

"A sennight tomorrow."

"Food and drink?"

"Some." The man had the wherewithal to look gutted, but that didn't make Edan's desire to run him through any less, for he was certain *some* meant mostly *none*.

"Hold this while I go down," Edan said, holding out the torch.

"Aye, my laird. Be careful." The guard took it swiftly. Edan had the flickering thought that once he was below, this man could very easily return the iron cover in place. But that would cost him his life, as

Raibert was sure to be close behind him. Edan had no doubt that he was innocent in all this..

Edan lowered his feet into the dungeon, sinking his body slowly in, holding his weight up on the rim with his arms. His feet just barely skimmed the bottom, a feat a man of lesser height would not be able to accomplish.

He let go, settling on his feet, and the guard lowered the light. Edan reached up, took the torch from him and held it out in front of him, watching rats scurry into the darkness. Bones littered the floor. Prisoners past. None that he knew, as he'd never made use of the hole himself, and he hadn't been home enough before to know better.

"Blair, 'tis Edan."

Still no answer.

"Come into the light, love." He moved forward slowly, not wanting to step on her by accident.

He listened carefully, still only hearing the scurrying of rats as they scattered into their burrowed holes. The scent of the hole was of death, and the silence just as macabre. Edan's heart was pounding, his stomach twisted up into knots, as he worked hard to thrust aside the images his mind conjured.

"Blair," he said softly again, "Where are ye?"

As a lad, he'd always thought the hole was just that, a hole big enough for only a man or two, but now that he was down there, he could see it was much wider, the size of small chamber. Edan turned in a slow circle, holding out the torch to light the entire place. When it seemed he'd finally come in a full circle, he saw her at last, huddled in a small, very still heap against the wall.

Edan let out a curse and rushed forward. He knelt where she lay, dropping the torch, too. It fell to the ground and was out snuffed, but he didn't care. He gathered her in his arms, trying to see into the darkness from the little light that shown from the hole overhead.

"My laird," the guard called down in a panic.

"I need a ladder."

She wasn't going to be able to help him get her out of here.

"Aye, my laird, right away."

Edan smoothed her hair from her face, touching her cool cheeks and pressing his finger beneath her nose. Shallow breaths fanned over his finger.

She was alive.

"Thank God," he said through a throat tight with emotion. Tears of relief and anger stung his eyes. Only a day or two more of this and she would have perished.

There was the sound of wood scraping behind him, and he saw a ladder being lowered, and then the guard climbed down with a torch.

"I'll light the way, my laird."

Edan didn't speak, though he did nod, not caring whether the guard saw or not. He lifted his wife into his arms and carried her to the ladder, and from there, to their chambers.

Inside, Blair's maid, Willa, stood before a steaming bath. "Let me take care of her, my laird."

He didn't like her tone, or the shift of her eyes, but more telling was the way that Blair jerked at the sound of Willa's voice. Though she said nothing and did not open her eyes. It didn't matter; the suspicions laid by Agnes and Mary were confirmed.

Willa was the guilty one all along.

"I've got it. Leave us."

Willa started to protest, but he gave her a look that promised death if she did not obey, and so she slinked from the room—though he wasn't certain how long he'd be able to keep her at bay.

Edan kicked the door shut and carefully laid his wife on the bearskin rug before the hearth, disrobing her and tossing the grimy garments into the flames. Bruises marred her flesh, whether from an attack or from being pushed into the hole, he didn't know, but every one of them made him want to punish someone. His wineskin was still attached to his belt, and so he opened the cork and let her sip from the whisky he had inside it. She drank heavily and sputtered but begged for more.

"Not too much, else ye'll be spilling it back out again."

He washed her gently in the tub, and as he smoothed the sweet-smelling soap over her fingers, she tightened her grip on his hand.

"Ye're safe, my love," he murmured, leaning down to press a kiss to her temple, and then her hand. "I'll never let anyone hurt ye."

She opened her eyes, searching him out, and tears brimmed the edges. Her lips parted, but nothing pushed past save a croak.

"Ye need not speak just yet, sweetling," he said.

Blair shook her head, her forehead wrinkling. "I... I need to tell ye."

"Only if ye're up for it."

"Willa... She is..."

But before she could finish speaking, Blair's eyes widened, and Edan turned instinctively to see that Willa stood behind him with a dagger, poised to strike.

He knocked her to the ground, grappling with her arm, which seemed to hold a strength unnatural for a lass of her slight figure. But he was able to get the dagger from her and pin her in place with his knees.

Raibert burst into the room, eyes on Willa. "Sister, what are ye doing?"

"It was her, Raibert, all along," Edan shouted. "Guards!"

Raibert looked stunned, as though he didn't want to believe what he was seeing. The man had still held out hope his sister was innocent, a hope Edan had shared for his guard's sakes. He backed away, shaking his head and muttering, "How?"

"Get over here and save me, Brother, ye spoiled whoreson. I killed that bitch, too, ye know. She was vile, and I hated everything about her." Willa was raving and spitting on the floor.

"What in bloody hell are ye talking about?" Raibert's eyes widened, and he met Edan's. "I didna know."

"Our mother, ye bloody, puss-filled cock. Watched her drown in her porridge after I tried out my special ingredient. Dried-up bloody old bitch."

Willa spewed other words that made Edan rage with anger, but seemed to snap Raibert into action.

He dropped to his knees beside Edan and the struggling Willa and helped to bind her wrists and ankles. With the task complete, he said, "I've got her, my laird."

"To the hole," Edan growled as he climbed back to his feet, staring down with shock at the woman, sister to his dearest friend in the world, and daughter of the housekeeper who'd faithfully served his family for so many years.

Raibert hauled the woman from the room, and as soon as they were both gone, he returned to the tub, slipping his arms around his wife, needing to feel her breathing and alive in his arms.

Edan pulled her from the tub, dried her carefully and dressed her in front of the hearth. He then brushed out her hair until it dried and crackled, and she told him all that had happened while he was gone. When she started to tear up, he let her collapse in his arms, and pressed kisses to her face, murmuring words of love and comfort.

"I'm so verra sorry, my love," he said. "Would that I could take it all away."

"When I tried to tell them that it wasna me, that it was one of their own, they only mocked me. And she, Willa, was amongst them, mocking, shouting, egging them on, even when I knew it was her all along."

"'Tis over now. Those responsible will be punished, I swear it."

A soft knock at the door startled them both. Edan called for it to be opened, and Agnes did so. She stood there wringing her hands and looking very worried. Blair sucked in a ragged breath.

"Nay," Blair whispered.

"Shh," Edan said against her ear. "She is not to blame."

"My laird," Agnes croaked. "We brought some food."

Edan narrowed his gaze, still uncertain who to trust. "Taste it first," he said. "Everything on the tray."

Agnes nodded emphatically as she sipped the wine and took bites of everything. They waited in silence, and when nothing happened, he nodded for her to leave the tray.

"Is there anything else, my laird?"

"Nay."

Agnes backed from the room. As soon as she was gone, he carried the tray to the floor where they'd settled before the hearth and he fed his wife every bite.

"I can eat on my own." She offered him a small smile.

"I know it, but I was not here to protect ye before, and I've the need to make up for it."

Blair sighed, took his hand in hers and brought it to her lips. "'Twas not your fault, and ye need not pay for what was done to me, nor make up for anything. Ye saved m; ye cared for me. Ye love me."

"I love ye with all my heart." His voice cracked. "If anything should have happened to ye…"

Blair pushed the tray of food aside and crawled her way over to him, curling herself up in his lap and pressing her lips to his. "I am safe now, in your arms. Make love to me and let us forget all of the horrible things that have happened."

Edan laid her gently down on the soft bearskin and braced himself over her. "Ye're my everything."

"And ye're mine."

WHEN BLAIR WOKE the following morning, she reached for Edan, but found his side of the bed cold. She jerked awake, suddenly fearful that his return had been a dream, and she was still stuck in the nightmare. But she was in her chamber, and the water that had cooled still filled her tub. Their leftover dinner was still on the floor before the hearth. A sob of relief escaped her, and she flung back the covers, determined to dress quickly and find her husband, if only to reassure herself of his presence.

But she needn't have gone far, as he was standing in their solar, staring out the window.

"Good morning," she said with a soft smile.

Edan started and came forward to wrap her in his arms and kiss her thoroughly. "I didna wake ye, did I?"

"Nay. I slept more soundly than I can ever remember."

"Good." A frown creased his brow.

"What is it?"

"The women who mistreated ye, save for Willa, have been placed in the stocks. If ye wish to face them, to say something to them, I will go with ye."

Blair sucked in a breath. She shook her head. "I dinna want to see them that way."

"It is a just punishment."

It was. She knew that.

"And Willa?"

"She awaits execution."

"When will that be?"

"As soon as ye will it. She is already tied to the stake."

"The stake?"

"She will be burned."

Blair shook her head. "Nay, please, I beg ye show her mercy."

"There is no mercy for a sinner such as this, Blair. The woman killed half a dozen people. Maybe more. How can we let her live?"

Blair bit her lip, uncertain of the answer to such a question. She didn't know. How could they allow her to live? She was a murderer, and very likely evil to boot. How else could she have so heinously harmed so many people and maintained her charm and care for Blair? She was cunning, conniving.

"Your da would have her executed."

She nodded. "Aye."

"Your brothers, too."

"Aye."

"But not ye?"

"Is there not a fate worse than death for a woman such as her?"

He shook his head. "Nay. But if ye prefer it not be done on our lands, I can have her sent to the Guinns and give my sister-by-marriage, Mary, the chance at her own revenge."

"Aye. Then her fate is not in our hands. I'd hate for ye to go to Hell for taking the life of the woman who killed your brother."

"Lass, hers would not be the first I've taken. I'm a warrior. Dispatching of life in the name of our cause and protecting our way of the world is what I do."

Tears burned her eyes. "I'm afraid I'm not cut out for being the wife of a laird. If I canna even mete out a death sentence to a woman who deserves it. My sisters would be ashamed of me."

"Nay, *mo chridhe*, they'd expect nothing less of sweet Blair."

He took her hand and led her reluctantly outside.

Willa stood on tiptoe tied to the stake, a pile of wood surrounding her. A loud curse blew from her snarling lips. "Whore! Ye sicken me, standing there discussing my fate as though ye were God. Ye're not God! Ye're nothing but a lowly whore. And ye're no laird." Her gaze shifted to Edan. "Only half a man. Ye know I fucked your brother? Every night. The reason his wife couldna get pregnant was because I took all the seed he had to give."

"She lies," Blair murmured.

"Aye," he answered. "If I know one thing, it is that my brother was honorable."

"And she'd have had a bairn by now, yet her belly is as a flat as the wall."

"Aye."

"Are ye going to light the flames? Or have ye not the ballocks for it? I curse ye. Curse ye and your whole family." She was screaming now, her head yanking from side to side.

Mothers in the bailey hid their children behind their skirts or ushered them away. People were crossing themselves as Willa begged the lord of Hell to come and avenge her.

Even Blair felt like looking at the ground to make certain no demons were coming up to grab at her ankles.

"I'm sorry, my love," Edan said. "I want to give ye everything ye ask. But I canna give ye this."

"I know." Blair pressed her quivering lips together. "I know."

"But I will make it swift. That is all the mercy I can show."

She nodded, turning her back on the woman who spewed even more vile things their way. Words and actions and curses that Blair was certain would haunt her dreams.

Edan shifted at her side, and she heard him say, "Bow," in a low tone to Raibert, who was distraught enough that his sister had killed their own mother, that he'd offered to enact the punishment himself.

Edan had denied him however, stating that if he were to give the executing blow to his sister, it was an act he might never recover from.

Still, Blair didn't turn around. She squeezed her eyes shut, ready for the nightmare to come to an end. The raving screams grew louder, shriller, as she demanded Edan end her.

There was a short whistle as his arrow flew, and then sudden silence from Willa, as his aim rang true.

Strong arms came around her. "'Tis over."

Blair couldn't find her voice. She circled her own arms around his waist, pressing her face against his chest.

"And now we can start anew."

"Aye. The way it should have been all along." He lifted her in his arms, cradling her against him as he took her back into the keep and up the stairs to their chamber.

Bluebell scurried over from her wee bedding on the floor to nuzzle Blair's hand. She kissed her sweet lamb's nose.

"Out with ye, cherub, I've a need to make love to my wife."

Blair clucked her tongue and led Bluebell to the door, letting her out into the corridor where she'd find her own way outside. Now with Willa gone, there was no more threat to her sweet lamb.

Edan came up behind her, his hands on her shoulder as he pressed his lips to the back of her neck and started to pluck the pins from her hair.

"I think when ye called yourself Blair the Not So Fair, ye spoke not of your beauty, for that would be a lie. Ye're the most stunning woman I've ever seen. With breasts as lush as fields of heather, and hips that keep me anchored as I fall into a deep well of lust. I have figured it out, though."

"Ye have?"

"Aye. Ye meant *not so fair*, as in the way in which ye planned to torment me. For ye've been verra, verra unfair, my love."

She turned in his arms, kissing him with all the passion she possessed and murmured, "Love is not fair, but it is kind."

"Just like ye."

EXCERPT FROM THE
HIGHLANDER'S TEMPTATION
WHERE THE SUTHERLANDS ALL BEGAN...

PROLOGUE

Spring, 1282
Highlands, Scotland

THEY GALLOPED THROUGH THE EERIE moonlit night. Warriors cloaked by darkness. Blending in with the forest, only the occasional glint of the moon off their weapons made their presence seem out of place.

'Twas chilly for spring, and yet, they rode hard enough the horses were lathered with sweat and foaming at the mouth. But the Montgomery clan wasn't going to be pushed out of yet another meeting of the clans, not when their future depended on it. This meeting would put their clan on the map, make them an asset to their king and country. As it was, years before King Alexander III had lost one son and his wife. He'd not remarried and the fate of the country now relied on one son who didn't feel the need to marry. The prince toyed with his life as though he had a death wish, fighting, drinking, and carrying on without a care in the world. The king's only other chance at a succession was his daughter who'd married but had not yet shown any signs of a bairn filling her womb. If something were to happen to the king, the country would erupt into chaos. Every precaution needed to be taken.

Young Jamie sat tall and proud upon his horse. Even prouder was he, that his da, the fearsome Montgomery laird, had allowed him to accompany the group of a half dozen seasoned warriors—the men who sat on his own clan council—to the meeting. The fact that his father had involved him in matters of state truly made his chest puff five times its size.

After being fostered out the last seven years, Jamie had just returned to his father's home. At age fourteen, he was ready to take on the duties of eldest son, for one day he would be laird. This was the perfect opportunity to show his da all he'd learned. To prove he was worthy.

Laird Montgomery held up his hand and all the riders stopped short. Puffs of steam blew out in miniature clouds from the horses' noses. Jamie's heart slammed against his chest and he looked from side to side to make sure no one could hear it. He was a man after all, and men shouldn't be scared of the dark. No matter how frightening the sounds were.

Carried on the wind were the deep tones of men shouting and the shrill of a woman's screams. Prickles rose on Jamie's arms and legs. They must have happened upon a robbery or an ambush. When he'd set out to attend his father, he'd not counted on a fight. Nay, Jamie merely thought to stand beside his father and demand a place within the Bruce's High Council.

Swallowing hard, he glanced at his father, trying to assess his thoughts, but as usual, the man sat stoic, not a hint of emotion on his face.

The laird glanced at his second in command and jutted his chin in silent communication. The second returned the nod. Jamie's father made a circling motion with his fingers, and several of the men fanned out.

Jamie observed the exchange, his throat near to bursting with questions. What was happening?

Finally, his father motioned Jamie forward. Keeping his emotions at bay, Jamie urged his mount closer. His father bent toward him, indicating for Jamie to do the same, then spoke in a hushed tone.

"We're nearly to Sutherland lands. Just on the outskirts, son. 'Tis an attack, I'm certain. We mean to help."

Jamie swallowed past the lump in his throat and nodded. The meeting was to take place at Dunrobin Castle. Why that particular castle was chosen, Jamie had not been privy to. Though he speculated 'twas because of how far north it was. Well away from Stirling where the king resided.

"Are ye up to it?" his father asked.

Tightening his grip on the reins, Jamie nodded. Fear cascaded along his spine, but he'd never show any weakness in front of his father, especially now that he'd been invited on this very important journey.

"Good. 'Twill give ye a chance to show me what ye've learned."

Again, Jamie nodded, though he disagreed. Saving people wasn't a chance to show off what he'd learned. He could never look at protecting another as an opportunity to prove his skill, only as a chance to make a difference. But he kept that to himself. His da would never understand. If making a difference proved something to his father, then so be it.

An owl screeched from somewhere in the distance as it caught onto its prey, almost in unison with the blood curdling scream of a woman.

His father made a few more hand motions and the rest of their party followed him as they crept forward at a quickened pace on their mounts, avoiding making any noise.

The road ended on a clearing, and some thirty horse-lengths away a band of outlaws circled a trio—a lady, one warrior, and a lad close to his own age.

The outlaws caught sight of their approach, shouting and pointing. His father's men couldn't seem to move quickly enough and Jamie watched in horror as the man, woman and child were hacked down. All three of them on the ground, the outlaws turned on the Montgomery warriors and rushed forward as though they'd not a care in the world.

Jamie shook. He'd never been so scared in his life. His throat had long since closed up and yet his stomach was threatening to purge everything he'd consumed that day. Even though he felt like vomiting, a sense of urgency, and power flooded his veins. Battle-rush, he'd heard it called by the seasoned warriors. And it was surging through his body, making him tingle all over.

The laird and his men raised their swords in the air, roaring out their battle cries. Jamie raised his sword to do the same, but a flash of gold behind a large lichen-covered boulder caught his attention. He eased his knees on his mount's middle.

What was that?

Another flash of gold — was that blonde hair? He'd never seen hair like that before.

Jamie turned to his father, intent to point it out, but his sire was several horse-lengths ahead and ready to engage the outlaws, leaving it up to Jamie to investigate.

After all, if there was another threat lying in wait, was it not up to someone in the group to seek them out? The rest of the warriors were intent on the outlaws which left Jamie to discover the identity of the thief.

He veered his horse to the right, galloping toward the boulder. A wee lass darted out, lifting her skirts and running full force in the opposite direction. Jamie loosened his knees on his horse and slowed. That was not what he'd expected. At all. Jamie anticipated a warrior, not a tiny little girl whose legs were no match for his mount. As he neared, despite his slowed pace, he feared he'd trample the little imp.

He leapt from his horse and chased after her on foot. The lass kept turning around, seeing him chasing her. The look of horror on her face nearly broke his heart. Och, he was no one to fear. But how would she know that? She probably thought he was after her like the outlaws had been after the man, woman and lad.

"'Tis all right!" he called. "I will nay harm ye!"

But she kept on running, and then was suddenly flying through the air, landing flat on her face.

Jamie ran toward her, dropping to his knees as he reached her side and she pushed herself up.

Her back shook with cries he was sure she tried hard to keep silent. He gathered her up onto his knees and she pressed her face to his *leine* shirt, wiping away tears, dirt and snot as she sobbed.

"Momma," she said. "Da!"

"Hush, now," Jamie crooned, unsure of what else he could say. She must have just watched her parents and brother get cut to the ground. Och, what an awful sight for any child to witness. Jamie shivered, at a loss for words.

"Blaney!" she wailed, gripping onto his shirt and yanking. "They hurt!"

Jamie dried her tears with the cuff of his sleeve. "Your family?" he asked.

She nodded, her lower lip trembling, green-blue eyes wide with fear and glistening with tears. His chest swelled with emotion for the little imp and he gripped her tighter.

"Do ye know who the men were?"

"Bad people," she mumbled.

Jamie nodded. "What's your name?"

She chewed her lip as if trying to figure out if she should tell him. "Lorna. What are ye called?"

"Jamie." He flashed her what he hoped wasn't a strained smile. "How old are ye, Lorna?"

"Four." She held up three of her fingers, then second guessed herself and held up four. "I'm four. How old are ye?"

"Fourteen."

"Ye're four, too?" she asked, her mouth dropping wide as she forgot the horror of the last few minutes of her life for a moment.

"Fourteen. 'Tis four plus ten."

"I want to be fourteen, too." She swiped at the mangled mop of blonde hair around her face, making more of a mess than anything else.

"Then we'd best get ye home. Have ye any other family?"

"A whole big one."

"Where?"

"Dunrobin," she said. "My da is laird."

"Laird Sutherland?" Jamie asked, trying to keep the surprise from his face. Did his father understand just how deep and unsettling this attack had been? A laird had been murdered. Was it an ambush? Was there more to it than just a band of outlaws? Were they men trying to stop the secret meeting from being held?

There would be no meeting, if the laird who'd called the meeting was dead.

"I'll take ye home," Jamie said, putting the girl on her feet and standing.

"Will ye carry me?" she said, her lip trembling again. She'd lost a shoe and her yellow gown was stained and torn. "I'm scared."

"Aye. I'll carry ye."

"Are ye my hero?" she asked, batting tear moistened lashes at him.

Jamie rolled his eyes and picked her up. "I'm no hero, lass."

"Hmm... Ye seem like a hero to me."

Jamie didn't answer. He tossed her on his horse and climbed up behind her. A glance behind showed that his father and his men had dispatched of most of the men, and a few others gave chase into the forest. They'd likely meet him at the castle as that had been their destination all along.

Squeezing his mount's sides, Jamie urged the horse into a gallop, intent on getting the girl to the safety of Dunrobin's walls, and then returning to his father.

Spotting Jamie with the lass, the guards threw open the gate. A nursemaid rushed over and grabbed Lorna from him, chiding her for sneaking away.

"What's happened?" A lad his own age approached. "Why did ye have my sister?"

Jamie swallowed, dismounted and held out his arm to the other young man. "I found her behind a boulder." Jamie took a deep breath, then looked the boy in the eye, hating the words he would have to say. "There was an ambush."

"My family?"

Jamie shook his head. He opened his mouth to tell the dreadful news, but the way the boy's face hardened, and eyes glistened, it didn't seem necessary. As it happened, he was given a reprieve from saying more when his father and men came barreling through the gate a moment later.

"Where's the laird?" Jamie's father bellowed.

"If what this lad said is true, then I may be right here," the boy said, straightening his shoulders.

Laird Montgomery's eyes narrowed, jaw tightened with understanding. "Aye, lad, ye are."

He leapt from his horse, his eyes lighting on Jamie "Where've ye been, lad? Ye scared the shite out of us." His father looked pale, shaken. Had he truly scared him so much?

"There was a lass," Jamie said, "at the ambush. I brought her home."

His father snorted. "Always a lass. Mark my words, lad. Think here." His father tapped Jamie's forehead hard with the tip of his finger. "The mind always knows better than the sword."

Jamie frowned and his father walked back toward the young laird. It was the second time that day that he'd not agreed with his father. For if a lass was in need of rescuing, by God, he was going to be her rescuer.

CHAPTER ONE

Dunrobin Castle, Scottish Highlands
Early Spring, 1297

"I'VE ARRANGED A MEETING BETWEEN Chief MacOwen and myself."

Lorna Sutherland lifted her eyes from her noon meal, the stew heavy as a bag of rocks in her belly as she met her older brother, Magnus', gaze.

"Why are ye telling me this?" she asked.

He raised dark brows as though he was surprised at her asking. What was he up to?

"I thought it important for ye to know."

She raised a brow and struggled to swallow the bit of pulverized carrot in her mouth. Her jaw hurt from clenching it, and she thought she might choke. There could only be one reason he felt the need to tell her this and she was certain she didn't want to know the answer. Gingerly, she set down her knife on her trencher and took a rather large gulp of watered wine, hoping it would help open her suddenly seized throat.

A moment later, she cocked her head innocently, and said, "Does not a laird and chief of his clan keep such talk to himself and his trusted council?" The haughty tone that took over could not be helped.

After nineteen summers, this conversation had been a long time coming. It was Aunt Fiona's fault. She'd arrived the week before, returning Heather, the youngest and wildest of the Sutherland siblings, and happened to see Lorna riding like the wind. Disgusted, her aunt marched straight to Magnus and demanded that he marry her off. Tame her, she'd said.

Lorna didn't see the problem with riding and why that meant she had to marry. So what if she liked to ride her horse standing on the saddle? She was good at it. Wasn't it important for a lass to excel in areas that she had skill?

Now granted, Lorna did admit that having her arms up in the air and eyes closed was borderline dangerous, but she'd done it a thousand times without mishap.

Even still, picturing her aunt's look of horror and how it had made Lorna laugh, didn't soften the blow of Magnus listening to their aunt's advice.

Magnus set down the leg of fowl he'd been eating and leaned forward on the table, his elbows pressing into the wood. Lorna found it hard to look him in the eye when he got like that. All serious and laird-like. He was her brother first, and chief second. Or at least, that's how she saw it. Judging from the anger simmering just beneath the surface of his clenched jaw and narrowed eyes, she was about to catch wind.

The room suddenly grew still, as if they were all wondering what he'd say—even the dogs.

He bared his teeth in something that was probably supposed to resemble a smile. A few of the inhabitants picked up superficial conversations again, trying as best they could to pretend they weren't paying attention. Others blatantly stared in curiosity.

"That is the case, save for when it involves deciding *your* future."

Oh, she was going to bait the bear. Lorna drew in a deep breath, crossed her arms over her chest and leaned away from the table. She could hardly look at him as she spoke. "Seems ye've already done just that."

Magnus' lips thinned into a grimace. "I see ye'll fight me on it."

"I dinna wish to marry." Emotion carried on every word. Didn't he realize what he was doing to her? The thought of marrying made her physically ill.

"Ye dinna wish to marry or ye dinna wish to marry MacOwen?"

By now the entire trestle table had quieted once more, and all eyes were riveted on the two of them. However she answered was going to determine the mood set in the room.

Och, she hated it when the lot of nosy bodies couldn't get enough of the family drama. Granted at least fifty percent of the time she was involved in said drama.

Lorna studied her brother, who, despite his grimace, waited patiently for her to answer.

The truth was, she did wish to marry—at some point. Having lost her mother when she was only four years old, she longed to have a child of her own, someone she could nurture and love. But that didn't mean she expected to marry *now*. And especially not the burly MacOwen who was easily twice her age, and had already married once or twice before. When she was a child she'd determined he had a nest of birds residing in his beard—and her thoughts hadn't changed much since.

She cocked her head trying to read Magnus' mind. Was it possible he was joking? He could not possibly believe she would ever agree to marry MacOwen.

Nay, Lorna wished to marry a man she could relate to. A man she could love, who might love her in return.

"I dinna wish to marry a man whose not seen a bath this side of a decade." Lorna spoke with a reasonable tone, not condescending, nor shrill, but just as she would have said the flowers looked lovely that morning. It was her way. Her subtlety often left people second guessing what they'd heard her say.

Magnus' lip twitched and she could tell he was trying to hold in his laughter. She dared not look down the table to see what the rest of her family and clan thought. In the past when she'd checked, gloated really, over their responses it had only made Magnus angrier.

Taming a bear meant not baiting him. And already she was doing just that. She flicked her gaze toward her plate, hoping the glance would appear meek, but in reality she was counting how many legumes were left on her trencher.

"Och, lass, I'm sure MacOwen has bathed at least once in the last year." Magnus' voice rumbled, filled with humor.

Lorna gritted her teeth. Of course Magnus would try and bait her in return. She should have seen that coming.

"And I'm sure there's another willing lass who'll scrape the filth from his back, but ye willna find her here. Not where I'm sitting."

Magnus squinted a moment as if trying to read into her mind. "But ye will agree to marry?"

Lorna crossed her arms over her chest. Lord, was her brother ever stubborn. "Not him."

"Shall we parade the eligible bachelors of the Highlands through the great hall and let ye take your pick?"

Lorna rolled her eyes, imagining just such a scene. It was horrifying, embarrassing. How many would there be in various states of dress and countenance? Some unkempt and others impeccable. Men who were pompous and arrogant or shy or annoying. Nay, thank you. She was about to spit a retort that was likely to burn her Aunt Fiona's ears when the matron broke in.

"My laird, 'haps after the meal I could speak with Lorna about marriage...in a somewhat more private arena?" Aunt Fiona was using that tone she oft used when trying to reason with one of them, that of a matron who knew better. It annoyed the peas out of Lorna and she was about to say just that, when her brother gave a slight wave of his hand, drawing her attention.

Perhaps his way of ceasing whatever words were on her tongue.

Magnus flicked his gaze from Lorna to Fiona. Why did the old bat always have to stick her nose into everything? Speaking to her in private only meant the woman would try to convince Lorna to take the marriage proposition her brother suggested. And that, she absolutely wouldn't do.

"'Tis not necessary, Aunt Fiona," Lorna said, at the exact same time Magnus stated, "Verra well."

Lorna jerked her gaze back to her brother, glaring daggers at him, but he only raised his brows in such an irritating way, a slight curve on his lips, that she was certain if she didn't excuse herself that moment she'd end up dumping her stew on his head. He had agreed on purpose —to annoy her. A horrible grinding sound came from her mouth as she gritted her teeth. Like she'd thought—brother first, chief second.

"Excuse me," she said, standing abruptly, the bench hitting hard on the back of her knees as so many people held it steady in place.

"Sit down," Magnus drawled out. "And finish your supper."

Lorna glared down at him. "I've lost my appetite."

Magnus grunted and smiled. "Och, we all know that's not true."

That only made her madder. So what if she ate just as much as the warriors? The food never seemed to go anywhere. She could eat all day long and still harbor the same lad's body she'd always had. Thick thighs, no hips, flat chest and arms to rival a squire's. If only she'd had the height of a man, then she could well and truly pummel her brother like he deserved.

She sat back down slowly and stared up at Magnus, eyes wide. Was that the reason he'd suggested MacOwen? Would no other man have her?

Nestling her hands in her lap she wrung them until her knuckles turned white.

Magnus clunked down his wooden spoon. "What is it, now?"

"Why did ye choose MacOwen?" she whispered, not wishing the rest of the table to be involved in this particular conversation. Not when she felt so vulnerable.

He shrugged, avoiding her gaze. "The man asked."

"Oh." She chewed her lip, appetite truly gone. 'Twas as she thought. No one would have her.

"Lorna..."

She flicked her gaze back up to her brother. "I but wonder if any other man would have me?"

Magnus' eyes popped and he gazed on her like she'd grown a second head and then that head grew a head. "Why would ye ask that?"

She shrugged.

By now everyone had gone back to talking and eating, knowing there'd be no more juicy gossip and Lorna was grateful for that.

"Lorna, lass, ye're beautiful, talented, spirited. Ye've taken the clan by storm. I've had to challenge more than one of my warriors for staring too long."

"More than one?" She couldn't help but glance down the table wondering which men it had been. They all slobbered like dogs over their chicken.

"None of the bastards deserve ye."

She turned back to Magnus. "And yet, ye picked the MacOwen?" She raised a skeptical brow. Ugh, of all men, he was by far the worst choice for her.

Magnus winked and picked up another scoop full of stew, shoveling into his grinning mouth.

Lorna groaned, shoulders sinking. "Ye told him nay, didna ye? Ye were baiting me."

Magnus laughed around a mouth full of stew. "Ye're too easy. I'd see ye married, but not to a man older than Uncle Artair," he said, refer-ring to their uncle who had to be nearing seventy.

"Ugh." Lorna growled and punched her brother in the arm. "How could ye do that? Ye made every bit of my hunger go away and ye know how much I love Cook's stew."

Magnus laughed. The sound boomed off the rafters and even pulled a smile from Lorna. She loved to hear him laugh, and he didn't do it often enough. When their parents died, he'd only been fourteen, and he'd been forced to take over the whole of the clan—including raising her, and her siblings. Raising her two brothers, Ronan and Blane, and then the youngest of their brood, Heather was a feat in itself, one only Magnus could have accomplished so well. In fact, the clan had pros-pered. She couldn't be more proud. If anyone deserved a good match, it was Magnus.

Her heart swelled with pride. "Ye're a good man, Magnus. And an amazing brother."

He reached toward her and gave her a reassuring squeeze on her shoulder. "I'll remember that the next time ye wail at me about nonsense."

Lorna jutted her chin forward. "I do not wail—and nothing I say is nonsense."

"A true Sutherland ye are. I see your appetite has returned."

Lorna hadn't even realized she'd begun eating again. She smiled and wrapped her lips around her spoon. Resisting Cook's stew was futile. The succulent bits of venison and stewed vegetables with hints of thyme and rosemary played blissfully over her tongue.

"My laird." Aunt Fiona's voice pierced the noise of the great hall.

Magnus stiffened slightly, and glanced up. Their aunt was a gem, a tremendous help, but Lorna had heard her brother comment on more than one occasion that the woman was also a grand pain in the arse. Lorna dipped her head to keep from laughing.

"Aye?" he said, focusing his attention on their aunt.

"I'd be happy to have Lorna return home with me upon my depar-ture. Visits with me have helped Heather so much."

Lorna's head shot up, mouth falling open as she glanced from her brother to her aunt. Good God, no! Beside her on the bench, Heather kicked Lorna in the shin and made a slight gesture with her knife as though she were slitting her wrist. Lorna pressed her lips together to keep from laughing.

"I'm sure that's not necessary, Aunt," Lorna said, giving the woman her sweetest smile. At least she'd not told her there was no way in hell she'd step foot outside of this castle for a journey unless it was on some adventure she chose for herself. She'd heard enough horror stories about the etiquette lessons Heather had to endure.

"Magnus?" Fiona urged.

There was a flash of irritation in his eyes. Magnus didn't mind his siblings calling him by his name, but all others were to address him formally. Lorna agreed that should be the case with the clan, but with family, Lorna thought he ought to be more lenient, especially where their aunt was concerned.

Aye, she was a thorn in his arse, but she was also very helpful.

Before her brother could say something he'd regret, Lorna pressed her hand to his forearm and chimed in. "Haps we can plan on me accompanying Heather on her next visit."

That seemed to pacify their aunt. She nodded and returned to her dinner.

Ronan, who sat beside Magnus on the opposite side of the table, leaned close to their brother and smirked as he said something. Probably crude. Lorna rolled her eyes. If Blane was here, he'd have joined in their bawdy drivel. Or maybe even saved her from having to invite herself to stay at their aunt's house.

As it was, Blane was gallivanting about the countryside and the borders dressed as an Englishman selling wool. Sutherland wool. Their prized product. Superior to all others in texture, softness, thickness, and ability to hold dye.

She stirred her stew, frowning. Blane always came home safe and sound, but she still worried. There was a lot of unrest throughout the country, and the blasted English king, Longshanks, was determined to be rid of them all. It would only take one wrong move and her beloved brother would be forever taken away.

Lorna glanced up. She gazed from one sibling to the next. She loved them. All of them. They loved each other more than most, maybe because they'd lost their parents so young and only had each other to rely on. Whatever the case was, they'd a bond not even steel could cut through.

Magnus raised his mug of ale. "A toast!" he boomed.

Every mug lifted into the air, ale sloshing over the sides and cheers filled the room.

"Clan Sutherland!" he bellowed.

And the room erupted in uproarious calls and clinks of mugs. A smile split her face and she was overcome with joy.

She'd be perfectly happy never to leave here. And perfectly ecstatic to never marry MacOwen.

Even still, as she clinked her mug and took a mighty gulp, she couldn't help but wonder if there was a man out there she could love, and one who just might love her in return.

*Want to read more? Check out **The Highlander's Temptation** and the rest of the **Stolen Bride** series wherever ebooks are sold...*

ABOUT THE AUTHOR

Eliza Knight is an award-winning and *USA Today* bestselling author of over fifty sizzling historical romance and erotic romance. Under the name E. Knight, she pens rip-your-heart-out historical fiction. While not reading, writing or researching for her latest book, she chases after her three children. In her spare time (if there is such a thing...) she likes daydreaming, wine-tasting, traveling, hiking, staring at the stars, watching movies, shopping and visiting with family and friends. She lives atop a small mountain with her own knight in shining armor, three princesses and two very naughty puppies. Visit Eliza at http://www.elizaknight.com or her historical blog History Undressed: www.historyundressed.com. Sign up for her newsletter to get news about books, events, contests and sneak peaks! http://eepurl.com/CSFFD

facebook.com/elizaknightfiction

twitter.com/elizaknight

instagram.com/elizaknightfiction

bookbub.com/authors/eliza-knight

goodreads.com/elizaknight

Made in the USA
Lexington, KY
23 June 2019